"A 'new' west is flourishing amid the beauties of nature in the northern Rockies, and Jeff Hull does a brilliant job of sizing up its dimensions in *Pale Morning Done*. Strong characters, vividly conflicted lives, heartbreak and passion—he's got my home territory dead on. And, in addition, this is one fine fly-fishing novel. Bravo."

—William Kittredge,
author of *The Best Stories of William Kittredge*

"What can be better than a love story on a Montana river—a story about love and sex, friendship and death? Jeff Hull's *Pale Morning Done* is authentic and vivid and true to life in the contemporary West. It is a story about creating life out of fresh spring waters, about the art of work and work as art, and about how finding ones self and discovering home may be the same thing."

—Annick Smith,
author of *In This We Are Native*

"Jeff Hull has written a wonderful novel. Human tension and environmental tension lay side by side on every page. The characters and emotions are raw and real. It's a view of the New West through the eyes of good and passionate people caught in the vortex of impending loss."

—Dan O'Brien,
author of *The Indian Agent*

"Young men in love with trout. Young women in love with trout. Young men and women in love with each other—and with the great riverine landscape of southwest Montana. Jeff Hull's humorous, stream-smart novel, *Pale Morning Done*, will appeal to anyone who loves fly fishing and the West. Anyone, for that matter, who enjoys fine writing, never mind those rainbows and browns."

—W.D. Wetherell,
author of *A Century of November*

"Jeff Hull has elbowed his way into the august company of great Western writers who evoke a sense of place with a sense of humor and a sense of purpose. *Pale Morning Done* is very well done, indeed."

—Daniel Glick,
author of *Monkey Dancing: A Father, Two Kids,
and a Journey to the Ends of the Earth*

"Written with clear-eyed love and an intimate knowledge of the land and its rivers, Jeff Hull's debut novel tells the story of Marshall Tate, drinker, lover, fly-fisherman extraordinaire, who yearns both for love and to create a home on his own spring creek in Western Montana. Hull's descriptions of rivers and fly fishing are exquisite, better than those in *The River Why* or *A River Runs Through It*, and Marshall's story is funny, exhilarating, and sad. *Pale Morning Done* is a wonderful float trip down some of the great fishing rivers of the West."

—Kent Nelson,
author *Land That Moves, Land That Stands Still*

PALE MORNING DONE

PALE MORNING DONE

a novel

JEFF HULL

THE LYONS PRESS
Guilford, Connecticut
An imprint of The Globe Pequot Press

To buy books in quantity for corporate use
or incentives, call **(800) 962–0973, ext. 4551,**
or e-mail **premiums@GlobePequot.com.**

Copyright © 2005 by Jeff Hull

ALL RIGHTS RESERVED. No part of this book may be reproduced or transmitted in any form by any means, electronic or mechanical, including photocopying and recording, or by any information storage and retrieval system, except as may be expressly permitted in writing from the publisher. Requests for permission should be addressed to The Lyons Press, Attn: Rights and Permissions Department, P.O. Box 480, Guilford, CT 06437.

The Lyons Press is an imprint of The Globe Pequot Press.

10 9 8 7 6 5 4 3 2 1

Printed in the United States of America

Library of Congress Cataloging-in-Publication Data

Hull, Jeff, 1962–
   Pale morning done : a novel / Jeff Hull.
     p. cm.
   ISBN 1-59228-684-4 (trade paper)
   1. Fly fishing—Fiction. 2. Montana—Fiction. I. Title.
PS3608.U43P35 2005
813'.6—dc22

                                       2005003123

For my brother, Chris,
who lent us courage when ours failed,
and gave us laughter in the darkness.

SKWALAS

It was not dust but distance that kept Marshall Tate from seeing what approached. Marshall was jouncing down a dirt road on an ancient Massey Ferguson tractor, newly bemused by the sensation of his cheeks jiggling against his teeth. The dust funnel unzipped from an advancing point, two miles or so across the valley. Marshall knew it angled at a vehicle making speed in his direction, about which he thought: *oh, joy.*

Marshall had been so pleasantly immersed in his surroundings, too. Only moments before he had been involved in something close to reverie. He had observed rich late-afternoon sunlight punching rents through furrows of blue-bottomed clouds. He had noticed, across the broad valley, swatches of light burnishing specific ridges and snow-clad peaks deep in the Scapegoat Wilderness. Marshall had closed his eyes to inhale the dense fragrance of early Montana springtime . . . and opened his eyes to see the dust vector, closing distance.

The rig raising it veered over folds and pockets in the terrain before revealing itself as the red pickup Marshall sort of dreaded. He suspected a matter of minutes would have him greeting either Daisy Klingman or her father, Bruce, who owned all the land Marshall could see to the south. Each presented a particular kind of worm can. Marshall clattered the tractor over a wood-planked bridge spanning the

West Fork River, feeling suddenly weary beyond his thirty-three years. On the other side he aimed the tractor on a lean into the borrow pit, where he yanked the gears out of mesh. Resigned to a stab at civilities, Marshall climbed down from his seat and pretended to restack the bags of grass seed in the tractor's bucket for a while.

The red pickup skidded to a halt in front of him, the following dust cloud sweeping forward to envelop, then unveil it. Randy Klingman drove and Bruce, wearing a black feeding cap, sucked a toothpick in the passenger seat. Marshall had come to understand that Randy, who was a few years older than himself, would inherit the Klingman ranch because he had studied his father's politics and aped them passably. Randy was problematic in that he believed people he didn't like were still walking around chiefly because he hadn't shot them yet. But Marshall felt he could be easily outmaneuvered. Bruce was the crafty bastard.

Bruce and Randy sat watching the dust cloud overtake them, then dissipate. The truck was running rich, and Marshall could smell the uncombusted gasoline. Randy switched off the ignition, rolled down his window, and nodded. Marshall stepped up to the truck. "Randy," Marshall said. He leaned to look across the pickup's cab and added, "Mr. Klingman."

"Heading over to work on your project?" Randy asked. From Randy's mouth, "project" sounded like a synonym for "shit pile." Randy let his right arm hang down the side of the pickup. His fingers rolled and popped, beating an incomprehensible rhythm on the metal of the door. Bruce stared at the windshield like it was a campfire.

"I'm planting some grass," Marshall said.

"Boy, we heard you've got a hell of a deal over there," Randy said. "Water everywhere."

"Just the usual amount," Marshall said, "in slightly different shapes."

Randy turned to glance across the cab to his father. Marshall sensed an I-told-you-so element to the gesture. Bruce Klingman pumped his eyebrows once and let his head nod to one side. Randy was looking at Marshall again. Randy's eyes were pale blue and his eyebrows formed arcs of constant emphasis. There was no doubt that Randy Klingman was a hit with the local ladies, but Marshall thought Randy's face generally held the already-drifting but still-surprised expression of somebody who has just been whanged over the head with a shovel.

Then nobody spoke. Marshall felt the creeping impression that he was supposed to feel guilty about something. He staged an obvious glance back at the ten fifty-pound bags of seed—all native grasses, precious and pricey—stacked in the bucket of his tractor. He had about two more hours of daylight to broadcast as much seed as possible, part of an ongoing effort to revegetate the banks of a spring creek he had spent the past two years carving through the heart of the 2,200-acre Fly X ranch. "Welp," he said, "I'm burning daylight."

"About that," Randy said. "How much water you taking out of the ground?"

Marshall felt gravity suddenly work with increased efficiency on his stomach. He was afraid it would be about this. He said, "Couldn't know," and let his grin acknowledge that perhaps he was foolish for not knowing.

"The reason why is we got the feeling Alice Creek is way down all of a sudden," Randy said. "You know we've renegotiated some water rights so we can divert from Alice Creek."

Marshall didn't need, or take, much water from Alice Creek, though he had a legal right to. The moment his father let Marshall have his head in terms of running the Fly X, Marshall launched an ambitious experiment—he was letting the land go to seed, return to its natural form. He'd ceased the leasing of pasturage, instantly antagonizing the Klingmans—who had grazed cows in Fly X meadows for decades—but also obviating the need for heavy irrigation. He maintained a wheel line and poured a trickle of Alice Creek water over the southern pastures only because in the world of water rights a predominant legal mechanism was: use it or lose it. Plus a little irrigation kept the fire hazard down and the elk and deer in graze, which made the bears and mountain lions—and, if one believed the latest reports from the U.S. Fish and Wildlife Service, suddenly a pack of wolves—happy.

"So," Randy was saying, "we're trying to suss out why the creek's so down. But I think you might have solved our dilemma."

Marshall noted that, over in the truck's passenger seat, Bruce had taken to picking at the dashboard. "Runoff hasn't started yet," Marshall said. "All the creeks are down. Doesn't look any different from any other year to me."

Without turning his eyes from the windshield, Bruce said in a dreamy voice, "Creek's named after my great-grandmother. Guess I ought to know what it looks like."

"Well," Marshall said, fed up now, "you got a new right from Alice Creek, you must have put a flow meter in, right? May first you just read your meter. You'll get your water." He started to swing a little on his feet, making moves like he might walk right off. "Lots of snow in the high country." Marshall suspected his jiggering of the local subterranean hydrodynamics over the past two years left him standing on shaky ground, but he knew the flow meter jab was a stopper.

Bruce had taken off his feeding cap and was glaring across the interior of the cab at Marshall. Randy was talking. The effect was vaguely ventriloquial. Randy was saying, "A fella can't just dig wherever he wants and lay tile, you know. That's an unadjudicated groundwater right you've got there. All this nonconsumptive usage . . . we're gonna follow up on that, we don't get our water. Bet your ass."

Unadjudicated right? Nonconsumptive usage? Marshall had no idea what any of that meant, and he doubted Randy did either. But Bruce might. That undercut any freewheeling he might have been tempted to try on Randy.

"Just keep an eye on that flow meter," Marshall said. He slapped his fingers on the roof of the truck cab as if *slam-bang* he might have solved everything. What he needed right now, Marshall realized, was a lawyer. A real prick. "You feel like you're a little low later in the year, give me a call. Better to settle that stuff between neighbors then go to Missoula about it, right?"

He wondered how long he could hold off a full-scale legal donnybrook. Marshall was pretty sure his reconfiguring of some upland springs had not affected the water levels in Alice Creek, but he had no idea how his engineering would bear up under the scrutiny of regulatory agencies like the Water Court. On top of that, he was broke. Legal costs alone could pull his plug. He wondered if the Klingmans knew that. How could they? But here they were, at his most precarious financial moment, pressing the issue. He knew from past concerns over water rights that even the slightest alteration to an existing right in the West Fork basin required the installation of a flow meter—this because government agencies had for a century blithely overallocated the amount of water actually in the watershed's creeks and riverbeds at any given time. Marshall knew the Klingmans hadn't installed a flow meter when they built their headgate on Alice Creek. He knew this not from any direct observation, but rather from a familiarity with the family character.

He knew because the first year he had come to live on the Fly X full-time, fifteen years before, the winter was a particularly hard one, awash with deep snows. Marshall, on some naive neighborly jag or perhaps a whimsical impulse to see Daisy, had driven into the Klingman yard and found nobody home. So he had searched around the outbuildings. At the back of the pasture nearest the house—maybe a quarter mile away—he saw round bales of hay stockpiled and surrounded by a fifteen-foot-high fence. The fence was draped with brownish towels. It became apparent to Marshall that no Klingmans were home, so he trudged down the tractor lane toward the hay bales, curious about the towels. At the time he was keen to borrow secrets of ranchcraft wherever he could find them.

When he drew closer, Marshall saw that the towels were in fact the carcasses of whitetail deer. The Klingmans had used four-inch-square wire fence to sequester their round bales, and winter-starved deer attempting to leap it slipped their hooves into the openings, hung there high above the ground, and died. Marshall could see that some were reduced to shanks of legs jutting from ankles at sickening angles. Others might have perished the night before. What Marshall knew about that fence was that it still stood around the Klingman winter bales. These were not people who installed flow meters on irrigation lines.

And yet the Klingmans were considered fine neighbors in the upper West Fork Valley, good ranch folk. Marshall always thought of Bruce and his right-hand son as primarily stoic and dangerously stupid, but in the past year, just as the long toil of his spring creek project came close to fruition, Bruce and Randy Klingman had ratcheted up a level of aggression he had never anticipated. In another time frame he might have guessed that the ongoing travesty of his dealings with Daisy had catalyzed matters, but he hadn't even seen her since she returned to the valley and she'd been in Reno for a year prior to that. Marshall could only suspect that the trigger was his decision to build the spring creek—an act the Klingman clan might interpret as an indication that, despite fifteen years of evidence already available, Marshall planned to stick around for a while.

Now here were Randy and Bruce, riddling him with water rights. Marshall wasn't sure he and the Klingmans had said their good-byes when he wandered away from the red truck and back to his tractor. The pickup hitched and rolled through a three-point turn in the middle of the road and began to shrink with distance, returning from whence it had come. Marshall closed the gate behind him and climbed aboard the Massey Ferguson, then drove along a two-track path paralleling the arc of the West Fork River.

It was almost a mile from the bridge to where Marshall needed to broadcast his grass seed, but halfway there he could see the banks of the brand new spring creek puffing up from the gray-brown meadow grass like lips of an infected wound. He needed more grass. He needed more aspens and alder and willows and serviceberry—everything. He needed a prick lawyer. He needed money. He needed Mike Shadford. He thought: *fuckitty fuck, fuck, fuck.*

When the sun burned clear from the occasional mare's-tail cloud sidling across it, the afternoon could have been July, although the sky's blue seemed brushed a bit thin for summer. It was late March, anyway. To the west the massive peaks of the Bitterroots stood, their shoulders blue-green plaid with pine and larch forests sloping up to snow-sealed ridges. The granite peaks threw up a palisade against incoming squall lines, vaulting them aloft, but miles to the south the gray fuzz of rain or snow had completely outflanked the range and was infusing the valley. A wind would soon gather and make the second part of the day an exercise in well-timed sallies between implacable gusts.

But while the sun still shone, a drift boat bobbed along on the river's surface, its hull a forest green trimmed in high-varnished spruce. The boat floated through a corridor of gray-white cottonwoods, their bare branches poised like a hoarfrost around extended trunks. In places the fat twiggy nests of heron rookeries blotted the screen of branches. Marshall Tate stood at the bow, thighs pressed against a curving teak brace. Though he'd caught no fish yet, Marshall had been having a marvelous time—an afternoon reminiscent of the early years when he and Molly Huckabee and Alton Summers wasted countless afternoons floating water together—until the boat coasted around a bend and he saw, plunked dead solid still in one of his favorite spots, a white-hulled boat with three people in it.

Marshall immediately began trying to convince himself he could still be having a marvelous time. It was only one other boat. There were lots of nice spots on this float. He was thinking this way, but also thinking: *yeah, but that's my favorite goddamned place on the river.*

Marshall twisted at the bow and said, "What do you think about holding up for a bit?"

Behind him a woman with fine, shoulder-cropped blonde hair dropping from a suede-billed cap sat and handled the oars. She wore waders, too, and the shoulder straps bowed around her breasts. She had pulled the brim of her cap low over her eyes, which worked behind dark sunglasses so that, besides a healthy splash of crimson on each cheek, it was difficult to make much of her face.

"They'll move when they see us," Molly said.

"He's working," Alton said, about the other boat. A short plug of a man, Alton sat in the stern seat, fuzzy in a deep-pile fleece jacket, eyes cocooned in narrow wraparound shades. The extra-long bill of a cap, festooned with chewed-out, unraveling flies, lidded down over his sunglasses.

Marshall looked back at the white-hulled boat. He could see an anchor rope taut and angling from the stern into the river. The rower was a younger man, the fishermen in the bow and stern seats older, heavier, bedecked in plackets of gear. Marshall sized it up as a guide and two clients. The client in back had a fish on his line and the guide bent over the rail to scoop at the water with a long-handled net.

"You know him?" Alton asked Molly.

"I think it's Dean Stone," Molly said.

"He a guide?"

"Not really," Molly said. "Let's just work this bank. They should get the hint."

"I really wanted to fish that hole," Marshall said. "I've been thinking about it all week."

"Don't worry about that hole," Molly said. "I'll show you one of my secret spots."

Marshall struggled to rescue his plummeting spirits. He stood in the bow with scrolls of orange fly line scribbled across the hip-high foredecking before him. He waved his rod a few times and shot a length of line toward the bank. After waiting out the winter, the spring sun on his skin felt like a new kind of vitamin. He felt he could go either way, the balance made delicate by the pervasive bitchiness of the Bitterroot River, water Marshall had learned to hold in dubious regard.

This small window—two or three weeks in late March and early April—was the only time Marshall could be convinced to float the Bitterroot. When overnight lows hovered above freezing for a few consecutive nights, when water flows remained stable a few days running, when the sun climbed high enough in the spring sky so that its rays no longer glanced from the river's cold water, but stabbed downward and sank in, Marshall and Alton and Molly and everybody who did what they did for a living hitched up the drift boats and headed for Darby.

By then, on the bottom of the river millions of thumb-sized stonefly nymphs called Skwalas scrambled their way from behind one rock to another, angling through the current for the banks. Armies of nymphs would scrabble onto dry rocks, or scale downed logs, where they would squirm and burst from rippled bug-shaped exoskeletons to emerge shiny and supple in the brilliant spring sunlight. The Skwala bugs, two inches long, dark gray with greenish bellies and tiny hexagonal heads, rose into the air, hovering like baby Hueys, impregnating each other in midflight. The males fell, exhausted, onto the water. Females endured longer and heroically launched themselves again, buzzsaw wings filming a halo around themselves until they dropped to the water, releasing the tens of thousands of tiny eggs dripping from their abdomens. Hundreds of millions of eggs drifted beneath the surface slick, sinking to the bottom, repopulating the river with Skwalas. And the huge and handsome trout of the Bitterroot River raised their snouts above the surface, opened their jaws, and slurped unfortunate adults.

After a winter crunching the kernels of nymphs, trout looked up and saw these, the first surface bugs of the season—coincidentally massive hunks of succulent protein—and imbibed without reserve. Big trout, in particular, forgot or just ignored all of the savvy that let them grow big and made the Bitterroot such a prickly river any other time of year. Shining, broad-shouldered rainbows and snaggle-toothed browns sucked in Skwalas like fat cousins at a spaghetti social.

In a few short weeks would come runoff, the end of everything for a while. The swollen flows of runoff would thunder through the flood plains, transforming rivers into wild white horses—palominos, actually, tawny with mud and white with froth—tearing down trees, gouging banks, scouring freestone beds. Fishing would be spotty until the salmonfly hatch on Rock Creek, months away. By then Molly and Alton would be booked solid, guiding—already they each had bookings for the Skwala hatch later this week—and Marshall would be wrangling with a whole new world: his spring creek, at which he desperately hoped people, lots of people, would pay to fish.

So these were supposed to be days of friendly calm, an annual ritual wherein Marshall, Molly, and Alton spent a brief afternoon or two enjoying the very thing that had brought them all together in the first place years ago, something they rarely had time to do together anymore. Marshall found his attention focusing downstream, where the fisherman in the front of the white-hulled boat now shouted and his rod bent and jerked. Amidships, the guide Molly had called Dean Stone scrambled for his net. He landed the fish, showed it to the man in the front of the boat, and released it. Then he dug in his shirt pocket, removed a small black object, and held it to his mouth while turning to glance upstream at them.

"And here I've already promised myself not to be surprised by anything I see on the river this year," Alton said.

Marshall swiveled to ask him, "Is this a new thing?" A foreboding sense of the obvious made Marshall glance past Alton at the river upstream. Another boat glided around the bend and slid toward them. Marshall noticed how fast the second boat was coming, the oarsman rowing steadily. Neither of the passengers were casting. Alton peered over his shoulder, then swung his seat to stare directly back at the oncoming boat.

"Looks like they're pulling out," Molly said. She was still watching the white-hulled boat downstream. She let her arms drop, lifting the oars from the water and allowing her boat to slip into the current. Marshall looked to see Dean Stone hauling up the anchor line from a block mounted next to his seat.

"Can you believe this shit?" Alton said. He spoke upstream.

"They're leaving," Molly said. "We're up." But Molly's enthusiasm was nipped by no response from the boys. She glanced around in time to see the upstream boat looming, then drawing past them, the oarsman rowing hard. Marshall scanned the oarsman carefully, and spotted what he thought he would find clipped to the man's wader belt: a black walkie-talkie. The boat stretched a thirty-foot gap downstream, then dropped into the line of their drift, heading directly for the hole where the white-hulled boat lay.

Alton stood from his seat and stepped up beside Molly. "Here, let me row a second." He gripped the oars over her hands.

"I'll row," Molly said.

"Just . . . let me," Alton said. He had stepped over the thwart and used his hip to nudge her shoulders.

Molly let go of the oars and slipped from the rowing cushion, moving back onto the stern seat. "Damn, Alton."

"You'll see," Alton said. He sat down at the oars, spun the boat around so the bow faced upstream, and began rowing them backward down the river, his spine arcing with the effort. He made none of the usual attempts toward etiquette and instead plowed through the hole where the new boat was settling in. Alton sliced his oars into the river until he had caught up with the white boat, which was slowly drifting out of the pool.

Only a few feet separated their gunnels as Alton drew abeam. Marshall took a close look at the guide in the other boat, Stone, who sported an enormous panhandle of chin. Stone let his oars drift through a stroke. He copped a scowl, but it overlaid a smug grin. The clients fore and aft frowned outrage. "Hey, watch it!" one of them shouted. Alton said nothing. For a moment it seemed that the oars of the two boats would clash, but Alton timed his strokes perfectly to miss the other man's. He waited until Stone's oar blade lifted from the water, then reversed his direction with a sharp swift backstroke. Alton's oar stem cracked Stone's, jarring it from Stone's hand, and smacking the handle of Stone's oar into his chin. Stone's head snapped back on his shoulders.

"Oooo. Sorry," Alton sang out with counterfeit dismay. "Gettin' a little tight in here. *Lots* of boats."

Alton was four boat lengths downstream by the time Stone recovered enough to yell, "Hey, you little son of a bitch!" His lips couldn't hang tight to the words.

"Just an accident," Alton called back. "It's so crowded all of a sudden!"

Stone half rose from the seat, then seemed to remember he had clients in his boat and sat back down. Alton erupted in a burst of power, his ass lifting from the rowing seat as he stroked them away from the scene. He called out to the white boat, "Tight lines!"

Marshall looked at Molly—who now sat in the boat's stern seat wearing a quizzical frown—and said, loud enough to still be heard in the other boat as they retreated, "And people wonder why I quit guiding."

Nobody actually wondered, Molly knew, why Marshall had quit guiding. Quite a few had at first, because over a course of a dozen or so years Marshall had become one of the most respected and re-quested guides in western Montana. But once he quit most people assumed they knew why, and nobody wondered at all anymore.

"They tag-teamed us with walkie-talkies," Marshall said, still bal-ancing bemusement with outrage as Alton pulled the boat down-stream. "Can you believe that?"

"It's not exactly . . . out of character," Molly said.

"Who are they?"

"You've seen them around," Molly said.

"Yeah, but who are they?"

"Oh, there's four or five of them. Their dads are all partners in a law firm in Santa Barbara," Molly said. "They bought Microsoft early and often and then started buying Montana. They own a couple ad-joining ranches, the dads do, up high on the Blackfoot. The juniors all came to the university and during the summer the dads pay them to take law clients out fishing. The clients figure they're being guided by regular guides and they pay regular guide fees."

"And the guides don't have actual guides' licenses, because why would you need one of those to be a nonactual guide?" Marshall asked.

"Like that," Molly said.

"That's an insult to our profession," Marshall said. "I think. Hard to tell anymore."

"One of them got busted by the fish cops last year. Kid named Jimmy Ripley."

"I'm sure Daddy paid the fine," Alton said. It was the first addition he'd made to the exchange since his ire began fueling furious strokes downriver.

Which reminded Marshall to note, "You know, Alton, we're giving up a lot of good river."

"There's a lot . . . of good river . . . left," Alton said, speaking in bursts between heaves on the oars. "I'd rather . . . give up all this . . . than have to see . . . those two boats . . . again."

Alton rowed another five solid minutes before easing and allowing the boat to settle into the current again. He angled the bow at the bank. Without a cue, Molly and Marshall started casting.

Marshall said, "I'm surprised Shadford hasn't thought of that walkie-talkie trick yet."

"If I told Shadrat about this he'd have us all wearing hands-free headsets by June," Alton said. "Did you hear he made us sign contracts?"

"And you signed one?" Marshall said.

"Well, that was before he slept with my girlfriend. At the time he was only threatening to freeze me out of the guiding rotation altogether." Alton shrugged.

"What are you now contractually obliged to do?"

"Guide exclusively for Shadrat. Whenever he wants. And in the event I leave his employ after the season, never guide any of his clients independently."

"And what is Shadford contractually obliged to do for you?"

"Book me at least a hundred days," Alton said.

"I could have booked you a hundred days," Molly said.

"So where were you when the documents were unfurled?"

Molly knew it wouldn't have mattered where she'd been. When the contract signing had gone on, Amy Baine was still Amy Baine; she was still a few weeks away from becoming Amy the Bane of Alton's existence. At that point Alton would have seen working for Molly as a strain between him and his girl, particularly on the overnight trips. Sorry she'd spoken, Molly flicked a new cast at the bank, hoping the afternoon would pour away in any direction that wouldn't bump Alton toward his semicontinuous dwelling on Amy the Bane and Mike Shadford.

The sun continued to shine, though with a sense of derring-do, as if it were awaiting the last possible moment to flee before the encroaching storm clouds. The afternoon sucked away the outrage of the white boat incident the way trout collapsed the river's surface beneath the poised Skwala bugs. Marshall offered to take a turn on the oars, and Alton let him. The sun lasted into midafternoon until the squall line behind them lost its cool. Then a bank of fuzzy white clouds with gray cores stepped up and blanked the sky, and in moments fat snowflakes twirled down around them, hesitating before melting when they struck the river's surface. The colors faded from green and blue in the river and rich brown and yellow on the bank to a monochrome gray, and the river's surface melded pewter. By then Molly was back on the oars and let the boat free-drift for a moment while they all scrambled for the dry bags, encasing themselves in SST jackets. By the time they'd geared up, a wet, heavy snow dumped like confetti, but the boys fished on.

Molly loved watching Marshall and Alton working the water. Alton was perhaps the best fly fisherman she'd ever seen—outside of her father—though of course there was no way to prove something like that. But Alton caught fish on slow days and consistently boated more big trout than anybody she knew. He cast beautifully, even with double beadhead rigs and split shot. She'd floated with him one day when Alton heard a fish rise behind them—a rise nobody else in the boat had heard—stood up in the bow, whirled sixty feet of line back upstream, threw a long mend, and hooked the fish.

Marshall could probably do all those things, but nobody knew. His concentration wandered and he missed strikes, which Molly found endearing. Marshall targeted individual fish, trout he saw or knew from previous floats that lurked under specific cutbanks or in certain pockets. He'd float to one of his spots, catch his one fish, and be ready to move on, which Molly found irksome—but in a somewhat touching fashion. Marshall disdained nymphing—he had a bumper sticker stuck to his raft cooler that implored HATE WEIGHT—whereas Alton possessed an uncanny ability to imagine the streambed and drift beadheads through every seam.

Molly could catch fish better than almost all the men she knew, could even force her clients to catch a fish or two on a bad day—which was the gift of a guide. But she was still learning from Alton and Marshall the magic of making things happen when conditions decreed that nothing much should. Now the sudden turn in weather had them fishing silently as they drifted down the river. Just that quickly the world had turned quiet and a little still. A pair of mergansers paddled ahead of the boat, looking like a couple straight out of the fifties with their Phyllis Diller hair. Molly said to Marshall, "You got everything ready to open?"

"Everything but the clients," Marshall said. "Creek's full of fish. Need some grass to grow. I want to print up some maps, build a little warming hut, that kind of stuff."

Molly glanced over her shoulder, and asked, "How about you? Are *you* ready?"

"That . . . well, that'd be your question, right there."

"All those yahoos running all over your place, sticking your fish?" Alton said. He said "yay-hoos" and put some steam into "sticking." He shook a dubious smile onto his face. Then added, "All in the name of commerce."

The word "commerce" punched Marshall into a funk that lasted the next two bends in the river, made not less uncomfortable by his inability to understand what to say about the concept. Then Molly rowed the boat through the confluence of a side-channel reentering the main stem. She slowed them and jumped out of the boat hip-deep into the pool.

"I'll just be ready," Marshall said, searching for a different entry into the conversation that had set him back so solidly. "I'll keep it under control. I'll just kick people off. People are going to fish the creek right or they're going to sit in their vehicles and watch bugs splatter on their windshield all the way back to Missoula."

"This is the secret spot I was telling you about," Molly said to Alton.

"Hmmm," Alton said. His face burlesqued discovery. "A pool, where two currents converge."

Molly pointed upstream beyond the pool to where a cottonwood with a burl of root bared stood on the bank. "See that tree?" Molly said. Nothing seemed remarkable about the water below it.

"I see the tree," Alton said, "but why are we standing in the spot where all the fish should be?"

"Because I'm going to show you something," Molly said.

"I'll give them their money back," Marshall said. "If they don't respect the stream, they'll just be gone. I don't need it that bad."

"I thought you did," Alton said. "I thought that was the whole point."

"Yeah," Marshall said, and he started shaking his head. "But still—"

"I can hit that tree from here," Alton said, focused upstream.

"I know you can, but don't," Molly said.

"What are you telling me?" Alton asked.

Marshall remained seated in the boat's stern, mired in private depressions about potentially disgusting clients, but also their juxtaposition against property tax assessments, credit accounts coming due at the ranch supply stores, and water rights he knew so little about. Molly stood just below him, the river up over her hips, her hands on the boat's gunnel. To Alton she said. "Pitch your junk two feet off the bank, three feet upstream of that tree." She reached up into the boat and shook Marshall's thigh. "We'll need you overboard, big guy. *Upstream, Alton.*"

Marshall dropped over the side, his attention still gliding along at some remove. He noted that he was now standing both in the river and in the middle of a heavy snow squall. He saw Alton exaggerating stealth into ridicule, creeping along the side of the boat. Alton's rod hand whipped back toward his shoulder in a short burst, then halted completely, no drift, while he waited for the line to unfurl behind him. His left hand stripped and released and his right hand exploded forward, and line shot ahead in a flat, tight loop that bulleted outward, unwinding itself.

Marshall vaguely followed Alton's fly as it flew upstream, sailing amid the pouring snow. Marshall saw the gray flake of foam touch on the river's surface and float back to them, unmolested. *Gray foam rubber and green thread. How could such beautiful fish be so goddamned dumb?* There was something about the fly's drift, its solo course and artificiality that made him feel like its movement should be instructive, but his hard-earned wariness of river metaphors conflated with a general mood-fog to scotch any momentum for making more of it. Alton bent and, with his face inches from the water's surface, watched the fly float just under his nose and into Molly's leg.

"Well!" he said. "That sure beat hell out of catching a real live fish in this attractive pool we're all standing in."

"Give me your rod," Molly said. She slid upstream, feeling for the bottom with her feet, and made three false casts before dropping the fly two feet farther upstream than Alton had. Four seconds into the drift a flash of pink rolled over the fly and Molly struck the fish. She turned and held the rod out for Alton to take. "I told you three feet upstream of the tree," Molly said. "They eat with their heads, you know."

"I am shamefaced," Alton said.

"There's a slot up there," Molly said. "I spotted it a few years ago during some really low water. You'd never see it otherwise. There's a bunch more fish in there." She still held the rod for Alton to take. "Large ones."

The trout bent the rod into a parabola and it was apparent that something would give quickly. Alton took the rod just as the fish turned and burst downstream past them. He plunged through the side-channel confluence without hesitation to consider how deep the water might be in the middle—navel-level on him, it turned out—and staggered up onto the ensuing gravel bank.

Molly turned and waded so she was just in front of Marshall, and he could see all of her face, the skin of her cheeks glowing like a waxed apple, the bow of her upper lip drawn. She shifted her feet like she might be finding the right rocks to stand on, leaving her leg pressed against his up to the hip. The bill of his cap cantilevered over hers. She placed a palm on each of Marshall's shoulders and said, "You're gonna do fine."

Marshall took a long look around him, at all the snow falling into the river. "I wish I knew that," he said. "I spent so much time getting it just right, you know? And now I don't even know if it was the right thing to do. I mean, I made up a stream so I could charge people to fish there. Isn't that kind of what's wrong with fly fishing these days?"

"Hey, *you're* not paying to fish. You're taking money from other people who are paying to fish."

"Worse yet," Marshall lamented. "I'm driving the consumer culture."

"Tate, you're backing and filling now. Just run the best spring creek you can. Make it good for the fish and it will be good for everything else. What's better than that?"

"I guess nothing, unless my hilljack neighbor keeps feeling sparks in his brain pan."

"Klingman?" Molly asked. She stroked his triceps without thinking, and when she did think, she noticed he hadn't flinched, which pleased her. Everything she knew about Marshall told her that little things triggered sudden responses in him. She'd seen him leave parties because somebody yelled at a dog for nosing the chip dip. He might quit fishing when he cast a little wind knot. Most of the boys capitalized on every poor excuse to loop an arm around her and give her a squeeze. Marshall seemed to recoil when he accidentally touched her, as if he'd insulted her flesh somehow. Molly was trying to learn how to avoid the trip wires, and she felt like every day drew her a little closer. She said, "Why? What's he up to?"

Marshall heard her asking a subtext question: what're *they* up to? Which meant: what's *she* up to? Molly had never met Bruce Klingman, but knew more than she needed to about Daisy. "Oh," Marshall said, "he's pissing and moaning about unadjudicated nonconsumptive groundwater rights."

"You've got the rights all straightened out, don't you?"

"I have done some things I'm not real sanguine about."

"Marshall," Molly scolded. "First rule of the West: whiskey's for drinkin' and water's for fightin' over. Get a lawyer."

"Can't afford one," Marshall said.

"You wanna guide a few days?"

"I don't have time," he said.

Molly looked at Marshall, saw him swathed in falling snow and clearly uncomfortable, as if the melt of each wet flake were a prick of doubt. More than anything she wanted to lift her fingertips to his cheek, let her lips press against his. She wanted to kiss him until he either believed everything would be fine or ceased to care about it. But Molly settled for wrapping a loose hug around him, thinking: *it could be a friendly hug.* She didn't push her luck. "It's going to work like crazy," Molly said, and patted him on the back. This was the longest he had ever allowed her to touch him without stiffening.

"Sure," Marshall said.

"And now you're going to catch a large fish, and that's going to make you feel better." She pivoted, slowed by current to an aqua ballet, and pointed back toward the tree and the barely discernible tongue of slower water beneath it.

Catching a large fish might make him feel better. So far the day had not been what he'd hoped for. Marshall looked downstream, at Alton, and saw him holding a broad silvery slab smeared with a rose blush, the fish drooping like a cut of meat off both sides of Alton's hands. The mealy sky and snow made the trout's red flanks seem like the only colored object in a grayscale scene. A fish like that might change the way he eventually remembered the whole day, and fishing, Marshall had come to understand, was nothing more than a method for assigning the days you mark time by. Alton's teeth were plastered by a disbelieving grin about how easy things had suddenly become.

Beside Marshall, Molly was smiling, too, her mouth wide but still round, and Marshall saw how sweet she looked, like a child when she first understands that she's made somebody else happy. Then his eyes turned back to Alton, who was returning now. But Marshall saw beyond him, to the bank far downstream where the river turned hard to the right against a jacketing of riprap boulders. Something there made him keep looking.

"What is that?" he asked. He jutted his chin at the distant patch of dark fur against sand-colored rock.

"I don't see," Molly said.

"On the riprap," Marshall said.

Molly lifted onto tiptoes and stared. "Oh yeah. Maybe a beaver?"

Alton waded into them, blocking the view momentarily.

"Where?" Alton asked. Marshall directed his gaze. Alton said, "Maybe a dead beaver."

"It's moving," Marshall said, "but something's . . ."

Molly stared, her mouth only slightly open. She couldn't guess how this might go, but knew that they'd all be getting back into the boat now, even though she had had every intention of revealing the startling number of large fish hiding in her secret spot.

Downstream the river ran straight against a wall of boulders designed to deflect the current from private property, then bent hard to the right. As they approached, Marshall couldn't help noticing that the animal was clearly a skunk, and that it made no effort to flee. He knew from life on the Fly X that skunks scoured riparian areas for frogs, turtles, and bugs, but also that they were primarily nocturnal. It was around three o'clock in the afternoon as they closed on this animal.

"Something's real wrong," Marshall said.

The skunk rocked back on its haunches as the boat drew near, lifting its right paw, which was crunched between the rusty curved bands of a leghold trap.

"Put us in," Marshall said. He felt a dome of nausea building in his gut.

"What are you going to do?" Molly asked. "There's no way to let it loose."

"We can at least put it out of its misery," Marshall said.

"We don't have a gun. What, are you going to beat it over the head with the oars?" Molly asked.

Marshall shrugged. "If I have to."

"And get doused with skunk stink?" Molly said. "Not if you want to float the rest of the way out in my boat."

"Who knows how long it's been there," Alton said.

"At least since last night," Marshall said. "Could've been the night before."

"They go numb," Molly said. "After a while."

Marshall recognized the sickness in his stomach from when he was young, when something happened that his father would interpret as wrong, or bad—unacceptable grades, the loss of a schoolyard fight, the time he was caught stealing a case of champagne from a family friend. He remembered it from the day he had seen the deer hanging from the hay fence on the Klingman place. It was a wash of awfulness alerting him that what was happening had real consequences, and the naked and irreversible essence of the wrong seemed inconsolable.

"They're supposed to drown," Molly said. "If you set the trap right, they drown."

"You know this from your lengthy experience in leghold traps?" Alton said.

"Don't act like this is my fault," Molly said.

"Sorry," Alton said. Molly turned from her rower's seat and inspected him for candor. Satisfied, she patted his knee. Alton said, "I just hate seeing stuff like this."

The skunk had taken to shuttling back and forth as far as its trapped paw would let it, waddling to the left and then turning with desultory regularity, as if it had figured this part out long before the people showed up.

"Put us in," Marshall said.

Molly rowed the boat into the riprap bank below where the current bent. Marshall climbed onto the boulders. On top of the bank, he scanned the surroundings. A half mile away he could see the flashing colors of cars racing down Highway 93. Closer, off to his left a few hundred yards away, he saw a tractor working the field. He started hiking over rowed dirt clods. When he came close, a farmer dropped down from his tractor cab. Marshall felt acutely aware of the fact that he was wearing the latest in breathable waders.

"Terribly sorry to bother you," Marshall said, "but are you running traps down along the river?"

"Nope," the farmer said. He wore Carhartt overalls, and his black hair made short straight jabs over his forehead. Marshall had the sense that the man and his forefathers had been working this plot of ground since long before the highway and realtors whittled it down to a quarter section.

"Because somebody's got a skunk in a trap down there."

"God*damn*it," the farmer said. He turned his chin toward the river. "We find 'em, we pull 'em, they keep puttin' 'em back. They caught a raccoon and a beaver and now this. No telling what they got we didn't know about."

"Do you have a gun I could borrow?" Marshall said. "I'm going to feel awful the rest of the day unless I know that animal gets dealt with."

"I'll go get one and take care of it," the farmer said.

"Thank you," Marshall said, knowing the man didn't have to react so kindly. Bruce Klingman, for instance, would have told him to go roast a goat.

Marshall returned to the river and stepped down the bank. Molly and Alton were both looking back to where the skunk huddled in a curl, as if it could perhaps go to sleep and wake up when the bad part was all over. Marshall legged back into the boat and, facing downstream, said, "Guy said he'd come shoot it. I wish we could stay until I know he's done it."

"Well, we're not gonna," Molly said.

Marshall turned and looked at her. "That part about them going numb after a while? It's wishful thinking. That's all it's ever been."

The notice came via mail three weeks later, in a plain white envelope, monogrammed in a tasteful but authoritative blue font in the upper left corner: JOHNSTAD, KALEVA & SEYBOLD, ATTORNEYS AT LAW. This was, purely by chance, also the first day Marshall would host clients on the Fly X spring creek, two men Molly was bringing, longtime repeat clients of hers. She'd called them slam-dunks. She'd said that if she told them they were having a peak fishing experience, then that's what they'd be having. Marshall had been up since five-thirty, waiting for them. It was around ten in the morning when the mail arrived.

Marshall opened the envelope, but didn't expend much effort puzzling out the legalese. He discerned it was a notice of the Klingman clan's not entirely unexpected intent to challenge certain water diversions on the Fly X, and that was enough to get him hopping into his pickup and bouncing down the drive. Though on a life-plan basis he fought mightily to control the blind rages that occasionally swept through him, he felt fine letting this one combust. He wouldn't mind if the morning evolved into a free-for-all. A litany of the foulest words he could muster scrolled through his mind in a soothing sort of mantra. The body of his truck tried to lift its wheels from Klingman's bridge as he hit its deck at fifty. Traveling at a high rate of speed was generally the best way to telegraph an emotional state in this neighborhood.

He didn't touch the brakes until he was nearly upon the Klingman house. His boots clomped across the porch floorboards and he had every intention of battering the door with his fists, but the screen flung open before him. Daisy Klingman half-stepped into the space and leaned against the door frame.

"Marshall Tate," she said, "you swain." Her eyes looked up from beneath tangles of hair, piles of light brown banana curls with sunkissed highlights city girls paid ninety dollars a month for. He had not seen her for over a year, but she always looked just the way he knew she would. "To what do we owe the pleasure?"

The top two buttons of her blouse were undone and he could see the spattering of freckles bridging her breastbone. Daisy had a bony, angular frame laced with ropy muscles that come from working outside. Her smile let Marshall know she could eat him alive. He felt the further disadvantage of never knowing when she was toying with him. For instance, he wasn't certain he knew what a "swain" was.

"I really don't have time for it today, Daisy. I need to see your dad." Marshall suddenly wondered if she had seen him coming and changed into this unlikely outfit—the blouse, a denim miniskirt wrapping her hips and not much thigh.

"You always used to make time for it," Daisy said. He couldn't tell if she was disappointed or not. "Daddy's not here. He and Randy went to town." She looked at him like this would be a shocking revelation if one fully understood its ramifications. In the tone of further hint, Daisy said, "Had to meet the lawyers."

"Shit," Marshall said. "So now they're hauling me to Water Court?"

Daisy shrugged. "You know I don't pay any attention to that crap."

He knew she knew exactly what was going on. "Why are they suddenly so out to get me?"

"Well, the deal is," Daisy said, as her eyes lifted above him and she squinted vaguely at the sky, "they don't like you. You know that."

"I don't need them to *like* me. But they've never been so vicious before. They've never gone legal on me."

Daisy put both hands behind her on the doorjamb and leaned back into them. Her eyes fell back on his face and he could see from the play in them she was still puppeteering. "It's so nice to see you, Marshall. Haven't seen you since . . . when was it?"

He hadn't *seen* Daisy in any meaningful way in over a year, since before she left for Reno, though he'd known for several weeks she was around again. He'd *seen* her in the sense that he sometimes saw her truck out on the road.

"Look," he said, "this water bullshit . . . it has no effect on your family's operation."

"I thought maybe you'd stop by and see me when you heard I was back in the valley," Daisy said. She lowered her chin to her chest and gazed down at the buttons of her blouse, then flicked at something on her chest. She cut her eyes up to catch him staring. "You did know I was back in the valley?"

"You've driven by my place how many times since you've been back? I haven't heard the doorbell ringing off the hook."

"Girls are coy," Daisy said. "Didn't you know that?"

"OK, but for right now, can we talk a little bit about this water situation? Because it's a big deal to me."

She shrugged again, then lifted an eyebrow in a sarcastic vamp. She said, "Tell you what, big boy, take me away from all this and I'll see if I can't put in a good word for you."

"Daze, if I took you away from all this you'd be living right next door."

"Yeah, now. But one of these days you'll get tired of playing cowboy. Then you could take me far, far away. Back East, to that fancy place you have there?" Daisy's voice lilted off toward dreamy. Marshall suspected she was toying with him. He prevented himself from biting on the "playing cowboy" line.

"I don't have any place back East. My family has places back East, but I guarantee you, you wouldn't want to live with them any more than you want to live with your own family."

"Why not?"

"My stepmom? Come on. She's a swamp Yankee and a drunk and a small-minded . . ." his voice pressed against the roof of his mouth, making small noises while he struggled for the right words, "Presbyterian bimbo."

"I could learn," Daisy said. It took twenty years of knowing Daisy to appreciate how close she could approach earnestness before shearing off into sarcasm. Now she stood with one foot inside the house and one on the porch, which had the effect of making Marshall think he should go inside. Moments before, it had been the last thing he wanted to do.

"I wouldn't do that to you, Daze. I like you too much the way you are," Marshall said. Not entirely true; he liked great chunks of her the way she was. He wanted to despise other parts of her, and could convince himself that he did when she was not around. Her crass desires, for starters; shameless appetite, is how Marshall had taken to thinking about it. But the truth was, whenever he stood in front of Daisy he found himself dissecting his biases and generally, within a few moments, understood that he would always see something to admire: teeth-gritting determination, a willingness to hold herself up for ridicule, a patience that might have something to do with foresight. "I could learn." That line slew him.

Daisy occupied the more livid dioramas of his past. Marshall's father, Jack "Skipjack" Tate, had bought the Fly X when Marshall was six. Skipjack was a wealthy man who had made his fortune early in life, in upstate New York, by purchasing a tanker truck and contracting out to county governments to spray herbicide on highway berms. Within only a few years he had amassed a fleet of trucks and branched into painting white lines on the highways, then leasing Jersey barriers and Port-O-Lets, and manufacturing road signs. Eventually his money started breeding on its own, even as he and his wife ceased to. Skipjack moved the small family to Watch Hill, Rhode Island, to an oceanfront manse more suitable to his portfolio.

Shortly thereafter he began his quest for the ultimate cocktail party and the ultimate place to host it, which led to the purchase of the Fly X from a member of the Klingman clan—Daisy's great-uncle—who could no longer deny his Arizona dreams. When he had learned of the impending sale, Bruce Klingman had tried to have "Crazy" Uncle Bud declared mentally incompetent, though ultimately he could articulate no specific grounds that didn't describe the whole family—or any family that had spent four generations in one valley—and the attempt failed, leaving only hard feelings and residual nomenclature.

That had been twenty-seven years ago, during which time Marshall had developed a fundamentally different relationship to the Fly X than his father had. The early ranch days, when his parents were still married, he cherished. But Marshall retained more vividly disturbing memories of the days following his parents' divorce, after Skipjack remarried and the cocktailing really ramped up—his father's new rich-and-tumble friends, savagely bored people belching in the ranch house kitchen and surreptitiously wiping cocaine boogers on the bottom of their scotch glasses. His early cognizance of wealthy people was marked by the impression that they would respect nothing they thought they could purchase, and this included certain groups of people—second spouses, for instance, or realtors. Marshall strained mightily to bear up during these parties, greeting incoming guests like a chipper buckaroo, nodding at their bellowed attempts at conversation. After an hour or so, Skipjack would be stoked out of his mind on adrenaline, and his second wife, Lila, who as far as Marshall could determine was largely a life-support system for vodka bottles, would have half collapsed—a loopy, potentially vicious grin splayed on her lips—on some man who was belching in the kitchen.

Then Marshall could grab his fly rod and sneak out the back door into the night, dodge between the pools of spotlight scattering the outbuildings, and make his way through the pastures toward the faint silhouettes of cottonwoods until he saw moonlight spangling the black gown of river. There nobody frightened him, and he needn't worry about walking in on his stepmother being groped by some sodden character in plaid pants. Along the river the night was pure and quiet and fish rose to his fly when he cast it right. Sometimes he would fish all through the night, until a pale morning light fell across the stream. On the initial outings he found it impossible in the darkness to guess where his fly might travel across the tapestry of current. That every once in a while a pulse or impulse told him to strike, and that the subsequent rip of line from the water foretold living, swimming weight on the other end, well, that was as close to a miracle as his young life knew. The other close-to-miracle thing in the early days was what Marshall did after he caught a fish, or quit trying, when he sat on the cobbles under the dark sky and smoked dope until he thought the stars would pour right down through his eyeballs into his skull and drip onto his brain. At thirteen, fourteen years old, these were the two most influential forces in forming Marshall's impressions of the possibilities in life.

Daisy came along and caught him one night, after which he'd spent a considerable amount of time closing in on some other possibilities. Back then Daisy was the only Klingman who didn't terrify him, though he was plenty scared of her. Sometimes she let him watch her plink gophers or magpies with her .22. Once, when they were about eight or nine, she had taken him to the rotted corpse of a winter-killed bull elk on his own family's property on the bench west of the river. Before revealing that treasure, she had made him join a secret society, inventing an initiation ritual the details of which Marshall could not recall, though it had something to do with dropping live worms into his mouth. At that age Daisy had been wiry and tougher than any boy Marshall knew. She was bossy and mean and she ceaselessly ridiculed his city-boy inadequacies. She could beat him up until . . . well, he wasn't sure she couldn't still beat him up.

"Have a drink?" Daisy asked.

"Can't," Marshall blurted. "I've got clients . . . people over at the place."

She ignored his refusal and stepped into the cool dark of the house as if she expected him to follow. Over her shoulder, she said, "Right, the fish pond."

"It's not a fish pond," Marshall said, finding that he had to enter the house to make that point.

"Whatever," Daisy said. She passed through the parlor and into the kitchen and Marshall followed her onto the linoleum. "Dad thinks it's ridiculous. What about gin and tonics?"

Their relationship had contained a chemical component since the summer he was fourteen and Daisy busted him smoking pot by the river. She would no sooner have squealed on Marshall than she would have complimented him, but her first demand was that he hand over the spleef and let her try a few mouthfuls. That began a long series of clandestine meetings at the river's edge that later progressed to various hideaways primarily featuring haymows in the Fly X barn, where they shuffled bales to form hollows within the stacks and climbed inside to

secretly smoke, surrounded by some of the most highly combustible material within miles.

One thing led to the other. Throughout their adolescence Marshall
and Daisy carried on a secret itinerant romance that began every year
when Marshall arrived at the ranch in June with a prickly re-feeling-out
of the territory. Marshall would tell Daisy about the girls he was seeing
in Rhode Island—lies, primarily—and grind his teeth while she remained closemouthed about what she'd done all winter. With each new
meeting he feared she might have become a slut, though at that point in
his life he had no understanding that it wasn't nice to think so, or even
wish it was true. By July they'd be partners in crime again, hiding out
and exploring the winter tales the summer retained on the landscape.

All of it had happened right here, in this valley. Daisy became the
first girl to kiss him. She was also the first to let him feel her nearly
nonexistent breasts and, eventually, she allowed him to slip a hand
into her Wranglers. Concurrently she was the first and boldest to
plunge a hand into his. Their affair continued—furtive and intermittent—even as he moved permanently to the ranch to attend college in
Missoula, and she began a rhythm of charging off full of vigor and
bright ideas, then returning to the valley to recoup. First it was a tele-
marketing scheme in Spokane. In Phoenix, real estate beckoned. In
Reno, she'd told him when she'd left, she was going to emerge as a
blackjack dealer. After each sally, she returned to the valley, remarkably unfazed by her inability to make things stick. One day, Marshall
suspected, she would go for good and then it would be over, everything
he had known with her. He sometimes wished it would happen soon.

Daisy reached into the custard-painted cupboards for glasses and
her blouse rode up to bare her midriff. Marshall leaned against the
Formica counter. He'd been in this kitchen before, on neighbor-relations
assignments, always stiffly accepting a glass of tea from Mrs. Klingman, knowing Bruce would prefer she not give it to him. He'd never felt
welcome here, and found disconcerting the prospect of pretending he
was having a relaxed conversation over a few drinks with an old friend
at this hour of the morning.

Daisy poured tall tumblers half full with cheap gin, then topped
them with tonic. During the first drink Marshall heard about how
blackjack dealing had come a cropper and serving cocktails to the
smoked-out octogenarians and small-time scumbags of Reno had worn

on Daisy's nerves—though a couple mentions of a buddy with a yacht and Baja dreams jabbed at Marshall's old jealousies. The second drink was on him and his relationship with Yacht Girl from Rhode Island. This was a young woman he'd met while visiting his father over Memorial Day weekend the year before. He'd gone sailing with her, leading Alton and Molly to dub her Yacht Girl before her first visit to Montana. When he met Yacht Girl, Marshall had been trying mightily to convince himself that Daisy was a bad person and that it wasn't necessarily her fault, but that she came from a bad bunch. The Rhode Island–Montana relationship lasted six months, and he and the girl had been remarkably polite to each other even while they both understood the whole thing never stood a chance.

"Sounds like a disaster from the get-go," Daisy said, once he'd encapsulated the entire failed affair.

"That's what my friends all said. You know, but nobody ever tells you that until it's over."

"Everybody drops hints, Marshall," Daisy said, "it's just your dick doesn't have ears."

"Nice, Daze."

Daisy swung her drink, causing some of the gin and tonic to splash over the back of her hand. She stuck a finger in her mouth to suck it clean. They were sitting at an oak harvest table, scuffed and gouged from decades of use. Both of them slouched in ladder-back chairs alongside the table. Marshall noticed that their legs were extended and overlapped and could touch if either moved to one side or the other. He wondered when that had happened. The comfort level was what he wanted to be bothered about.

He said, "I want to talk about what's up with your family and their vendetta against me."

"I want to talk about your dick," she said.

"Can you just for a minute . . ."

She scowled at him as if he'd been an ass for taking her seriously. Whereas he was pretty sure she'd been serious.

"Why do they hate me?" Marshall asked.

Daisy made a production out of stirring the bluish liquid in her tumbler. "Maybe because you won't make an honest woman out of me."

"They've hated me for years, long before they knew . . . How do they even know about that?"

"Oh, Christ, everybody knows," Daisy said. She dipped her finger in her drink and flicked it at him.

"Did you tell them?"

Daisy said, "People know shit, Marshall. They just . . . ," she swirled her tumbler around trying to hit it with a phrase, "see shit and know other shit. They've known for years." She stood suddenly, the chair honking across the floor. She snatched Marshall's tumbler from the table and whirled to mix new drinks.

"Ah, Daisy, you know, it's only eleven in the morning," Marshall protested.

She whirled back to face him. "I knew you when you ate pot because you were too stoned stupid to roll it up in papers and light it. Don't 'Ah, Daisy, you know' me."

"I'd like to think we're a little more grown up now," Marshall said. "I have a business to run, for instance. Kind of changes the way you have to behave a little."

"Well, change back," Daisy said. "I don't like it."

By the time she was done building the drinks, she had abandoned her cranky tone. She sashayed up to Marshall, spread her feet on the floor, and lowered herself on his lap, facing and straddling him. Marshall felt it incumbent upon him to act like this was run of the mill, though given the late-morning cocktails and the absence of contact with a female body throughout the entire winter, he may have been guilty of lifting a little to meet her weight.

"You know what I kept thinking about in Reno?" Daisy said, her eyes trying to lock his down. "Whenever things went to hell down there, I kept thinking about that time you and me took your raft and drove it way up all those logging roads, way up the river, and we put it in and we floated down toward here and we stopped overnight on that island. Remember?"

They had floated all day, occasionally anchoring so Marshall could fish. Eventually they had hauled out on a small island in the middle of the river, perhaps fifty square yards, pitched a tent, and built a bonfire with driftwood. The fire had escalated, at some point burning out of control until every stick of brush on the island went up in a rippling conflagration.

"We should have been killed that day," Marshall said.

Daisy burst into laughter and had trouble speaking. "We had to run around and quick take the tent down—"

"We should have burned to death," Marshall said. Her giggling made her wiggle on his lap.

"But we didn't," she said, "we just sat in the water and laughed and laughed."

They had moved the boat into the eddy pool downstream from the island and had plunked themselves in the water, sitting so it came up to their chests. He remembered feeling the heat in waves over his head and watching the flames ululating against the night. Orange sparks crackled into the deep blue dome of night sky. You couldn't fake something like that.

Daisy's laughter tittered into a long sigh. "And then we made love." She dipped her head so her hair brushed against his face. "In the cool water, with the heat from the fire and the light flickering on our skin—"

Daisy's mouth descended on Marshall's. A few frantic moments later he found himself lifting his buttocks so she could slide his jeans down to his knees.

"Uh, Daze . . . I'm not so sure . . . ," Marshall said with what ragged breath he managed to catch.

Daisy lifted her skirt and lowered back into his lap. She held her face close to his ear and said, "Mar*shall*." She moaned the second syllable.

"Mmmmmmmshit," Marshall uttered, and then his hands were filled with hanks of her hair and he was done talking for a while. When it was over, Marshall felt afraid to open his eyes. He assumed Daisy would be laughing at him, self-satisfied and somewhat triumphant. But when he peeked he saw the fragile press of tension on her forehead, her eyes squeezed shut. He knew nobody could concentrate so intensely on frivolity or irony.

Thirty minutes later Marshall strolled through the field, uncomfortable with how much lilt he felt, and more than a little worried that he'd step in a gopher hole and break his ankle, walking around this buzzed. Several geese feeding near the creek intermittently chased each other around, hooting like a band of party chimps. Molly Huckabee stood on the bank of the creek where it flowed from the big pond—the "fish pond" Daisy had sneered about, though it was only one feature in a complex system.

Below Molly, even closer to the water, stood two older gentlemen wearing or carrying, Marshall quickly estimated, a couple thousand dollars' worth of gear apiece. Before he'd closed the distance Marshall could see Molly pointing and describing strategy with sweeps of her arms and hands, but when he saw her miming casting motions—pausing between the backcast and forward cast seemed the meat of the lesson from a soundless distance—he knew the fish living in his creek were safe for this day. Then he caught himself thinking that he couldn't think that way. Clients had to catch fish or they wouldn't come back.

So instead he worried about the appearance of the place, worried these first clients would find it too bare, not grown in enough yet, too obviously *contrived*. He wondered if his own bewitchment with this water had to do with his conjuring it up in the first place. If he had arrived here out of the blue, he might see all the engineering and go cold. But years of experience with people who came from other places to go fishing led him to understand that how things looked mattered only somewhat, stacked against how the catching went. In other words, how nice it was "just to be out there" weighed in only when the fishing went south.

Exclusivity had a lot to do with it, Marshall knew and counted on. Some guys were dumb enough to pay five hundred dollars a day to catch almost nothing, provided they felt convinced they were the only people with the opportunity to catch nothing in that particularly sought-after place. But that was all a function of cachet, which this creek had yet to accrete. At any rate, in a year, maybe two—if he could stay afloat that long—the banks would grow in. There would be willows and alder, and he could peel away the deer fence from the small groves of aspens he'd transplanted from higher ridges. Cottonwoods and maybe some saskatoon or huckleberry would fill in along the pond. The Fly X Creek would look as natural as Alice or Bird creeks, streams that had flowed from the mountains for millennia.

Right now it looked a little . . . exposed. The creek Marshall had built rose from a series of natural springs that bubbled from the earth at the base of a long, treeless bench that reflected the curve of the West Fork River through the Fly X. The largest literally poured out of the side of the hill. Marshall had taken to calling this area the Fountain-head. The springs had previously spilled in several rills in various paths of least resistance eastward across a wide alluvial plain toward the river. Marshall had used a relatively dinky Kubota backhoe and many man-hours of labor to coax those separate springs from their beds and braid them all together into one brand new stream he imagined as he carved it across the plain.

This had required brutally hard work, and he'd hired the youngest Klingman, Kyle, a high school junior, to help him drag and roll and place the heavier structure. He dug deep, broad holes to back the water up before spilling it into high-grade, speedy turns just as the stream hit riffles of fine gravel he'd mined and strewn strategically across the bed. This was no simple gouge through the dirt, but a reflection of everything he'd seen in fifteen years of professionally floating down rivers—and hours of reading hydrology and aquatic biology and geomorphology textbooks. He'd studied the sinuosity of the flow to ensure a stream that would hold its shape over time, width-to-depth ratios that determined the transfer of sediment loads, helical flow, and its effect on scour patterns.

The upper mile of the creek was narrow, only ten or fifteen feet across in the runs. On this higher gradient, a mile of stream ran fast, a carillon of cold, clear water broken by rocks and logs, stepping down the streambed into deep emerald pools. Halfway to the river, Marshall had excavated the broad, five-acre pond with a kidney bend to it. The pond backed up enough water that Marshall could draw the lower two miles of creek into a wide, S-curving meadow stream. Through this lower stretch, the water fattened to fifty feet in places, and flowed in broad, casual arcs that appeared shallow because the clarity was so acute. But along the banks on the outside turns, current continually scoured holes that plunged over Marshall's head, and some of the undercuts went back five or six feet beneath the bank.

The lower stretch of water, hemmed by lush sedges and slender-stemmed rushes, was so clear and flat that beneath the surface flags of elodea and duckweed visibly waved over clay-striped bare bed and scrims of small cobble. Sometimes, when Marshall walked along the stream here, he would spot a discoloration, like faint brown smoke hanging in slack water, where a fish had disturbed the streambed as it jetted out immediately prior to his arrival.

It was at the head of this section, at the outlet of the pond, that Molly stood with her arms crossed and one hip jounced as Marshall approached. One of her clients, a balding man whose crown already burned bright red in the mountain sun, stood staring at the water, befuddled. The other had walked up the edge of the pond a bit. Marshall could see he was chasing a fish, hoping it would slow down long enough to cast to. Marshall couldn't tell if Molly eyed him suspiciously while he approached or if he was being more paranoid than usual. What he knew for sure, looking at her in her river shorts and fanny pack, hanks of wheat-blonde hair lustrous in the light where it hung beneath her cap, was that she sure looked cute. By the time he arrived, Molly had corralled her nearest fishermen and had him waiting to meet Marshall.

"Morning, Romeo," Molly said.

"What?" Marshall asked, shocked. How could she *possibly* know?

"You're supposed to say something like, 'Morning, Juliet.' It's clever banter that way," Molly said. In a way her client couldn't see, she scowled at Marshall. "I want you to meet Roger Poirier. Roger, Marshall Tate. Roger's in telecommunications. Marshall's in trout."

Up close, Marshall could see that the sun was harder on Roger Poirier than he had previously guessed. The man's scalp looked peeled. Roger was extending a hand to be shaken and Marshall liked the way he did it—straightforward, economical. He knew there would be no squeezy-wrestling.

"Hope you find the place to your liking," Marshall said. He had been suspecting that one of the secrets to success in the business he was about to enter might be his ability to curry a little character. He figured clients would want him to be cowboylike, or rancherlike, or wily-old-fishing-guidelike. Perhaps some combination of the three. He understood this from the way his father and their friends discussed guides and owners of lodges. The thought of faking it had always struck Marshall as repugnant; on the other hand, there was no use being a dumb ass, and half in the bag was as good a starting place as any. He felt just loopy enough to shoot for a laconic wrangler voice. "I'm real happy you all decided to visit." When he heard it out loud, he felt vindicated for consciously choosing "you all" rather than "y'all."

"These fish are, uh, difficult," Roger said.

Marshall reeled for a witty riposte, but he held enough remnant sobriety to know that forcing something stupid would only sound drunk. He rocked back on his heels and smiled dumbly.

"Missed you when we checked in this morning," Molly said.

"I was negotiating some water rights with the neighbors," Marshall said. He liked that he could talk about water rights. It sounded Western and ranchlike.

Molly—rudely, Marshall thought—clapped her hand on Roger's shoulder and used the momentum to turn him back toward the creek. "We'll stop and see Marshall on the way out," she said. "Better get back after those hogs before Steven catches them all." Marshall noticed that Steven, whom he assumed was the other client, still prowled the bank, looking like at any moment—*now!* . . . nope—he might be about to start casting. Molly walked Roger a few steps toward the stream bank, then turned back to Marshall, snatched his arm, and jerked him up the bank.

"What's wrong with you?" she asked, her whisper a hiss. He could see she hadn't decided yet: she was ready to be either highly amused or two days' worth of pissed off.

Marshall cocked his head back. "Nothing," he snorted.

"What's with the truck driver's accent?"

"What accent?"

"I've never heard anything so stupid." The closer Molly examined him, the more she leaned toward pissed off. "Are you drunk?"

"A little."

"Jesus, Marshall. It's noon."

"Ah," Marshall said, "I knew it was noon somewhere."

"What the hell have you been doing?" She seemed to be sniffing him, or the air around him.

Marshall, meanwhile, was halted midchuckle. He'd thought his previous response was really funny. Apparently they were going to be serious now. He recalibrated and said, "I've had to talk to my neighbors, who are threatening to haul me to Water Court to dispute some rights they allege I have violated. I promise it's enough to make anybody drink."

Molly scanned him with a weather eye. "I'm thinking this may not be the best way for you to begin your career as spring-creek host," she said. "Wandering around shit-faced and doing bad J. R. Ewing impressions?"

"Oh, don't be so dramatic," Marshall said. He noticed that Roger had never started fishing and was instead trying surreptitiously to observe the confab between himself and Molly. Marshall lifted two fingers to acknowledge Roger with a small wave, which led Molly's head to swivel toward Roger, then back at Marshall.

"I told you I'd bring you clients," Molly said, her voice a register lower, "but I've got to make a living, too. I can't afford my clients thinking I'm hauling them all over hell's half acre to fish with some hiccup buddy of mine. There's an element of respectability involved here."

"You know as well as I do that this whole . . . today . . ." His hand waved in a circle below his wrist, "This . . . it's a freak thing."

"Well, don't be a freak thing in front of my people," Molly spit. She began walking away with long, bouncy downhill strides.

RUNOFF

Marshall noticed the airy ramp of dust rising and angling toward the ranch from the meadows a mile to the east, recognized the glint of black at its vanguard as Mike Shadford's late-model Suburban. Marshall felt a long-incisored gnawing in his chest, the sense that what he was doing next was very wrong. What he wanted most to do was grasp Shadford by the shirt placket and smack his face back and forth at least three times. But he couldn't, and he hated that he'd put himself in a position wherein he so critically understood how he couldn't.

Marshall had once considered Shadford a friend, but over fifteen years of guiding for Fly Guys he had seen a certain development of the man, or perhaps a long devolution. Shadford had never screwed Marshall directly, but he'd manage to screw nearly everyone Marshall knew, which included everyone Marshall liked. The latest example, sleeping with Amy Baine, a twenty-three-year-old shop clerk and the girlfriend of his best guide. Marshall simply failed to see anything canny about that. Perhaps Shadford had reached a station in life where he construed the quixotic pathos of it as more gripping than loyalty or general human kindness or any of the other goody-two-shoe considerations. Perhaps he was closing too quickly on that fiftieth birthday, and flailing for handholds without regard for whether or not they could support his weight.

Maybe he was just confused about reality. Before Shadford pulled in the drive, Marshall could see he'd brought a passenger. If this was Amy Baine, Marshall might feel forced to resort to the back-and-forth face slapping. But he saw that the passenger was, instead, Scott Wadsworth, which chapped Marshall's ass in a different direction. Shadford nosed the Suburban into the drive, stepped out, and said, "Hey, babe. Ready to test-drive this creek?"

Shadford's forehead rose like a tanned tombstone from his eyebrows. His body was a runner's: lean and corded. This was a relatively new thing. When Marshall met him fifteen years before, Shadford had been well on his way to seed. "I brought Scotty along to help pound these sheltered fish of yours a little."

"See that," Marshall said.

"Hey," Scotty Wadsworth said. Scotty was fresh out of college. He stood short, chunky, and sloppy. Earlier in the season, Alton had taken to calling him Scotty the Wad.

"Thinking about giving Scotty a guide's license this year," Shadford said, striding past Marshall and gazing out into the fields, in the direction of the spring creek. "I wanted to check out his skills a little. Figured this would be a great place to test-drive him. You know— spring creek, spooky fish. You can catch spring-creek fish, you can catch anything."

Marshall knew that the demand for float trips overreached dependable guides, but . . . *Scotty the Wad?* Marshall tried to imagine how pissed off he'd be if he flew all the way from Tallahassee or St. Louis and found Scotty the Wad as his guide. Shadford turned, took a few deliberate steps, clapped a hand onto Marshall's shoulder, and squeezed the muscle. A smile flitted in his eye.

"Relax, chief," Shadford said. "You're gonna have to get used to other people whaling on your fish if you want to run a cash-generating business." He kept squeezing the shoulder muscle, and Marshall was dying to twist away from the pinching fingers and hypnotic green eyes, but he stayed stock-still. *I am jelly,* he told himself. *I am cool as jelly.* His glance cut back to Scotty, who stood unsure, his feet pointed away from each other, cow-hocked knees buckling inward, his thumbs resting in the belt loops of his jeans.

"Well, let's see what we can do," Marshall said, stammering around for nice-sounding phrases.

Marshall was not oblivious to the plight of the Wad. Scotty was a rich kid. You could see Scotty and his friends on any given night at the Rhino bar, letting the world know that they had it by the balls. Scotty's saving grace was that he was fat and a little homely, which lent some humility to the boy when you cut him from the herd. He had finagled a cash register jockey's job at Fly Guys, which, Marshall had noticed through the years, was not difficult if your family was rich. Marshall remembered, a little bitterly now, how Shadford had befriended, then hired him shortly after the first time his own father had sprayed cash all over Fly Guys. Scotty had been at the shop two summers now, and worked a little fill-in at Christmastime, which did not, Marshall couldn't help but see, make him a fishing guide.

"What'd you bring?" Marshall asked Shadford.

"My Winston four," Shadford said, strolling to the back of his vehicle. "Seven-and-a-half-footer."

"You got any four-weight rods, Scotty?" Marshall asked.

"Nope. I don't have any."

"Seems like a three and a five ought to pretty much cover it, is what I've always thought," Marshall said, sidling over to the now-open tailgate of the Suburban, where Shadford and Scotty both worked at joining their rods. "A four-weight seems like that second pecker on a billy goat. But then, I don't own my own fly shop."

"Don't even try it, Tate," Shadford said. "If I had your money I'd throw mine away."

"You must have me confused with my father, who *is* a wealthy individual," Marshall said. "I, on the other hand, am dead flat busted broke. This is all me, Mike. Pops contributed *nada* finances-wise."

"Why not?" Shadford asked, turning Marshall away from a longer pronouncement.

Marshall paused a moment. "It's stand-alone time," he said at length. "One of those things."

"Seems sort of stupid," Shadford said, "when there's so much to go around."

"It's about something a bit more," Marshall said.

"Yeah, yeah," Shadford said. "Don't go Shakespeare on me."

"Well, at the moment it's about me needing clients fast," Marshall said, "before this whole shebang becomes a tidy little exercise in earthmoving."

"Tell you what, chief, you show me all the fish you say live in this drainage ditch and I'll show you some fishermen," Shadford said.

Marshall loaded them into the Fly X's black Chevy one-ton and headed down the county road, then Klingman's road. The Fly X ranch consisted of three sections of land, 640 acres each, with a few extra slivers tacked on over the years. Two sections stacked atop each other on a north-south axis. From the upper half, an adjoining section jutted westward toward high ridges—three square miles in an upside-down L. The West Fork River entered from the west and followed the arc of the property, slicing the ranch roughly in half through both legs of the L. The house and outbuildings all stood on a rise to the east of the river.

West of the river, the high bench stepped above the floodplain, a relatively treeless interruption before evergreen ridges marched into the Scapegoat. There were springs all along the bench—to the south, a significant amount of springwater made the Klingman cattle operation hum, although those springs had long ago been gridded into irrigation canals.

The river itself was blue in the shallows and green where it poured over deeper holes, but crystal clear so that it took on the mottle of its rocky bed when you looked straight down into it. There was the beauty. It was all about the beauty. By the time Marshall had reached his late twenties, he'd realized that his father was bored with the Fly X and Montana in general. By then second-tier movie stars and dentists from Cincinnati were snatching up ranches with equal zeal and making the whole scene, to Skipjack's taste, look gaudy. Skipjack himself was remarried and busy manufacturing a brand new stepfamily while simultaneously discovering fishing bonanzas in Mongolia, French Polynesia, Slovenia, and the Seychelles.

Perhaps it was these expanded horizons. Perhaps it was Skipjack's remarriage and his involvement in the lives of Marshall's stepfamily, or perhaps it was the pressure that Marshall's mother brought to bear—he knew she had much to do with how long he'd been able to stay on the ranch in the first place, though she had retreated to Canandaigua, never again setting foot on the Fly X after leaving Marshall's father. In any event, a certain caginess began creeping into Skipjack's end of his relationship with Marshall, until it felt almost as if he were waiting to see which way Marshall was going to come at him. Marshall's feeling all along was that the old man had to know it would be the ranch. Things had come to a subtle head on a Rock Creek float trip during the salmonfly hatch two years before, when his father dropped in for one of his spotty fishing trips—unforeseen appearances that invariably married a quickie drop-in at the ranch with a potential business partner who wanted to be impressed by the place. Marshall's job, during those occasions, was to row them down the river and agree with his father about how wonderful everything was.

"We sure assholed them today," Skipjack had said as they glided downstream, a few hundred yards above a takeout. "You did a hell of a job of getting us into fish," Skipjack told Marshall, making sure to speak loudly enough so that the man in the front of the boat, a retired Air Force colonel, could hear.

Marshall would have taken that seriously, except he knew that Skipjack lavished praise on all his guides when the fishing was good. "This isn't exactly difficult," Marshall said.

"Sure, sure," Skipjack said. "Guide's biggest job is making sure the client's erection doesn't subside. Most of it's foreplay and knowing when to let the wad blow, hah?"

"All in the chitchat," Marshall said.

"Sure would like to see a way to let this little ranch of ours keep itself afloat," Skipjack had said, as if he was bemused about it. This was a conversation bomb Marshall knew enough to scurry away from. Speaking now to the colonel, Skipjack said, "Boy, now Chile, Chile's like this, only bigger fish. I took Scooter"—Marshall's ten-year-old stepbrother— "down there in February. Unbelievable. You can buy whole watersheds. Scooter just loved the place."

A few days later, looking back at that snippet of conversation, Marshall realized the color of the balloon his father was floating: Skipjack was thinking of off-loading the ranch in favor of a grander, more exotic spread in South America. Marshall realized next that it would be incumbent upon him to pony up a solid contraposition or start house hunting.

What Marshall knew he'd have to do would be to adduce the ranch from the scope of his father's concerns. Pay off the property taxes and upkeep—perhaps even turn a nominal profit—and Marshall could go on living there forever. But how? Cattle were not an option; Marshall hated everything about commercial meat production, what it did to both the animals and the land. He didn't know the first thing about horses. Crops were unreliable.

His answer came late one afternoon that same summer as he hiked atop the broad, bare bench from the foot of which the Fountainhead springs emerged. Below him the West Fork River had been sheathed in the reflected green of leaves and lined by low-water beaches of cobblestone textured in blue shadow. In every direction before him lay pastures that had gone fallow for years. Along the foot of the bench, dollops of greenery bundled around the springheads. Marshall had breathed the scene in, felt it, and had come rather abruptly to the conclusion that the beauty of this place would have to be what saved it, and that it could not be compromised in the process. *What, Marshall has asked himself, can I do with the beauty?* He invented the spring creek. It had not seemed like a great idea even at the time, though now he felt incapable of explaining how deeply in love he was with the thing.

Marshall had completed most of the work during the grip of winter, often in the dark, after driving home from working at Fly Guys for Shadford. There were also many late nights during the guiding season spent digging, screening, rolling, dragging, filling, hauling, then replanting and fine-tuning. But as soon as he connected the spring creek to the river, squads of very big fish moved up into it without compunction, as he suspected they would, and now it was time to talk commerce. Shadford and Scotty the Wad would be a perfect test because he sort of despised them both, though he needed Shadford in a fundamental way. He drove the truck over the Klingman bridge, then angled off north into the meadow, bouncing along the two-track tractor path.

"Need some signage," Shadford said, "a little atmosphere."

"Way low on the list," Marshall said.

"Just trying to help."

Marshall stopped the truck where he had mowed down grass for parking and walked through the field until the meadow opened onto a clear stream.

"There are fish in here?" Scotty the Wad said.

"Trust me."

"There's hardly any water," Scotty said.

It was the clarity, Marshall understood, that deceived Wad. There was plenty of water. Marshall had known before he'd started—it was, in fact, why he'd started—that the constant temperature of a spring, a function of its birth underground, combined with constant clarity and pH and constant flow levels, provided a stability that allowed riparian vegetation to flourish, which in turn encouraged aquatic insects to grow in gobs. At every other spring creek he had ever seen, big trout inhabited little water, and even the little trout grew fat fast.

Marshall directed Shadford and Scotty to the obvious spots, skipping over other less likely niches he knew held monster fish. In one stretch he spotted a hand-sized tail fanning the shadows beneath a mat of watercress—and walked right by it. He pointed out the long, dark streaks of trout holding against the banks, or folded in seams of current. Scotty cast in rapid, impatient stabs, which resulted in him catching nothing in the slow, lower stretches of the creek. Shadford fished upstream. He seemed rapt with his own ability, which occasionally resulted in his pausing too long between strokes and throwing tailing loops. But Shadford knew where to put his fly, and he hooked and released three very nice trout.

Marshall found himself silently rooting for each fish to shake Shadford's hook, barely suppressing a shout when a fourth one did. It was important that Shadford had a good time on this creek, that he saw lots of fish and caught a few big ones. Shadford owned a fly shop, so people thought he was a guru. All Shadford had to do was utter a few magic words—"this sweet little spot I know"—to the multitudes of anglers looking for the Next Great Place, and Marshall would float through his first season.

When they reached the point where the creek paused in the long kidney-bent pond, Marshall pointed Shadford toward the bluish cigar-shaped silhouettes of four big trout finning in place just above the outlet.

"Those are all twenty-four-inch fish," Marshall said.

"Let's see what you can do," Shadford said to Scotty Wadsworth. Marshall had noticed previous to this Shadford not paying a bit of attention to this prospective guide he was allegedly evaluating.

"Why don't you give it a try," Marshall said to Shadford.

"Naw, it's shiny time for the Wad," Shadford said. "Show us your stuff, Scotty."

"You got a little nymph?" Marshall asked Scotty. He found himself unexpectedly on the Wad's team, wanting Scotty to catch a fish.

"I thought I'd try dry."

"Not a chance," Marshall said, stepping over to where Scotty stood. "Maybe in the evening, but it's too bright now. Gotta go subsurface. Do you have a little Copper John, or a Disco nymph? Any kind of midge larva, real small, twenty, twenty-two?"

Scotty dug a fly box from a vest pocket, opened it, and started strafing the compartments with his index finger. Marshall peered over his shoulder to examine the contents of the box. All store-bought patterns. Scotty pointed to a green scud in a size Marshall guessed to be about eighteen.

"Hey, Shadrat," Marshall said, "you got any flies this guy can borrow?"

"Sure, babe," Shadford said, but he stood with his hands clasped behind his back, not moving, his smile glutinous and smug. Marshall was the only person who called him Shadrat directly, though even Shadford was aware that everybody did behind his back.

"I'll just try this," Scotty said, holding up the scud.

"You'd have to do everything perfect, and even then it wouldn't work," Marshall said. "What's your tippet?"

"Five."

"Five?" Marshall blurted. "No wonder you haven't caught anything. Go with three feet of six-X and at least a foot of seven."

Marshall stepped back to where Shadford stood—Shadford rearranged now, his rod jutting from his crossed arms like an outrigger. Scotty tied on tippet. Shadford said to Marshall, "Always the guide."

Marshall didn't say he'd rather Scotty caught one of the trout than provide Shadford with a good excuse for failing to, because he knew with more disappointment than he cared to delve into that Scotty wasn't going to catch shit.

"You're gonna miss it," Shadford chided.

"Guiding?"

"Yep."

"Not a bit."

"Being out on the river every day," Shadford said, "Here you're going to have to deal with clients wanting this and wanting that. Cheating. You'll catch people killing fish. Wading on redds, trashing the place."

"How's that different from guiding?" Marshall asked.

Shadford smiled. "It'll all be on your property."

"This is my dad's place," Marshall said, angry at Shadford for not knowing that clients trashing the place pissed him off no matter where it happened. But Shadford was right about one thing: Marshall viewed most rivers as big, forgiving places, resilient and redolent with second-, third-, four-hundredth chances. Whereas, rightly or wrongly, he envisioned his spring creek as a new and delicate phenomenon, easily shattered. Marshall had spent countless hours sawing mats of sedges and their associated soils from the old springbeds and laying them in along the new creek. He had cut willow shoots and cottonwood seedlings from the river and replanted all of them along the watercourse. He had hiked up onto the bench and the ridges above and dug ten-foot aspens and carried them on his back, root-ball and all, to plant in groves along the new creek.

In its second season, mosses, algae, and sedge had begun to colonize the spring creek. Mats of watercress clung along the banks, and the glowing green string-of-pearls duckweed leaves waved in the current. That fall, he had seen spawning redds gleaming like porcelain platters on the streambed, oblong scoops where the tails of brown trout whisked away algae and muck. The females would lay their eggs and males would swoop over them like crop dusters, discharging clouds of milt. He had counted sixty-two redds the second year, twenty-four of them above the pond. Next would come the fly-fishing hordes with their much-trumpeted sensitivity to nature, which Marshall knew was pegged to convenience and often just a friendly batch of crap.

He had seen clients snap off willow saplings to clear backcasting room, or tread thoughtlessly over spawning redds. While guiding in Alaska his one and only fall, Marshall watched a client blow away a back screen of alders with repeated blasts from a shotgun. Another client had caught and killed 152 grayling, and when Marshall complained to his boss, he was told: money talks, guides don't. Marshall remembered this as he watched Scotty the Wad finish tying on his fly and plod toward a budding cusp of reeds along the water's edge.

"Wad, hands and knees, man," Marshall said.

Scotty looked at him as if he would not be made an ass of.

"I'm serious," Marshall said. "If you want to catch those fish you gotta approach on your hands and knees. And you have to cast at least ten feet ahead of them, give them a long time to see it."

Shadford shrugged when Scotty looked to him for confirmation.

Marshall watched the Wad drop to his knees and shuffle along before leaning all the way over and placing weight on his hands, too. Near the water Scotty rose to a kneeling position, let one foot step forward in a team photo pose. He waved his rod, let out enough line, dropped the fly onto the pond. The four blue shadows jetted into its depths.

"Who else you got guiding this year?" Marshall asked. He knew all about the timing, but he kept it conversational and aimed at Shadford. Shadford played along.

"The regular crew, plus Scotty. Alton, of course," Shadford said. Now they were two old buddies engaged in chat, which let Scotty Wadsworth wander up the pond bank in search of other fish, unshackled from the weight of their attention. Shadford added, "The thing with Amy, by the way, is not all the way Alton probably says it is. I mean, they were having problems, whether he saw it or not."

Marshall took a moment to sift through his approach before saying, "Can't imagine how it's too smart either way."

"Well, Alton really didn't—"

"Ahp!" Marshall barked, his palm flying open in a flat *Stop!* gesture. "I'm done hearing about it."

"OK," Shadford hurried to say. "All right. To be perfectly honest, though, it's going to be hard working with Alton, with all this going on."

"You made him sign a contract."

"Yeah, well, that was before—"

"Seems like it doesn't matter when," Marshall said. "Contract's a contract."

"You don't go to happy hours with many lawyers, do you?" Shadford said, and Marshall could see that he was trying to gussy it up as a joke.

"That's your business," Marshall said. He started to walk away toward Scotty. "I'm out of it now."

"But you're still friends with everybody in it," Shadford said, following. "And you want to do business with me."

"I want you to send fishermen here," Marshall corrected.

"Same thing," Shadford said. "Business is all about relationships, Marsh."

Marshall, though he didn't feel that way at all, didn't know how to draw the distinction subtly enough to risk speaking. He walked on, growing angrier at the position Shadford seemed to need to squeeze him into. *What would be wrong,* Marshall wondered, *with letting me off the hook.*

"You think about it; if you hadn't quit, I wouldn't be in this spot," Shadford said. For a moment, after he heard it, Marshall thought with alarm that Shadford was reading his mind. But then he replayed the statement and it became apparent that Shadford was once again merely covering Shadford's ass.

"How do you arrive there?" Marshall asked. They were close to Scotty again. Scotty had quit casting and moved toward them as if he were coincidentally done fishing at the moment. Marshall had stopped and turned to Shadford. He stood in the greening sedge a few yards back from the edge of the pond, equidistant between Scotty and Shadford as each of them converged on him.

"Hey babe, if I still had you, I wouldn't need to move Scotty up," Shadford said. He seemed immediately to know that was the wrong thing to say, or that he'd said it at the wrong volume. "Or," Shadford said, louder, "I could go ahead and move Scotty up and let go of Alton."

Marshall didn't let Scotty see the scoff he flashed at Shadford.

"Give me an exclusive on the creek," Shadford said. Again, Marshall took a moment to replay what had just been said. He felt like Shadford was pulling things out of hats. He wondered how much of what had gone on all day was simple misdirection. Why hadn't he seen this coming? But it had never crossed his mind.

"What?" Marshall said.

"Give me an exclusive on the creek, I'll keep you booked solid through runoff," Shadford said. "Tell you what, I'll guarantee it."

"What about the rest of the summer?" Marshall said.

"Well," Shadford said, as if what he was saying were only natural, "I'd want the exclusive all season. I mean, frankly, Marshall? To be perfectly honest with you, I can't imagine taking it on without an exclusive. I mean, exclusivity among outfitters."

"Really?" Marshall said, gauging the meaning of the new term: *exclusivity among outfitters—how would that work?* Everybody had stopped walking, as if one more step might push the negotiation over the crux.

"I don't know, Mike," Marshall said. "I didn't really build this to be your own private creek." He stared away, into the pond, watched the form of a big trout coast along the bank toward the outlet, then carve out a graceful turn and halt, facing the outgoing current.

Shadford asked, "What are you going to charge?"

"Sixty a rod this season," Marshall said.

"You could get a hundred."

"Bargain rate to build a customer base. Then I'll see," Marshall said. He just couldn't think about this now, not so urgently.

"How many rods a day?"

"Six," Marshall said. He had worked this through before and answered now by rote while the rest of his attention disengaged, floated somewhere in the surface film of the pond, floating over the holding trout, entering the bright white reflection that was the sun's imprint on the water, where everything disappeared into a ball with the burning of oblivion at its core.

"You could handle ten. Including the river? There's all that river to fish. You could handle twelve. That's great water, practically private. With twelve at sixty you'd be looking at seven hundred and twenty dollars a day this season," Shadford said. "If it goes well, you double to one hundred dollars a rod next year. Give me an outfitter's exclusive. I'm the only outfitter who can book it—that includes your girlfriend Miss Huckabee, too. Six rods guaranteed and I take a fifteen percent commission. Anybody who books through you on top of that is yours."

Marshall's gaze flicked to Scotty Wadsworth, who stood watching the two of them with what Marshall thought was the incipience of a grin twitching in the corners of his lips.

"I'll have to think about it," Marshall said.

"Sure," Shadford said. "But you don't have much time. Runoff's starting. I need to get the word out that I have this available. Have to market a little."

"Start marketing," Marshall said. "The creek isn't going anywhere."

"There's the matter of exclusivity, babe," Shadford said. "Positioning, you know. I have to be able to offer my clients something they can't get just walking in off the street. It isn't like the old days when people walked in and asked, 'Where's the fishing?' and you just said, 'In the river.' The movie changed everything. I need to give people things they can't get at Troutfitters. It's all about the edge, now."

"Yeah," Marshall said. "Edge. Huh. I'll let you know. Listen, you guys fish on, there's good stuff above the pond. Smaller but faster, not as technical. I'll let you know on the other. I've got some things back at the house . . ." Marshall hooked a thumb over his shoulder back toward the ranch house. "Take the truck back. Keys are in it. I'll walk. Find me if you want before you leave," he said.

Marshall didn't go back to the house. He stalked off across the field of spring grass until he felt he was either out of sight or they'd quit watching and gone back to fishing. Then he cut straight across the pasture to the river. Shadford had been right. The river had already begun to swell, tickling the roots of willows and sedges along the bank, and its clarity had fallen off, its midlevel browning. The real runoff, the high-country melt, had begun. Marshall could hear it in the tone of the water spilling over rocks that had not been wet since the valley snow melted off. He sat on a flat slab of boulder and watched the brown water slide by beneath the vault of cottonwood branches bursting with new leaves. *Edge? When had it ceased to be just fishing?*

Marshall sat in his house—a log structure his father had had built after demolishing an existing house on the site—and dreaded the thought of calling that very man. The house was T-shaped, two stories. The stem of the T described a great room with vaulted ceilings and an accent on windows. A broad porch wrapped this room. Beyond it stretched a patch of yard, bordered by patchy aspens and a few pines. Inside, the rooms had featured slouching sofas and overstuffed chairs when Marshall's mother originally furnished it. A redecorating blitz by Marshall's stepmother and a designer from New York had for a brief while created a case of Rocky Mountain splendor: buffalo guns mounted on the wall, wrought-iron and cowhide director's chairs, deer-antler chandeliers. Gradually, with pack-rat determination, Marshall toted all that stuff into the barn, took the lavish art he didn't understand off the walls, and the house crept back to being the sort of place where visiting dogs could sleep on the furniture and nobody minded boots scuffing kernels of dried mud on the runners.

Marshall's stepmother had not been to the ranch for over a decade, and he frankly thought his father preferred his more functional decor. In a small, creeping way he could not exactly articulate, Marshall was beginning to understand that the viability of his spring creek project would form a watershed in his relationship with his father that had been a long time coming. He had strictly avoided seeking financial assistance from his father during construction of the creek, though it would probably have been made available for the asking. All of Marshall's life, Skipjack Tate ran the checkbook of love like an interest-free account. Marshall understood that the handouts were gestures meant to convey an emotional gamut his father had trouble running in the open field. He felt his father meant well and that, Marshall thought, was about as much as you could ask from anybody. He was not so naive as to ignore the obvious power dynamic involved in the rather one-sided concentration of wealth in the family, though Marshall was able to excuse this as simply too easy for his father to resist. But Marshall could resist it, and he had so far during the birth of the spring creek. The thought of a phone call soliciting aid now made him cringe.

Skipjack had visited the ranch once since the transformation began, had seen the creek work in progress. Marshall thought his father had decided to appear quizzical about the whole thing, and possibly sardonic. Whereas he never so much as shrugged to indicate he doubted the viability of the project, Skipjack was clearly going to wait and see how things turned out. This was a test. Everybody involved knew it. Marshall's spring creek project was something Skipjack had rather conspicuously never thought of; also, Marshall had cleverly put into play his father's craving for cachet. Skipjack had fished the Livingston spring creeks many times through the years, and was well aware that, sitting in the upper warming hut at DePuy's, a man shared space with a cultural history. Every famous fly fisher had been within those walls, every personage in the realm of trout. If his ranch could develop into something similar, well, then even Skipjack would have to admit that Marshall had pulled off quite a coup.

Skipjack despised lawyers but used them like junkyard dogs. Marshall believed he could broach some obscure confusion about the details in a way that let Skipjack believe the idea to bring a lawyer in was his own. Mention any problem and the elder Tate's first-look reaction was to huck money at it. So Marshall picked up the phone and punched the numbers to his father's office in Providence. The conversation very quickly whipped out of control.

"Oh, Marshall . . . right. Listen, I was going to ask you, I want to send some, ah, associates out to your spring creek," Skipjack said. "I've been talking it up around here and I'll tell you, I've generated no small amount of interest. Will you be ready for them?"

Because Marshall understood that his father was not asking out of concern for Marshall's state of mental preparedness and was instead saying: *this place will be as good as I'm telling people it is, right?* he was able to frame the comment in a working context. There had been a time, early in his life, when Marshall actually enjoyed fishing with his father and his father's friends, but his father had run with a different crowd then. For starters, those folks had been actual friends, as opposed to "ah, associates." Ocean fishing was what Marshall remembered about liking fishing with his father. Saltwater fly fishing was something at which his father excelled by any measure. It was, in fact, Jack Tate's landing of a tippet-class world-record bonito off Lobsterville Beach on Martha's Vineyard that prompted the invocation of the longer nickname—Skipjack. Marshall's father found a symmetrical beauty in that, and told Marshall about it years before, late into the Macallan one night in the sitting room of their Watch Hill "cottage."

"Marshall," his father had mused. What followed sounded like something he'd been thinking about for quite some time, trying to figure out how to make it sound just so. "It's more than mere irony or coincidence when destiny arranges for nomenclature to complement accomplishment."

"Does that mean I should shoot for a career reviewing parades?" Marshall had asked.

His father reacted as if he had received a blow, and responded by delivering one. He slapped his son straight down on the top of the head with the flat of his hand. Marshall's eyes closed of their own accord, then popped open wider than he would have liked. His father had never struck him before, but Marshall was only beginning to understand how seriously Skipjack would be taking this nickname business. Nevertheless, Marshall was perplexed by how little gravity he placed on the fact that his father had assaulted him—possibly, he thought, because it had been such a silly whack. The lightness of the moment had bothered him. What bothered him more was the counting back to how long it had been before that moment since his father had physically touched him in any sort of gesture.

"You don't have to be a goddamned smart-ass just because you know how," Skipjack blustered.

Skipjack held his ground shakily, obviously scared about what he had done but feeling the propriety of hierarchy at stake. Marshall couldn't fathom a way to work it out cleanly. He said, "Sorry," and rose from the wing chair, floating up and away to his bedroom, where he hung out his window listening to the tide rip on the Watch Hill reef and sucking his bong long enough to make the ringing slap on his skullcap fade into tingling ripples, until all sensation dissipated.

About the new "ah, associates" his father wanted Marshall to entertain, Marshall said, "Send them in late June. I'll have some people under my belt by then, and if things really go to hell they can fish the river."

"They're awfully keen to get out there later this month," his father said.

"It's runoff. That kind of limits things if they don't like the creek. I'd be loathe to give you any guarantees," Marshall said, remembering diction tricks and simultaneously sparking a notion of how to spin the dialogue to an element that would let Skipjack glow. "Which reminds me . . . Shadford wants an outfitter's exclusive. I set aside six rods a day for him and give him fifteen percent of the fee. What's your take on that?"

After a short pause, during which Marshall hoped his father was relishing the fact that his son was asking for business advice, Skipjack said, "There's a myriad of avenues to approach this thing, and those are delicate determinations you're going to have to execute. What about your guide fees?"

"Which guide fees?"

"I assume you'll be guiding fishermen yourself. I certainly don't want to send people out there without the knowledge that they'll be in good hands. These guys are no experts."

Marshall hadn't thought about that, but didn't want to admit it. "Yeah, but there's a lot of work to do around here. The fence along the southwest quarter is a disaster."

"Let Klingmans fix that goddamned fence. You've got to learn to prioritize, son. You're at a time in your life where you've got to start placing a monetary value on your time," Skipjack implored. Marshall could tell he was working himself up to get on a roll. He could picture the old man kicking back in his high leather chair. "What happens if you don't fix the fence right away? Cows get in our pasture and you call Klingmans and Klingmans piss and moan and they come and get the cows. Big deal. You've got bigger fish to fry. You have to decide policies and strategies about this spring creek. Do you let other guides work it? Do you let Shadford send his guides with his clients, or does he send the clients and you guide the ones who want guides? Do you hire and train your own guides? Quality control seems imperative. Who pockets the guide fees? I would assume given the timescape and the development process, you're going to—for a while, anyway—be drawing clients who would otherwise be fishing with a guide, floating the Clark Fork or the Blackfoot, because western Montana has no reputation as a spring creek destination. Have you talked to any writers?"

This last seemed to Marshall a radical departure from a garden of topics he hadn't thought through to a forest of ideas he hadn't even spied on the horizon. But this was what his father did best—concentrated in manic bursts on solving specific problems, then shifted far away to something else. It had, Marshall understood all too sadly, nothing to do with him.

"Writers?" Marshall asked.

"Fishing writers. Christ, Marshall, growing up you read every issue of *Fly Rod & Reel* that came in the mail," his father said. "Didn't that make you want to go to all those places you read about?"

Marshall suspected Skipjack would be talking more about himself now, but he conceded the point.

"Establish who are the premier fishing writers in your area and appropriate their appreciation. Give them free days—hell, it doesn't cost you anything if you're not booked up. Understand, Marshall, you've targeted an elite clientele." Now Marshall *knew* his father was talking about himself; Marshall hadn't targeted anybody. "So traditional forms of advertising are not the most viable options for you. Do you see Nelson's or DePuy's or Armstrong's spring creeks advertised anywhere? No. But they're booked solid. Milesnick's? *Never been advertised.* But you have to reserve a year in advance. Why? They're famous. Who made them famous? Tom McGuane. Jim Harrison. The editors of *Fly Fisherman*, who, as you know, I'm on good terms with, and it wouldn't hurt to exploit that sort of contact. The people you're trying to reach value exclusivity, which, incidentally, is why I think you've vastly undervalued your fee structure."

He did? Marshall's fee structure was not something he'd ever imagined on his father's things-to-think-about list. Marshall said,

"Yeah, but Dad, I can't just call Tom McGuane and say, 'Hey, man, wanna go fishing?' "

"Why not?" his father bellowed. "Who the hell is he, special? Listen to me, Marshall: you stepped right into the bigs. You've skipped the minor leagues. How many times have I told you that people respond to carriage, to presentation. You've got to approach these personalities as their equal. You've been around the world, son. You've hobnobbed with industrialists, media personalities. Who the hell could possibly intimidate you?"

You, Marshall could have said. He decided furthermore not to note that fifteen years of guiding for Fly Guys might count on some scorecards as the minor leagues. If Skipjack wanted to think he'd hatched a superstar, fine. Let the man have his shiners.

Marshall was busy being disappointed in the dawning discovery that he had allowed the conversation to stray far from his intended tack, and he wasn't going to be able to sheet it in. His father had moved on to offer the opinion that Marshall should not feel beholden to Shadford. "He'd screw you in a minute if he could, wouldn't he?" Skipjack asked.

Marshall suspected that his father harbored smoldering resentment for the man who had employed his son as a lowly fishing guide for so long, but he also had to admit that all evidence indicated Shadford would probably screw him.

"Then screw him first," Skipjack said. "You want to establish a reputation as nobody's pushover, you don't have to screw a whole lot of people. You just screw a couple real thoroughly."

"Actually, Dad, establishing a reputation as nobody's pushover isn't high on my agenda right now."

"Look, save the fucking altruism for your Nature Conservancy friends," Skipjack shot back. "You're going to learn, my boy, that when you build a successful, high-profile business, people will come crawling out of the woodwork looking for a piece of you. And you'd better quickly establish a pattern of quashing that sort of behavior or you'll find yourself nibbled to death."

Marshall had begun to feel like this was the sort of self-empowerment lecture certain people in major metropolitan areas listened to on audiotapes while they commuted to and from their middle-management careers. But with the last exchange, he thought they might have crossed over from talking about a spring creek and entered into a whole field of discussion about Marshall's character flaws and the many lessons he had failed to learn from his success-ridden father. So he began scrambling to get off the phone, leaving unturned the stone under which water rights lawyers lived.

Just after he hung up, still feeling dazed, Marshall caught a glimpse of two dark hurtling shapes at the same moment he heard a briefly tympanic *wang!* against the picture window. He stood and looked out. The dive-bombed body of a robin stuck beak-down in the grass. Beside it another robin spread its wings over the corpse. Marshall walked outside and around to the birds. One was clearly dead, beak down in the grass, its body straight as a spear. The living bird continued to mantle and cranked its head back to watch Marshall with a beady black eye. Marshall had to assume this had been a mating mishap. He looked at the living bird and said out loud, "You pushed it."

At almost exactly that moment, Molly Huckabee sped east down I-90 in her white 4Runner. She drove eight miles, exited, and hopped on State Highway 200 angling north and east for forty-five more, then turned northwest on a county road and chugged along the improved gravel for twelve before the road bent at right angles to the southwest and began running along the Tate property. Molly noted the immediate and pleasing change of landscape the moment she began paralleling Marshall's place, how the land that had been for centuries oppressed by agriculture—mostly hay cutting and cattle grazing—suddenly sprung back to life around her. Still not unbent from the weight of winter snow, long stems of grass leaned in tawny clumps, and even the fence line flourished with shrubs and creeping plants.

She drove her rig down Tate's dirt lane and pulled into the yard. She saw Marshall on the flagstone veranda of the main house, sitting in a hewn pine rocking chair with a notebook in his lap and a pen slanted between his fingers. She squinted at the sunlight and smiled as she approached him.

"Hey there," Molly said, dropping into a rocker beside his.

"My father," Marshall announced, "after owning a Montana ranch for almost thirty years, still does not know how you determine who's responsible for fixing a fence between neighbors."

"How do you?"

Marshall turned on her. "You're a Montana girl!"

"I grew up in Havre! We lived five blocks from the high school. We didn't have to fence off our neighbors."

Marshall looked scolded and Molly wondered if she'd used a harsh tone. "How do you determine who's responsible for fixing a fence?" she asked.

"You meet your neighbor in the middle of the fence line, each on his own property. You face each other. All the fence to your right is your responsibility. All the fence to his right is his baby."

"The things I learn from you," Molly said. "I take it you spoke to ol' Skipjack about paying for a lawyer."

"I had every intention." He let his gaze unfocus on the cottonwood scroll marking the river in the distance.

"Bulldozed?"

"Just rolled right over. Exposed my soft underbelly. Now I feel wounded and contused."

Since she'd understood what Marshall had planned to do on the ranch, Molly had appropriated every opportunity to fish the spring creek. She knew the creek project would work, and that she could both profit from and contribute to its success. Although she wouldn't put a finger on it, she now and then allowed a warm flush to overtake her as she thought in notions of this partnership and how it might define the way she and Marshall moved through the future. She'd known him for over ten years, and initially had wondered why he seemed content as a fishing guide when his other life, the life of his father and his upbringing, seemed such a rich pageant of not only wealth, but fame and the attendant opportunity to go places and see things few people could. Molly had grown up on the Hi-Line. Her parents had split when she was sixteen, only a year after her younger brother had died of leukemia. Neither parent understood how to live with the other's form of grief, but neither remarried, and both remained active in Molly's life. They were both schoolteachers in Havre, and her father coached the Blue Ponies football team. Molly grew up dreaming of the life Marshall could live.

When she first met Marshall, she pegged him for a rich boy right away, and was amused at his constant attempts to repudiate his status. At first she assumed Marshall's stance was mostly posturing, but soon enough she realized he was in full retreat, tail tucked between his legs. Marshall once told her that it wasn't money he despised; rather, he hated how one-dimensional rich people let themselves become. Given the opportunity to pursue interesting and meaningful lives, all they had to show for themselves was acquisitions, and he found that repulsive—which she found charming. Molly had gone through phases with Marshall—initially a mad but completely concealed crush, followed by a casual acquaintance that had built into a rich and complex friendship. Then, while she watched, Marshall was building his spring creek and things turned again; Molly feared she might be profoundly in love with him.

"Let's go fishing," Molly said. She slapped the back of her knuckles against his leg.

Marshall evinced no reaction to the contact. "I need to call Shadrat while I'm feeling like shit."

"Marshall, you know you're going to get the business. You *know* you will. Don't let Shadrat control a significant portion of the access to your own water."

"Point is, I need the business right now."

"I looked at my books," Molly said. "I'm pretty sure I can bring two to four guys out here for at least four days a week through runoff."

"Pretty sure?"

"It's a matter of how many will demand a float trip. But they're mostly repeaters. They trust me."

"When is 'through runoff' over?" Marshall asked.

"Salmonfly hatch. I've got some pretty die-hard Rock Creek fans. Some guys are going to insist on salmonflies."

"So you keep all your regular guide fees, and your clients fork over an additional rod fee to me?"

"Yeah," Molly said. "They'll pay. Most of them figure the more they're spending the better fishing they're into." She felt secretly willing to eat some of the rod fee if it came to a crux, but she didn't need to tell Marshall that.

Marshall did quick math. She was telling him four hundred to eight hundred dollars a week if she came through, although the skeptic in him wondered how much of her enthusiasm was simply a desire to see Shadford not get his way. Since his conversation with his father, Marshall had been sitting in the rocker making a list of guides and outfitters he should invite to fish the creek. He was also puzzling over the kind of letter one might send to fly-fishing writer-type personalities, but struggling with the wording. He wanted to sound enthusiastic and friendly without glad-handing, but feared everybody would see right through him. It was very hard for him to imagine the creek as a product, or a commodity, and also he did not want to bray.

"You're sure," Marshall said to Molly.

"I think so, Marsh. I think I can tell you that sitting here right now I cannot imagine anything that would keep me from bringing you that many clients."

"I'm not quite sure how I feel about that sentence construction."

"You do the English," Molly said.

"All right, I'm calling Shadrat." A cordless phone lay on the end table to his right. He picked it up and beeped out the number to Fly Guys.

"I'll give you preference for three rods a day until forty-eight hours previous," he said when Shadford came to the phone.

"That's not really what we talked about," Shadford said.

"It's the arrangement I'm willing to make."

"Exclusive," Shadford said. It wasn't a question.

"I can't see how that would benefit me, Mike."

"To be perfectly honest, I'll have to think about that," Shadford said. "Let me ask you this: we've been friends for how many years, Marshall? I mean, that should count for something, you would think. Frankly, I feel an obligation to tell you that you're kind of screwing yourself here."

"Well, it might not be the best screwing I ever got, but it's one I'm real familiar with," Marshall said. He glanced up at Molly, whose face had turned with his comment into a semidisgusted frown. He shrugged. "Look, there's another shop in town and over twenty outfitters in the general area and God knows how many guides, and the demand is booming. We both know I'm going to get the business. The question is when, and do you want in. Take some time if you want, but I'm already booking people through several outfitters." Primarily a lie.

Marshall beeped off, set the phone back on the table. "Welp," he said, "that's that. Let's go fishin'." He reached over and clapped a hand down onto Molly's thigh and gave one hard squeeze. The heat and surprise sat her straight up.

SALMONFLY

Molly was out of bed by five-thirty. She stumbled through her dark kitchen and swung open the refrigerator door, pulling light into the room. In a quick scan she saw on hand all the provisions she would need for the day: a slab of defrosted salmon, a Tupperware container of tortellini salad, a huckleberry cheesecake, peaches, plums, and apples, juices and sodas. She started the coffeemaker and popped an English muffin into the toaster oven. She stepped out the back door to find her breath steaming from her mouth in white plumes, ridiculous for early June. Clouds clotted the waning night, thickening the darkness while not revealing themselves as anything but overcast. She picked the newspaper off her doorstep, then grabbed the cooler resting on the concrete of her driveway, feeling her back ache as she straightened to carry it into the kitchen.

When she was done loading the cooler and packing it with ice, Molly poured a cup of coffee, spread jam on each half of the muffin. She ate the muffin and whipped through the pages of the newspaper, stopping to focus on the editorial page. Molly rarely read the syndicated opinion columns because she felt they were largely tripe. Her attention focused, a little indecently, on the *Missoulian*'s own uneducated guesses and, even more pruriently, the Letters to the Editor that

daily decried wolves, cows, grizzly bears, hunting, antihunters, logging, tree-huggers, zoning, ranchers, open space, development, gay and
lesbian rights, growth, Christian ethics, and all manner of modern
blight throughout the state. What Molly found most enthralling about
the Letters to the Editor was only in part the blind stridence of their
writers. The big kick was knowing that someone who probably held a
university degree in journalism read all these letters and still thought
it would be a good idea to print them in a newspaper.

This morning, though, the *Missoulian*'s own editorial snagged
her interest. It was titled "Hey Outfitters: Time to Help the Fish" and
it read:

> The fly-fishing industry brings over $300 million to the state of Mon-
> tana annually, in the form of license and guide fees, tackle purchases,
> lodging, food and gas outlays. Over 30,000 people come to this state
> every year with fishing as their primary goal.
>
> Now whirling disease has been discovered on the Madison River.
> This spore-borne ailment, which causes spinal deformities in juvenile
> trout and destroys their sense of balance, causing them to swim in
> whirling motions, has long existed in Europe, where fish have had
> centuries to adapt to it. In the western United States, whirling dis-
> ease is far newer. It was first discovered in Colorado five years ago,
> and much of that state's blue-ribbon fisheries have been annihilated
> by the disease.
>
> But Colorado is a put-and-take fishery. Their rivers are stocked
> from hatcheries, which are no doubt the source of initial contamina-
> tion. In Colorado, it should be a relatively easy matter to breed trout
> that are genetically resistant to whirling disease, then release them
> into the rivers.
>
> Montana, however, has made a commitment to wild trout. We do
> not stock our rivers and we don't want to. Wild trout have made Mon-
> tana the premier fly-fishing destination in the world.
>
> It would seem obvious, then, that for the sake of the trout, and
> for the sake of the people whose economic survival depends on them,
> outfitters and guides need to band together to aid the resource in any
> manner they can. If that means canceling guide trips on the Madison
> this summer until biologists can formulate a plan for recovering the
> Madison River rainbow stocks, then outfitters and guides should see

the clear long-term benefit in doing so. If it means donating a portion of their profits to research efforts, ditto.

Give the fish a break.

Well, thought Molly, that was an interesting little ditty and another fine example of the blind leading the clueless. While Molly didn't personally know anything about whirling disease save what she had read in the papers, she doubted that anybody had to make any decisions today or tomorrow about how the problem might best be solved. Bad press they didn't need. Fly fishermen were such a finicky bunch—just a whisper that Montana's trout streams were infected and summer flights to Anchorage and Jackson Hole would book up in an instant. Molly didn't guide on the Madison at any rate, so the problem was not much hers except in spirit. Though her spirit did wonder, *what the hell is killing all the fish?* It couldn't be good.

Already the day was trying to dawn, though the overcast held light at bay. Molly dressed in polypro longies and fleece pants. She lugged the full cooler out to her driveway, unsnapped the cover to her boat, and heaved the cooler up into it. The cold air made re-covering the boat difficult, and clicking the snaps in place hurt her fingers. It was almost seven now, and morning had built enough momentum to spill beneath the clouds. She had booked new folks today, people referred by one of her regular clients. Jeff and Nancy Sloma were their names, although she would instantly begin thinking of them as Mr. and Mrs. Johnson. Years before, Alton had told her that he thought of all his clients as Bill and Marge Johnson—even if both people in the boat were men—and that grabby little revelation stuck in Molly's mind like a tick.

A few hours later, the Rock Creek current was rollicking. Thick clouds hung like fog halfway up the mountains, showing snow on the slopes just beneath their hems. Green and wet saturated the landscape. Rain spattered the heaving fabric of the river's surface. Molly knew when she launched the boat that it would rain all day, as it had the day before, injecting even more water into the rock-and-roll spring runoff. With temperatures in the mountains reaching only the mid-fifties, the Johnsons would get cold early and get to bitching long before noon. The only effective tactic for avoiding a miserable day was to catch fish early and often.

Which no doubt would have happened had Mr. Johnson possessed the rudimentary skills needed to throw his fly out of the boat. His wife was a tungsten babe who sat in the back swathed in a rain poncho and asked when he was going to start catching them. Molly wondered how much the questions had to do with Mr. Johnson's frequent insistence on changing flies.

"It's nine-thirty," Molly explained the first time he wanted to switch tackle. "I don't see a lot of fish moving. They'll pick up here in the next half hour or so."

"I haven't seen shit working this fly," Mr. Johnson said.

"But I haven't seen much working naturals, either," Molly repeated. "If you really want to get into them right now, we could drop a nymph off your dry."

"I am not fishing nymphs," Mr. Johnson said.

"If they're not on top yet, there's nothing we can do except go subsurface," Molly said.

"I did not come all the way to Montana to fish nymphs."

"You might want to try getting your fly closer to the bank," Molly said. "They're going to sit very close to the bank."

Mr. Johnson made a face like he'd eaten a ball of cat shit.

"I'm happy to tie on any fly you'd like me to," Molly said, and smiled, "but it's not going to matter unless you can get it closer to the bank."

"Can't you get the boat closer to the bank?"

Sometimes Molly liked her clients so much she practically ached for them to catch fish. This guy bored her senseless. Too, Molly had done this stretch of river five times in the past five days. Her mind began to wander, first returning to the editorial she had read about whirling disease. She wondered if she should try to capitalize on the fact that, west of the Rockies, Montana's streams were uncontaminated. WD-free. Maybe she should make bumper stickers, or paint the bow of her boat. She could change the little brochure she printed up to read, "Clark Fork, Bitterroot, and Blackfoot: All Three WD-Free." Although who knew how long that would last.

Alton had said something about calling Fish, Wildlife and Parks and talking to somebody about what was happening, get the scoop from the source. Of course, he spent most of his time with fishermen, not many of whom were reliable fonts of information. *How do you know when a fisherman is lying? When his lips are moving.* Molly remembered Marshall's riff on trout talk, what real-world quantitative phrases meant when uttered by fishermen.

Fisherman says:	Fisherman means:
"a couple"	got skunked
"a few"	two
"a bunch"	more than three, less than five
"ten or a dozen"	eight or nine
"a pretty good day"	ten or a dozen

Ah, Marsh. When was he ever going to give her a sign? Never, she feared. Some things seemed so obvious. She could wait. She was learning that. Molly remembered how sick she had felt the previous summer when Marshall was carrying on a long-distance relationship with some willowy, raven-haired beauty from Rhode Island. He'd gone back there to fish for stripers with his father over Memorial Day weekend and met this siren at a party. Molly imagined the party being at an oceanfront cottage with gray shake-shingle sides and white trim and French doors opening onto a sprawling emerald green lawn where men stood in madras shorts and women wore Laura Ashley sundresses and single strands of pearls. Beyond the perfectly cropped lawn, surf pounded the rocky shore. Frank Sinatra crooned from discreet stereo speakers.

The girl Marshall met was the type who, during her visits out West, would sit in a Montana bar and order cosmopolitans, then protest that the drink was done "medium rare." She knew a lot about boats and enjoyed spending time on the water, so she wasn't a pain in the ass on all-day float trips, which probably extended her stay in Marshall's life by a few months—that and the distance factor. But anybody could see the relationship was going nowhere, unless they were Marshall. Even so, Molly felt acute distress throughout the life of the coupling.

When it did tear asunder, Marshall was aptly crushed, and while he was, the three of them—Marshall, Alton, and Molly—had gone over the hill into Idaho and packed into the St. Joe River. They hiked ten or a dozen miles the first day, climbing forested sidehills before dropping to the river bottom where sedges and ferns clotted the ground beneath massive aromatic cedar trunks. Eventually they stumbled into a grassy clearing dotted purple-blue and carmine with lupine and Indian paintbrush.

There they set up a campfire and hurried to the river to catch a few smallish cutthroats. They vented the fish, wrapped them in foil, and broiled them over a fire. Alton boiled instant polenta in a camp pot, heated black beans in the can. They shaved slivers of Asiago cheese into the beans and polenta, then wrapped the mix with flakes of white trout meat in fire-warmed tortillas, and devoured them, dirt- and fish-blood-flecked hands not even measured as a hindrance. Marshall unveiled a bottle of tequila.

Later, they all lay on their backs, listening to the fire crackle. The speckled wailing of coyotes wafted from nearby ridges, answers warbling in from outposts across the river, and then a full moon was up. Cranking her head Molly saw Marshall in his sleeping bag, head propped up by a log. She watched the flames paint Marshall's face against the darkness. The fire died and its light eased away, leaving the nightscape of the clearing and the stream. The moon cast distinct shadows out from under the trees and into the meadow. Molly watched the stars, suspicious that they might be moving, dancing among themselves, until the moment that she cut her glance to them, at which instant they froze and twinkled.

She drifted in and out of a chilly, shallow sleep. At some point she heard a clomping, a sound like horse hooves on wood, from the edge of the woods thirty yards away. She made out a swath of movement, a darkness rolling against the shadowed stand of tree trunks. The bear came clear as it entered the meadow, a smallish black bear, his muzzle lighter than the rest of him. He moved in an arc around their camp but tilted his nose toward them like a hand trying to grasp the scents flowing to it from the campfire. Molly realized the clomping sound she'd heard were his jaws chomping together. And then he was gone as quickly as he had appeared, his course a goofy amble back into the woods. It took her a while to return to sleep.

She awoke to the pure rose and liquid lavender of a high and brightening morning sky, and the first thing she heard was the sound of the river. Marshall was not in his bag, but within moments tromped up wearing only soaking wet shorts, his hair dripping water. The morning sun lit the dome of each water droplet clinging to his bare chest and shoulders.

After coffee they headed for the river. Huge orange October caddis floated through the air, sparkling like chunks of fairy dust in the slants where sunlight slashed through the picket of firs and pines. Marshall charged off, determined to see as much water as he could. Alton and Molly spent the day fishing together. They met Marshall again late in the afternoon, working his way back downstream. Then Alton took them to a place below camp, where a long pool opened below a rare, treeless hillside. Clearly visible from above, the blue shapes of trout hovered in the current. Molly and Alton sat on the sidehill above a rock outcropping where a warm spring gushed from the ground, pouring over the rock and dashing the lens of the pool's surface.

Marshall waded across the river below the pool and walked up from the other side until he was opposite them. Molly and Alton called in the casts: "Six inches closer in," "OK, four inches out now," "A foot upstream." And they watched while Marshall's big Orange Sedge provoked individual blue shadows into breaking from the pattern of the pool's bottom, tilting upward, drifting back beneath the float of the fly, and piercing the surface with a barely audible *glip* or *gloop*. The cutthroats he caught featured fluid orange-red slashes beneath their chins, sometimes pouring down to stain their pale bellies. Their backs were deep green mottled with black spots.

Alton sat on the sidehill with Molly and torched up a joint, and knowing the other two weren't interested, stoned himself. Eventually, Alton scooted to the edge of the rock outcropping and tumbled down into the pool. A soft *plop* followed, and Molly noticed that what had made the noise was Alton's drenched shorts, which he'd heaved up onto the hillside.

Marshall's reaction was initially pique, but quickly he decided to try catching a fish somewhere near Alton. He did hook one upstream from Alton's head, which sent Alton diving to try to grab the fish while it fought on Marshall's line. Marshall's attention was stripped away by the sight of Molly standing on the sidehill opposite him, lifting her T-shirt over her head. The sky was going soft now, and her body shone against the cool blue behind her. Molly bent, worked her fingers around her waist, then made a kicking motion and her shorts flung out onto the grass. She heard Marshall across the stream say, "Wow." In three steps Molly was airborne, her arms held over her head, and then the surface of the pool collapsed.

Marshall quit fishing and joined them, and the evening sky deepened, and soon Alton clambered from the stream, gathered up his clothing, and headed back to camp. Molly was aware that she and Marshall each held onto juts of rock beneath where the outcropping spilled its warm springwater into the pool. They faced each other, naked, treading water with their free hands. The spring was warmer than the river, making it possible to stay in the water only if they remained where they were. Even a few feet downstream the flume of warmth blended into the cold mountain stream.

She watched the water reflect in shimmering panes of light beneath Marshall's chin and less distinctly on his throat. His free hand waved figure eights in the water, occasionally brushing against her hand, with which she was describing similar shapes. There were probably other sounds, but she remembered the trickle of the warm springs sheeting into the cold pool, its xylophone tinkling. And she remembered the trout rising around them, the counterpoint *glip, gloop, glip* stippling the night. She looked at Marshall watching her, trying to determine if anything about his eyes looked hungry. This, she remembered feeling at the time, had to be when it was going to happen. She could feel her breasts buoyant in the water, sensed the slow frog-kicking of Marshall's legs beneath the surface, the mesmerizing wave of his hand treading water. He seemed to tuck a wry smile onto his lips, but she wanted to be careful that she wasn't only wanting to see these things.

"What an amazing place to be," Marshall said.

"I saw a bear last night," Molly said. She saw the smile on Marshall's mouth grow undeniable. "He walked through the meadow, but he was sniffing our camp."

"Why didn't you wake me up?"

"I didn't want to make any sudden movements."

"Why didn't you wake me very gradually?"

"I think I was frozen in the moment."

His arm bumped hers and she felt the jolt of it in her spine. She hated that she didn't know what to do next, despaired that she had never been a flirty girl, never understood really how to make the faces, make her eyes say what she wanted without making herself look what she felt sure was pathetic. The sexual encounters in her life had mainly been obvious and too often involved perception-dulling substances and, once those wore off, a sense of profound shame about what parts she could remember. Aside from one beloved and, to her mind now, almost legendary high school boyfriend, there had not been a long list of repeat offenders—though, as tendentious as the evidence seemed, Molly did not consider herself the one-night-stand type. She didn't have, she felt, the élan.

Instead, in her own mind, she explained the itinerant character of her love life with a line from a Suzanne Vega song, which she heard in her head with its definitive spacing and emphasis: *It's a one . . . time . . . thing. It just happens . . . a lot.* She also continually viewed the phenomenon as temporary. At the moment, Molly wished she would have paid more attention all along to the process. She suspected, for instance, that Marshall's Yacht Girl would have known exactly how to turn her eyes down and when to reach to tuck a lock of hair behind her ear. Marshall would be used to those sorts of signals. What drove Molly even more mad was that Marshall seemed poised and waiting.

"This is," Marshall said, "well, it's an amazing place to be. We have to thank Alton."

For what? she thought. *For leaving them alone?* Molly's mind was busy assembling templates of the way she imagined Marshall's hands would feel at the base of her throat, on the small of her back—instead of formulating a response to what he was saying. What would he do if she reached between his legs and wrapped her hand around him? She would never do it, not without him somehow signaling that he wanted her to.

In precisely this manner—though they held themselves in the pool, naked and inches away from each other, for some time longer—Marshall Tate became another man she craved as a lover who never slid out of his role as a very good friend. To this day—almost every day—Molly wondered how you go about changing something like that without losing it altogether.

Her reverie dissipated with the whip of Mr. Johnson's fly line wrapping around her shoulders. He had missed yet another strike. "God*damn*it," he said.

Now that she was paying attention again, Molly saw that trout heads tipped up everywhere along the bank, quick-sipping and dropping back into the green water. This was no surprise—it had been exactly the same for the past five days. Fish were up everywhere, smacking orange-bellied salmonflies off the surface. It was a bonanza.

"I think this hook's bent or something," Mr. Johnson said. He had turned in the boat while Molly once again lifted his line from her bedecked shoulders. Most of the problem was Mr. Johnson's consistent failure to mend his line with each cast. The current bulged an instant belly across the length of Mr. Johnson's line almost the moment it hit the water, which caused the fly at the far end to drag. The fish were trying. They were doing everything they could to suck up the fly Mr. Johnson skated across the current. With the fly zipping along faster than the current, they just couldn't time it right.

"It's not the fly," Molly said. "You gotta mend. You gotta mend as soon as the fly hits the water."

She tossed Mr. Johnson's line back overboard and said, "Cast and mend." Mr. Johnson cast, but did not mend.

"Mend," Molly said, "mend, mend."

"Men, men, men," the wife said behind her, then giggled.

Molly had long since quit being amazed by people who would spend several hundred dollars to float Rock Creek during runoff without first learning to mend their line, though she wasn't sure she was finished being annoyed by them.

"It's the goddamned fly," Mr. Johnson said. "I can't see it on the water. And I think the hook's bent." He sat with his rod resting against his shoulder, like a weapon at arms.

"What kind of fly do you want?" Molly asked.

"I thought that was your job."

There was going to be this education process, she could see, possibly lasting the entire day. It happened with the more hot-headed male clients. They never wanted to believe a woman could tell them anything about fishing. And it always started with the fly. Anything that wasn't working, change flies. Molly said, "Just turn your wrist and lift the rod tip and make a flip so the line flips upstream." She lifted her right hand from the oar handle to illustrate, but felt the boat careen into a new line of current and quickly dropped her fingers back to the handle, and then *bonk*—another rock bounced her bow. And the rain. But hers was a service job, and she took it seriously. *If you can't be happy,* Molly thought, *at least be less obtrusive.* So she strained to make conversation with the wife, and made every effort not to lift an oar clear of the locks and poleax the dipshit sitting in front of her.

• • •

Marshall wrestled the Massey Ferguson off the road and ran it through the grass up the fence line. The ground was wet and he worried about getting stuck, but there was no delaying what he had to do and, without another hand, he'd need to use the tractor. His plan was dangerous, and he was a little nervous about it. Winter drifts had plucked strands of barbed wire from the fence between the Fly X and Klingmans' property. The wire was rotten in places, but Marshall had no room on his Quality Supply charge account to buy new. Any day now, Klingmans might let their cows loose in the border pasture. The last thing Marshall needed was cows dredging through his spring creek, gnawing his new grass, busting saplings, shitting in the stream, trampling the fine gravel, and generally mucking up the place.

Marshall puttered up to the first gap in the four-wire fence, drove through it, dismounted, and walked down the fence line to the last place where the wire remained tacked up. He began yanking the wire off the ground, freeing it from mats of grass. He marched off ten or a dozen posts, found one that was tamped in solid, and looped the wire around it before bending it back to the tractor. The tractor's front bucket had a tow ball welded to the center. Marshall twisted the wire tight around it with a pair of fencing pliers. He jumped on the tractor and shifted into reverse, pulling the wire taut using the post as a fulcrum.

Marshall backed the tractor as far as he dared, jump-stopping the gears with frequent stomps of his foot on the clutch. Nervous. Though the clatter of the engine drowned out most sound, Marshall saw the wire stretching in the sun and imagined he could hear it humming with the strain. He dropped the tractor out of gear, stepped on the locking brake, and rolled off the seat. With a fencing pliers and a leather pouch full of fencing staples hanging from his belt, he made his way from post to post, darting in at each to tack up the wire, then arcing out in a long curve on his way to the next post.

For reasons he felt at a loss to explain—perhaps a change in the quality of sound in the air—he glanced over his shoulder in time to see an off-road four-wheeler bouncing down the road from the Klingmans' ranch. He saw the black feeding cap and the blue-and-black-checked coat and recognized the old man, Bruce, coming toward him. Marshall ducked into the fence line to tack another post, then retreated and started for the next one. The four-wheeler slowed, then jerked to a stop a hundred yards away. Bruce Klingman rose from the seat like a man on horseback standing in his stirrups. He looked at Marshall, his face blank. Marshall waved with the fencing pliers. Bruce Klingman cranked the steering bar and turned the four-wheeler in a tidy circle, then high-geared it for home. *Now what,* thought Marshall, *was that?*

He wondered if Bruce was heading back to the house to collect the whole clan, or at least the male members, and bring them out to look at what foolishness the dumb-ass neighbor was up to now. Nothing Marshall did on the Fly X measured up to Klingman standards. He heard it from Daisy, or sometimes Kyle, the youngest boy. This fencing job would be half-assed. If Marshall had hired a professional fencer, well then, that would be that East Coast money not wanting to get its hands dirty, and anyway the job would be subpar because nothing really counted unless you busted your own knuckles. There were no easy victories. With the top wire stapled as far as the fulcrum post, Marshall returned to the tractor, shifted into a forward gear, and eased the tension. He untied the wire from the ball. He went back down the fence line and began uncurling the next wire from the grass that winter had pressed it into.

In addition to coming unstapled, this wire had broken. Marshall had, through the years, clipped off still-good sections of broken wire, coiled them, and hung them randomly on fence posts for use in just these instances. He walked along until he found the nearest one, uncoiled it, and began splicing it into the break. He had the piece whole, tied to the tractor and stretched taut around the fulcrum post, and was walking back to start tapping staples when he saw the four-wheeler approaching again. Bruce Klingman veered the vehicle off the side of the road and it jounced over the grass at Marshall. Bruce squeezed the handbrake and shut the vehicle off in one smooth motion.

He was less fluid lifting his leg over the seat and dismounting. Bruce hoisted from a utility box mounted behind the seat a length of ratcheted steel with a long handle. He walked over the grass to Marshall with it.

"Ever seen one of these?" Bruce asked, twisting his wrist to hold up the wire stretcher.

"I have one. It broke."

"You're going to goddamned kill yourself like that," Bruce said, pointing toward the tractor with the wire wrapped to its towing ball.

"I couldn't think of another way."

"How about buy a new wire stretcher? What's that, a thirty-dollar item?"

Marshall moved up to the next fence post and rapped a staple into it. "I had to get this done today," he lied.

"Well, come on then," Bruce said. He pointed to the tractor. "Only back that thing off before I get too close."

"Oh, I don't need any help."

Bruce stopped, turned to look back at Marshall. "No use seeing you get killed. Daisy wouldn't like to forgive me."

"Huh," Marshall said.

This would not be the first time Marshall and Bruce Klingman had been jointly involved in a work project. Marshall had helped Klingmans hay since he was boy. Living the way they did, chores came up that pitched neighbors together. There was a way of putting personal feelings aside in order to get things done. But it was rare that Marshall stood alone beside Bruce with the subject of Daisy raised. Which made Marshall wonder about taking a chance. He said, "And here I thought you disapproved of pretty much everything that happens between Daisy and me."

Bruce nodded, and looked at Marshall as if he were waiting for the thrust of his statement. When he sensed nothing more forthcoming, he nodded again and said, "Pretty much everything so far."

"You see how that might not leave me much room to do any right things?" Marshall asked.

Bruce leaned forward, as if now spotting the opportunity to make the point he was waiting for. "When you two were young, it didn't matter then. You're not young anymore."

"I guess I feel like we're both old enough to make our own choices."

"I don't like to see things getting in her way," Bruce fired back.

Marshall wanted to say something about Bruce getting in her way, about the ties to the ranch getting in her way. He said, "I thought you always get unhappy when she leaves."

"You feeling your oats a little?"

"No," Marshall said. "Just don't feel like taking the blame for everything today."

"Well, tell you what. My oats are mostly all through the horse, but I'm not near so stupid as you seem to think. I miss my daughter when she leaves, but I sure as hell don't want her staying here to rot. Christ, there's no future on a ranch. It'll be all over by the time my kids are grown. The only segment of the ranching business worth pursuing anymore is real estate. We've got a nice piece here, nice water. That's the only real value. Goddamned out-of-staters coming in here now with more dollars than sense, buying everything up, inflating the prices. That's the only value I've got left, the price of the land I own."

There followed a short silence, from which Marshall felt a staring match brewing. But he had no heart for it. He narrowed his eyes once, then dropped his head into a half shake before striding toward the tractor. On board, he looked again at Bruce, wondering what the old man was up to. There had to be something going on here he hadn't yet surmised. Bruce knew he could fix the fence by himself, particularly with a wire stretcher. Marshall jammed the gear shift and released the clutch. The tractor lurched unexpectedly in reverse. Marshall stomped on the clutch again, but too late. The wire snapped with a warbling twang of a singing sword and sliced through the air. Bruce Klingman plunged backward onto the ground. The tractor stalled.

"Goddamnit!" Bruce cried out. Marshall felt an impulse coursing through him to leap from the tractor and rush to the fallen man, but he hesitated, ass raised from the seat, waiting to see Bruce's face. Bruce was slow to rise, pulling himself into a stiff sit-up. Marshall could see that he was holding the shirt on his right forearm with the fingers of his other hand. The sleeve hung torn. Marshall could tell nothing about Bruce's face for a moment because it had flushed a deep red. By now he knew that no matter what had happened, he needed to be hurrying over there.

"Jesus, Bruce, I'm sorry. Are you OK? Are you hurt?"

Bruce's hands dropped to his lap and he stared at Marshall, as if to let stand as noted the hesitation Marshall had shown in coming to his aid. "You'll have to try harder than that to hurt me," Bruce said. He rolled onto his hands and knees and pushed himself to his feet.

Marshall had rushed up to him by then, laid a hand on Bruce's forearm. Bruce pulled his arm away. "I'm fine. Just nicked my shirt is all. Christ, Marshall, a fella can't just go around like his equipment is a bunch of toys. Act like you know something."

"I don't know what happened," Marshall sputtered. "I just . . . I thought I was in first, but I must have been in reverse. I'm so sorry."

"Let's get this wire up before somebody gets killed," Bruce said.

Marshall felt his hands quivering with leftover adrenaline and fear. He picked up the wire stretcher from where Bruce had dropped it, feeling his fingers weak, barely strong enough to lift it. He doubted he could make the tool work right now—he needed a moment for some stomping around, some deep breathing—but didn't want to admit that to Bruce. Bruce took the wire stretcher from his hands as if he expected no resistance.

"I'll stretch, you staple," Bruce said.

Bruce hooked the bracket onto a post. Marshall found the wire where it had backlashed into the grass. He lifted it and walked it over to Bruce, who threaded it through the guides on either end of the tool. Using the post as an anchor, Bruce pumped the handle and the wire creaked tighter. They worked a five-post span. Bruce held the wire tight, Marshall rapped staples into the posts. He was shaky in the beginning, still wobbly from the near decapitation of his neighbor, and it took him several more whacks with the fencing pliers than it should have to punch in the staples. He pulverized his thumb on the third staple, and again on the eighth one, but Bruce wasn't looking, so Marshall let a mask of pain roll his lips toward his teeth and press his eyes shut and uttered no sound.

"How many other holes you got?" Bruce asked.

"Two more big ones, then just some places to splice."

The process was slower than the way he had devised with the tractor. Bruce worked silently, in a steady get-her-done pace. Marshall suspected the old man's expression carried a touch of disdain, as if somehow Marshall wasn't keeping up his end of the operation. He tried to imagine how he could work faster. He began to think there was nothing wrong with the way he had been fixing the fence with the tractor, that it was only a matter of paying a certain degree of attention. The mechanics were perfectly legitimate. He could have had the whole thing done by himself. They had finished the two middle wires and were working on the bottom one before Bruce spoke again.

"Seen them wolves yet?" Bruce asked. He pronounced it more like "woofs."

"Nope."

What Marshall knew about the wolves that had moved into the upper West Fork Valley he had read in newspaper accounts and heard on the NPR station. A radio-collared black female wolf had left a pack near the Canadian border and set off on her own, crossing Glacier Park, then trotting down onto the plains somewhere on the Blackfeet Indian Reservation. There she'd turned south, threaded through the Badger-Two Medicine and the Bob Marshall Wilderness areas before entering the Scapegoat. At some point she'd been seen on a piece of property just north of the Fly X owned by a family from Cincinnati named Ballou. The Ballous, not knowing a wolf from a Weimaraner, called a Fish and Wildlife Service agent, who camped out for days before eventually identifying the wolf from her radio collar signal frequency. She'd made about a five-hundred-mile trip. The agent further observed that somewhere along the way the female wolf had picked up a big silver-gray male. Nobody had a guess about from where he had materialized. It was as if the male had lived somewhere in the hills for years, just waiting for a female to come along. The Fish and Wildlife agent said he suspected the pair had mated and had a den nearby, and probably already had pups. A meeting was scheduled for the valley residents to learn all about it. Marshall had every intention of attending.

"I don't know why they had to go and put those woofs here," Bruce said.

Marshall lined up a staple for hammering, wondering what to do with that assertion. Cautiously, he asked, "Who did?"

"The government."

"What makes you think they *put* them here?" Marshall asked. He could feel Bruce waiting for him to start hammering the staple. Instead he straightened and regarded Bruce, the stooped man against a blue sky where clouds stretched into thin discs. Bruce lifted a hand from the wire stretcher and raised it, gloved fingers spread against the sky.

"This kind of bullshit has been going on for years. How do you think the grizzy bears all got here? Grizzy bears were shot out of here back in the 1920s and '30s, same like the woofs," Bruce said. "Now all of a sudden we've got grizzy bears on the place every summer because the Feds bring them here in a helicopter, is why. Every time some bear gets in trouble down in Yellowstone or up in Glacier, they move it up to one of these little valleys, just dump it in and hope nobody notices. Those woofs are the same way. They showed up here in the back of a pickup truck."

"My understanding with the wolves was the one came down from a pack near Canada, wearing a radio collar, and the other came from nobody knows where, and they showed up here on their own," Marshall said.

"Now, Marshall. You don't really believe that, do you?"

Marshall bent to the post again and started hammering at the staple with the fencing pliers. Bruce disengaged the wire stretcher, moved down five more posts, and ran the wire through the calipers. The clank of the handle rang across the meadow.

Bruce said, "There's a time and place for everything and the time for those animals in this place is gone. The first woof I see is going to die of lead poisoning, sure as shootin'."

"They're on the Endangered Species list," Marshall said. Waiting to start tapping in a staple, he cocked his head to see Bruce. He got only the back of Bruce's head, a smoke curl of white hair wisping beneath the black feeding cap.

"How endangered could they be if they're living right in the valley here?"

Marshall straightened and said, "Do me a favor, Bruce, and don't make me know about it." He walked to the next post, fumbling in his leather pouch for another staple.

They finished patching the big holes in the fence and Marshall insisted on not wasting any more of Bruce's time. He could fix the smaller splices himself. They had worked their way almost a mile from the vehicles. He and Bruce walked back along the fence line toward the tractor and four-wheeler, and though he hadn't meant to, Marshall noticed that he'd somehow started walking on the Fly X side of the fence, and that Bruce was on the other side. Bruce walked crooked-legged, as if something had once broadsided him from the left, wiped him out at the knees, and they never quite came back straight.

About halfway back to the rigs, a notion began brewing in Marshall's thoughts, and he let it build anxiety until that bubbled in his guts. He felt like a young boy trying to invent an opportunity to kiss a girl. The comfort Bruce felt walking along silently agitated Marshall more. It apparently never occurred to the old man to have conversation while they killed all this distance. When they reached the rigs, Bruce reached up, pulled off his feeding cap, and scratched the back of his head. He looked over the valley at the mountains to the north.

Marshall decided he would have to say something now. The key would be to remain colloquial without revealing signs of weakness.

"So how can we make this water deal work out good for everyone?" he said.

Bruce looked at him and took to rubbing the inside of his cheek with the point of his tongue. Marshall kept expecting a grin to break out, but Bruce's face remained sealed until, after a long moment, Bruce nodded as if to confirm with himself that he'd made an agreement. He said, "Marshall, it ever occur that not everything under the sun is about you?"

Molly Huckabee walked into the Rhino and knew heads were turning as she made her way down the bar, knew eyes were shifting with her breasts. This poked at her angry streak. *Screw the dolts.* Molly was a big girl in so many ways. Not excessively tall, but broad-shouldered. Not fat, but strong-limbed. Her upper arms were dense from rowing. She had a big smile, and a big, round face suggestive more of her father's Irish background than her mother's Norwegian ancestry. A big ball capped her upturned nose, or at least she thought it was big, despite assurances from her friends to the contrary, that in fact her nose was "cute." Molly had a big problem with "cute."

She spotted Alton at the pool table, standing with the cue clutched in both hands, its butt floored, so that if he leaned forward an inch he'd chalk the end of his nose. Alton still wore his winter beard, a tightly woven rim of woolly brown, black, and red fur, and Molly wondered how long until that was shaved for the summer and Alton became baby-faced again. Usually it was gone the day after he spotted his first salmonfly—and started growing again on the opening day of big game season in October. As she made her way toward the pool tables, Molly idly wondered why he still wore it now, with the salmonfly hatch in full swing, but then she remembered Amy Baine and Shadford and actually felt a twitch. Molly had never thought much of Amy Baine, at least not as a match for Alton—too young, too fancy, too much money and its breezy pathology—but she knew he thought the world of the girl.

Approaching the table, Molly saw Billy Mills bent over the table, ragged and stained Carhartts hanging off his ass. Mills was well into his thirties, but dressed fly-guide grunge and talked a slang Molly was pretty sure the college kids weren't using anymore. She saw Marshall sitting around the bend of the bar. He was turned on the stool with his back to the bar, facing the pool table, trying to balance a half-full beer glass on one fingertip. He watched himself balancing the glass with an expression that indicated he was annoyed to find himself bored enough to be trying it. Molly smiled to herself, guessing how much Marshall was suffering. He hated Billy Mills.

"Hey, Shitbird," she said to Marshall, sliding onto the stool beside his.

"Evening, Sugar Boogers," Marshall said, his voice flat. The fingers in his free hand cupped the air around the beer glass, catching it when it teetered from the tip of his finger.

"*Sugar Boogers?*"

"I don't know," Marshall said, lackluster. He shifted his finger in quick, short scoops to keep the beer on a balance point.

"Jeez, Marshall."

"Yeah. I just don't know," Marshall said. "I spent the day on the phone with water rights lawyers." He scooped his finger away from him and then back quickly, averting a disaster with the beer glass. "Actually, I was on the phone with their secretaries, because as it turns out, I can't afford to talk directly to a water rights lawyer."

Molly reached for the pitcher behind him on the bar and the empty glass beside it. "Buy a gal a beer?"

"Sure. I wonder if there are better shapes for balancing liquids." Marshall again scooped his finger away from him, but this time the beer glass crashed to the floor. Marshall looked down at that. "How'd it go for you today?"

"We probably boated fifty," she said. Then, checking Marshall's inevitable skepticism, "Serious. Know who I had?"

"Who'd you have?"

"The lieutenant governor."

"No shit?" Marshall asked. "What's his name?"

"Hawkins."

"That's right. He as dumb as his boss?"

"He was a surprisingly good guy," Molly said. "Damned good fisherman. Seemed like you could talk right to him, too. A bunch of us did a big party float for some political retreat. I had him and a guy who's, like, the governor's chief of staff. That one was a little pompous, but the loot was a pretty decent fella, seemed pretty open to things. Said he was going to book me later in the year for some sort of trade mission from one of the Stans."

Marshall waited.

"Googy-oogy-stan, Marshall-tate-istan, one of those former Soviet places."

Molly hoped she'd get a response from all this news, but already she sensed she wasn't going to pry much witty repartee out of Marshall tonight. "Sugar Boogers" had been a weak enough gambit. Alton looked just as tired and frustrated. Some nights that wouldn't matter, but this was a bad mood going around. She said, "But it was a Chinese fire drill. I bet I saw thirty goobs."

"Thirty what?"

"Goobs. Guys On Other Boats," Molly said.

"Where am I when all these fun phrases get coined?" Marshall asked.

"Playing in the dirt up at your fish farm."

The crack of pool balls rang, then Billy Mills stood beside her, saying, "We spanked them up high. Caught ten over twenty."

"Did you now?" Molly said. Billy Mills was a rangy guy with too much Adam's apple and not enough beard. Molly figured he measured his penis the way he measured his fish, until she realized he might be just the kind of guy to actually measure his penis. Marshall slid off his stool and walked around the corner of the bar. Alton moved in front of Molly, eyes on the array of pool balls before him. Instead of saying hello, she stuck her tongue out at him.

"My mother told me never to stick that out unless I intended to use it," Alton said, still examining the table before him.

"She did not."

Alton shrugged, though Molly knew better than to buy the sheepishness he was foisting on her when he said, "My mother said a lot of things she never really said."

"Right."

"How'd it go?" he asked.

"Good," she said, then, springing a disingenuous appreciation of her own, added, "Spanky here landed ten over twenty."

"I heard," Alton said, cutting her a glance, and then, turning it dubious, toward Billy Mills. "He's my hero."

"Dude, I am not shitting you," Billy Mills said.

"Oh, I know," Alton said. His eyes drifted back over Molly before he stooped to shoot.

"Mills, how long is twenty inches?" Molly asked. "Just show me."

Mills stood gripping his pool cue and his smile turned dopey.

"Is it this long?" Molly asked, holding her hands apart. "This long?" Moving them farther apart. "Come on, I want to see what you think twenty inches is."

"Shit," Mills said, snaking it out over a few syllables.

"Exactly."

Marshall came back with a broom and dustpan and started sweeping the broken glass from the floor around Molly's feet. When his hip bumped her knee, she felt the touch shoot up her leg. She felt fully aware that part of why she always reacted so strongly to Marshall was that he showed absolutely no romantic interest in her. Mills, on the other hand, she considered pretty much a squirrel. Mills wanted to be a guide—Shadford had hired him for the summer as a clerk at Fly Guys—and thought that hanging around with Alton would somehow accelerate the promotion. These days anyone with testicles and a 6-weight Sage wanted to be a guide. Why Alton suffered this one was beyond Molly. She suspected Mills won Alton's audience with garlands of free pot, and that Alton was too nice to give him the boot. Alton was sweet like that, too laid-back to actively court antagonism, friendly to everybody in his smart-ass way. He knew as much about fishing western Montana as anybody she was aware of, but he still asked advice of her, of everybody, and not just for lip service—he tried it out on the water. And he laughed at himself when he botched. Marshall tried that, but somehow Molly always felt that Marshall's self-deprecation came with an edge that cut himself deeper than he was willing to admit.

"Read the paper?" Molly asked Marshall when he was done cleaning up his mess.

"Nope," Marshall said.

"They found whirling disease in the Gallatin, the Ruby, and the Jefferson."

"Inexorably marching westward," Marshall said.

"Fish, Wildlife and Parks is full of shit," Mills said, splayed over the table for a long-green shot. "They said all that about the Madison, it's bullshit. I was over on the Madison for the Mother's Day caddis hatch and we smoked them. There were plenty of rainbows."

"Yeah, Billy," Molly said. "They're just spreading this rumor around so nobody will come to fish the Madison and they won't have to fit all that out-of-state license revenue into their budget."

"It's a government bureaucracy," Mills said.

Molly looked at Alton, who seemed to be checking with her for something he might have missed, like a point.

"Those guys run around starting fires so they have something to put out," Mills said, standing straight, his shot missed, his arms flung apart. "That way they get more budget. You gotta invent a crisis to get funds."

"You know . . ." Alton said. He pinched an unlit Camel Light between the joints of his first and middle fingers, stabbing it at Mills. "I'll bet that's it."

Molly turned away from any response, and pushed an elbow into Marshall's arm. "It's good to see you out, buddy."

She noticed an odd look on Marshall's face, and then felt herself gripped tightly from behind, arms wrapped under hers, a chin on her shoulder, and sloppy lips on her cheek.

"Hey, baby!" a voice said into her ear. She recognized from the easy drag of the words that the speaker was drunk. That he was also stoned she deduced from the musty after-odor of breath. Molly recognized the voice as Jimmy Ripley's, and set her beer on the bar beside Marshall. She wrapped her fingers around Jimmy Ripley's wrists, poised to lift and separate. Ripley's weight, vectored into her shoulder but sliding around with a drunken shuffle, kept her off balance. When she cranked her head to look at him, his face held too close for comfort. All she saw was teeth and lips and dim, bloodshot eyes.

When finally he let her go, Molly found herself pinned to the bar, and Ripley stood a sliver away from her, his hips knocking against hers, his face weaving to stay right in front of hers. Not a particularly big guy, Ripley could nevertheless be tough to outmaneuver. He stood close to the ground, held a low center of gravity, and he kept his arms always on hers. She knew this drill. He thought she was hot, he was drunk, he thought he was hot, he needed his ego stroked. She'd have to hear about what a great day fishing he had, and how they should get together and hit the river soon. She'd say yes, that's true, and Ripley would leer at her to let her know just what she'd be in for in such an instance, and she'd raise her eyebrows to let him know she'd heard that one.

Ripley was harmless in the way that Molly found all womanizers harmless if you take them at face value. He was a guy who frequented this particular bar and wanted everybody in it to know who he was. He should have been a year or two out of college, but wasn't. Molly wondered how Marshall was reacting to this sudden appearance—because it wasn't just Ripley now, but two or three of his buddies all pressing in, all occupying space where Molly and Marshall had been seated comfortably—and when she was able to see past Ripley, she saw Marshall had given ground, had in fact fled to where Alton stood on the other side of the pool table. Both of them were looking over with their chins down and their eyes up underneath their brows. It didn't take much to see what they thought of the Ripley crowd, but that was how the Ripley crowd liked it. They had money and looks and unclimbed ranges of stupidity to be scaled and named in their honor.

"Who is that guy?" Marshall asked Alton. They stood side by side, both isolated from the beer pitcher still on the bar and walled off by a group of young men in river shorts and fishing caps. Alton still held a pool cue, butt firmly planted on the floor between his feet.

"Name's Ripley," Alton said. "Sort of a jackass around town."

"One of Scotty the Wad's buddies, right?" Marshall asked. In fact, he noticed Scotty Wadsworth among the group of young men. Scotty saw them, tilted his head back in a cool greeting.

"Yeah. Remember the guy that day on the Bitterroot with the walkie-talkie?" Alton said. "Same crowd. They come into Fly Guys all the time now. Shadford's plucking them clean."

"That guy ever say anything to you?"

"The guy with the chin? Just dirty looks," Alton said. "Ripley here's the one got busted for guiding without a license."

Marshall found himself nodding, though not from any great motivation to agree. He was watching the grope-fest, the guys all bustling and shoving against each other, bouncing off other patrons in the bar, bouncing up against Molly.

Once Molly had extracted herself from the drunken rowdies who had taken to standing around slouch-hipped, surveying the room in search of the next good-looking girl they could smother with their attention, she walked directly to where Alton and Marshall stood at one end of the pool table. Indicating in an apologetic tone the boisterous boys from whom she had just removed herself, she said, "Ah, high on life and taking themselves out for a walk."

"I think Marshall wants to take them out and rub their teeth on the curb," Alton said.

"Jimmy?" Billy Mills said. He had just finished racking the balls and handed a cue to Alton. "He'll kick your ass in a skinny minute."

"Trust me," Molly said, "as rarely as it happens, Mills is right about this one. You don't want to mess with those guys. They're crazy."

"They're punks," Alton said, making his way around the pool table to break. Mills moved down to stand beside Alton and intimidate his shot.

"Except they're amoral punks," Molly said. "Jimmy Ripley's hit people with tire irons, broken beer bottles—you name it, he'll hit you with it. And he'll hit you when you're not looking. He's got no feel for a fair fight." Molly could see Marshall digesting that. "I'm sure the world would be a better place if somebody beat them senseless now and then, but unless you want to get seriously hurt doing it, let somebody else be the action hero."

"Somebody'll kill him one of these days," Alton said, bent over the table. He stroked the cue and the balls exploded over the green felt. Molly heard the wooden thunk of two balls dropping in pockets, then rolling with a hollow wobble through unseen tunnels into the holding box in the guts of the pool table.

"Probably," Molly said.

"So how come he doesn't go to jail?" Marshall asked. "Hitting someone with a tire iron?" Alton squinted through his cigarette smoke, lining up his next shot. Mills was following him around, standing just beside him.

"Daddy's a big-time lawyer in a big-time firm in a big-time city," Molly said. "Jimmy's been in a lot of trouble, but Daddy always gets him out of it."

"Well," Marshall said, as if that solidified his point and she'd do well to see it. One of the very few things Marshall didn't understand about Molly was her ability to see people so clearly and still tolerate them. "Anyway," he said, "I think I'm taking off."

Molly knew that somehow her interaction with Jimmy Ripley had decided that course of action for Marshall, and she was suddenly furious, though she wasn't sure if she was more furious with Ripley or Marshall. *Enough,* she thought. *Enough with goddamned Marshall.*

"Listen, I have an open day on Monday, if you need any help up at the place," Molly said. "Fencing or whatever."

"Sure," Marshall leaned away.

"I'll give you a call," she added, because he wouldn't offer to call her.

And then Marshall was gone, leaving Molly feeling like he'd turned his head right before she kissed him, though she hadn't even tried. *Enough,* she thought again. She watched Marshall walk out of the bar, and on the return sweep her eye caught Alton. Alton sucked on his cheeks a little and she knew he understood what was happening. She didn't want him to. As much as anything, she didn't want him to feel left out of it.

"He's just being Marshall," Alton said.

Molly sidled over to where he stood waiting for Mills to finish shooting. She reached to start a friendly rub of the muscle over Alton's shoulder blade.

"So how's working with Shadrat?" Molly asked.

Alton wasn't about to move. The sore muscles of his back rolled to meet the pads of her splayed fingers.

"It's hard," Alton said. "Seeing him and Amy?" His shrug lifted a wave of empathy into her heart. They stood where they were, her fingers reaching for the ridges of his back, feeling the cords slide under them. Billy Mills missed a shot, walked over to the bar, and topped his glass from the pitcher of Alaskan Amber. He sipped and waited for Alton to shoot. Alton stood with his eyes on the table but his face quartered to Molly. Everything about Molly felt too good.

Molly, meanwhile, sensed Alton going gooey under her fingers, and began to enjoy the power she seemed to have over him. He was so easy to please, and Marshall was so . . . Marshall. She suddenly understood that desire to be pleased, for something to be easy. Lowering her voice, she said, "You got any weed at home?"

"What's this?" Alton said, leaning away just enough to pretend surprise without disrupting any of the places their bodies met. "When did you start breathing fire?"

"Sometimes a girl needs to relax," Molly said and pulled away, sensing it was precisely the right time to deprive him of her touch. *How,* she thought, *could she know these things so simply with Alton and never ever ever with Marshall?* Alton's arm followed her miniature retreat, looping over her shoulder.

"Well, we'd better get you to some relaxation aids before the situation reaches crisis stage," Alton said.

Molly smiled. Alton tossed his pool cue on the table, scattering the contested geometry of the remaining balls.

"Dude," Mills said, standing straighter. "That's so utterly."

"You won," Alton said. "Damsel in distress. I'm outta here."

"We've got all this beer," Mills said. He very quickly saw what was going on and just as quickly pouted.

"I just bought you a pitcher," Alton said. "Catch me later."

"Aw, man," Mills said, "you're sad."

"Not at the moment," Alton said, and he followed where Molly had already made her way through the crowd.

There was no such thing as a grand opening of the Fly X spring creek. There had been the day when Molly showed up with two men, the men handed over $120 cash money, and the three of them left to wander around the creek all day. Marshall hadn't even thought through a system for dealing with the money and had been embarrassed to fold the bills and shove them in the front pocket of his Carhartts. Low tech was fine, but he wanted to look like he'd done this before.

Then there was the next day, when Molly showed up again with two more fellows and a woman, and the next day when she showed up with two more, and Dan Bennett of Troutfitters called and booked four rods for the next two days. Afterward, obviously happy, Bennett called Marshall and booked twenty rods over the next few weeks. Molly brought more. By then Marshall had bought a cash drawer, the kind that slides into cash registers, and stocked it with different denominations for making change.

Avoiding a personal capitulation, Shadford had Billy Mills call with a series of bookings. In fact, deprived of exclusive access through sugar-daddy dealing, Shadford seemed intent on monopolizing the creek through sheer force of numbers. Marshall couldn't have cared less. Save a couple slots for Molly and he didn't give a damn who filled the rest. Things were moving right along, Marshall thought as he sat at 7 A.M. on the front porch of the Fly X ranch house. His mullings were abrogated by the appearance of a car quite a way down the lane leading to his house.

In addition to mulling, Marshall had been on the porch peering through his spotting scope at the elk herd grazing in the meadow across the river. About sixty animals, all cows as far as he could tell, stood knee-deep in the burgeoning grass. The more distant animals seemed muscular and dark. Closer to the river he could see individual faces, the black eyes and bony noses, lower jaws swinging sideways while they chewed. The yellow circles on the elks' rumps glowed against the green grass. In between all the big bodies moved the red flanks of deer, and as he gazed at the scene he kept thinking—as he often did when he saw a herd of animals grazing peacefully in an open meadow—that this was what it looked like here before white people came.

Marshall loved moments when he could imagine that. He wondered if the wolf pack was nearby. Marshall hadn't spotted any wolves yet, and he very much wanted to. He glassed the far hills every dawn. At the moment he wanted to see them emerge from the high woods and trot onto the plane to assess the elk herd. The wolves apparently did not care about their roles in his fantasies and continued to make no appearance. But elk and wolves aside, the truth was Marshall had originally plopped onto the cushioned chaise on the front porch because he intended to wonder if he should have a sign professionally made, if he should build picnic tables, if he should rope off the parking area, if he should place garbage cans near the creek, and what about some sort of structure—a warming hut, someplace to change, maybe a tyer's bench? Then he'd become charmed by the elk herd and wolf fantasies.

Which brought him to a curious crossroads, a place he found himself often standing these days. Marshall found himself again facing the undeniable paradox of what he had done: he had built a spring creek that had never been there before. He characterized the process as attempting to invent a piece of nature. It was new habitat for many animals—birds, mammals, amphibians, and fish. The fish loved it, moved in from the river in droves. They would feed prodigiously on the abundant crops of insects and grow to great lengths. They would spawn in the spring creek with far greater efficacy and, Marshall liked to think, a touch more brio. Inescapable remained the notion that next the goal was to let a lot of people come and jab curved spikes into the fish's heads. Would it have been more wrong if the stream had already existed?

The car, when he spotted it, was not moving. Marshall watched, relieved to be tugged away from his weighing-of-conscience. This from the car: more not moving. It was a long American-made dinosaur, a Pontiac or Cadillac or Oldsmobile with just the slightest hints, or vestiges rather, of fins creased over the trunk, which Marshall could see because the car sat sidesaddle in the road, its nose poking off toward pasture. The vehicle could have been white, but a slight pink seemed to flush its cladding. Marshall rose and walked inside the house, but looped right around to the kitchen windows and gazed through the gauzy curtains. He saw the car lurch, bounce on its springs, straighten on the road, and roll forward perhaps a hundred feet, where it halted again.

About those trash cans, Marshall decided to think, *be a shame if trash started fluttering into the creek.* But if he placed trash cans any-where convenient, clients would empty all the trash they owned into them, and eventually would allow litter to spill over or flutter away. *Trust them to be decent,* Marshall thought, but then he couldn't over-come the car, and stalked off the porch. He tilted a mountain bike, an old bangtail Rockhopper, from where it leaned against the side of the house and legged over it. He'd taken to riding the bike around the ranch the last couple years, which he liked to consider one of his ec-centricities, although his choice had more to do with having no money for runaway fuel costs.

He stopped the bike and let it fall to the grass, walking the last few yards to the vehicle. As he approached, he could hear the engine happily slurping fuel, even at idle. A rev startled him, but the car seemed geared in park, and the revving only served to rock it on its springs. Marshall walked to the driver's side door, and the window de-scended to reveal a pale man with the nose of a beagle and florid stains across his cheeks. He was completely bald, with long ears. The man couldn't have been a day under seventy.

Marshall nodded, said hello, bent and peered into the passenger seat. Another oldster, a small-faced bald fellow, blinked studiously at the windshield. The yellow-gray hair in the front of his head seemed to have collapsed in a landslide and piled down onto his brow. He ap-peared frail but not frightened about it.

"How can I help you gentlemen?" Marshall asked.

"Wellhell," the driver said, eliding the two words into one, "no need to be so curt." His breath became nearly visible with the sharp saturation of booze. Nor was it stale liquor; the guy had been pounding already that morning. The passenger held his hand down under his leg, but Marshall could see the bottle.

Marshall apologized, torn between an instinct to display civility to potential clients and a deep desire to not have a couple of septuagenarian drunks staggering around the property. He let his enduring smile tell them whatever they wanted to hear. "I'm afraid I missed your name—"

The man in the passenger seat turned full of vigor and stated, "We've brought the guns."

"Huh," Marshall said.

"It won't do to ignore the Captain," the beagle-faced driver said, "but at the moment you may find it instructive to note that he's had a nip or two." He stuck his thumb to his lips and made a quick tilt with his fist to indicate, just between the two of them, the old glug-glug. "Medicinal."

Marshall nodded with his lips pressed together.

The Captain leaned across the driver's lap and, with his tiny face and bushy brow pointed up at Marshall, croaked, "Where's the Tater ranch?"

"It's not to be helped," the driver said. He used an elbow to lever the other man back into his seat. The Captain capitalized on this reversal of momentum—though almost allowed his drive to falter when his first two flailed attempts at the door handle failed to unlatch anything—and, when he could finally swing the passenger-side door open before him, stumbled from the vehicle. Moving as if he'd only now discovered that his legs were a size too long for him, he stepped to the front of the car, unzipped his fly, fished out a tab of flesh, and began to urinate on the fender. The stream made a steady splash underlain by a metallic drumming. Marshall could see the man took some pride in that.

"I'm Marshall Tate. May I offer you gentlemen some breakfast?"

"Food makes me sick," the Captain replied.

Marshall heard a snipe *whooring* in the field.

"Some coffee, at least?" Marshall implored the driver now. "Can you see what I'm aiming for here?"

"Yes, and I'm beginning to resent it," the driver said.

"What is your name?" Marshall demanded, more stridently than he wanted.

"Sim!" the man shot back at him.

The small man at the fender made a sallying gesture with the bottle. He moved around the front of the car toward Marshall, each step an inverted accident. As he approached he drew from his pocket a hefty dollop of money. Hands shaking tremendously, he stripped two hundreds from the wad, crumpled them, and threw them at Marshall, his wrist flipping like a girl's. "We'll be fishing today," he said.

"You fellows drive a long way to get here?" Marshall asked.

"Just over from Billings," Mr. Sim, the driver, said.

"Can I ask how you heard about the creek?"

"Mike Shadford," Mr. Sim said. "He spoke to our Trout Unlimited chapter last month."

"Really?" Marshall asked.

"He said it's the greatest secret in western Montana!" the Captain chimed in.

"Last month this was?"

"Oh," Mr. Sim said, "month, six weeks ago. Where would we sign up for the guides Mike was talking about?"

"And Shadford said there would be guides?"

"Yeah. Said we'd need them here."

"When did he tell you this, do you remember?"

"Remember?" the Captain snapped, "I guess we can remember yesterday afternoon!"

"We called over yesterday," Sim said, "and Mike told us the owner out here would provide guiding."

Marshall again experienced a brief synopsis of the two oldsters wandering unchaperoned around the property, drunk and injury prone. But he had quit Fly Guys partially because he no longer wanted to spend his days with people he could not stand simply because Shadford arbitrarily assigned him to them. It was a risk, but he felt it crucial to his mental stability and the momentum of his unexpected success not to let Shadford prevail. He told the men there would be no guides.

"No guides?" Mr. Sim sniveled, his face drooping in doglike disappointment.

"No guides," Marshall said, feeling cavalier about it.

The Captain glared at him.

"Not part of the deal," Marshall swashbuckled. Then he shrugged. "Also, you overpaid. It's one-twenty for two of you." He smoothed one of the hundreds and handed it to Mr. Sim, who held it out for Marshall to regain. "Perhaps for a guide?" he asked, near a simper. "Surely you could—"

"No guides," Marshall said, dipping his knees and expanding one arm outward and upward with it.

"I'll be goddamned," muttered the Captain.

Mr. Sim flung the hundred onto the dashboard. "Captain!" he called. "Let's off."

Marshall gave them directions to the creek and went back to mount his bike. As much as he dreaded the notion of leaving his stream in the hands of such heathens, he hedged his bet on the strong chance they'd already limited their abilities to do much damage. Anyway, Marshall reckoned it was time to drive into town, have himself a palaver with Shadford.

Marshall was pissed, but he got in his rig and drove through such a lovely morning that he didn't attempt to hold on to his annoyance during the trip. He was happy to be tooling along the dirt road, watching the pastures and trees scroll by. He had a Greg Brown CD to listen to, a cold Diet Coke to sip from. Once he joined the main valley road— improved gravel, the tourist maps called it—he spotted an outfit coming toward him, a red pickup. Out here, it could belong to anybody going to one of a dozen or so ranches in the area, or some outdoorsman headed for the high country trailhead at the end of the road.

Marshall lifted the first two fingers of the hand that gripped the top of his steering wheel, a courtesy he'd long ago learned the locals expected. He liked this little custom, cherished it in the recognition that most communities were too big to wave at everybody who drove by, but that in his life vacancy was a virtue. At the last moment, Marshall saw framed in the oncoming vehicle's windshield Daisy Klingman's coils of curls. Her mouth was set in a thin line and her eyes seemed riveted to the road before her, as if she expected trouble from the roadbed at any moment—a turn she'd never seen before, a hump buckled up during the night. She flashed by, but Marshall was pleased to see she had lifted a finger from the wheel to return his wave. It wasn't until a bit later, as he slowed to turn onto the pavement road, that he thought about what he found odd in her gesture. It had taken a little extra effort, it seemed. Then he realized she had actually rolled her hand off the wheel, and the finger she'd lifted to him had been her middle one.

Even as Marshall embarked on his hour-and-a-half journey from the ranch, in downtown Missoula, in a gravel parking lot separated from the river by only a stretch of green-lawned city park, Alton Summers sat in his pickup truck, door swung open, pausing for a moment before heading up the wooden staircase to the back door of Fly Guys fly shop. He made some silent wishes about his clients arriving before Amy Baine showed up for work. Alton was, as was nearly always the case, the first to arrive this morning. He jingled his keys as he mounted the stairs, stuck one in the lock, then scrambled to outpace the security alarm. He flicked lights on in the shop, watching each new bank of illumination shine on another rack of Orvis flannel shirts, Filson waxed-cotton shooting jackets, T-shirts scrawled with clever fish puns, trout-head salt and pepper shakers, Patagonia fleece vests, Patagonia sport shirts, Patagonia shorts for women, Patagonia for Kids, Patagonia this and Patagonia that, plus socks with trout on them, ties in trout motifs, tie tacks shaped like trout, trout-shaped money clips, keychains, kitchen aprons, license-plate holders, and hats, hats, hats. Up in the very front right corner stood two racks cradling fly rods, and just inside the back door, closest to him, were fly bins, most of them empty or woefully in short supply. Alton wondered when, exactly, the place had ceased being a fly shop and had become a souvenir stand for dilettantes.

He made his way forward to the cash register and the counter full of reels—no more than twenty reels in the entire store, most of them either $500 Abels or $120 Battenkills. Beside the cash register he found the guide book and leafed through it to today's date. He glanced at the entries, saw he would have two men from North Carolina. He wondered idly which of the two would be Marge Johnson. He glanced farther down the entry list, assuring himself that all parties were matched with suitable guides. He spotted Scotty Wadsworth's name on the list, and wondered who were the lucky devils who wound up with the Wad. Scotty was a perfectly fine young goofball to hang around with, but Alton shuddered at the thought of slapping down five Cs for a guide and having the Wad show up to row him down the river—particularly since it was salmonfly season, which meant Rock Creek during runoff. Ideally on a stream as fast as Rock Creek the guide should be rowing nonstop, hauling on the oars, holding water, trying to slow the boat's descent all day long. Otherwise it was like casting out of the back of a pickup truck zooming down the interstate.

Alton heard thuds on the stairs out the back door and looked up in time to see Shadford's wiry body bounding up the last few stairs. Shadford glanced Alton's way, documented who the person standing behind his checkout counter was, grunted, and turned into the small private office in the back of the store. He closed the door behind him. Alton didn't care. He had already decided this was his last season with Shadford. He didn't care what happened next.

A long series of fixture-rattling steps pounded up the back entrance and Scotty the Wad rolled in, followed by a lovely midforties couple. He wore Sansabelt slacks, and for her, white mules. Scotty said, "Hey, Alton," in that offhanded way a young Turk might use when he's trying to create for his clients the atmosphere of comfort and experience, the notion that he belongs here, that this fly shop, this circle of fly-fishing guides, is his home water. And all Alton had to do was play along, say hello, as if seeing Scotty the Wad with a lovely pair of clients was the most usual thing in the world.

"Hey, Scotty," Alton said. "They found that last couple you took out."

Scotty stuck on pause for a moment before saying, "Ha ha."

Alton spotted Shadford's head thrusting from the private office, scowling at him then sucking back into the door frame, quick as the flicker of a lizard's tongue. That only spurred him on. Alton slid across the room and disappeared into the stockroom. He'd been waiting for this chance. He found two small, round plastic canisters, one of which contained an unwrapped cherry Starburst candy. The other held a piece of something called strike putty, which looked just like a cherry Starburst. Alton strolled casually back onto the floor. Scotty had his people at the fly bins, where he was trying to sell them salmonfly patterns.

"Scotty," Alton said, copping a helpful tone, "have you used this stuff?" He opened his fist to display a canister.

"Naw," Scotty said. "I've seen it. I haven't tried it."

"Oh, you should really try it," Alton said. He opened the canister with the cherry Starburst candy wedged into it. "New this year from Orvis. You know what a hassle it is every time you want to affix a new strike indicator when you're nymphing?" Alton sized the client up as a fellow who didn't spend much time nymphing, so he didn't wait for an answer. "Well, this stuff you just glom onto your leader. And it's reusable. Pretty nifty, huh?"

"That is," the man said. His wife was nodding. Scotty watched with what Alton noted was a healthy dose of reserve. "So you like this stuff," Scotty said.

"I do," Alton said.

"Better than those stick-on indicators?" Scotty said.

Alton smiled. This was too easy. "See, the thing I really hate about those stick-ons, every time I'm standing by a good nymphing run, I see where somebody has ripped off a stick-on indicator and just thrown it on the ground. I hate seeing litter on a trout stream, you know?"

The clients nodded with sincere appreciation.

"Well, this stuff's biodegradable," Alton said, "A piece comes off by accident, it'll disappear in a few days."

"That's cool," Scotty said.

That's cool? Alton thought. *Jesus, Wad.*

"Yeah, hell, it's even edible," he said, "so if, say, a deer or a bird comes along, or a fish eats a piece—zip, right through them. And here's the surprising thing, it actually tastes pretty good." Alton pried the cherry Starburst from the canister in his hand and popped it into his mouth. After a couple closed-mouth circular chews, he said, "Try it," and tossed Scotty the other canister.

The Wad's countenance was dubious, but his clients clearly stood waiting for a review. Scotty opened the canister, picked out the square of strike putty, and bit it in half. Alton could not imagine what that crap tasted like. Mostly dry, he guessed, and musty with esters and other chemicals. The gag was watching the dye run from the putty, mix with Scotty's saliva, and paint his lips, teeth, and tongue bright red. Scotty's chewing slowed and his face fell into a studied frown, then segued into a glare. Billy Mills chose this instant to stride in through the back door, take a look at Scotty, and hoot. Mills actually slapped his thigh and laughed out loud. Scotty's client started to chuckle, then realized he was booked for a trip with the guide everybody made fun of.

Shadford emerged from his office to see what the noise was about, took a look at Scotty's tongue pushing a masticated wad of juicy red something onto his palm, saw the red dye all over Scotty's mouth, and grew so instantly furious that he had to retreat once again into the office. Not before he summoned Alton, though. Fortunately for Alton, his own clients appeared at the back door of the shop just then. Alton ignored Shadford, introduced himself to his clients, father and son from North Carolina, they drawled. They mentioned "brown" in reference to a drink. Alton liked that. It meant they were hung over and he could sort of ease into the morning. Alton sold his clients a few flies, fixed them up with tippet and some floatant and, on his way out the door, popped his head into Shadford's office. "You wanted me?"

"No, but I'm stuck with you."

"It's no less a blessing for me," Alton said.

"Why don't you just quit?"

"Why don't you gather together the balls to fire me?"

"The scene with Scotty was not cool," Shadford said. "In front of clients? You want to fuck around, do it offstage."

"Right-o," Alton said. "Must run." Surely Shadford would get around to understanding that the scene with Scotty was all for him.

When Marshall arrived at the Fly Guys shop almost two hours later, Alton was already on the river, rowing merrily down the stream. Shadford was absent from the shop as well. This from Billy Mills. Marshall didn't know whether to trust Mills. Shadford could easily have been behind his closed office door. Marshall didn't know whether to push the issue, but his alternative was asking Amy Baine, who sat crosslegged on the floor in the back of the room, folding T-shirts. Marshall sort of wanted to avoid her as much as possible.

"Tell Mr. Shadford I'd like to speak with him when he gets a chance," Marshall told Mills.

"Whatever," Mills said.

Marshall made his way toward the back door and almost reached it when the door swung in and Palmer Tillotson followed it.

"Palmer, how are things?" Marshall asked.

Palmer Tillotson set sail a smile and said, "Things get any better, I'm going to have to hire someone else to help me enjoy them."

Palmer Tillotson had guided for a few seasons, but now ran a shuttle service for all the guides in town, shuttling rigs from put-ins to takeouts so that when the guide arrived at the end of a float, his vehicle and trailer awaited. Like so many other guides, Palmer had come from elsewhere—Gulf Shores, Alabama—as a young man wanting to go fishing, and had fallen into guiding to support his habit. He had built a solid reputation, then quit guiding so he could enjoy fishing again. He was a lanky fellow, late twenties, with a long, black beard and a softness around his eyes that, Marshall suspected, was born of the amusement he found from observing people. His southern manner and the occasional sprinkling of folk language—this was a man Marshall had heard use the phrase "box of sunshine" in a sentence—had won the hearts of his clients. Marshall doubted he'd ever seen Palmer without a cap on.

"So I was wondering," Palmer said.

"What were you wondering?" Marshall answered, because this was how you had to talk to Palmer.

"The thing is, Katy and I are getting married here soon," Palmer said.

"Yes. I'm aware." Still trying to get a feel for the shape the conversation would take.

"Well," Palmer trickled an illustrative little chuckle, "this'll jar your preserves. What it was, pure just dumb luck . . . we wanted to get married at the Triple Creek Ranch, down the Bitterroot? And then some things happened and we ended up calling down there to find out when we could get in to, you know, start setting things up, and it turns out we didn't get it booked after all. Only I thought we had. So we've just discovered that the two hundred people or so that we've invited, including all her aunts and uncles who are flying in from New York and Philly, don't really have any place to stand around while we get married. It's one of those things where the wheel's still turning, but the hamster's dead."

Marshall saw it coming now. "These 'things that happened,' they didn't involve you forgetting to book the lodge, did they?"

"Well hell, I mean, Katy, generally she's varying degrees of wonderful until you get her started on this wedding. Then she's just relentless. She makes up a thousand lists of things to do and each individual item has to have a thirty-minute discussion with it. She keeps saying we have to talk about this or that, and I say, But we've already talked about that. Except that's where I've made my mistake, because it turns out that we haven't talked about anything until I've capitulated. Only I don't know this. I've just now figured it out. But in the meantime, I thought we'd already talked about who would book the lodge. Only we hadn't, see?" Palmer reached a hand to gather in his beard and tug it.

"You want a place to have the wedding?"

"You know I would never, not in a million years, drop this on you if the situation hadn't fully bloomed into a clusterbumper."

"What's the date?"

"July the thirty-first."

"We should be able to throw a wedding together in a month," Marshall said, wondering if that was at all realistic.

"I want to apologize in advance, though, for my wife-to-be," Palmer said. "She'll be kind of aggressive."

"It'll be fine. I won't have much time to help organize," Marshall said, "but she can have free run of the place."

"Oh," Palmer laughed vaguely, in a way that, had Marshall been a little sharper, would have clearly indicated that he had no idea what he was in for. But Marshall was distracted by Amy Baine breezing by, silky brown hair winging out behind her, and Palmer was heading to the other side of the shop. Amy wore a black sleeveless blouse and batik-print harem pants in gold and black.

"Ames," Marshall said.

"Marsh," Amy said, dropping her chin to lower her voice in a parody of gravity. Marshall glanced askance.

"I hear the spring creek business is going quite well," Amy said, still forcing the baritone.

"The business would be going much better if your boss—or should I say boyfriend?—would stop screwing with me."

Amy clucked her tongue. "He's not my boyfriend." With that, she became a twenty-three-year-old girl again. "Speaking of which, I suppose you've heard about Alton and Molly?"

"I have not," Marshall said.

"He bagged her," Billy Mills chirped, all the way from the front of the shop.

"Doubt it," Marshall said.

"Mills saw them leave together," Amy said. "I knew it all along. I don't know how many times he tried to deny it. I knew they'd hook up the minute I stepped out of the picture."

"He saw them leave where together?" Marshall asked.

"Rhino," Mills called.

"Amy, do you know how many times Alton and Molly have left the Rhino together?"

"Not like *this*," Amy said. Marshall was amazed at how seamlessly she was able to don the cloak of the wronged party.

"Dude, I saw it," Mills said. He was making his way back toward them. "I promise you, it wasn't the usual thing."

"Dude," Marshall argued.

"Dude," Mills argued back.

"You know they've just been waiting to hook up," Amy said.

"I don't know any such thing," Marshall said.

"And it's just like you to defend them!"

Marshall interpreted the turn of events as his cue to leave. The problem with living an hour and a half out of town was that when you drove an hour and a half into town to see someone and he wasn't there, you rarely felt like turning right around and going home. Marshall rarely made spur-of-the-moment trips, but his ire with Shadrat had overtaken better judgment. Now he sensed he'd somehow created at Fly Guys a hostile, free-fire zone for himself. He didn't believe for a moment that Alton and Molly would hook up in the Biblical sense, but he understood how Amy Baine might want to believe it. He felt like he probably should not go back inside the shop for a long time.

Furthermore, he felt seriously remiss, all of a sudden, for allowing two drunk old men to wander around his father's ranch, and he began to imagine every liability pratfall they could possibly perform, the first of which being that they fall into the creek and drown—and that seemed the least problematic scenario. Shouldn't he have an extra insurance policy to cover these sort of exigencies, and why hadn't he thought of that before? He was beginning to understand how his scorn toward understanding the world of "business" could bite him in the ass.

Marshall wandered around downtown Missoula, admiring the old facades and hating the boxy, flat-faced buildings in between. He felt uncertain about the retro-frontier stuff, the teal and puce cutout detailing and parlorlike facings of certain storefronts. Coffee shops had migrated from Seattle to nearly every street corner. The hills south of town, tawny gold and wide open when Marshall had moved West, now bristled with vapid box homes and subdevelopments featuring hideous mauve, chocolate, and peach walls. That the West lacked an

architectural vernacular—save vague and unfinished gestures like a
penchant for piling derelict automobiles alongside houses—did not excuse the common man for being tasteless. There were trailer parks
with more subtlety than the claptrap erected on the South Hills.

Still, the old Northern Pacific building hunched at the north end
of Higgins Avenue, its red tile roof capping an impressive expanse of
yellow-red brick. The Wilma building stood above all others, only thirteen floors high, a remnant monolith with an opera house inside and
the town's only on-duty elevator operator. Marshall took himself to the
public library and decided to read a bit about water rights, and when
he could find nothing that made any sense, he drove out Third Avenue
to a shopping center where, wedged between a Save-On drugstore and
an organic grocery store, he found the Department of Natural Resources and Conservation, Water Rights Division. He pulled the file on
the property his family owned and spent a long time looking at the
sheaves of paper covered with dates and words and phrases describing his privilege to the applicable waters in the West Fork drainage.
The words and terms lay like clusters of nettles before him—probably
penetrable but awfully intimidating if you weren't feeling full of patience. He thought leafing through the Klingman claims might lead
him to ring a bell. But the Klingman file was absent from the cabinet.

"What's that mean?" Marshall asked the clerk.

"Means somebody's examining it. An attorney, most likely."

Marshall's heart fell. The Klingmans and their attorneys. Were
he involved in this fray, Skipjack Tate would blow the Klingmans out
of the water. He'd surround them with lawyers and lay siege, then
bury them with countersuits. Ultimately, the Fly X water rights meant
everything to Marshall's spring creek. Moreover, his plan had been to
adduce the ranch from the scope of his father's attentions, not spark
up new concerns. A disaster this colossal so early in the game would
let Skipjack think exactly what Marshall feared he might already sur-
mise—something Marshall himself often suspected—that Marshall
was in no way capable of operating any kind of going concern.

Marshall no longer wanted to stay in town, but he felt no momentum for driving all the way to the ranch. What was left to do? He took
himself to the early movie at the Crystal Theater, a French film
wherein everybody sat in a train car and talked with flat affect so that
the only means of gauging emotional expression was the ferocity with

which the actors smoked. But the popcorn, sprinkled with yeast, cay-
enne pepper, and Parmesan cheese, was outstanding. When the movie
let out, the sky outside had deepened only slightly. The sun had
slipped around to the north and fired the bricks of the Milwaukee Station's mission-style watchtower a rich, pulpy red. Marshall realized he
had nobody to call, nobody he could drop in on casually and say, "How
ya doin'?" His friends were guiding. All the others, friends from college,
friends from the fly shop, friends from living around town, had either
moved or now had lives Marshall had slid away from. For two years he
had concentrated singularly on building a trout stream. He knew
nothing about what people did in town anymore.

Marshall wandered into the Rhino around nine o'clock. It was stupid to start drinking, so he did. The sour apple tang of Rolling Rock
made him salivate. The bottle was crisp, cold, beaded with condensa-
tion. The first beer helped, but not as much as the second and third.
This was foolish, and he knew it. A ninety-minute drive lay ahead in
his evening. Sitting in a bar alone, with nothing to do but parse things
out, the facts started facing him: he'd been drinking a lot lately. When
he stayed at the ranch—during the winter, when he worked on the
spring project for hours and days on end—he would go for weeks without cracking a beer. Not even miss it. *Town,* Marshall thought. *It must
have to do with coming to town.* At any rate, he decided, it might be an
idea to put the brakes on. Of course it was too late to start that tonight.

There were people he knew in the bar, but none he knew to strike
up a conversation with. Mostly he recognized folks. At this hour most
of the drinkers were men. He could talk fishing to any of them—the
way most of them could talk skiing or kayaking or fishing to each
other, even if they hadn't done any of those things for years—but, God,
he'd grown tired of that. Marshall ordered a cup full of peanuts, then
another. Popcorn and peanuts comprised his nutritional intake for the
day. Squirrels ate better. The cold beers relaxed his mind enough that
it began to conjure images of drunk old Mr. Sim collapsed in his spring
creek, beagle face pinched, lips carping for air while cold water rushed
over his skull. A worse scenario would include either of the oldsters
suffering grievous bodily harm and living to sue about it. The Captain
might blunder into a cow elk protecting her calf, have his collarbone
cracked by flung hooves and lie around injured for hours. He'd take
Marshall for everything he had.

Determined to cease with the fretting Marshall turned his attention to a baseball game, but found himself repeatedly unable to appreciate why anybody enthused over a "sport" where the players could complete an entire game without ever touching the game ball or breaking a sweat; and yet tens of thousands of people nationwide seemed to care. But of course he'd grown up with the Red Sox. Marshall noticed Scotty the Wad's friends arriving in a pageant of river rat panache. Jimmy Ripley, Marshall remembered, was the blond with his hair cropped close, the billboard forehead, and hooded eyelids. The other one, the guy with the walkie-talkie, was . . . *Rock?* His chin stretched comically long and flat, and his neck seemed to thrust it forward, as if that was how it got flattened, repeatedly running into things face-first. *Flint, was it? Pebbles? Bam Bam? What was his name? Stone,* Marshall thought, *something Stone.* Marshall could see that the guy might be handsome if his features showed more relief. He watched Stone talk to a girl, saw how he wrapped himself in a broad-legged stance, folded arms, an expression untouchably swell. Trust me, he seemed to be saying, I don't need your opinion of me.

Marshall wondered what made young men so enormously enthralled with purveying their visions of themselves. Women were seldom such buffoons. He watched them absently, watched the bar begin to fill, tried to guess what night of the week it might be based on the crowd. He figured Wednesday, but then did the calculations and came up with Thursday. Marshall thought about ordering a fourth beer, then wondered what he was doing here. The original excuse had been the hope that Alton would wander in. But it was ten-thirty now, and Alton clearly had better designs on his evening. Marshall tossed off the contents of the bottle and wandered out the door. He drove to Alton's apartment, the second floor of a pestilent Victorian house plagued by decades of rentals to college students.

Alton hunched over a fly-tying table in a room that served as library, tying bench, gear closet, dinette, and living room. The furniture in the room consisted of the chair Alton sat in, a knock-kneed couch wrapped in tie-dyed cotton drapery, a coffee table strewn with detritus, and a beanbag chair. Marshall opted for the beanbag, stuffed into a corner amid bookshelves. Aside from David James Duncan and Norman McClean, the library was one big advice column—how-to and reference tomes focused on fishing. Alton owned—and had pored over—Lefty Kreh's flats-fishing books, even though he'd never fished in saltwater, books about fishing Maine's Allagash River, the Restigouche salmon run, and a guide to riparian terrestrials of New Zealand. The collection was, as much as anything, a catalog of desire.

Whereas the tying bench was a zoo of animal parts, real and artificial. Shelves stuffed with hackles, piles of pheasant and partridge skins, receptacles brimming with biots, stacked packets of CDC, drawers stuffed with calf tails, interspersed with Antron dubbing, holographic tinsel, Mylar ribbon, foam strips, and micron fiber bundles—the effect was that perhaps when Alton wasn't working at it, the entire bench might rise, shake its shaggy head, and take itself outside to pee. Beside the bench, on a table, stood an aquarium Alton used to hatch out insects. Alton's wrist spun at an unnatural speed as he wound thread around a hook. At the moment he was whipping up piles of his ZAP PMD cripples. His secret was the shuck.

When Alton had become involved in fly fishing, he immersed himself almost immediately in the bugs. Fishing was the engine that drove his initial interest, to be sure, but Alton found himself mesmerized by the seemingly infinite array of fly patterns. He learned quickly to tie, found that his small fingers and quick hands allowed him to assemble flies with preternatural consistency and pace. He was good at it, and he liked that. Alton had not been good at the obvious things as a youngster. He was not unathletic, only small, which limited his options. He read books, only to find out that other boys his age didn't read the same kinds of books. In his high school, ornithology and entomology, it turned out, were not inspiring lunch-table conversation starters.

When he moved to Montana to start college, Alton found himself standing in rivers, sometimes forgetting to cast. He watched bugs like he might eat them himself, and then he did. It was weird, eating bugs; he understood that. Probably unnecessary for the basic understanding he'd need as a fisherman. But he wanted to know what fish were getting out of the deal. He'd chewed three-inch salmonflies to see what about them could create such a fuss—softer, more custardlike than he'd anticipated, except for a few disheartening kernels. Ants had a fizzy citrus bite. They were what he fished by default now when nothing else was going on—ants and beetles. It was merely the relative lack of anybody else doing it, Alton suspected, that made trout on heavily fished rivers susceptible to terrestrials. All the goobs floated Adams patterns with prince droppers when the action was slow. Ants and beetles, though, could light up an afternoon.

The signature discovery in Alton's professional life so far had come while watching pale morning duns. Several insects comprised the hatches known locally as PMDs—all members of the genus *Ephemerella*, that tragi-poetic group of balletic bugs that existed in the air for an hour or perhaps a day, never longer, before floating above a river, dipping to the surface to lay eggs, then falling, spent-winged and dead, back to the water. In the western PMD category, you primarily had your *infrequens*—meaning scanty or uncrowded—and your *inermis*—defenseless, without strength—mayflies with a cream or yellowish body and three long tails. Alton doubted the trout made much distinction between the species, but he did know that the individual bug size diminished as the season progressed. A PMD hatch in late August called for a smaller fly than one in June. A further observation, gleaned while wallowing in the river with a snorkel and mask, nose at surface level, formed his hopes of securing a niche in the local fly-fishing establishment.

Alton sat in the shallows of various rivers and creeks on cool, overcast days and observed over and over again PMDs struggling against the confines of their nymphal shucks as they lifted from the bottom and approached the surface slick, then emerging as duns. The duns might float long distances with their wings down, Alton had noticed, but once their resin-thin wings levered upright and began to dry, they lifted off the water within a few seconds, levitating in an unwavering arc toward the streamside foliage. But any hatch contains some evolutionary backwash, the thousands of bugs that don't emerge from their cases, or that die trying. Repeatedly Alton noticed a prevenience in trouts' attitude toward the cripples in a hatch—which bugs, he also noted, were often invisible to someone standing thirty feet away on the bank.

Alton had studied dozens of hatches and the ways fish reacted to them before experiencing an *aha!* moment and sitting down at his bench for several hours of creative biomimicry. The sun had set and rose again before Alton had the blueprint of his ZAP flies—a cripple pattern featuring a micron bundle for the wing casing with crinkled slivers of clear plastic jutting out to imitate emergent wings. On the

tail he twirled more plastic—he used what he had handy, in the initial
case the cellophane wrappings from one of the packs of cigarettes he
occasionally bought in the bar, only to repudiate the next morning—to
approximate the trailing shuck. Later he would smoke the cellophane
over a butane lighter to add color and a bit of distortion.

It didn't look good, but its effectiveness was deadly—indeed, the
pattern name declared itself to him when, on their first trial run,
Alton fished the fly aswirl in the surface slick and found it worked
'Zactly As Planned. Word got around and guides started clamoring for
ZAPs. Shadford had snatched up an exclusive twelve-month contract
for the things at a time when Alton wasn't thinking farther than next
month's rent, which hindered his ability to sell the pattern nationally
via the big mail-order catalogs, or on the Web, even while he received
phone calls about the possibility on a regular basis. At one point a
writer from *Fly Fisherman* magazine had written a how-to story about
ZAPs, though all orders went through Fly Guys, and Shadford profited
handsomely, leaving Alton with his measly piecemeal contract. But
the contract expired at the end of the summer, and Alton was now in
the midst of assembling inventory and diversifying the product line.
He'd knocked off several mayfly variants, and Marshall's new enter-
prise had inspired him to develop some tiny spring-creek patterns.
Next he was trying to imagine a way to apply the thinking to stoneflies. Alton could crank out twenty dozen of these flies in an evening,
and was on his way to that when Marshall had rapped on the door
while moving through it.

"How was the fishing?" Marshall asked, once ensconced in the
beanbag chair.

"I bet we caught twenty, thirty," Alton said without looking up.

"Oh, you're going to hell for lying," Marshall said.

"No, these guys could really fish. Nice guys, too. I hung with them
a bit after."

"What'd you do with them?"

"What you always do with clients you're getting along with."

"You took them to the Depot and scored a free meal."

"Yup." At this Alton quit tying for the first moment since Marshall
had arrived. He saw that Marshall was holding a six-pack of Moose
Drool in his lap. Alton's attention seemed to goad Marshall into better
manners. "Oh yeah," he said. "Want one?"

Alton looked at the half-finished beer on his tying bench, calculating how warm it was. "Yeah. Can't have too many, though. I want to get some serious tying done. Hear what I did to Scotty the Wad?"

"No, but I heard what you did to Molly," Marshall said.

"Here we go," Alton said. Alton copped a grin that played over only one side of his mouth, but hooked well up that cheek. His head cocked to open one eye right at Marshall, and he seemed to rise in his seat. "I'd much rather talk about what I did to the Wad," Alton said by way of offering an out.

"OK, what'd you do to Wad?" Marshall asked. Alton told him about the strike putty.

Marshall said, "That's pretty funny. Now what did you do to Molly?"

Alton whip-finished a fly and dropped his hands. He turned in his chair and said, "Why is it any of your business?"

"So you did it."

"Whoa, whoa, ho there, big boy," Alton said. "Where's your stake?"

"You guys are my two best friends."

"Yes, that's what everybody is thinking about these days," Alton said. "How will my private life affect Marshall?"

"You know how these things work out between friends," Marshall said.

"That's your only interest? Amicable concern?"

"What?" Marshall said.

"I think you're full of shit," Alton said. "Frankly."

"That's not how things are," Marshall said.

"How are things then?"

"I'm not jealous if that's what you're trying to get at," Marshall said. "God, Molly's hooked up with other guys."

"Maybe you should be jealous," Alton said.

"Why would you say that?"

"Do you really think it's me Molly wants?" Alton asked. "Or do you think she figures I'm what she can get?"

"What kind of thing is *that* to say?"

There was a long silence, longer than a pause—a stillborn moment filled from the background with the gurgling of the bug aquarium while the people in the room reflected. *Well,* thought Marshall, *what we've learned here is that the worst time to shoot yourself in the foot is when it's in your mouth.*

Marshall drank some beer. He didn't believe for a second what Alton was trying to pull on him. There had been the one moment with him and Molly, back in the St. Joe, but you could just as completely write that off to the magic of some rivers. *Huh uh.*

Alton meanwhile was trying everything on, seeing what fit. "Are you nervous at all about this whirling disease stuff?"

"I guess I should be," Marshall said, unable to think of a good reason not to answer the question.

"Everybody who comes into the shop asks about it. Shadford's pretending it isn't happening," Alton said, "though I don't see what a lot of the fuss is about. Seems like nature to me."

"Nature?" Marshall said. "It's a disease from Europe that's wiping out entire fish populations here. How's that nature?" Then he felt like he was just arguing, so he eased off to say, "I guess if it's as bad as they say, potentially it could wipe me out."

Now Marshall felt awful about the way the conversation had taken to circling the drain. On a mission to get some lift back under this exchange, Marshall asked, "You still liking guiding?"

"Some days better than others."

"Why do you think people like guiding?"

"Different reasons," Alton said, though Marshall could see he wasn't being deliberately obtuse. Alton seemed to be thinking about some of the different reasons. "I really love rivers and fish and fishing. And I hate it when I see things that I think are bad happening out there. I figure I can have some influence if I'm guiding. I'm out there every day. I'm teaching people. I just figure I can have something to do with it."

"Yeah, me too," Marshall said. "Except, of course, not anymore."

Another long silence slid into the room, though each man seemed to be thinking that he'd got out ahead of trouble, got a rope on its nose and turned it. They both seemed willing to show the other that they were open to a softening.

"After all these years," Marshall asked, "what do you know about guiding that you can say in a sentence?"

Alton smiled. " 'Why don't we grab a quick bite at the Depot.' "

"Nice, nice," Marshall said, nodding, appreciating. "What do you know about fly fishing that you can say in a sentence?"

Alton's lower lip slid over his upper for a second before he answered. "I wouldn't say a thing."

"Perfect! That's it exactly, isn't it?" Marshall said. He settled back in the beanbag chair and looked around the room at Alton's books. "I remember when all I wanted to do was talk about fishing. When I first stumbled into Fly Guys, I thought, here's this place where a bunch of guys sit around and talk about fishing all day and get paid to do it. I thought I was in heaven."

"Yeah, yeah," Alton said, his head bobbing with the same rhythm, though half time with his hand wrapping thread around the hook. "Me, too."

"And now—"

"Yeah," Alton agreed. "It's not that I don't like it anymore, or don't like talking about it. It's still good every time I go out. I mean, there's different things I like about it now. The places matter more. Who I go with. But I still love it."

Neither said anything for a moment, and the room held a reverberant hum from the contentment they both felt, for not only sharing a mutual evolution but for recognizing it in each other—and for correctly suspecting that they were exactly the only other people they each wanted to talk about it with.

After a while Marshall's feel-good buzz flattened and he thought about home and said, "I'd better hit the road."

"You OK to drive?" Alton asked.

"If I close one eye," Marshall said, holding his palm over one squinted eye. "I'll be fine—there's rumble strips on both sides of the road."

Marshall pulled out of town and drove home with exaggerated caution, though he worried that might make him a target for some sharp-eyed statie. He watched the roadsides for the green glow of deer eyes, slowing when he spotted them along the highway. He'd come close to pushing too far with Alton, to digging them both into disgruntled positions, but then they'd pulled it out together. On top of that, Marshall was kicking around the edges of a discovery, something about saying things, about placing them in the presence of someone close to you and making those things more true. *Say it out loud and there it is. You just can't deny the connections that information makes.*

Marshall sang along to an Allison Moorer CD, which took him far into his country, where he felt safe on the roads under any condition. He turned off the state highway onto the gravel, now howling out Jerry Jeff Walker songs, completely relieved once the sound of gravel popped and crunched under his tires. Nobody would arrest him on the gravel, and he was only half an hour from home. And what he was going to do next would be no more of this boozing in town. He was going to obviate the need to feel this relief. Marshall slowed to twenty-five miles an hour, rolled down his window, filled the cab of the truck with the thick smell of field grasses heavy with dew. He stared into the fringes of his headlights' reach in the hope that he might spot a wolf skulking away—his eyes were always looking for them now.

Instead he swept around a turn and his headlights flashed on the reddish flank of a whitetail doe standing at the roadside. She stood with two legs in the grass and two on the road. Marshall always slowed and swerved at deer near the road, honked his horn, anything that might scare them deeper into the fields. People flew down even the gravel roads, and he liked to educate the deer that roadside grazing was not a winning survival strategy.

Now he swerved and shouted. He half hung out the window and growled, like he thought a wolf might, and when he did he saw beneath the doe's belly another set of legs. The doe uncoiled one long bound, cleared the fence, and disappeared into the dark. From underneath her a fawn sprang the exact opposite direction onto the road. The fawn's body was only the size of a spaniel; its legs were as long as yardsticks. The fawn tried two seesaw leaps—bucking farther upward than forward—before landing wrong on the second leap, its soft hooves skidding on the hard road surface so that its back legs did the splits until its belly hit the gravel. The fawn immediately curled its forelegs under its chest, sucked in its back legs, and dropped its chin onto the road surface.

Marshall had seen fawns hiding in the grass before, particularly fawns still in the first weeks of their life. He knew they were scentless for those first few weeks, and that they hid in the grass for hours on end, hoping some bumbling predator didn't wander into their patch of vegetation. Marshall's heart broke when he saw a dead doe on the side of the highway during this time of the year, because he knew that somewhere nearby a spotted fawn curled in the high grass, waiting for its mother to come and release it from its hiding spot. The fawn would wait until it began to tremble from malnourishment or dehydration, then die, too. Once, while walking through the grass along the spring beds to choose the route he wanted to dig for his creek,

Marshall had come across the perfectly whole skeleton of a fawn, its spine curled in a half moon, its legs folded into itself. No predators had found and disturbed the carcass. Its flesh had simply melted away through the seasons.

Still, he was surprised to see the fawn in his headlights fall into that behavior in the middle of a gravel road. The fawn held completely still, as if somehow the gravel might conceal it from whatever danger had exploded into its night, as if by freezing it could simply disappear. Marshall stopped his truck, happy he was going so slow, and got out. He circled around so that he approached the fawn from the side opposite where its mother had disappeared. He felt an enormous sadness for the small creature, so inexperienced, resorting to genetic memory as a last hope for its short life, and choosing such a poor place to try its best trick. He talked to it as he approached, saying, "Come on, little guy. Up and out."

He stepped so near that his boot toe almost touched its body, and he could see its spotted pelt lying loosely over its spine. He could see the thin membrane of its nostrils distended, trembling while the fawn exhaled. The creature did not move. Marshall bent over even closer and clapped his hands softly. That did it. The fawn unfolded in a burst, levered itself to its feet, and managed to assemble three long leaps that carried its gracile form off the road and into the dark grass. Marshall heard another vector of noise in the night, the doe moving through the field to intercept her baby, guide it back into the dark safety of the tall grass. Marshall stood for a few moments. He loved living where he did for the little emotional responses the land continually provoked in him.

He had another one coming, though it was less about the place as how it tended to shape its denizens. Marshall finished the drive home in such swelling spirits that he felt it was safe to sing "Morning Song for Sally." He was having enough fun with it that he brought the disc into the house with him and plunked it in the CD player. He felt exhausted but a bit exalted, too, and put off washing his face while he looked around the house for something to take out his energy on. Then that problem was solved by a knock on the door, and when he opened it, Daisy Klingman stood in the rectangle of night, all lines and angles slanted with a shaky veneer of savoir faire.

"What are you doing here?" Marshall said.

"Oh, just out for a drive . . ." Daisy said.

"At three A.M.?"

". . . And I saw the lights on."

Marshall took a look at her, bugged that he was drunk. He couldn't imagine any reasons for her to show up like this that were different from any reasons she had showed up like this in the past, so he said, "I'm really tired. You wanna go upstairs?"

"Whoa. Damn, Marshall. Wherever did gallantry go?"

"Hey, I'm not the one who blew in here with the night breeze."

"Yeah, even still, a girl wants to be treated with a tiny bit of respect," Daisy said.

"Aw, shit, I'm sorry," Marshall said. "I don't know what I was thinking. You just look so . . . I just got foolish. Sorry."

"And now you're going to be all Sweet Boy!" Daisy said. She clapped her hands together, strode into the house, whirled, and pressed her butt against the back of a sofa. Marshall noticed the tendons rising from her forearms where her hands remained clasped in a clap. Daisy said, "This is funny. I had no idea there was so much comedy happening over here so late at night."

Momentum jiggered, Marshall paused to take stock. He was aiming toward keeping things floating within reach of a quick rescue. Then he watched Daisy's eyes bleed to another feeling. They fell away, and her chin dropped to her shoulder, arcing her bare neck. Daisy said, "Why are we so awful to each other?"

To Marshall's thinking, that was quite the puzzle. He was willing to hazard a guess: "Familiarity breeds contempt?"

"Maybe that's it," Daisy said.

Marshall didn't like her taking him at face value. He tried, "Or maybe we feel comfortable enough with each other to take some shortcuts."

"Or that," she said.

"And maybe we like each other and trust each other enough to know we'll be forgiven when we cut too close," Marshall said.

Daisy lifted her fingertips to her nose and squinched her face as if she were going to rub it. But she dropped her fingers and a smile leaked onto her mouth. "You *are* going to be a Sweet Boy. Look at you . . ." Then her eyes narrowed. "No, wait. That's not it. You're drunk, aren't you? Oh shit, I should have thought of that. This isn't fair. Let's just go upstairs."

"All right," Marshall said.

They did go upstairs, where they both undressed and got in bed and Marshall felt himself living everywhere he felt her cool lips touch his skin.

Marshall's next day found him standing on the banks of the spring pond readying to pitch rocks at mergansers. It was six-thirty in the morning and a flat dawn light seemed to subtract a dimension from the landscape. Out of sight, a fox yapped in a field, sounding like a violin bow barked against its strings. Marshall could follow the fox around the imaginary map of the land in his head, even tell which way the fox was facing when it called. Before him the pond's surface lay rippleless, stained with a rose glow. Marshall reflected that, prior to building a spring creek, he had never thrown rocks at birds. But the previous spring, waterfowl collected on the pond in rafts pushed about by the breeze—teal, shovelers, widgeon, mallards, pintails—and the mergansers.

He began to see through an equally jaundiced eye blue herons and the inimitable prehistoric insouciance that he had long admired. He found himself standing by the pond, waving off ospreys that hovered high above, their wings folding-flapping to hold them stationary in midair as they prepared their dives. None of these trends startled him until one day Alton had come to see the work in progress and caught Marshall stalking around the pond stockpiling rocks of good throwing size. Alton pointed out that this was a bit kooky. "You didn't stock this place," Alton pointed out. "All the fish came up from the river on their own. It's a limitless supply."

The irony—the one Marshall chose to dwell on, anyway, in his weakened, blue hangover—was that now he waited for predators he had actually invited to the pond to invade this vivid habitat. For money. How could anything mergansers do compare to that? He looked down at the collection of wet rocks in his hand, then opened his fingers and let them drop in a stuttered thud to the ground. The worries allayed during the swell of business he had seen over the past six weeks had begun eating at him again. Runoff was done. The Rock Creek salmonfly hatch had peeled away clients. The summer's regular hatch cycles were setting up on the big rivers, clockwork predictability for guides wanting to get their goobs into fish.

He still hadn't talked to a water rights attorney, and now the issue of insurance was scratching his neck. Of course he needed extra insurance—how could he have been so stupid as to not see that? Driving back from town this morning, Marshall had been prickled with the anxiety that he would find one of the old farts—Sim or the Captain—floating facedown in the pond. All across America, if somebody comes onto your property and hurts himself, it's your fault. Given the sharpers they were cranking out of law schools who knew how you could make yourself safe?

Instead of withdrawing the ranch from his father's concerns, Marshall had created a new liability. Lovely. He would have to get on the phone the moment the insurance agency opened for business, and even preliminary guesswork concluded that a huge chunk of his proceeds to date would plunge into that rat hole. By then Marshall spotted an automobile moving down the county road toward his house from the direction of the Klingmans. Closer inspection revealed the great pink-white land yacht of the Captain and Mr. Sim. The car rolled along barely above idle. Marshall leaped on his bike and pedaled to cut it off.

He caught the car, a Cadillac he could see by the logo on its tail, from behind just after it had crossed the bridge. Marshall rode up beside the Caddy, though neither Mr. Sim nor the Captain turned their concentration from the road before them. Neither could see over the dashboard without craning their necks. Marshall, still riding alongside the vehicle, reached over and whapped the roof of the car. Mr. Sim started violently and the car swerved, clashing against the bike. Marshall's front tire bit into the door of the car, his handlebars wrenched from his grip, and Marshall found himself sailing through an endo. Before he landed, the Caddy dodged away. Marshall splashed into the dirt.

"It's you. Well, I don't feel so bad." Marshall rolled and looked up at the Captain, bent from his waist, hands on hips, scowling down. His bushy brow sprang at Marshall with fantastic disarray. The Captain, however, seemed considerably soberer than the previous morning.

"Oh, wow," Marshall said.

"I suppose you thought that was funny?" The other face hovering over him belonged to the beagley Mr. Sim.

Marshall squeezed his eyes shut, but when he opened them, the two old farts still stood looking down at him like doddering surgeons revisiting their favorite operating theater. He felt a sharp throbbing on his chin, and his teeth had new edges.

"Sending two old men all over hell's half acre? That's your idea of a good time?" the Captain said.

"We paid you a hundred dollars!"

"Didn't you like the fishing?" Marshall asked. He squinted. He ran his hand around his chest and shoulder, trying to determine if he could localize the pain. He rolled over and pushed himself to his knees. Everything took his weight.

"Fishing? What fishing?" the Captain roared. He rained spittle on Marshall with his outburst.

"We drove forty miles of Forest Service road, and only by a stroke of goddamned good luck did we come out where we went in," Mr. Sim said. "Spent the night with some horrid family up the road."

"Maybe you should have your money back," Marshall said. He was amazed and grateful to find that he hadn't broken any limbs, that his terror at the thought of being left to the paramedic graces of Mr. Sim and the Captain could begin to subside, and into its place eased a sort of retrograde, but nonetheless profound, relief that the two had not, after all, spent the previous day staggering around the spring creek in episode after episode that approximated a lawsuit. They'd spent the night at the Klingmans'! He wondered why Daisy hadn't mentioned it, then wondered if their unexpected presence had cued her to come looking for him.

Marshall found in his pocket the same hundred-dollar bill they'd given him the morning before and returned it. Mr. Sim made the Caddy's tires spout gravel on his exit, though he never exceeded fifteen miles an hour. Marshall allowed himself a more extensive self-examination. Alone and finding himself unwounded in any heroic fashion, his mood plummeted again. It was all fine and well and good to play the smart-ass to two old drunks, but everything about those men suggested they had connections. Who knew what word they'd spread. And that hundred was a half hour of time spent in the hallowed advisement of a water rights attorney.

Already in a frangible spirit, Marshall wanted to absent himself from the ranch before Molly arrived with her clients. He simply didn't know what he felt about her and Alton, but knew it wasn't good. There was nothing concrete, nothing you could throw on the ground and kick around, but he was ill at ease and would prefer to pretend nothing was different until he could put his finger on exactly what bothered him so. It was fortunate timing, then, that he had planned this day to go fishing with Kyle Klingman. He limped back to his house, walking the bike.

Marshall had at the beginning held severe doubts about hiring Kyle Klingman to help with the spring project. Kyle was a hulking teenaged male, running around stoked on hormones and bad ideas; who knew what he might blurt out? For instance, how else but Kyle would Klingmans know the extent of his water-moving activities? If anything Kyle was an unwitting dupe. Marshall and Kyle would have to have a sit-down, talk about awareness and savvy. In fact, Marshall sensed the boy was suggestible to many things. He took to fly fishing, under Marshall's tutelage, with great enthusiasm and no small amount of natural talent, agitating some members of his clan. Marshall intended to teach Kyle to guide, partly as a matter of convenience—he could use a local boy to take on the Mr. Sims of the world—although he could not dowse his delight at the subversive nature of his intent.

When he arrived, Kyle took one look at Marshall and asked, "Are you all right?"

"Just a little mob-out," Marshall said.

Kyle Klingman kept strawberry blond hair cropped short atop his head. He had white-blond eyelashes and pinkish lips surrounded by cinnamon freckles. His face was pale, smooth, and deep, with an extraordinary distance between his forehead and his chin. But what you noticed first about Kyle were his shoulders. The boy had a throwback-strength upper frame. When Marshall watched Kyle lifting heavy objects, he thought about bullfights, how the picadors stick the rolls of muscle on a bull's shoulders, and how the bull, stacked with muscle to spare, is able to continue fighting with mortal capacity. Marshall wondered how Kyle found shirts that fit him. Today he wore a yellow and blue windowpane-plaid shirt with the sleeves ripped off, unbuttoned down the front.

Kyle had with him someone Marshall assumed was a girlfriend. He hadn't known anything about Kyle and a girlfriend, but the last he'd spent any great deal of time with Kyle was months ago, back in late March. This one bounced when she walked, balling her calf muscles.

Her body was hard and round and full of energy. Her name was Cait-lynne and she watched Kyle like she couldn't believe how much of him there was to be had.

In Marshall's rig, towing his bright blue inflatable river raft on a trailer, they crossed Klingmans' bridge and followed the dirt lane up onto the bench and past the turnoff to the Klingman house, a collection of tin roofs winking in the distant field. On a skein of Forest Service logging roads, none boasting any recent maintenance, they wended their way up and over a saddle in the ridge that fingered down into the Tate ranch. The trailer skipped around behind the truck as the road switched back down the steep, north side of the ridge in a three-mile drive that took almost forty-five minutes to cover. There Marshall stopped at remnant pilings from a long-gone bridge. The bridge had been exploded back when Kyle's great-uncle, Bud, owned the property, partly as an antigovernment gesture meant to prevent access to the wooded hillsides beyond, once the Forest Service took over from the Anaconda Company in a land swap.

Caitlynne stripped off her shirt, revealing a Lycra bikini top. She pulled her bottle-blonde hair in a ponytail through the back of a ball cap and smiled relentlessly. Nobody bothered with waders on such a warm day. The water, draining snow-clad ranges for miles upstream, delivered a sharp slap to Marshall's genitals, but then he settled in and let himself go numb to it. Kyle carried the cooler by himself, grin-ning widely when he stuffed it into the raft frame and tilted back the lid to reveal beer cans blended with ice.

"Oh good," Marshall observed, "we'll be drinking."

"You fuckin' betcha," Kyle said.

Just when Marshall had the night before decided to flag down the wagon. He could of course simply choose to not indulge, though when he'd seen the cooler back at the house he'd assumed Kyle had it stuffed with sodas, and so he'd brought not even a bottle of water. Kyle had never struck him as the type of kid to tote around coolers loaded with beer. Nor had he uttered indecent language the entire time he and Marshall had worked together digging the spring project. In two years, Marshall didn't think he'd said anything stronger than "shoot." Mar-shall cocked an eyebrow. Kyle shrugged. Whole new ball game.

For the first part of the float, Marshall let Kyle row. Caitlynne re-clined in the backseat with her eyes closed and her face tilted to the sun. Marshall sat in the front seat and fished and corrected Kyle's positioning of the raft vis-à-vis the bank. Kyle had little feel for subtlety, and the strength of his oar strokes was sweeping. Linked oversteerage led to drifts that were by turns too close, then too far away from the bank to which Marshall cast. For Marshall this was no problem. He could throw a fly nearly across the West Fork at almost any point. But if Kyle wanted to guide . . .

"OK," Marshall said, struggling not to sound patronizing, "here's the thing; when you have clients in a boat, well, most clients can't cast more than thirty feet. It's stunning how bad these people are."

"They pay all that money and they can't fish?" Kyle asked.

"Right. If you can't actually fly-fish well enough to catch fish on your own, you spray four hundred bucks on some guide and think he's supposed to do the work for you."

In a tone meant for Kyle, Caitlynne said, "And you're dumb to want to do it for them."

Marshall regretted the heavy cynicism—far heavier than he actually believed—but was struggling to communicate with the Klingman worldview. He decided to switch to instructional and told Kyle how to angle the boat toward the bank so the guy fishing up front could aim at the bank a little downstream and let his backcast sail harmlessly over the upstream side. "The other thing," Marshall said, "tell them thumb to nose."

"Thumb to nose?" Kyle asked.

"Take the thumb of the hand that's holding the rod, bring it up to your nose for the backcast. If you touch your nose with your thumb, it's virtually impossible to hook somebody behind you in the boat."

"Why's that?" Kyle asked.

"I don't know," Marshall said. "Physics or geometry. Everything about casting is either physics or geometry."

Marshall let Kyle row until he evened out his feel for the bank, then he put Kyle up front. Kyle knew as much as anybody about where to find fish in a river, but his presentation needed polish, and he could use some experience casting out of a boat just to understand the breakdowns. Marshall took over the oars. He'd stretched one beer through his entire fishing spell, then cracked another when he moved to row, and it was cold and crisp and he liked it too much. Searching for an easy justification, Marshall decided, *well, if you can't get on the wagon,*

no use getting run over by it. He knew that was fancy and glib, but facility was a shortcut he felt he could take, if for only this one afternoon.

He fed Kyle advice. "Always be looking downstream, spotting fish
for the client. Then you'll know how and when to set something up.
Even if you don't see any, you should now and then say you do."

"And they believe you?" Caitlynne said.

"Just fuckin' with them, eh, Marsh?" Kyle said.

"That's it."

"See, that's what I need to know. How to fuck with the clients. I
need the secrets."

"Well, first off cool the foul language," Marshall said. "After that
the secret is primarily in the secrecy." He could tell by the quality of
the ensuing silence that he'd soared over both their heads. Marshall
thought about explaining, but he'd cracked another beer, and anyway,
what he said wasn't even always true. When the fishing's good, the
wise guide keeps close counsel, but Marshall had noticed that when
the fishing sucked most guides would tell you anything you wanted to
hear. Kyle went back to casting and hooked a cutthroat in the swirl behind a rock.

Then the sun that had lit most of the day took a dive in intensity
and Marshall glanced skyward to notice dark clouds bulging from the
mountains. Within twenty minutes a hard hail hit them. Caitlynne
squeaked and whooped and held the cooler lid over her head. Marshall
dug in the dry bag for his raincoat, which he gave to her. Kyle plunked
a baseball cap onto his head, hunched his shoulders, and let the hail
sting him. He said, "Jesus barefooted Christ."

"It'll go away," Marshall said. But it didn't for a long time, and
Marshall finally conceded and rowed to shore. Kyle heaved the raft up
onto the bank and he and Caitlynne scurried for the shelter of the
trees. Marshall plucked some extra beers from the cooler. He was
thinking purely in terms of buzz maintenance. He strode across the
cobbles to join his compatriots, hearing hail on the water like a long
tear and more hail clicking off the rocks with the *ping* of well-struck
golf balls. He felt ice balls zip him on the clavicle and cheekbone.

From the cover of tall cottonwoods, Marshall watched the storm.
In spite of the downpour before them, the sun shone from beneath
the clouds to the west. In front of them the sky was dark and hail
glinted, flashing as it fell through bands of sunlight. They drank the

beers Marshall brought and Kyle dashed out to fetch more, leaving Marshall with the young girl in his raincoat, her bikini top and river shorts trembling beside him. Was this what Shadford was after when he started in on Amy Baine?

He took a long look at the girl to see if he felt himself touched by any of the urges that motivated Shadford and concluded with relief that, sure, there was a sense of physicality to her, but Caitlynne looked mainly like a kid. Then she caught him staring and Marshall flustered, wanting to explain why he was gawking at her but knowing it could never come out right. Caitlynne shied, dropped her eyes. Marshall flung his gaze away and stared out at the river, shivering with the breeze moved by dropping ice nuggets and a chill of embarrassment. The hail subsided before they could finish the second round. Just that quickly the sun returned, driving the chill before it. Back on the river, Marshall regained his swimmy sense of splendor and well-being. In more prosaic terms, he was drunk. It amazed him how quickly he forgot to continue being embarrassed.

Kyle said, "Are you going to marry my sister?"

"Am I going to what?" Marshall asked.

"Marry Daisy."

"Why would you ask that?"

"I don't know. Seems natural," Kyle said. "Daisy gets mad about a lot of shit, but you're the only thing she stays mad about."

"That's touching, I guess," Marshall said. "Ah, we've just known each other a long time."

"God, Kyle," Caitlynne said, "how rude do you know how to be?"

Marshall caught a whiff of sweet beer on Caitlynne's breath. He found himself thinking about being her age, Kyle's age, how beer tasted in the mouth of a seventeen-year-old girl when you're a seventeen-year-old boy. Daisy was the girl he was kissing when he was seventeen, and for a moment a channel opened to a sensory memory of how beer tasted on her breath so long ago, the smell sweet but the taste sour, the booze softening her mouth.

"She's a pain in the ass," Kyle said, and for a moment Marshall was confused about whether he meant Caitlynne or Daisy, "but you could do worse."

Marshall had spent a good many years fantasizing about marrying Daisy, but those were years before he had any idea what marriage meant, pre- and early-teen years; most notably, those were presexual years. Now the very existence of those fantasies seemed to occlude any possibility that they might ever come true. It seemed like something one day Daisy and he—separately, married to other people—would have a good laugh about.

The connection to how the past felt remained open and Marshall let himself spend the time remembering without feeling guarded about it. Caitlynne sunned herself, and Kyle became intensely serious about catching fish. They floated silently through most of the Tate ranch, although perspective limited their vision of the place to the slopes of the banks and the cottonwoods cresting above it, nothing visible above the bank except the distant Scapegoat peaks. Marshall felt a little happy jag, came back to the present when they passed the small delta where his spring creek entered the river, knowing the cold, clean water practically sucked fish up into its sparkling habitat. They swung around a corner and approached the Klingman bridge.

"Watch out for the wire," Kyle said.

"Huh?"

"The wire! The barbed wire!"

Marshall felt the raft shift dramatically, buck under Kyle's forward lurch. Kyle thrust himself over the bow to wrap his finger around two strands of barbed wire stretched across the river a few inches from its surface. Marshall dropped the oars and dove to catch the wire as the raft pivoted on Kyle's handhold and swung athwart.

"What the hell!" Marshall grunted. He felt Caitlynne scramble to be of assistance.

"I should of remembered," Kyle grunted back.

"When did this go up?" Marshall said. Current bulged behind them, squeezing the raft against the wire. He could see the tendons in Kyle's wrist popping with effort.

"What do we do?" Kyle said.

His raft about to become linguine, Marshall had reflexively already begun digging for the Leatherman tool in his pocket. With one hand and his teeth he unfolded it until he could fit the wire into the cutters.

"Hold the top wire," Marshall said. Kyle levered his grip on the upper wire, shifting the wire down and providing a force to push against. Marshall clipped the bottom wire, Kyle lifted the top wire above his head, and they slid downstream.

"What the hell was that about?" Marshall asked.

"Randy strung it. He said it was for the cows, so they don't get up onto your place. But actually he did it right after he saw some guys floating down through here on those ciccararfts. Those one-man raft things?"

"So he just thought he'd fence it off? You can't just do that."

"I know," Kyle said, angry at being lumped in with his brother.

"It's illegal," Marshall said. "There's a goddamned stream access law in this state."

"Hey, I know it!" Kyle bellowed in a voice that resounded off the water, amplifying the sudden silence that swept in behind it. Kyle sat and fumed. Marshall wrestled with his own silent rage. Caitlynne seemed embarrassed for both of them.

At the bridge they hauled the boat ashore. They broke down the frame, deflated the raft, and carried everything up the bank. Kyle had left a pickup parked in the grass before the bridge decking earlier that morning. The three of them piled into the bench seat of the truck and drove out to the county road, then in the loop that took them past Marshall's house. By then fits of pleasant-sounding conversation sputtered up, questions about summer jobs and future plans. Marshall felt bad about yelling at Kyle and tipped the kids to two new restaurants in Missoula. At Marshall's they pulled in briefly to off-load all the gear. Kyle smooched Caitlynne in that long, don't-want-to-quit way that high school kids fondle each other, and she reapplied her T-shirt and disappeared from Marshall's life in a blue Subaru, headed for town. Kyle drove Marshall back over the Klingman bridge and the Forest Service roads to pick up his rig and trailer.

"Sorry about the wire," Kyle said as Marshall was getting out of the truck.

"No. Not your fault," Marshall said. "Don't worry about it. I'll deal with Randy."

He let Kyle leave and followed him. Marshall tapped the horn as Kyle turned into the drive that led to the Klingman house. He pulled into the field and followed the two-track to the parking area for the spring creek. Molly's white 4Runner stood in the lot, but Marshall had a low-grade sense of awfulness concerning Molly just at the moment and he really did not want to talk to her. He decided to head back to the house and take a shower, because, he realized a bit too late, he smelled.

When he emerged from the shower, he slipped into a pair of jeans and a T-shirt and thought about reading a book, but wondered if he wasn't too hammered to focus on words. He had wanted his shower to scrub a clean edge onto his day, but it hadn't. Marshall had been drunk for too long without adding any new booze, and the old stuff was going south on him. He felt cranky and ill at ease, awkward in his skin. He found himself squinting at things. Then he was peeved about it. What was it, exactly, that all this drinking meant to avoid? Yes, there was the easy forgetting. Laughter might be the best medicine, but in Marshall's life there had been a pretty high street value on forgetting. And booze wore off a lot faster than several other disillusionments. There was all that.

But it seemed like tossing beer bottles—and, previously, other substances—at his anxieties had separated him from some things that were going on in his life. Hadn't he noticed the difference in the two winters he'd spent sequestered at the ranch, digging the spring creek? The world had seemed like a brighter, more colorful place with all that exertion. What, then, was with the backsliding? Then Molly stopped in after sending her clients off happy and well-fished, so he took it out on her.

"Nasty little hailstorm we had there," Molly said.

"Yeah," Marshall said. "So I guess you're shacking up with Alton now?

"Who told you that?"

"That's real nice. You guys have been friends for how long? And you think this is a good idea?"

"Whether it is or not, it's nothing for you to get mad about," Molly protested.

"I'm not mad," Marshall shot back. "But what happens every single time friends start sleeping together? Every single time? I mean, you can't tell me you've been harboring this suppressed desire for Alton all these years. That he's your dream man, but you've been keeping it a secret?"

"That would be unbelievable, huh?"

"It would have been a little more obvious, for starters."

Molly glared right at him. "Really?" She was a little dumbstruck by the obtuseness of what he was saying.

Marshall had the sneaking sensation he might be getting glared at. He felt like maybe he was acting foolish, like maybe a jealous high school boy who wasn't smart enough to know what he was jealous about. Trying to figure a graceful segue, he fell to the obvious. "Look, it's been a long day. I'll drive down to Trixie's with you and buy you one of those thirty-two-ounce T-bones."

"Oh boy! You know just how to pluck a girl's heartstrings," Molly said. Even Marshall could see she was sort of disgusted. "Tonight: insults, followed by beef."

"I just meant I might have overreacted," Marshall said. "Let me buy you dinner."

Molly stewed for a moment, rinsing Marshall with the full heat of her gaze. Without letting the tightness around her eyes go, she said, "What I was going to tell you about the hailstorm was, you know where my clients hid during the hail?"

"I hope in the work shed over there."

"No, too far away," Molly said. "They hid in the porta-potties."

"Why didn't they hide in the work shed?" Marshall said.

"What I'm saying is maybe you should build a couple little shelters over there."

"I'm going to build warming huts, with woodstoves for late fall and early spring," Marshall explained. "I just have to . . . the materials."

"Think about it: huddled in a porta-potty for half an hour," Molly said. "With the hail and the smell?"

"They don't smell," Marshall said.

"All porta-potties smell."

"They're called Port-O-Lets and they don't smell. They're chemically treated not to smell."

"Marshall, please. Just . . ." Molly closed her eyes and sighed. "Just slide that shelter building up on the priority list. Did you have a few cocktails on the river today?"

"Oh sure," Marshall said.

Trixie's stood unsurrounded atop a small rise beside the highway. The town of Ovando lay on the other side of the hill, though you could see none of it approaching from the east. The bar was a clapboard building peeling barn-red paint. The front door, constructed of thick slabs of ponderosa pine, weighed two hundred pounds. Posted on the door, a sign said NO GUNS OR HORSES ALLOWED INSIDE. Marshall had been present during many violations of that first provision and on at least one occasion when the horse ban was breached. A few years back a local ranch hand and his gal-pal had ridden a pair of Appaloosas right on into the bar. It was winter and everybody suspected boredom. Likewise, nobody complained until the ponies started dropping road apples on the wood plank floor.

Marshall said hello to the bartender, Dotty, who stood a shade over five feet tall and nearly as wide. Stout was a wasted adjective on this woman, who wore her brown hair cut short and straight like a man's. Marshall asked for a pitcher of beer.

"No longer offering the pitcher format," Dotty said.

"Breakage?"

"On Cody Ingermaier's head," Dotty said, offering up two cans of Busch, which made Marshall's lip involuntarily curl. "That was the straw that broke the cowboy's head." Dotty laughed at her joke and Marshall sensed she'd had some practice doing that.

Molly wandered toward the back of the room where a pool table stood centered beneath a rectangular hanging lamp shaded with plastic panels advertising Schmidt's beer. Beyond the table a door opened to the darkening evening outside. Molly double took the pool table, thinking maybe she'd been spending too much time on trout streams. But no, an insect hatch was erupting over the green felt. But it wouldn't be a hatch. A mating? A massive clustering, at any rate, some sort of signal and life-affirming arthropod event. Marshall wandered over and clunked the beer cans on a small side table.

"Look at this," Molly said. She was trying to decide whether to be fascinated or repulsed.

"What are they?"

"Flying ants, looks like," Molly said. Hundreds of glossy red-brown bugs crept across the scraped green of the table's surface. A few lifted upward toward the overhead light. She noticed a faint but steady stream of airborne insects departing and arriving via the open door. "You'd think they'd spray these things. They serve food here."

"Let's rack 'em," Marshall said. He levered two quarters into the chrome game handle.

Molly glanced askance. "You're serious?"

"It'll give me a chance."

Molly doubted that. Marshall had never, to her knowledge, beaten her at pool. At the other end of the table he racked the balls and lifted the plastic triangle from them. Molly placed the cue ball, and tried to imagine a line of attack that didn't involve crushing hundreds of moiling bugs. She let fly and the balls cracked but nothing dropped. Marshall lined up a touch shot on the one for the side pocket, stroked the ball smoothly. The cue ball lost momentum as it crunched over bunched carapaces, and dribbled to a halt two inches before it struck its yellow target. Marshall said, "Holy crap."

"What a lovely evening," Molly said. "I think I want to sit down."

"You want a steak?" Marshall asked.

"Does that come with the flying ant sauce, or just A-1?"

"You want the big one?"

"I think twenty-five ounces should do me tonight," Molly said, remembering that the thirty-two-ounce entrée looked like something Fred Flintstone would grill.

"I'm starving. I'm getting the big one."

Amazingly, while they sat at a table and waited for their meals, things got worse. The front door opened and the change in Marshall's face made Molly turn to see Daisy Klingman striding in, looking a little tipsy. Daisy placed her feet a bit out in front of her as she came toward the bar, casually testing the floor with each step. While Daisy seemed oblivious to their presence, Molly watched hard, seeing in stark relief her narrow waist, the slimness of her torso. That's what turned Marshall on, Molly thought, the skinny hips and high, stand-alone breasts. You couldn't design on commission a body type more different from her own. For a moment Molly let herself think that no, maybe it was more, maybe it was the past. She knew how people sometimes became involved in misguided affairs and then simply let them drag out because it took less energy than forcing an end. But the Yacht Girl had been a tall, skinny thing, too. There was little avoiding the obvious; that's what Marshall liked.

Molly turned away before Daisy caught her looking, but she noticed Marshall's eyes angled over her own, toward the bar. She followed the continued tightening of his face as his eyes tracked what she could easily discern was Daisy's approach, until Marshall was looking at something just behind Molly's shoulder. Daisy was teetering at table side now, and there was no longer a reason to pretend not to see her.

"Why hello there, Marshall Tate," Daisy said. She swayed a can of beer at him, and then at Molly. "What an interesting coincidence."

"You remember Molly," Marshall said.

"Yep," Molly said. "We've met—," Molly started, but Daisy was having none of the pleasantries.

"Oh, I know who Molly is," Daisy said. She stood with her hips thrown forward, her knees bent a bit too far. The net effect was that she leaned away from the table. The hand that held her beer can extended a pointing index finger, which oscillated between Marshall and Molly. "Seems like we've been seeing quite a bit of Molly 'round here lately. Can't hardly drive by the Tate place without seeing ol' Molly's rig parked over there somewhere. Is this a little romance we've got cooking? Am I, uh, *interrupting* something here?"

"Daisy," Marshall said. "Please. We're friends having dinner."

Molly quickly looked away so that no one would notice her disappointment in that statement. Which, of course, Marshall, sitting directly across from her, instantly did. The quick, simple gesture skewered him with humiliation. A hot flush filled his face. Because discoveries don't ask who makes them, Daisy also took note of Molly's deflection.

"Boy, you're really something," Daisy spat at Marshall. She seemed to be speaking exactly as each new thought clicked into place. "You know, I could understand the rich bitch from back East. That made sense to me. This one . . . well, I mean, shit, it's been a long time coming, I guess . . ." Daisy paused, then in a more comprehensively contemplative voice, started, "You know, Marshall, I could have . . ."

Here Marshall felt a bizarre wave of awfulness inspired by a near certainty that what Daisy would say next was "really loved you once"— though she didn't, which left him wondering why it came so quickly to his own mind. Instead, Daisy finished with, "just stayed home last night. Been about the same thrill."

With that Marshall saw Molly's face, open and round and registering new information. She seemed sad, though it was hard to know who the sadness was supposed to cover. Molly said, "I thought you were done with that."

"Done with that?" Daisy made a noise with her tongue and, simultaneously, a snort through her nose that sounded like a loud "Tuh!" "*Done with that?!* Is that what you tell people? I'm a *that* that you're *done with?* That's not even fickle, that's just punk-ass!" Daisy seemed to want to say a great deal more, but grew tangled in where to begin. She spun and marched to the bar and said to the bartender, "Dotty, can I get a go cup?"

"Sure, baby," the bartender said. She handed Daisy a plastic party cup. Daisy poured her beer into it, then strolled over to the table and threw the beer on Marshall. He heard from Molly what he thought was a gasp, but turned out to be a bit of poorly stifled laughter. "You think that's funny?" Daisy fumed.

Marshall wiped beer from his face with the back of his forearm and opened his eyes in time to see Molly sit back in her chair, look up at Daisy, and say, "It's either funny or sad, depending on how I decide to feel about you."

Daisy screeched, but Dotty had already come out from behind the bar and strong-armed her. Dotty dragged her toward the door, a flurry of slashing arms and legs and wet hissing. "Can't do that here, baby," Dotty was saying. "Out you go." For all the motion, Daisy did nothing to impede Dotty's crossing of the room. Through the window, in the lights from the bar Marshall could see Dotty jam Daisy up against the red pickup and give her a talking to. Daisy began flinging her hands around, and then pointing back at the door she'd just been hauled through. Dotty shook her head and Daisy whirled, jerked the truck door open and heaved herself in. But she didn't drive away. Marshall watched as Daisy gripped the steering wheel with both hands at the top and rested her forehead on her knuckles, and then he thought he could see her shoulders shake.

The next morning, Marshall rose in the first light of dawn, dressed, stepped out onto the front lawn, and looked longingly at the bent front rim of his mountain bike where it leaned against the side of the house. He walked to the shed, slapped the dust and cobwebs off an old three-speed Schwinn his mother had abandoned at the ranch decades before, hopped aboard, and pedaled down the drive. He made it to the Klingman house before sunup. The bike had been subterfuge, no tell-tale dust to announce his approach. Marshall straddled the bike in the lane and examined the Klingman place. About a hundred yards from the more contemporary buildings huddled remnants of the original homestead—a single-roomed house, a shed, a barn with a parabolic collapse hanging its shingle-shedding roof. The entrance to the homestead house was no more than five and a half feet high. Knowing it had been on this spot since the turn of the century, Marshall looked at the squat building, its gray logs missing in chunks, a nap of green

moss growing from the roof. Hard to believe people lived in those little, lightless boxes.

The new house, which was probably seventy years old, exhibited
little flair, no departure from standard farmhouse design. A large
gable tented above the front porch. Add-on dormers jutted from the
second-story roof, symmetrically, two on a side. The house was painted
white. The tin roof held a dull luster in the early light. Behind the
house the yard light still burned. Marshall could never understand
why people would live in the country, then light up their yard at night
like a Vegas casino, but almost everybody did. Skipjack had originally
installed spots on poles in their yard, but Marshall talked him into
motion-sensor lights. Even then, Marshall disarmed most of them. He
preferred nights dark.

The reflection on one of the dormer windows dissolved, letting
Marshall know an interior light was on. So somebody was up and he
prayed God it wasn't Daisy. Just showing up at Klingmans' was tor-
ture enough, but after yesterday evening in Trixie's he had serious
doubts about the wisdom of an encounter with her. But Randy needed
a talking-to for Kyle's sake, so Marshall had chosen early, early morning, hoping Daisy was still sleeping it off. Marshall slipped quietly onto
the porch and rapped with his knuckles in an effort to make contact
only with someone who might be listening. You couldn't sneak up on a
farmhouse in the morning. Somebody already knew he was there.

Marshall waited, wondering who was watching him. He scanned
the surroundings for living human beings. A barn and two machine
sheds clustered beyond the house, and to the side a wide shed for vehicles stretched leftward. At the edge of the shed, and forming the border of the lawn, ten or a dozen derelict vehicles heaped in various
stages of dissolution, waiting to be "parted out." Western landscape ar-
chitecture, Marshall thought. You haven't really made it as a rancher
until you've stuck some old rigs up on blocks and let them rust for a
decade or so. Marshall noted in this lineup the cab and arm of a track-
less old crane, three tractors circa the 1940s, a Plymouth Road Runner, a Valiant, and the once-beautiful frame of a 1957 Ford half-ton,
pitted, dented, crumpled, scratched, scraped, stripped, and missing
doors. What this place needed was a pair of really vicious cow dogs.
But lately Marshall had noticed that the Klingmans herded their cattle around with their balloon-tire off-road vehicles.

When the front door of the house opened, Marshall saw Colleen Klingman. Bruce's wife had been a tall, raw, big-boned lady when Marshall was a boy first coming around the house, but had long since gone deep, thickened in every aspect, and seemed to gather strength and density. Her features grouped in the center of a long face, like the map of a town surrounded by desert.

"Hello, Mrs. Klingman; would Randy be up yet? I need to speak to him."

"I'll see," she said. She let her gaze linger on him in a blank expression Marshall found inscrutable, then disappeared into the house. Marshall walked off the porch and down onto the front yard. He didn't want to confront Randy so close to the domicile, in case screaming commenced.

Randy banged through the door and stepped out to the edge of the porch. He had on jeans and packer's boots with untied laces. Up top he wore a dirty T-shirt that he might have slept in. "Heard you cut up my fence," Randy said.

"I did," Marshall said. He noticed a shadowy figure just inside the front-door frame, and guessed from the shape it had to be Bruce. A larger patch of light material stepped up behind the shadow, which Marshall figured was Kyle, also in a T-shirt. "You know, Randy . . . you can't just string a fence across a river."

"Why the hell not? My property," Randy said.

"If you'd come down here and talk to me, I'd be happy to explain why you can't," Marshall said.

"If I come down off this porch I'm liable to stomp your ass," Randy said. "And I'd rather not do that so early in the morning. People are sleeping." Randy thought this was funny and set a smug grin on his face to let Marshall know about it. Then he added, with portent, "Like Daisy."

"Randy—" a voice said from inside the house. Bruce.

"Look, it's against the law to build a fence across the river," Marshall said. "Rivers belong to everybody in the state. You cannot impede navigation on a river. You cannot exclude people from using the river corridor up to and including the mean high-water mark. That's the law. That's how it is."

Randy hesitated, squinting at Marshall. He pivoted his hips without moving his feet and glanced back into the doorway. Marshall heard a noise, a voice, but wasn't clear on the words. He thought they were "batch" and "crap."

"We can call FWP or the sheriff's office, if you want them to come out and explain it to you," Marshall said.

"We're not going to do shit," Randy said, and he came down off the porch much faster than Marshall would have liked. "And if *we* ever catch *you* snipping one of our fences again—"

"Randy!" Different voice, this one sharper with edges. Kyle. He emerged from the house and took two steps onto the porch, barefoot.

Then the old croak from inside: "Kyle—"

"No, Kyle, it's fine," Marshall said. Randy had come right up on him and they chested each other. Randy stood just shorter but much broader, and Marshall looked at Randy's eyes and knew he couldn't win a fight. Randy was crazy, and you'd have to kill him to stop him, or at least break all the bones that allowed him to keep moving. Moments like these, Marshall understood with chilling clarity, were what Randy Klingman lived for. The level of fear he evoked was exactly the scale upon which he measured himself as a man.

Still, Randy looked goofy, the eyes a touch crossed, his mouth squelched together. Maybe that was mockery, though. "Randy," Marshall said, "you can kick my ass six ways to Sunday, but you know what you're going to have when you're done? Sore knuckles, a night or two in jail, an assault suit, a big bill from your lawyer, and every same problem you had before you started. If you think slapping me around is going to back me down, you're out of your tiny mind."

He could see that threw a hitch in the grind of Randy's ratchetry. Randy snorted god-awful shots of breath—old saliva and some terrific gastrointestinal disorder—which made Marshall want to pull away. He didn't, but he did wonder if he was involuntarily making a funny face, and then he wondered if that made him look any fiercer. Marshall felt on his head—a twitch along his jawline, an imaginary pain around his eye socket—the various places Randy's first blows might land. He doubted after the first few he would feel very much. Time to aim a little higher. Marshall lifted his eyes from Randy's heliographic stare and directed his comments to the door frame, where he knew Bruce lingered.

"You people do whatever the hell you want and expect everybody else to take it. I'm not going to rustle your cows or violate your women, for Christ's sake, and I'm not going to fistfight with you. This isn't the wild frontier anymore. There are laws you have to pay attention to." Time to exit, turn slowly—no sudden movements, no opportunity for impulsive retribution—walk to the bike, leg over, and . . .

Randy stared and seethed, but his posture left his head, chest, and arms leaning, as if he were checked by an invisible choke collar controlled by someone back at the doorway. Silence.

"Morning, Kyle," Marshall said.

"Morning," Kyle said.

Marshall pedaled away. He could hear the voices mauling each other behind him for a while, then nothing but the gravel popping under his bike tires. The sky stretched clear in all directions, if a fellow was looking for indications that it could be a nice day.

GOLDEN STONES

Marshall filled the tractor bucket with fist-sized rocks from along the river and drove up into the field toward the spring creek. He knew two men from Grand Rapids were fishing the lower portion of the creek, and he aimed to cut across the field to place the rocks in the stream up above the pond. While he drove he kept busy with some low-level fuming and high-level dread about his most recent telephone conversation with his father. Skipjack had expressed shock that Marshall had not yet added an insurance rider to the ranch policy. Marshall suspected the shock was practiced, or at least preconsidered. A short but dynamic speech about how the hell do you ever expect to make it in this world if you can't think through the obvious? followed. That his father had a point led to Marshall's fuming; the part about the money lay behind his dread.

So he went and picked rocks. That day he'd planted over a hundred seedlings—red osier, serviceberry, currants—part of a plan to plant five thousand by the end of summer. It felt like a good day for working on incremental progress. What he was doing with the rocks was technically illegal, but he hadn't been able to imagine what harm he might inflict if he acted with circumspection. There were lots of rocks on the banks, and literally whole mountains of them upstream. True, each rock infinitesimally influenced the shape of the water, its

direction and velocity, which in turn shaped the landscape of the entire valley, but Marshall felt there was a threshold at work and he
suspected he was nowhere near crossing it. These very cobbles—
encrusted with the casing of caddisfly larva, and slithering nymphs of
other insect species—arranged cleverly in, say, a spring creek, would
hold finer gravels that fish could spawn on.

The day was waning. Marshall was hauling his load of rocks up
through the meadow when, above the rattletrap of the tractor, he heard
a round *pop!* sound. Then a second one. His first assumption was that
he knew exactly what the noises sounded like, though he didn't believe
that could be right. He choked the tractor engine to silence, and stood
up on the seat, scanning the lower meadow. A third *pop!* puffed through
the evening air, cuffed by a slight breeze. It was enough to let Marshall
locate the source of the sound. His two clients that day were a rail-
legged black-haired man who stood somewhere about six-five, and a
fellow with fat fingers, a soft face, and a chest that dripped in slabs.
Marshall remembered meeting them that morning, reaching up to
shake hands with the tall man and fearing the man might fall off of
himself. The other man's name was Peter Dodd, which Marshall immediately translated to "Pud." Ironically, Pud's manner brimmed with
confidence, or at least self-ease, and if it bothered him to be completely
without shape, Pud provided no clues.

It was Pud, Marshall now saw, who held the shotgun. The tall man
stood in the water by his side. Marshall revved up the tractor, then
just as quickly choked it down again, opting for stealth. He struck out
for the creek at a lope. He used a roll in the meadow to conceal his approach as long as possible. He needn't have. The two men were focused
entirely on the stream before them. The tall man had waded across
the creek and was holding an enormous brown trout by the gill plate.
Pud had pushed a pair of wire-rimmed Ray-Ban aviator sunglasses up
onto his forehead. When he saw Marshall he took two steps, casually
bent over, and laid the shotgun in some thick grass. He stepped back
to his original place, as if the distance disavowed any relationship between himself and the firearm.

Marshall had no idea how to begin, so he stared. Pud's mouth
fairly quivered with the grappling his soul must have been doing to
stave off a satisfied grin. Stranded without recourse, the tall guy stood
on stork legs and held the fish. Finally Pud spit on the ground.

"Well, goddamnit *all*," he said.

Marshall could see thin rivulets of blood dripping down the trout's flank from two or three pellet holes near its head.

"What exactly—?" he started.

"I floated every goddamned fly I had over that son of a bitch!" Pud cried. He was almost begging. The flavor was: *you'd have done the same thing*. "I mean, just *look* at that fish! He's *huge!*"

Pud seemed to surrender his entreating, and turned to look over the creek at the fish. The tall guy was rotating his wrist and paying close attention to examining the fish on both flanks, as if that scrutiny might make him invisible. Pud's chin trembled.

"Aw . . . shit."

"I think it'd be best if you leave," Marshall said.

"You gonna give us our—"

"Don't even ask if I'm going to refund your money," Marshall interrupted. He raised his voice to call across the creek. "Here's the deal: put the fish down on the bank, and leave."

"You gotta let us keep the fish," Pud said. He sounded like a desperate man asking for a last drink from a bartender who'd seen him every night for months. "I know it was wrong, but you gotta—"

"Put the fish down on the bank and leave," Marshall said sharply. "And don't come back. Ever."

He waited while the other two tromped across the grass toward their vehicle. He considered the three *pop!* sounds again. They must have failed to account for the glancing of pellets off the water in the first two. Shot high, as it were. Marshall knew the fish they'd shot, knew it specifically, knew it lived under a cutbank, fed primarily at night. He didn't know why he'd made them leave the carcass other than to deprive them of reward. Then he thought of taking a photograph of the huge, handsome brown with the pellet holes in its side. He could assemble a bulletin board of transgressions. That he'd thought of it so early in the game depressed him. Besides, he didn't have time to go back to the house and fetch a camera and still get his tractorload of rocks put down in the stream. He walked away, leaving the fish on the bank for an eagle or a skunk or a coyote to find.

Later that evening Marshall was still at the stream, working. At a spot where the creek was broad and shallow Marshall handpicked the larger rocks from his tractor bucket and arranged them in a shallow riffle. As in hundreds of other places along the creek he had built the streambed elevation up at the end of a pool, slowing the water down, then loaded finer gravels into the high spot, jazzing up the flow as it rounded a turn, before the water dumped down into the following pool. This allowed the water to aerate itself, and also created habitat for aquatic insects. The gravel riffle, about five yards broad, held a particular shape, a stretched-open S that didn't run directly perpendicular to the flow of water over it, but instead angled slightly upstream from foot to head. The foot end of the S was also significantly shallower in cross-section. Marshall had seen this shape subtly underlying so many riffles he had floated clients over in the past decade, but had not actually recognized that he'd noticed it until he'd decided to build the creek—after which point he saw it everywhere.

The shape caused water pouring in laminar flow to fold into itself, tumbling into a helical flow—better for scouring out pools and moving sediment downstream. Also, when viewed from above, the S riffle focused flows into its two nodal points, creating two convergent feed lanes that bounced into the pool below. The dead spot between them allowed trout to hold without expending energy and watch for food particles in both lanes. It was critical that the larger rocks, the spine of the curve, hold in place, and at this spot they hadn't. So Marshall had spent the last hours of daylight placing new rocks in the shape, jamming them tightly and hoping the current's pressure would lock them against each other.

He was also struggling mightily against depression and the attendant notion that what he was doing made not a whit of difference. He shoveled smaller pebbles into the high side of the riffle. They would be such happy little rocks in their new home, he tried to think, and in a few years nobody would know they weren't there by nature's very own design. Unless, of course, the Klingmans pressed their water rights complaint and Marshall had to relinquish his Fountainhead engineering, in which case these very rocks might be mainly dry and bare and not very happy at all in a month or . . . or when? Why were the Klingmans stalling on hauling him to Water Court?

He couldn't help but wonder if Bruce was having second thoughts. Marshall's experience with the family revealed them primarily as opportunists, and yet they stood to gain so little from suing him over water they didn't really need. Bruce had always been a cantankerous old ass-crack, but he'd never seemed so malicious that he would actively seek to put an enterprising young man out of business just because he could. He was, on the other hand, a rancher, with deep-seated ideas about the land. Once he launched even the most ludicrous display of principle, he'd feel a hidebound compulsion to follow through with it until everybody was crying. It was one of the many things that kept him from getting rich.

Marry Daisy. That could be Marshall's easy way around it all. The expectation must be there—hadn't Kyle been the one to bring it up? Maybe that was in some abstruse way what Bruce was angling for, and perhaps what Randy feared. Whenever the thought *marry Daisy?* popped into his head—and it had with alarming frequency since Kyle voiced it—Marshall had to admit that the notion was rushed into his cerebellum by one word crowding right behind it: *nightmare.* But that was mostly drama. Marshall always had fun with Daisy, even when she was tossing beer in his face. His only real fear regarding Daisy was that she might, in the wrong circumstances, turn into some kind of craven, tacky Montana socialite. Though she could just as easily decide to age gracefully. It depended, he supposed, on whether she ever got what she wanted—or figured out what that might be.

Marshall hadn't thought about marrying anybody in years. He had seen his own parents' marriage implode for no apparent reason other than that his father enjoyed wild business success and became a dickhead. Through much of his twenties, Marshall felt himself waiting to see if he, too, would become a dickhead. He didn't think he had, but he'd not enjoyed much of what is traditionally known as success, either. By then days had washed downstream, spawning yesterdays as they went, and here he was, thirty-three and well outside the frontier of marriage.

Marshall had always had a difficult time imagining long-term relationships, although it was perhaps time to admit he'd been in one with Daisy for most of his life. But that felt like something he could end at any time—only he just hadn't yet. He fully expected that at some point Daisy would go away and he'd never see her again. Anyway, at the moment he felt overwhelmed by the sensation that his heart was broken, though he couldn't point to anyone who had broken it. Molly, maybe, or Alton, or both of them, but that was convenient and facile, he knew. That didn't feel like the truth, although lately Marshall had begun to realize that there are many distances from the truth and the heart breaks in just as many ways. It's like anything else: once there's already a fissure or a crack, it doesn't take much to send spiderwebs through the safety glass.

As a deep blue dome of night built overhead, only a thin green-yellow streak along the western horizon pried light into the pastures. Feeling now mildly whimsical and tentatively safe from depression, though in touch once again with the heart he imagined broken, Marshall fired up the tractor and started across the field to the Klingman bridge and home.

Marshall drove east on Interstate 90, just west of Deer Lodge, where a conglomeration of ranches, a private collection of old automobiles, and the state prison provoked town fathers, in a fit of laconic jingoism, to erect billboards proclaiming COWS, CARS AND CRIMINALS. It was a pleasant late June evening, warm enough to crank vented air into the pickup's cab. Snaking along the highway, the Clark Fork River had settled out of runoff and into a tame green-brown ribbon. The sun was pulling one of its endurance acts—at ten o'clock at night it was still bright enough to read without artificial light. Bugs clicked against the windshield as the evening tried to wane.

Molly sat beside him, more silent than usual. He wrote this off to the endless badgering she had unleashed to convince him about this trip. They were off to attend a whirling disease conference in Helena the next day.

"You can't just stick your head in the sand and hope it goes away," she'd argued.

"There's no evidence of whirling disease west of the Divide," Marshall argued back.

"There wasn't any on the Madison last year either. And ninety percent of the fish are gone this year. They don't know how it gets from place to place."

Marshall had continued to balk until Molly pointed out that it behooved him to know everything he could just from a PR standpoint. All sorts of rumors about the virulence of the disease and its potential to poleax the Montana fly-fishing industry were reeling around the state and littering the angling media. Ignorance in this case, Molly insisted, would not be bliss. But the deal wasn't sealed until Molly had said,

"You know Shadford will be just spouting bullshit about it. You gotta be able to talk straight when he sends people out to your place all full of his crap." Then Marshall had agreed to attend the conference and even to pack a bag and head to Helena a night early because the meeting started at 8 A.M. pronto in the morning and Molly wanted to miss none of it.

Dusk made serious inroads as they hurtled along the asphalt, though it was almost eleven before the evening finally darkened. The Phosphate exit trolled by. Marshall flicked on the truck's headlights and Molly, apropos of nothing said, "So why do you suppose Alton won't sleep with me?"

"Gee, I don't know. I sort of thought he was," Marshall said, first taking a moment to get over the affront of the question. He had no desire to talk about what was happening or not happening between Molly and Alton, as the whole notion upset him for vague, shape-shifting reasons.

"Well, in the sense that sometimes we both get drunk at a bar and stagger home to his or my place and pass out on a bed together, yes, he is. But in the sense that we—"

"All right," Marshall said.

He could tell that Molly was smiling, and then, just as tangibly, that she wasn't. She said, "When I wake up in the morning, he's always as far away on the bed as he can get from me."

Marshall moved from feeling uncomfortable to feeling a levity he didn't want to pin down at the moment. He was a bit unnerved by how happily he received this piece of news. After all, it wouldn't be fair, Alton and Molly sleeping together, though fair to whom he could not identify. He suspected he was thinking of himself on the brunt end of the unfairness. They were friends, for God's sake. All of them. This just passing out together on a bed, this was a phase they could all look back and laugh about later. But then he wondered if Molly's line of questioning indicated that she really *wanted* to sleep with Alton, and that would be as bad as—no, worse than—falling into it out of, say, boredom or loneliness. Doing it could be a mistake, a drunken boo-boo. Forgivable. *Wanting* to do it implied yearning. That stuck.

"I suppose, then, that he's not sleeping with you for the reason you probably assume he's not sleeping with you," Marshall said. He didn't know what that was exactly, but wanted to proceed cautiously.

"He's still too upset about Amy?" Molly said, her sudden singsong indicating this was an obviously flawed state of affairs.

"Sure," Marshall said. He felt horrible for saying what he was going to say next, knew he shouldn't be saying it, guessed that her understanding why he was saying it could change everything—because Marshall suspected he was not cool and cavalier, and was, in fact, nearly transparent—but he said it anyway. "But so is this your new thing now?"

"What?"

"Hooking up with Alton?"

"I don't know," Molly said. "I have no idea."

"Whatever happened to the guy with the name? The photographer guy from Bozeman."

"Soren?"

"Right. Soren Rue." He crooned it. "Love that name."

"He's from Livingston," Molly said, "and that lasted about as long as the Mother's Day caddis hatch."

"What was wrong with him?" Marshall asked. Soren Rue was safe. Soren Rue had a preposterous name. He lived somewhere else and anything that happened between him and Molly happened offstage.

"He lives in Livingston," Molly said. "He's a freaking newspaper photographer. He's boring. And he's taken."

"Oh," Marshall said. "Sorry to hear that."

"That's been over for, like, months," Molly said. "Where have you been?"

"How am I supposed to know these things?" Marshall asked.

"You could ask. You don't need to be so blithe. Or do you not care, actually?"

"No, actually I do care," Marshall asserted, then wavered. "I care inasmuch as I'd like for you to be, you know . . . happy. But I don't want to be nosing into things that aren't my business."

"So when I ask you questions about your love life, you assume I'm being nosey?" Molly asked.

"I assume you ask questions about my love life so you can make fun of me." He was serious. Night had fallen now and the truck's headlights traced paths for Marshall to follow. At the Garrison interchange he exited and pulled onto Highway 12. They hadn't gone three miles before the headlights flashed on a deer, a whitetail doe, at the side of the road. The doe was down, forelegs curled beneath her chest, but her head stuck up to watch what went by.

"Oh," Marshall said, letting the word aspirate, "man."

"I hate that," Molly said.

Marshall slowed and pulled over to the gravel berm. He could see the yellow stalks of timothy beyond the road's edge, falling off down a steep slope toward the Little Blackfoot River below.

"Do you have a gun?" Molly asked.

"No," Marshall said. He legged out of the truck. "Let's see how bad she is."

He walked back down the road to the doe. He could see her eyes, dull pewter orbs in the slight reflection of his running lights, like fish eyes in the night. The deer lay with her legs gathered, head up, ears pricked forward. She watched Marshall come, but made no effort to move. Marshall circled around behind the deer. He snaked a hand to grasp her ear. The doe provided resistance, but did not flail or thrash. Marshall touched the deer's shoulders on both sides. Her muscles trembled at his touch, like a horse shivering flies off. He could see that the forelegs were intact. Then he pushed his fingertips into the doe's left hip and felt the dissolution there, a sandy disintegration of bone into chips and fragments. The whole joint was smashed. "Poor girl," Marshall muttered. "Poor, poor girl." He could hear the doe's breathing. He felt himself welling up to cry.

Marshall let go of the deer's head, and walked back to the truck. Molly stood outside her door, apart from the rig, both hands wrist-deep in her jeans pockets. "I don't even have a knife," Marshall said. "You?"

Molly shook her head briefly. Marshall dug around under the truck's backseat and emerged with a tire jack.

"Oh no," Molly said.

"You have a better idea?"

"There has to be a better way," Molly said.

"Tell me." Marshall stood, tire iron down along his leg. He turned his face back toward the doe so Molly wouldn't see the tears rimming his eyes. He'd love to have a better idea.

"You don't have anything else?" Molly asked.

"I got nothin'," Marshall said. Molly turned and climbed back into the truck. Marshall walked back to where the deer lay. He could see the animal crippled there, dead but not dead yet, attentive to what was coming to finish her off. Tears splashed down his face. He crushed her skull with three swings of the tire iron.

Back in the truck, Molly said, "Maybe she didn't have a fawn this year."

"I saw her teats," Marshall said, though he knew it would dent Molly's wishful thinking.

He drove five or ten minutes before either of them spoke again. Things had changed dramatically in the cab of the vehicle, but Marshall couldn't guess how. Eventually Molly said, "I'm sorry that had to happen."

"Me too."

"You know," Molly said, and before she finished Marshall could see that something had changed again, that she was more sour, "speaking of making fun of your love life, I guess you're sleeping with Daisy again?"

"I guess that'd be hard to deny after the scene at Trixie's," Marshall said.

Molly was pretending to be interested in her fingernails. "That was just confirmation. But I suspected before that. That very first morning I brought clients to the creek, and you showed up late to meet them? You said you'd been at the Klingmans'? You stumbled over, half in the bag, breathing booze, and your fly was undone, and your shirttail was sticking through it."

"It was not," Marshall said.

"Might as well have been. Even outside with a breeze you reeked of sex."

"I did *not*," Marshall said. *Jesus—even outside?*

"I don't know why you keep doing it," Molly said. "Or her, I guess."

"You make it sound like she's evil," Marshall said. "She's not."

"Probably a lot of fun in the sack."

Marshall declined to respond, which inspired Molly to stare out the window on her side of the vehicle for a while. Finally Marshall said, "There's so much history. You know, I had almost all of my firsts with her."

"Really?" Molly said. It seemed to strike her with an even more sour note.

"Yeah, that," Marshall acknowledged, "but also, I got drunk for the first time with her. I drove a vehicle for the first time with her—I think she was about thirteen and she was doing the teaching. I spent the whole night with a girl for the first time with her up on the bench above the springs. I got thrown in jail for the first time with her."

"What about?"

"Drunk and disorderly. We were pissing off the Higgins Street Bridge in Missoula—which was a lot easier for me than for her. The cops started threatening to make us register as sex offenders because we bared our genitals in public. We convinced them we just really had to pee and the trade-off was a night in the county lockup. Not as bad as you'd think."

"Hmmm, well," Molly said, and Marshall could tell that the next part would be sarcastic. "You say it that way, maybe there *is* something there with you and Daisy. Maybe you should pursue it, Marsh."

He waved her off. "There's all that sloppy Capulet and Montague stuff to deal with."

"The Klingmans don't hate your family, do they? They just hate you."

"Yeah, actually that's not accurate either. The more I deal with him, the more I think he doesn't really hate me. The old man, I mean, Bruce. He hates me in that vague, nonspecific way that he resents all people from somewhere else. But my new theory is that Bruce has an agenda. I feel like there's some measuring going on. When Bruce comes after me, it's always about some rule he's got in mind. 'A fella can't just do this,' and 'A fella can't just do that,' he's always saying. Randy, on the other hand, really does hate me, which is not such a good thing since he'll inherit most of the place." He sighed. "A big part of the problem is, if I didn't think involving myself with Daisy might be some sort of manipulation on my part, I might honestly try something more serious with her. But I always catch myself wondering if I might be using her."

"You didn't seem to mind using Kyle," Molly said. Though it was precisely what she'd moments before suggested, she found herself taken aback by his last statement. Thrown for a loss. Could he actually have serious, change-your-life feelings for Daisy Klingman? Was she going to have to start hating Daisy Klingman? Why couldn't it be just Marshall getting his rocks off? Molly had even appreciated Daisy for that, because Daisy had never been a threat to rise above—unlike, say, the Yacht Girl.

"I pay Kyle," Marshall said.

"Probably ought to pay Daisy," Molly said.

Marshall's glance let Molly know that he hoped she was kidding. And she had been for most of the conversation, sort of. She'd been skipping down the borderline between tra-la-la and what the hell? Now she huddled in the seat and stared out the window. She tried not to, but she could hear the wet smacks of the tire iron against the doe's skull when Marshall had killed it. She couldn't get the sound out of her head.

Why they had agreed to stay in a hotel—how they had agreed to stay in a hotel and when they had made such an agreement—was lost to Marshall. Both of them knew people in Helena, clients or guides or outfitters or college friends. If either had come to town alone, he or Molly no doubt would have stayed with friends. Maybe it had been part of the encouragement package that Molly used to browbeat him into attending this meeting in the first place. Once the decision had been made, Marshall—he was sure he would have said something like this—argued absolutely that they'd need to sleep cheap. Money was tight, tight, tight, and the client stream seemed to be dwindling. So how they ended up booked in a room at the Plaza on Last Chance Gulch was another development he couldn't explain.

And then the night on the town: Molly started with a Cabernet at the hotel bar, switched to Chardonnay immediately afterward, and never looked back. Marshall thought to monitor his intake, beginning with a variety of single malts. He felt that a scotch would help him relax when everything else about the evening seemed to be on such a high pitch. Later, he'd have an opportunity to look back and assign reasons for why he chose, yet again, to drink too much. For instance, Molly kept brushing against him as the night progressed, and each incidental contact seemed to linger longer than the last. Too, she was looking at him funny. At a point he couldn't identify in retrospect, he made a conscious decision to follow his building curiosity: he wouldn't be the first one to break contact anymore.

That proved interesting when they returned to the Plaza and entered their room. Molly stopped in the doorway, facing away from Marshall, and reached around behind her back to offer a friendly, goofy little backward hug. But when Marshall's arms looped around her to return the gesture, his hands went directly to her breasts—and though he was at first shocked by the accident, he just as quickly figured what the hell? Alton had—and then, with her back still to his chest, Molly's head dropped back and her mouth was open beneath his tongue and her hands had dropped to his hips and her fingers dug in. Marshall had every intention of this not becoming full-blown sex. He supposed he just wanted what Alton had known, the fooling around, the wrap of arms throughout the night. He liked the idea that he and Molly would share something to be mutually embarrassed about, too. Although there was also a curious attractive force that seemed to build with each moment that passed with their bodies pushed against each other. What happened in terms of Marshall's control of the situation was obliteration, and what happened next was nothing like any of his past experiences. Molly was so much more delicate than Daisy Klingman, even more so than his snooty girlfriend from Rhode Island the previous summer.

What happened with Molly happened so slowly, with such an air of caution, that, even drunk, Marshall had time to feel and observe the rebirth of body parts, these legs and arms, these eyes and lips, how these sections of flesh slipped into a realm that, for a while, was entirely new and exalted. His sense of himself as separate from her dissolved in a tingly, woozy fizz, and wonder existed in its most irresistible form.

Who ever would think that Molly Huckabee, fishing guide, rower of boats, drinker with men, could be so achingly vulnerable? She was the most awkward, fumbling lover he'd ever known. The slowness collapsed beneath dual pushes of want, and then the athleticism and the very strength of her pulled into play and everything went crash, over and over again. When it was finally over, Marshall tumbled off her like someone sideswiped by an ax—not because he wanted to be away from her, merely on a rebound from the energies that had collided between them. Then came the blackout.

In the morning Marshall woke long before he saw anything, partly because he felt so hungover that he feared if he opened his eyes he would bleed to death. But he was also terrified. He tried to tell himself that the paradigm defining his triangular friendship with Molly and Alton had been destroyed the moment Alton and Molly stumbled home from the Rhino and into bed together—regardless of what had or hadn't happened there. Didn't matter. Everything was blown to bits from there. This new wrinkle . . . well, now would be just the time to get the new wrinkle in there, wouldn't it? Do it while the situation was still fluid, still dynamic. The key next was to absolutely not act like a jerk.

There were things to think about: frilly underthings, for example. Marshall had seen Molly in various stages of undress throughout the years. He'd seen her peel off longies, shift from fleece pants to jeans at the end of a day, drop her shorts to pee. He'd even seen her fully naked once, back in the St. Joe River. He'd hovered right beside her in the river, both of them nude. He'd actually wondered, back then, if something was happening, but maybe Alton was too close for comfort, wandering around somewhere near their camp. At any rate, Marshall had the rootless sense that Molly was holding back at that moment, and when nothing transpired and the moment had passed, he figured that was that.

When Molly slid from her khakis the night before, Marshall's fingers had found her wearing something trimmed in lace. *Molly Huckabee in lingerie?* Which meant, Marshall conjectured in his funk, either Molly regularly wore fancy pants when she dressed up, or she'd done it for him. The latter would entail salacious forethought, and how should he feel about that? The funk pervaded. On the one hand: wow! On the other hand, it was Molly, and she was still in bed beside him. His hangover was stultifying. Underlying everything, he'd just screwed his best friend.

Unbeknownst to Marshall, Molly lay beside him, also wide awake and wracked with similar thoughts, in the midst of which flourished a fresh and fragrant batch of Catholic guilt. Lapsed or no, it was always there. She watched him from eyes she pretended were shut, watched him cradle his pillow with both arms—that's what he was supposed to be doing to her—and nestle his head into it. How could he be so calm? So . . . *sleepy?* She wondered if she should touch him, just to see how he would react. But the results could be crushing.

She breathed in deeply through her nose, pretending to wake. She rolled and stretched, letting herself brush against him. Marshall didn't flinch. By now Molly couldn't tell if that was good or bad. Marshall flipped his head on his pillow. She watched him smile at her and interpreted it to mean: *can you believe this?* She knew that however she gazed back at him she would look pathetic. She felt it imperative to pretend she was as baffled by the whole thing as he, so she hummed for a moment, then said, "Whew. What to think about this?"

"Um," Marshall said. "That it was . . . that it was really nice. Surprising, but very nice." He meant that, Molly could tell, and it was sweet, which left her briefly relieved, but then just as quickly made her wonder exactly how he reviewed performances in the aftermath with Daisy or Yacht Girl. The shithead probably told everybody the sex they'd had was "really nice, very nice."

"Well, one thing I know is, I don't want to lose you as a friend over this," she said, because it was truly what she was thinking. But also, why couldn't he roll toward her, loop an arm over her back, slide his leg over hers? Because that would be perfect, and perfect wasn't real. OK, so why wouldn't the bastard at least display some affection for her like a decent human being? She could go home with that.

"Of course, of course not," Marshall said.

"I don't want you to think badly of me," Molly said when she grew too antsy to wait for him to elaborate. *Try giving him more to talk about.*

"Nooo," Marshall said. "No, I don't think badly of you. Put that one away."

"I mean, kind of hooking up with Alton, but then sleeping with you." Tell him it was him all along, that she'd been wanting them to be like this for months? *No way.*

"Of course, Molly. Geez, I certainly can't pretend to corner the market on rock-steady behavior. People get confused. Things happen."

People were confused and "things" were "happening." Great. Marshall reached out and brushed her hair from her forehead, let his fingers press a lock to her temple, loop it behind her ear. He watched his hand do this. Then his eyes slid to hers, and he smiled again. "We're going to be late for the conference if one of us doesn't get in the shower soon."

Molly wanted to scream *JESUS GODDAMNED CHRIST!* but she felt that might place too much emphasis on the moment. She hoped her eyes veiled the frantic whirring and crackling of the neurons and synapses behind them. She said, as softly as she knew how, "You go."

He lingered long enough for Molly to begin to believe that he did crave more intimacy with her, then slid his feet to the floor. He sat on the edge of the bed, facing away, and she saw how his back angled toward his waist. Used to be he was gaunt. Two years of moving rocks around had added ridges. Modest crescents of looser flesh roosted over his hip, Rhino beer mostly. She liked them. She couldn't stand it if he were perfect. Molly lay in bed with her eyes closed and listened to the sound of the shower rushing over his body. *Hold your horses,* was all she could think to do. *Give him time.* It was brand new to him, she realized, and men, they do need some educating.

• • •

"There is now no reasonable doubt that whirling disease is the primary cause of the drastic declines in rainbow trout populations in the Madison River," the first speaker said. He was a slick young J-school graduate, the type you find throughout the halls of government, clogging up the works with hair gel, shoe polish, and pungent Canoe cologne. Anybody could see he wasn't long for the Department of Fish, Wildlife and Parks. "No other state stands to lose as much as Montana in terms of natural resources revenue. An estimated three hundred and fifty million dollars is spent on trout fishing in Montana annually. Montana is unique in the lower forty-eight in that we do not stock our streams with hatchery-raised fish.

"Montana Department of Fish, Wildlife and Parks biologists have determined that over one hundred thousand fish in the Madison River have died of whirling disease in the past five years. Responding to the loss of this valuable resource, Governor Foster has formed the Governor's Task Force on Whirling Disease. We are that task force, and this morning we are presenting our interim findings. I'd like to begin our presentation with a gentleman with whom you're all no doubt familiar, chief fisheries biologist Kipp Wessel . . ."

Marshall sat in a metal-frame chair with his legs sprawled out in front of him. His hangover whomped out a slow bass throb, counterpoint to his pulse. On top of that Molly sat beside him trying to casually let her knee bump up against his thigh while he tried with a little more intent not to let his leg casually bump up against her knee. He didn't know how he wanted to feel yet and he resented having to think about it when any mental activity sparked such flagrant discomfort. He resented having to be at this presentation so early in the morning. He resented the slick young presenter and his Bass Weejuns and his olive pants with the sharp pleat. He resented whirling disease. Furthermore, it pissed him off that more people hadn't attended the presentation. He'd seen better turnouts at Weed Board meetings.

Kipp Wessel had a body as scrawny as any junior high kid, and wore glasses too big for his face, emphasizing low-slung ears that seemed to anchor his face, but he had the deep stentorian voice of a god. "*Tubifex tubifex* is our culprit," Wessel was booming into the mike. Marshall's attention hit and skipped. He heard, "The protozoan parasite, which is the disease-causing agent in whirling disease, exists in spore form . . . spores are ingested by *Tubifex*, a bottom-dwelling worm present in streams throughout the United States . . . spores evolve into parasites . . . travels through the nervous system of young trout . . . clusters in trout's head, where an abundance of soft cartilage is found . . . excretes an enzyme which destroys the cartilage, producing deformities." Marshall sneaked a glance at Molly, her face pert and full of attention, as the speaker said, "It is the fish's immune system's attempt to battle the infection that causes swelling, which produces pressure on the neural pathways that control the fish's motor coordination. Hence we find the erratic 'whirling' or tail-chasing characteristics of an infected fish. The disease becomes so debilitating that infected trout cannot feed themselves, nor are they effective at avoiding predation. Infected trout die, and dead fish release new spores back into the water, where they settle into the mud of the stream bottom, whereafter the cycle begins again. The spores can survive in mud for over thirty years while it awaits the *Tubifex* reagent . . ."

Eventually the slickster regained the microphone and began to outline plans of attack. The science subcommittee would expand field-monitoring activities to test streams statewide for the presence of whirling disease spores, while also evaluating the susceptibility of various species of fish to the disease; assessing the concentration and distribution of *Tubifex* worms in various watersheds; investigating the role of birds like ospreys, herons, and mergansers as vectors of the disease; and cryo-preserving fish sperm as a "wholly precautionary" firewall in case the entire rainbow trout population in Montana should be decimated. This was war, Marshall was being led to understand. There would be full funding for the grinding of fish heads, the resultant soup to be studied under powerful microscopes. Later came a strident recommendation to communicate locally and nationally that the sky was not falling, and to figure out just how much this thing was costing the state in terms of bed-tax collection in the communities along the Madison like Ennis, Three Forks, and West Yellowstone.

Marshall wondered that the tone of the meeting and the delivery of information could produce such a neatly onomatopoeic reaction—the droning voices seemed to affect a swelling along his own neural pathways until he felt he knew exactly what the young fish were going through. He wondered if this could possibly have been intended, but then a speaker spent fifteen minutes dwelling on the spat between

Colorado and Montana over the proposed relocation of the U.S. Fish and Wildlife Service's Fisheries Health Lab from Colorado Springs to Bozeman, and he understood that his musings about onomatopoeia and sympathetic response gave the gubmint boys far too much credit. The last speaker of the day was the actual head of Montana's Fish, Wildlife and Parks department, a charismatic man in tweed with jet-black hair who imparted no new information, but spoke boldly of progress and funding sources and suggested, with feeling, that there was "no need to panic." Whereas, given the stunning and overwhelmingly miasmic nature of the scientific findings presented throughout the day, Marshall thought panic was exactly what was called for.

He left Helena confused and depressed. It was an opportune afternoon to allow certain revelations—foremost the notion that the trout of his spring creek could be wiped out willy-nilly should the disease be present there—to combine with the corrosive swell of rancid alcohol slushing through his veins and produce a mean, dispirited mood. *This,* he thought about the booze poisoning, *really is going to end.* Meanwhile, it appeared Molly had decided to be cheery.

She hadn't, really, but she was good at appearances. Molly sat in the truck's passenger seat and looked around at the bright sunshine and tried not to feel overwhelmed about what had happened the night before and what it might cost her. In a rare instance, she wondered how her mother might feel about her recent deeds. Growing up she had never sensed much enthusiasm from her parents. Her brothers got it, sure. You just had to go to a football game to see that, or listen to them talk about practice around the dinner table. Until her youngest brother died. Then a lot of the enthusiasm hissed away, and nothing more could be said about "the family." But independent of that, about her endeavors Molly's parents had always seemed either cautious or angry. Or, if all went well, relieved—as if then that was one thing else that wouldn't get untracked. Parents were always so dainty with girls, walking around on eggshells. She surmised it was the pregnancy thing, but couldn't imagine why the Pill hadn't blown that away.

Molly realized she had no idea what to say to Marshall. He hunched in his seat, his eyes vaguely lidded. He looked like a man-eating animal when it's bored. Out the window Molly could see where the river used to be, before the Corps of Engineers moved it to more conveniently fit the highway course. In long-gone oxbows, dead black cottonwoods stood like the skeletons of some war against trees. Long white streaks marked the trunks where sheaves of bark had dropped off. Closer in, she watched the flattened tufts of small dead animals whiz by on the road surface. They neared the turnoff for the ranch. Molly had left her rig in the service plaza parking lot just off the exit. She asked, "What are you up to tonight?"

"No idea," Marshall said, and when he seemed content to let that comprise the totality of his answer, she thought: *asshole.* She felt outraged and wholly unable to bear the man's failure to perceive his only acceptable response, which would have been an invitation to join him for dinner, or at least some sort of discussion of what had happened. Then she blamed herself. Of course he heard what she was getting at, and what he saw was her coming on strong and that deflected him. She sounded needy, and even though he felt bad about it, the neediness turned him off. Either way the second-guessing had begun in force, and Molly found herself hoping—but hope is a hellcat.

The Blackfoot ran high later in June than the other rivers, but visibility in the greenish-cast water was three or four feet. Dried casings of golden stonefly larvae pocked the rocks along the bank and midstream like bas-relief hieroglyphs depicting a struggle to be free. Alton had been happy to meet this Mr. and Mrs. Johnson because he'd been able to talk them into skipping the caravan of boats scrambling to capitalize on the tail end of the floating season on Rock Creek in favor of the Blackfoot, where, Alton had assumed, they would have the river pretty much to themselves. That was before Mr. Johnson hooked Mrs. Johnson in the face.

Today's Mr. Johnson, John, and his wife, Marie, hailed from Connecticut. They were nice people, midfifties, easy to get along with, and they seemed to trust Alton implicitly. Alton worked hard for the people who trusted him. John cast his 4-weight Sage with grace and some precision, making Alton's work easier. According to Shadford, John was some communications big shot. Alton couldn't care less, but was thrilled that John worked hard at mending his line, something he obviously wasn't familiar with, and that he put the fly six inches closer to the bank when Alton told him to.

Alton favored the Blackfoot over all other rivers, and the Box Canyon float above any stretch of water he knew. The river meandered through lush meadows before the North Fork kicked in at River Junction, and then continued through a high, yellow-walled canyon. Later in the summer, giant bull trout would rest and feed in deeper holes midstream as they wedged their way upcurrent to spawn. Alton found nothing more exciting than watching a client skid a small cutthroat toward the boat, only to see a spout of water, the flop of a broad tail, and the sudden doubling over of the rod tip when a bull trout ate the hooked fish. The look in everybody's eyes was the same: *Holy Moses!*

Alton chatted up Marie, speaking in terms of natural history and painting word pictures of previous floats, of elk swimming the river in front of him, ospreys folding their wings and plunging into the stream to snag fish, long-winged falcons swooping to their nests on the cliffs above the water. All the while John landed a healthy smattering of rainbows and cutthroats. The sun staked out shifting positions, the only feature in an otherwise empty blue sky. The day was idyllic and had Alton thinking, *nice tip*.

About midmorning Alton chanced to look upriver and spot a rower in a white-hulled boat ferrying two men down the bank toward them. Looking at the boat's color and profile and the shape and shading of the man at the oars, the long chin and flat face, Alton knew immediately who it was—Dean Stone. Just at that moment John, perched in the bow seat, unfurled one of his lovely backcasts and hooked his wife in the face. The hook, a No. 12 festooned with the makings of a bullethead golden stonefly, sank deeply into the subcutaneous fat of her cheek. Marie, who until that point had been talking about her children, peeped once and fell completely silent. Alton realized as soon as he touched the fly that he had forgotten to flatten the barb before tying it on John's leader. "Oopsie," Alton said. "No problem though, happens all the time."

He pulled a few strokes on the oars to push the boat's stern up onto the bank, then swung around on his rowing seat to deal with the goring at a more efficient angle. Marie held her hands beside her face, fingers splayed, and looked down her cheek at the fly. Her husband said, "Darling, I'm so sorry. Oh, darling," and repeated variations on that theme.

Alton cut a piece of 0X monofilament from a spool in his boat box and looped it around the shank of the hook as far down the bend as he could. He depressed the eye of the hook with one thumb and, with both ends of the monofilament gathered in the fingers of his other hand, he yanked it quickly. The fly did not budge. Marie's fingers, held near but not touching the fly, fluttered. Alton grew instantly wary.

"OK," he said, "you're going to have to trust me on this one."

Marie made a noise that, had it been louder, would have sounded like "Eeeeeeee."

"This won't hurt a bit. You might feel some tugging, but it won't hurt," Alton said. He began to deeply resent the husband for suddenly shutting up. Alton unclipped from the lanyard around his neck a pair of hemostats. He held the fly between his fingers and twisted it sharply, pushing the hook up and through her skin to expose the point. Marie was now completely skewered, and she was letting on that she knew this by ratcheting the "Eeeeeee" sound up to the level of genuine keening. Alton squeezed the hemostat down on the barb, flattening it. By then Marie had latched onto his wrist with both sets of fingers, pinching his blood flow. Alton had to fight her to back the hook out.

"There we go," he said, pulling away from her face, fly in hand, her fingers still crushing his wrist. "See? It's out." He reached his free hand and extended his index finger to caress away a droplet of blood that had seeped from the entry wound. "All done."

Marie continued strangling his wrist, now pulling her head back to gain perspective to inspect the freed fly. Alton regretted the fact that in the snag of the barb he hadn't quite smashed completely lodged a fleck of white flesh. Maybe, though, her face was too close to see that.

"I'm so sorry, darling," John said. He stepped back over the thwarts to lean over Alton and rub his own finger across the tiny mark on her cheek. "You're all right aren't you?"

"Don't do that again," Marie said. Alton fished around in the cooler and withdrew an ice cube for her to press to her cheek.

"All set?" John asked.

"All yours," Alton said, holding the fly so that John's cast could flick it away from his fingers. He jumped overboard to give the boat a little push off the bank and could not help but notice that Dean Stone's white-hulled boat was floating by, all three occupants' heads on swivels to watch the goings-on. Stone's boat skirted them and then dropped right back in along the bank below them—which under any circumstances was rude. Alton leaned on the oars, pulled into the current, and rowed past the white boat, favoring Stone with a silent glare. He stroked hard, using his effort as a cover for his failing attempts to think of things to say to Marie. Truthfully he was ashamed at his silence and could bear himself no longer, so that after he had rowed at least a quarter mile downstream, he let his hands come together and hold the oars above the water while he twisted his head over his shoulder to say, "Are you OK?"

Marie nodded her head yes, but he could see that she had already fitted sunglasses over her eyes and a wide-brimmed hat on her head, and that she'd turned up the collar of her blouse.

"That won't even leave a mark," Alton said as he used two or three effortless strokes to bring the boat back toward the bank and set up a drift for John. "I get hooked all the time."

As if to prove it, twenty minutes later John lanced Alton just under the point of his chin, through the smooth skin Alton had shaven clean of winter beard. The sun stood in mid-sky, heating up the rocks along the river, and golden stoneflies filtered through the air all around them. Fish popped in all the usual spots. John had already broken off the fly he'd hooked Marie with. Alton had replaced it in a hurry. He'd personally tied all these flies and felt certain he had pinched the barbs down. But he hadn't, and this fly sunk deep into his chin when John, unaware of his errant backcast, followed through on his forward cast, stretching Alton's neck a little.

"Oh boy," John said. "I don't know what's wrong with me today."

Alton fingered the fly in his chin, lifted the nippers from his lanyard, and clipped the leader. The fly rested with the hook pointing straight up toward Alton's jawbone. A few long tugs inspired a sickening in his stomach and the knowledge that he would never pull this hook out. He couldn't see to push it through and clip the barb. Nor did he want John to do it—not that he didn't trust the man, but there were certain things clients shouldn't have to endure. He spun another fly onto John's leader, noticing what he thought was a sliver of sneaky cheer in Marie's expression.

"Aren't you going to take that out?" John asked, twisted around in the bow seat.

"I'll get it later. Fish are working now, we'd better get after them."

Alton tried to ignore the fuzzy feeling under his chin. He noticed the white boat again crowding down on them from above. He saw that instead of rowing to slow the boat, Stone propelled his boat forward. The white boat passed them and about twenty yards downstream dropped in on the bank. Within moments Stone's fishermen began shooting out line, plinking away at the bank. Once again Alton pulled heavily on the oars, moved his boat to midstream, and leapfrogged Stone. Again he moved several hundred yards downstream before settling in and setting John loose on the various cutbanks, feed lanes, pools, and slip-streams formed behind partially submerged rocks.

They were approaching a pool Alton very much wanted John to fish before Stone's clients plundered it. The river poured directly into a towering brick-yellow cliff. Current ran tight against the wall but then bent left, where the river had eaten a deep, wide hole in the streambed reaching well downstream in a long emerald oval. After making the hard left turn, Alton oared his hull from the current and rowed across the pool to the left bank. He pointed out a peregrine fal-con perched high atop the cliff wall for Marie, its lead-blue cap and shoulders offset by black bars that lent a military bearing. He left Marie with binoculars and walked John over to stand knee-deep on the inside turn of the current, where water spread to riffle over cobble.

Alton wanted to fish the riffle first because it was just after lunch and he had to fill some afternoon. John could catch ten or a dozen smallish fish here, then they would move down to the glassy tail-out, where any number of truly handsome trout fed. Alton was also think-ing of tuning up his tip. With polarized sunglasses, he could see into the water and spot the forms of fish lifting up through the pool to his client's flies. John cast a big yellow Stimulator that jostled along the chopped surface. Deep in the water Alton spotted a green-brown move-ment that elongated as it rose into a trout wriggling to the surface. "Here he comes," Alton said.

The first time, John flinched, yanked the fly off the water before the trout could snatch it. Alton ladled out a big smile. John cast again, same sequence. The trout lifted up through the pool, accelerating as it approached the surface. "Aaaannd . . . another one," Alton said, timing it just so. This time John set the hook and the fish wiggled and flipped, digging for the depths. John gained line on the trout and used his rod to drag the fight over in front of Alton, who had stepped downstream a ways.

"How do you do that?" John asked, casting back to the riffle.

"It's a feel thing," Alton said. He scooped the fish in his net and re-leased it. "Plus I can see them."

"I can't see them," John said.

"That's the feel thing," Alton said, and just then he heard a loud, hollow *conk*. He looked up to see Dean Stone's white boat caroming off the cliff face. Stone worked the oars, accompanied by energetic splashing.

"Wow," John said. Alton didn't think he'd said it quietly enough.

The boat bounced back into a line of current that would carry it safely through the pool. Stone glanced briefly at Alton, but made no gesture of acknowledgment. Probably embarrassed, Alton thought. John returned to fishing. The boat angled slowly closer to his side of the river, and Alton caught Stone looking furtively over his shoulder. Disbelieving, Alton heard the boat hull grind against cobble, saw Stone hop overboard and haul his stern onto the bank. Dropping in on another guide was one thing. Horning in on their hole pretty much required confrontation. The two fishermen disembarked Stone's boat.

"John, just keep on doing what you're doing right here," Alton said.

He waded from the knee-deep water and ambled over the rock beach. He kept his gaze fastened on Stone, which caused him to stumble. Stone had moved his fishermen into the tail of the pool, waded them up to their waists, and pointed them toward the feedline. Alton could see fish breaking the surface, rising to the stoneflies he saw drifting through the sunlight. Alton wanted to give Stone an out, let him have this talk out of earshot of his fishermen, make it look like guides just trading river jive. But Stone made no move to leave his fishermen.

" 'Scuse me," Alton called. All three of them looked. Stone said something to the man he stood beside, then waded toward the bank. Alton stepped back upstream a ways and waited. Stone showed a grin as he emerged from the shallow water.

"What's up?" he said.

"You guiding these guys?" Alton asked.

"Why?" Stone said.

"You're right, that doesn't much matter," Alton said. "Point is, my people are fishing here and you just dropped in on me. That's the third time today. I'd like it if you wouldn't do that anymore."

Alton could see that Stone didn't know how to play him, but was planning on maintaining those winning ways. "This is a nice pool," Stone said. He nodded out to his guys. "Pretty big. I figured you could have the head, I'd take the tail."

Alton said, "You know the first thing about river etiquette? I'm serious here."

Matthew
1 - 4

7 -

through this, gaze serenely back
o was watching them. He said to

touch the yellow Stimulator still
look fierce, he imagined, with a
head tilt to one side, and looked
crutable, but Alton wondered if,
In't know how to act. Alton mean-
ith clients around.

"Act like you know something."

ostream wondering if he looked
een so stoked that he hadn't until
now bothered to check and see what John and Marie were making of
the scene. He was selling serenity here, an idyllic afternoon. Nothing
could screw that up quicker than naked antagonism. He took it things
weren't well when he noticed John had stopped fishing and climbed
back into the boat. Alton had tried to make his gestures and body language seem fairly casual. So that hadn't worked.

"Are there any places down the river where we might get into bigger fish?" John asked as Alton strode into earshot.

"I'd like to not stay here," Marie pointed out.

"Heh heh," John tried to chuckle, "we worried there might be some
sort of scuffle."

Floating through the tail-out, Alton purposely rowed down the
center of the feedline, hoping that would put the fish down for a while
and that Stone and his goobs would stay and wait for them to come
back up. He heard one of the fishermen say to Stone, "He's taking his
boat right through where we're fishing!"

"He needs some lessons in river etiquette," Stone replied, which
brought Alton's blood to a rolling boil. But instead of reacting, he
chirped on about an ouzel he saw standing on a rock, telling Marie
how ouzels dive under the water, then walk or "fly" along the bottom,
eating nymphs. Marie thought this was marvelous and missed the
heated stares the boat was taking from the wading fishermen.

John had caught and released twenty-six trout by the time they
reached Alton's last honey hole. Just below them the riverbed faulted,
dropping by two feet in a line straight across its width. Approaching
from upstream the water lay smooth, the sound of the short falls the

only indication that something was up. Downstream the water lay pocked by car-sized boulders. Because it was so broad, there were few well-defined chutes through the falls. In the duress of picking a chute and running the drop, it would be easy to miss Alton's honey hole, but Alton aimed his bow and rode easily over a tongue of current, hearing Marie whoop as the boat *whumped* down over the falls. Then quickly he swung the boat and pulled his stern into the edge of slack water formed downstream from a constellation of boulders in the falls. He dropped his anchor, and readied John to cast. Trout heads were tipping up in the pool, eating golden stones, and Alton concentrated on picking drifts over what looked like the biggest fish. They had hooked and released three fine rainbows when Alton was astounded to hear a solid *kronk*.

The white boat skipped off a rock as it dropped over the falls on the other side of the hole John was fishing. Dean Stone flailed at the oars, managing to pull his boat into the far edge of the slack. His fishermen cast into the water just beyond where John's line lay. Stone watched Alton for a moment, then reached up and flicked his fingers under his chin. Suddenly aware again of the metal hook of the fly lancing his skin, Alton understood at once the full range of the gesture's meaning.

"Can he just do that?" Marie asked.

Alton said, "John, are you feeling ornery?"

"What do you mean?"

"I want to teach this guy a lesson." Alton could talk at almost normal volume, confident the rush of the falls erased his voice by the time it reached the white-hulled boat. "I'm going to need you to show off your casting skills. Can you cast a little weight?"

"I'll try," John said.

"John, what are you doing?" Marie asked.

Alton saw he'd recruited a winner. John probably hadn't done anything improper in thirty years, and though nervousness vibrated his voice, he was thoroughly game. Alton pinched two split shot pellets onto John's leader, inches from the fly. When one of Stone's fishermen cast a line onto the water and let it drift, Alton said, "John, stand up and shoot that baby right over his line."

"Is this smart?" Marie asked from the backseat.

"The man needs to learn a lesson," John said. He stood and cast. The line plowed through the air then dropped onto the water, fly and BBs flipping forward to land with a tiny splash.

"Count to three, then start bringing in line as fast as you can," Alton said. "Now, strip it, don't reel. Fast, fast, fast." He turned to the white boat and called out, "Sorry about that! Ha ha! Guy doesn't know his own strength!" John pulled his line through the guides in long strips with his left hand. His fly, sinking with the weight of the BBs, hooked the other fisherman's line, snagged it, and pulled a crook into its layout. Alton raised up his hand and called, "We'll get it!"

The fisherman in the other boat pulled line off his reel, letting John drag the tangle toward Alton's boat. The man scowled. Dean Stone leaned out from behind him and watched. Alton lifted the snag. He pulled in more line until he had all of the other man's leader and the first ten feet of fly line in his hands. He held up one finger and pretended to bend to the task.

Alton said to John, "You know what a pain in the butt it is to tie a leader to the line?"

"I always have the guys at the shop do it for me," John said.

"Well, even if you do a lot of them, it's a hassle. Sometimes it takes me ten, fifteen minutes to do one—that's when I'm sitting at a table and have all the tools I want. I'm thinking that yahoo over there, the so-called guide who is not, I happen to know, a licensed guide but who is, I also happen to know, taking money to guide those folks, which is illegal and he's been busted for it before . . ." Alton had shifted in his seat and was speaking mostly to Marie. "Anyway, point is, that guy's a bad actor. I'm thinking he's also not so good at tying knots. So, if I were to clip off this line way up here above the leader-to-line connection . . ." Alton used a set of clippers on the lanyard hanging from his neck to sever the other fisherman's coated fly line a good ten feet above where the leader was tied to it. "I'm thinking they'll be sitting here a while trying to patch something together, and we can fish the rest of the river without them dropping in on us again."

Alton held up the two pieces of the snipped line for the other boat to see, making sure they understood just how far up he had cut the line, and called across the water. "Hey, it was a real mess. Had to cut the line. Sorry!"

He threw the other fisherman's line out of the boat. He looked at Marie one time and said, "He's been pulling . . . What he's been doing all day is wrong and inexcusable and deserves a little mischief. Just a little guide mischief." Alton winked, twisted toward the bow, and added,

"Well done, John. Beautifully handled." Alton hauled up his anchor, grabbed the oar handles, spun the boat, and began to pick his way through the rock garden blooming up through the ribbons of white water below them.

The Rhino was loud with too much music in too small a space. In a corner of the room a couple of would-be troubadours with ambitious amplifiers slaughtered songs. Everybody else cawed attempted dialogue at each other.

"I don't think they should be on the river," Alton was saying, standing at the bar beside Molly. He was talking to Marshall, who stood with his elbows tucked against his ribs, a glass of Sprite—in which he'd dunked a lime wedge so he could pretend it was a gin and tonic—held close to his face, not wanting to be bumped or brushed up against in this crowd. Marshall shrugged.

"I'm serious," Alton said, still on about his run-in with Dean Stone three days before. "They make us all look bad."

"They make *us* look better," Marshall said, running his hand around a quick loop to indicate all three of them.

"Yeah, to the couple hundred people a year who actually work with us," Alton said. "But to everybody who has these guys for guides . . . they've got no skills, they've got no respect for the river . . . and it's not just the people they guide, but all the potential goobs in Ohio and New Jersey who run into these clowns on the river and go home and tell their friends how shitty things are out here."

"I don't think it matters that much," Marshall said. "Everybody knows bonefish guides in the Keys are jerks, doesn't stop people from booking them. It's not like the old days. We're just a commodity now."

Molly looked at Alton with his shoulders thrown back and his chest puffed, a raptor's scowl full of disagreement. He was maybe an inch taller than she, although she always thought of him as a little guy.

"The point is," Alton was saying, and Molly could see that Marshall was bored, just arguing for something to do, "there's something . . . and I don't want to call it hallowed tradition or whatever insults your delicate sense of propriety . . . but there's something about fishing the Blackfoot and knowing—yeah, it's beautiful, it's wonderful all by itself—but there's also this *history*. You know? This *way it should be*. I do want to believe that."

"Here we go," Marshall said.

"It's knowing all the people who have fished it before you and knowing things, the place, the water, the fish, weren't really that much different then than they are—"

"Oh boy," Marshall said.

Alton suddenly switched and said, "Why do you go fishing?"

"No," Marshall said. "It's a river. That's all."

"Seriously, why do you fish? What brings you out to the river? It's a hassle and expense to round up all the gear, tie the flies, buy the boat or whatever, and drive out to a river to stand around fishing. Why do you do it?"

"I don't have time to answer that," Marshall said.

"You fish to get away from the crappy singers in crowded bars and the drunks spilling beer on your feet and the neighbors who want your water rights and the freaking insurance company who wants their money *now*. All that goes away on the river. Am I right?"

Marshall shrugged. He was so noncommittal tonight Molly could barely stand him. She nevertheless could not stop herself from staring at his hands. They were such long hands, and each finger had its own distinct musculature. The tendons along the back of his hands raised hints of veins. The skin was stained brown from the sun, though paler flesh rimmed the bulge of his palm where it pressed against the glass he held. Those were hands that could touch a gal.

Molly wondered if she was about to admit to herself that she had started going home with Alton in the hope that it would spur some lunging response from Marshall. Not on any conscious level, of course. Up to now she'd been convincing herself that hooking up with Alton had merely been an attempt to break free from the tyranny of hope in which she'd entangled herself concerning Marshall, that it had been all for her. But on some sort of last-ditch level, she had to have considered that it might lead to something like Helena. She could concede, for instance, that the first night she and Alton had gone home together from the Rhino, the next morning some of her first thoughts orbited around what Marshall would think if he found out. How to deny that?

"Yeah, well, and then along come these punks floating down the pike," Alton was saying, "acting like the river is their own personal playground and what's that do? Just reminds you of all the other shit in the world you came fishing to get away from."

"So do something about it," Molly said.

"What can you do?" Alton asked. "You can't call FWP, what are they gonna do after the fact? I suppose you could shoot holes in their boats, but suppose you hit somebody? Then you're a felon and it's off to prison to hang out with all those guys who flunked typing in high school."

"I'm sure there's something we can do," Marshall said. "You just have to drink about it a little more."

Alton feigned surrender to the notion, said, "Your turn, Mol," and lifted the empty pitcher to her. It was, Molly supposed, her turn, though Alton had been doing all the consuming; she'd not even finished a glass of beer from the first pitcher. Molly turned and held up the pitcher for the bartender to see. The musicians had taken a break and, looking around the room, she noticed how she heard whatever she looked at: shouted attempts at conversation from a table full of college boys near the door; the boop, boop, boop, BEEP, boop, BEEP, BEEP, boop of the video Keno games lined against the wall; the clinking of glasses as the bartenders washed pitchers behind the bars.

When she had first started guiding, hanging out in the bar with the boys afterward was most of the fun of it. A certain stretch of her social life had consisted solely of nights that started by going to the bar and allowing herself to drift into a lightheaded willingness to feel good for a while. Willingness was the key. That's how she'd always explained it to her girlfriends, when she'd had them in college and during her early years in Missoula. She liked feeling will as opposed to, say, intent, because it left her with less responsibility for the outcome.

Now she was twenty-nine and everything took more out of her, not the least this part, the bar part, and it was stupid, really. It had been fun once, for a while, to gather with the other guides after a day on the river, to drink beer and tell stories. When Molly started, there had been no other full-time female guides in western Montana. Maggie Merriman had been guiding and instructing out of West Yellowstone forever, and Molly had met her during a casting clinic. That chance encounter, Merriman's humor and style, captivated Molly, then led her to think: *I could do that.* She stumbled into a niche waiting to be filled, and soon was swamped with clients. It had been such a thrill when she understood that the boys in the bar—Alton and Marshall before anybody else—saw her as one of them, and then even more of a thrill when they began to understand she was going to be more successful at it than they were.

But twenty-nine and sitting on a stool swilling beer? Stupid. Co-incidentally, it seemed that recently she kept spending more time at the Rhino. It had to be this thing with Alton and Marshall, she guessed. Putting herself out there. Might be an idea to put herself less out there, Molly supposed. *Might help to change filters.*

What if she had gone home with Alton to prod Marshall? If that were, on some level, an operative factor, what did it say about her? She refused to see herself as the manipulative type—that looped back to intent. The difference between hypocrisy and unresolved contradiction was what you did on purpose, wasn't it? She'd been frustrated, maybe. Confused. Errant. Yes, what she could say for sure was some mistakes were made. But she'd spent a long time without a partner, what did it mean that she suddenly wanted one—a specific one, Marshall—so much that she was willing to take ridiculously selfish measures? Was she desperate? That would be unsavory. That would be not what she wanted to be. It seemed to Molly that things had gone on too long, lines had been crossed. It seemed like, for a long time, those lines hadn't much mattered, but now they were going to. Maybe she even wanted them to.

She turned around with her full pitcher to find Alton staring bla-tantly at a college girl whose halter top could not have been any tighter. The girl stood with her feet slightly splayed and a decided arch curled her lower back. Molly looked down at her own feet, shuffled her toes to point away from each other at a right angle. She tucked in her lumbar, experimentally. Then she felt dumb, and that made her mad, so while she poured beer in Alton's glass she said, "You know what I think? I think you two are full of shit. You," she indicated Marshall, "you'd let somebody drive over you with a pickup truck before you did anything about it. And you," she leaned at Alton, "you'll just yap your jaws until your molars fall out of your head."

"That's a fine thing to say," Alton said.

"I'm sick of hearing about it. All night last night. All night tonight. Go do something about it." A quick glance indicated that both Alton and Marshall were shamed to silence. "I happen to know," Molly said, "that Jimmy Ripley and Dean Stone are right now doing an overnight trip on the Blackfoot. They've got two boats full of clients, plus a gear boat, and they've got a camp set up with wall tents, coolers full of booze, Cuban cigars, and a camp cook."

"How do you know that?" Alton asked.

"I'm alert. I know people around here. Those guys have a camp on a piece of property that I think Ripley's parents own, although it all runs together and the law firm probably technically owns it. They rafted a bunch of gear and supplies down. There's no access on that side of the river for miles, and on the other side the only access is a private road that runs through Ripley's place. It's a pretty sweet setup, really."

"How far up?" Marshall asked.

"Above the River Junction access. They have a private put-in about eight miles up. They float down to the camp the first day—almost all untouched water because nobody can get on it. They camp, then the next day they float out. They can do one night, two nights, three nights; they just keep alternating stretches of river, shuttle boats back up along a private road, and ferry them across to camp. If they could market the place commercially, they'd make a fortune."

"But since they're not actually outfitters, or for that matter even fishing guides, they can't. What shit," Alton said. He hopped forward, interjecting himself between the other two. He said, "Let's go dick with their boats a little."

"Oh no," Molly said.

"Just a little," Alton said. "We'll just monkey with them a little bit."

"I've got nothing to do with that," Molly said.

"It was your idea!" Alton said.

"Nothing was my idea," Molly said, "I was just sick of listening to your whining."

"You know," Alton said, "I think you've got a thing for that flat-faced goon."

"Kids, kids," Marshall tried.

So Molly headed into the rest of the night knowing it was a bad idea. A discussion that took longer than it needed resulted in all three of them piling into Alton's Toyota pickup and stopping at the Orange Street Food Farm to buy beer and some ad hoc supplies. Then they hauled off through the night—Marshall sober and driving Alton's truck—with one of Alton's bootleg Dead tapes unwinding in elaborate free-form jigs. At the turnoff to the River Junction access Marshall bounced the rig onto the badly rutted dirt road. Darkness filled the world beyond the cones of light the truck's headlamps burned onto tree trunks lining the road. Twin sets of green night-eye glows stood beside the road as various deer watched them approach. Marshall kept his foot on the gas, letting the truck brawl its way over the ruts. The road branched half a dozen times, the way to the River Forks access clearly marked, but at one of the branches Molly reached up from the backseat and clawed Marshall's shoulder.

"Right here," she said.

Only a wooden post with numbers painted on it marked the road. Though narrower than the Forest Service road they'd been traveling, the private road had been graded recently, and a few hundred yards in the dirt gave way to a layer of fine gravel. Marshall doused his headlights and the night blackness rushed right to the bumper, forcing him to proceed at a near crawl. They came to another branch in the road, the main stem heading north. A gate blocked the right branch, the new chain of the lock a dull glimmer in the dark.

"This must be it," Alton said, though it was a question to Molly.

"Yeah, locked," Marshall said. "So now what?"

"Oh ye of little faith," Alton said. He hopped out of the rig, dug around in the toolbox in the truck's bed. Marshall could hear the clang and clunking of heavy metal instruments tumbling around. Alton appeared in the driver's side door with a set of long-handled bolt cutters, glinting in the moonlight. He chopped the air in Marshall's direction twice and sprang a demonic grin. "Fisherman's most valuable tool," Alton said.

The chain parted like butter. Alton swung the gate open while Marshall drove through. "Close it," Marshall said out the window. "Cows."

Alton looped the violated chain around the fence post, headed back, and the truck crawled slowly forward. Then they could hear and smell the river and feel the cool air drifting up from it. With his head out the window, Marshall could hear how much noise the truck engine made in the otherwise still night, and he was glad to have the sound of rushing water to cover it. When Marshall spotted the slivers of water, he saw that they were traveling on a bluff about forty feet above the river. He stopped the truck and everybody got out and trotted down the path to the river. The water slid before them, dark, muscular bulges broken occasionally by white streamers of foam. Across the river they could see three white-hulled boats hauled out onto a splinter of sand. The embers of a large fire glowed in a ring of orange. Marshall squinted to make out the tents' walls and peaks. He found himself feeling slightly afraid, but fine with that. It was important to do some things you were afraid of. Alton led them back to the truck. He lifted the grocery bag from the pickup's bed and took from it a roll of freezer-wrap butcher's paper. On the ground he kicked it open until he had a few yards of blank white paper stretched before him. He opened a package of indelible markers, uncapping a sweet smell.

"What should we write?" Alton asked.

"A big word that means something," Marshall said.

Both Alton and Molly stared at him.

"Like, you know, one of those . . . an acronym," Marshall said. "Like GAFFE. All capital letters."

"What would that stand for?" Molly asked.

"I don't know . . . Guides Against Fake Fishing Experts?"

"What does 'gaffe' mean?" Alton asked.

"It means a mistake," Molly said.

"Oh, they'll never get that," Alton argued. His face turned back to the blank paper and he said, "What about, like, SHITHEAD."

Molly snorted laughter.

"It needs to be short," Marshall said. "Think about it, Alton. All the good acronyms are short. PETA. MADD—"

"SCUBA. GORP," Molly said.

"Fishermen Revealing Illegal Guides," Molly said.

"What's that spell?" Alton asked.

Marshall and Molly prevailed on him to scrawl the acronym with the initial consonants in huge capitals—then Alton added the word "Off." He wrote out another sign, then ripped the paper free of the roll and folded it. Standing, he fetched a dry bag from his pickup bed and shoved the paper signs in it. "OK," he said, "we need a manifesto."

"You should have maybe thought this through," Molly said.

Alton ignored her. "What should we say?"

"Something like from here on out the actual licensed guides in this state will no longer tolerate unlicensed punks," Marshall said, thinking that for an occasion as silly as this he really should be drinking. But it was too late for that now, so he rambled on, ". . . and that we will do whatever it takes to run these phonies off the water. And our actions should teach unfortunate clients to hire accredited guides who work hard for a living, instead of punks who treat the river like shit."

Alton wrote it down word for word with a smaller Magic Marker. He detached this message from the roll, too, then tossed a can of spray paint into the dry bag and rolled it closed. He stretched his shirt over his head, dropped his jeans, and walked away from them in boxer shorts and Teva sandals. At the edge of the river, he stripped naked, leaving his sandals on. Marshall did the same.

"I ain't swimming in that," Molly said.

"It's not going to get any warmer while we stand here," Alton said. Looping an arm through the strap of the dry bag, he waded into the water until the current tugged his legs out from under him, then began to swim. Marshall followed, his lungs stapled short by the cold of the water. He could not seem to draw deep enough breaths for a few moments, instead gulped tiny bundles of air in rapid sequence. Then he dropped into the water over his head, and felt the current sweep him downstream with more power than he had anticipated. He had to swim hard to keep moving across, and thought that a smarter team would have started its swim quite a ways upriver. As it was, when he reached the far side he had to clamber naked over sharp edges of a rock face and then dodge the reaching scrapes of needled pine branches.

Ahead of him he could see Alton's naked body walking with an exaggerated bounce, as if pretending to hide from a small child. Marshall wondered if he knew he was doing that. By the time Marshall reached the boats, his heart had filled his entire chest, whapping away and preventing him from swallowing. He remembered Molly talking about Jimmy Ripley hitting people with tire irons. Alton had already strung one sign between two trees, puncturing the paper with branches to hold it up. At first he used hand signals to indicate that Marshall should hang the other one bow to bow on two of the boats, then he produced duct tape from the dry bag to secure it.

"What next?" Marshall said, barely audible.

Alton began shaking a can of spray paint, letting loose a liquid rattle in the night. Marshall hissed and grabbed at the can with both hands. Alton shouldered away from him, and Marshall became suddenly aware that he was wrestling naked with his friend. He stopped trying to grab the can and shushed, "Too loud!"

"All right," Alton snapped. He stepped over to the boat and sprayed the letters FRIG broadly across one of the white hulls. Marshall threw his arms in the air. "What are you doing?" he shot through clenched teeth. "Those are *boats*."

Alton had a marker in his mouth and, biting the cap from it, he filled in letters that said Fishermen Revealing Illegal Guides in vertical columns, then added OFF in the horizontal. He colored all three white hulls the same, on both sides. Marshall crouched on the beach and watched Alton and watched the tents, wondering how much the river covered the noise they made. Up close he could see two canvas-wall tents—for the clients, he guessed—near the smoking fire rubble. Back in the woods he spotted three smaller tents, two-man ripstop. Marshall picked a plastic trash bag from the kitchen tent and made a tear in its bottom. He began moving around the camp, scattering a trail of garbage that leaked from the bag.

"What are you doing?" Alton asked.

"Skunks," Marshall whispered, his hands describing the vectors by which skunks would arrive from the woods and infiltrate the camp, seeking garbage. "Raccoons, bears, whatever." But he really hoped for skunks.

"All right, let's get these," Alton said, moving to the boats. He had stuffed the paint can back in his dry bag, rerolled the seal, and shouldered it. He moved beside one of the boats and began lifting the oars from their locks.

"Are you crazy?"

"Inconvenience factor."

"They'll be stranded," Marshall said.

"Yep," Alton said, "Come on, I can't take them all myself." Alton's struggling clunked the oars against the boat as he tried to lift the second pair while holding on to the first one. He dropped the first pair with a clatter that shot Marshall three steps down the beach before he knew what he was doing. Marshall looked at Alton with the fiercest, most awful face he could muster, hoping the moon was bright enough to convey all his consternation. Alton waved a backhand at him. "You get the spares."

Alton took the third pair of oars much more quietly than he had the first two, lifting each singly and placing it on the sand. Meanwhile, Marshall unlashed the spare oars from two of the boats. The third one didn't even have spares, which let Marshall think about how much these clowns deserved what they were getting. Alton waved him upstream and took off up the bank, crashing through the brush along the side of the river with half of the oars gathered in his arms. Marshall bundled up the rest and followed. His chest held a huge cold hollow now, and he was sure at any moment that shouts would break from the tents behind them, and he'd be naked and caught. Thirty yards upstream Alton had come onto a rock face and launched himself into the river, swimming toward the other side. Marshall swam long before he reached the rock. He wrapped an arm around the oars and sidestroked. The current swept him far past the sloped put-in on the other side and he had to scramble back up the bank again. When he arrived, Alton was already wrapping a hand around his underwear and trundling the oars up the bank. Marshall collapsed, dropping his load of oars amid each other with a crack that rang through the night.

"Come on come on come on," he heard Alton sputtering, laughing as he ran. Marshall glanced back across the river. Except for the banners of butcher's paper festooned from the trees and boats, nothing had changed. Then he spotted the shape of a man wandering among the tents. Though he heard no voices, Marshall saw that other bodies were emerging from the tents. He picked up the oars and scuttled up the path to Alton's truck. Marshall forgot he was naked until he straightened, dropped the oars, and watched Molly's eyes follow them toward the ground and then hang up. Alton was doubled over in the dirt, leaning against a tire, laughing in hysterical manic wheezes.

PALE MORNING DUN

In mid-July, on the Clark Fork River just above Superior, Molly guided two men through the most prodigious hatch of pale morning duns she'd ever seen. At about one o'clock in the afternoon a cloud front that had been assembling in ragged wisps over the mountains set adrift across the sky and screened the sun. The river's surface darkened, a bit of sprinkle began, the vegetation along the bank seemed to swell and green, and then the PMDs appeared. Across the glassy blue-brown surface of the Clark Fork, dipping and twirling on bulges and swells, yellow bugs with their wings folded upright like lavender sails littered the river. The insects seemed to burst forth from just below the surface, the emergence so profligate and vast that Molly thought there should be sound effects—a Moog synthesizer doing popcorn popping, perhaps. Fish broke the surface across the entire river, rising in places where fish had no business holding.

Molly recognized the danger instantly: so prolific a hatch made suckering the trout into eating an artificial fly an act of extreme difficulty, requiring actual chicanery. Yes, the fish were crazed, genetically kicked into overdrive by this momentary phenomenon that might last for hours or only five more minutes, but selection was the issue. It was a puzzle of sheer multiplicity. How to make the trout select your fly among all the real ones?

Molly loved this conundrum because it allowed her to think about Alton in a warm, unfiltered way. She remembered him specifically wading into the Clark Fork, squatting down to watch a PMD hatch with his nose inches from the surface. But that was why he tied such incredible flies—it wasn't just studying bugs in an aquarium, but putting himself among them in their natural conditions, inserting himself into the dynamics of their life cycles. Whenever she found herself with clients in the midst of an overwhelming PMD hatch, she clinched Alton's ZAP flies on their tippets and pointed them at the water. Today she employed an additional trick, watching for fish rising regularly, shipping the oars, leaping overboard and, hip-deep in the river, walking the boat downstream. She held the boat until her clients could pitch a half dozen drifts by an individual fish. She got her Johnsons ten or a dozen fish each—not nearly as many as an observer might think they should hook, given the crashing activity as far as the eye could see, but, Molly knew, damned good for these bozos.

The fantastic PMD hatch allowed Molly's clients to marvel anew at their good fortune in having hooked up so long ago with such a knowledgeable and talented fishing guide who, it could not escape notice, sported an extravagantly pleasing figure. Today's Johnsons were Hal, who ran an advertising agency in San Francisco; and his buddy, Jay, who did something in the paper industry down the pike in Walnut Creek, a couple of middle-aged jesters tripping along toward dirty old men.

She had no problem agreeing by three o'clock, when the PMD show tailed off, that the day had already been "special," and when they floated through the town of Superior and the twisted neon beer signs of a bar perched up on the high bank caught Hal's sharp eye for drinking establishments, Molly could see no harm in stopping for a beer. In unspoken complicity lay handsome tips. She rowed to the shallows, released the anchor line from its cleat, hauled the inverted lead pyramid up among the bigger shore rocks, and dropped it behind a quadrangular hunk of feldspar. The boat was going nowhere.

"Should we bring our gear?" Hal asked. Hal sported a sandy brown comb-over that said: I know I'm going bald but that doesn't mean this isn't still the best cut for me. Jay featured a Hawaiian print shirt and wore his gray hair in a ponytail, but every now and then made a comment about drag queens or the Halloween parties of his past that Molly suspected he held too dear to his heart.

"Who'd steal a Sage?" Molly said.

"Sure. Belittle my equipment with guide snobbery," Hal said.

"Well," Molly said, "it's time you step up."

"Need to get you into the Winston-Abel combo," Jay chimed in.

"I see Hal as more of a Hardy man," Molly said, hoping he was taking that as flattery. They were climbing the bank now, rods left behind to jut from the boat like derelict radio antennae.

The darkness of the bar was a cool shock and negated boundary dimensions so that Molly had no sense of how big the room was. They took beers from the bartender and Molly figured that, as long as she wasn't paying for the drinks, and she maintained a modicum of sobriety, she could cruise along within the legal prescriptions. The river she had left to row was not particularly dicey.

"Do you think it matters that much?" Hal asked, back on the subject of gear.

"It's more of a feel thing," Molly said. "These graphite rods, clearly they outperform the old fiberglass, and yet some people still swear by bamboo. It's all feel."

"Is that your boat?" This from Jay. For a moment Molly thought she was being asked to expound on watercraft. Something seemed not right about that. She noticed Hal boosted off his bar stool, craning his neck to see out the bar's plate-glass window to the river below. She did the same. A boat that looked undeniably like hers moved casually downriver at a slice off the pace of the current.

Molly spouted a colorful phrase and dashed from the bar. Her feet trilled down the steep embankment, then became clunky and awkward as she tried to run over ankle-rolling rocks. It was July and she wore no waders or boots, only Chaco sandals. The rocks beat her feet to a pulp. Molly scattered a group of rat-faced preadolescent punks—the perpetually dirty-cheeked kids you see playing in garbage dumps or auto junkyards—who had gathered along the bank to . . . fish? throw rocks? swim? She had no idea and couldn't care, although she noticed that they seemed to be more or less laughing at her as she ran.

The boat had a good head start, a few hundred yards now, but she was closing fast—as long as the bank left her room to maneuver. But a glance downstream reminded her of something she already knew: the bank ran out. It sheered upright, became a steep plunge of dirt and moraine into the river. And then the water entered a bit of a chute, a riffle with rocks. The prospect of the boat cracking up on the rocks, dumping everybody's gear, swamping, and deep-sixing loomed very vividly at about the same time Molly's right foot rolled off a rock and shot down into a crack. She tumbled in a heap and felt something wrong with that ankle. When she rose she had to argue with herself about how much longer she should keep running and when she should take the plunge and swim. The running part was ruined by a sharp pain lancing up her leg from her ankle.

Molly plunged into the river and swam across and downstream as her boat headed for the collection of rocks that V'ed current into some mild standing waves. A rowed boat could maneuver this feature with ease. Empty? Her strokes came naturally; the breathing less so. She inhaled a few gulps, which only seemed to hasten the stiffening of her lungs. Kicking was a challenge because it felt like she was wearing a basketball around her right ankle.

When she caught the boat she clasped the anchor rope, wrapping her wrist in it. That she could catch the anchor rope as it floated behind the boat encouraged Molly to notch a thought for later: *why is there no anchor attached here?* She pondered how she might try to climb aboard while around her the current began to slice off protruding rocks. With just her head above water, she couldn't see beyond the curving freeboard of the boat above her. What she could do was hang off the stern and provide enough rudder weight to keep the bow pointed downstream, and guess what was happening next. She floated through the sluice, feeling the boat bob over standing waves. Underwater rocks bumped against her wounded foot, sending shots of pain skittering up her leg until she was sure she was done walking for the day.

If this were Rock Creek, or the Blackfoot in places, she'd feel a greater sense of urgency, she knew. Those rivers could kill you. Well, any river could kill you, in the right circumstances. But the urgency she felt now was all about saving her clients' day and not looking as ridiculous as she knew she must. Eventually Molly sensed the current ease against her skin, then the water was slow enough that she could heave herself over the gunnels athwart. She glanced at her right foot long enough to see she didn't want to look at it again, and set up to row the boat ashore. This time she knotted the bow line around a tree. She one-footed her way up the bank and began the long hobble up the road to the bar, well over a mile away.

Hal and Jay U-turned on the empty macadam to pull up beside her in a maroon Buick Skylark. They made her get in, but didn't immediately drive off.

"It's the bartender's," Jay said. He grinned with pleasure in himself. "We paid him fifty bucks to use it."

Molly felt overcome by how sweet that gesture seemed. She was surprised to witness an act of concern, rather than the motivation almost universally revealed to her by clients on the river, which was convenience.

"Let's see that foot," Hal said, turned around in the front seat. Molly lifted her right foot. The skin was shiny as an eggplant, but the purple was shot through with rotten-chicken yellow. "We're taking you to the hospital."

"We can float out," Molly said. "I don't have to use my foot for anything."

"Nope. Hospital," Hal said. "Jay and I will off-load the gear. Those kids untied your anchor. You know that? We found it on the rocks."

Molly was starting to see amorphous shapes floating away from the edges of her vision, which seemed curtained with a gauzy darkness. "Maybe the hospital would be OK."

"Is there someone we can call to come and get the boat?" Jay asked.

Molly thought instantly of Marshall, and then thought: *why is it always Marshall?* In a wave of visceral sensation she felt how much she would like for him to come for her. But . . . pressure. She settled on Alton. Then she realized he'd be on the river and out of contact. She said, "Marshall Tate. We can call him from the hospital." The men left to start shuttling gear up to the car. "Bring the oars," Molly called after them.

Eventually, Marshall was learning—and this was a lesson he'd learned a thousand times already in his life—putting things off, allowing them to generate crushing levels of anxiety, becomes a self-fulfilling prophecy. *Bad news does not get better with age,* was an old favorite adage in the abstract, though not one he could bring himself to live by. Concerning the notion that he should seek some definition of how legal his spring creek really was, for instance, Marshall felt devout paralysis. The more people came to fish the Fly X, the more the money started buoying him from debt, the more extrapersonal the source of his inaction felt, until it seemed some recondite and superhuman force in the sky prevented him from taking action. And the slightest occasional flashes of cognition—the phrase "water rights" or any associated language tickling his neurons—generated instant physical lancings in his chest.

But several days of sober reflection in a row finally convinced him he'd had enough. On the very afternoon that Molly wrestled her boat down the Clark Fork River, Marshall dialed the Department of Natural Resources and Conservation and asked for the Water Rights Division. A man picked up and identified himself as something Van der Wal.

"Hypothetically," Marshall started, then changed tack, "Let's say my neighbor and I have water rights from the same creek and they've been doing some development of springwater that may or may not feed into the creek. What's the legality of moving springwater around?"

"What was your name?" Van der Wal asked.

"Well, I just want to keep this hypothetical," Marshall said.

"Just your first name would be fine," Van der Wal said. "So I can address you."

"Uh, Summers," Marshall said. "It's a last name."

"All right, Mr. Summers. I should start by telling you that there are a couple of answers to your question. If you were to develop the spring at its source, by which I mean dig up the spring and sink a pipe into it, as long as the water flow that results is less than thirty-five gallons per minute, you can get a groundwater right for that."

"My neighbor," Marshall said.

"Right. Your neighbor."

"Because I'm thinking about filing a complaint," Marshall lied, though he wasn't sure why. There was something about being believed he found necessary at the moment.

"That would be an option, of course," Van der Wal said.

"What if it's more than thirty-five gallons per minute?" Marshall wondered what a thirty-five-gallons-per-minute flow looked like.

"You'd need a commercial-use permit."

"What if you, if they didn't develop right at the source?" Marshall asked.

"OK, if you're diverting surface water—"

"It's not me," Marshall said. "It's my neighbors."

"Let's just stipulate that I'm talking in the universal 'you,' OK, Mr. Summers? If you're diverting surface water you need a new water right and a commercial-use permit. Where are you located?"

Marshall felt a jolt—were they on to him that easily? "I . . . I don't want to say," Marshall said. "I don't know what I'm going to do yet, about my neighbors."

"Well, where you are matters a great deal, Mr. Summers. In a lot of watersheds the basins are closed and no new water rights can be issued."

"The West Fork."

"That's not closed yet."

"So, what if I want to follow up on this?" Marshall asked. "If I want to file a complaint, what happens next?"

"First of all, our advice is always to settle it between neighbors. I would strongly, *strongly* suggest, Mr. Summers, that you exhaust all avenues with your neighbors before you come to us. Because when a dispute comes to us it enters a procedure that, once started, can't be stopped. Our department will not respond unless a formal complaint is filed. But once one is, we'll come to the site and investigate. If we find an improper development, we'll shut down the use of the water and direct the party to apply for the appropriate use permits and/or water rights. In the meantime, we may levy fines of up to one thousand dollars a day for every day the water was used without a permit."

"A thousand dollars a day?"

"That's correct, Mr. Summers."

"That's a lot of money," Marshall said.

"Yes. We're allowed a great deal of discretion in levying fine amounts, but it can go that high if there seems to be egregious abuse," Van der Wal said.

Marshall thanked the man and by the time he beeped off the phone found himself immersed in a profound *Holy shit!* moment. So many times in the process of constructing the spring creek he'd faced some unexpected blitz that made him think if he could just get to the corner, he'd have a broken field to run on. Now this.

To a large degree he was sorry he'd made the call. Maybe later he'd see the wisdom in knowing what he was up against, but standing this close to it, Marshall could not clear his head of the zeroes that followed the number of days he'd had his spring creek running. Even if he fudged the figures and started with the date he'd pulled the final diversion plugs and let all the water start flowing into the streambed he'd built, he was looking at almost two years' worth of days. He'd just gigged himself—and Skipjack—for a half-million dollars in liabilities.

About which Skipjack would be livid. But more crushing was the notion that Marshall had strayed far from his purpose. He had wanted to reveal to his father a way that he could be important to the ranch, and that the ranch could be important to the world around it. And now . . . now he'd stripped himself naked of who he wanted to be and slipped right into the outfit of the half-assed failure he knew his father expected him to wear.

Marshall felt crushed, and sat in an overstuffed leather armchair in the dark house, staring out the window at the summer Montana sky, which deployed ever-shifting platoons of cloud from different quarters. The lawn and pasture beyond it curved in a sweep that would stop nothing from falling off the face of the earth. Marshall didn't move. His mug was shot. He wanted to guard against finding monsters under beds he'd never slept in, but the plain fact was the spring creek had come to feel like the fulfillment of an unknown need. The money, yes. Living down to his father's expectations, ditto. But losing the creek that he'd poured so much of himself into would deal a withering blow.

Eventually, though, as he brooded, a question pestered his mind. Marshall rose and went outside to the shed, where he fetched a five-gallon bucket. He cranked open the garden hose and timed how long it took to fill. About twenty seconds. Math ensued. His garden hose flowed about fifteen gallons per minute; two garden hoses would pour thirty gallons a minute. OK, he was definitely looking at some surface water rights. Then he was looking at the phone handset, which was sitting on the porch, ringing. He picked it up to hear Palmer Tillotson on the other end.

"We're thinking about roasting a pig," Palmer said. "For the wedding."

Marshall thought, *oh yeah, that.* Palmer's fiancée, Katy, had not delivered the storm of overbearing micromanagement Palmer had promised, and Marshall had forgotten he'd be hosting that particular bit of bliss in fourteen days. He said, "OK."

"Do you have any?" Palmer asked.

"Pigs?"

"Right."

"No," Marshall said, "I don't have any pigs."

"Well, you live on a ranch."

"I keep forgetting you grew up in the South," Marshall said.

"And another thing is, Katy's all upset about these wolves," Palmer said. "She said she heard on the news there's some wolves up there now."

"I don't think they'll crash the party."

"She's in a *lather* about it."

"Palmer, the wolves have been here for months and I haven't even seen them. Nobody I know up here has seen them. They're not going to feed on your wedding guests."

"I may ask you to speak directly to Katy about that," Palmer said.

"Tell her the wolves ate my pigs," Marshall said.

"See, you think that's funny, but wait until you get married. It changes your sense of humor."

"Tell her to call me, we'll work it all out," Marshall said, immediately returning in his thoughts to the pressing issues of the day. He was starting to approach his dilemma from the perspective of the Klingmans. What could he do to mollify them without selling his soul? Or was that just waving candles in the wind? But then it occurred to him that the Klingmans had been talking to lawyers; surely they understood the respective positions. They could have shut him down any time they wanted to. The question Marshall wanted to pay attention to was: *what's keeping them?*

When the phone rang next, Marshall thought perhaps he'd underestimated Palmer's choice of the word "lather." But it wasn't Katy; this call was from Molly's clients, telling him what had happened and where to find the boat. On the drive in, Marshall used his cell phone to call Fly Guys and asked whoever answered—which happened to be Amy Baine—where Alton was floating that day. Marshall would no sooner have bought a cell phone than he would have painted his ass red and glued feathers to it, but Skipjack valued the ability to, ironically enough, communicate with his son on a whim, and had bought the cell phones, insisting that Marshall at least keep one in his truck.

Marshall drove directly past Missoula on the interstate, watching, as he pivoted around the town, the sun soaking the Catholic church steeple; the flat, white slabs of the hospital walls; and the

Milwaukee station's tile-roofed brick watchtower building across the river. He noted construction had begun on what looked like a monstrous new hotel at the Reserve Street exit, which Alton called the Reverse Street exit because it led to Target and Home Depot and Kmart, Burger King, Best Buy, Taco Bell, Costco, Barnes and Noble, and the Chevy dealership, among other contrapositives to this small corner of the world.

He drove on through Frenchtown and past the Huson and Ninemile exits and then turned off at Petty Creek, crossed the river on the bridge, and whipped into the river access. A gravel road looped around to a concrete boat ramp and a brown wooden outhouse. Among ten other rigs, Alton's Toyota pickup waited, its trailer empty. He'd need Alton to drive Molly's rig back. With nothing to do but wait, Marshall rolled down his windows, tipped a cap over his head, and slumped down in the driver's seat. He felt exhausted by the emotional overwhelming he'd had earlier in the day and nodded off to the sound of the river slipping along the willow banks. He woke to a sudden free fall, his body whooshing to fill the space made empty by the swift opening of his truck door. He came awake like a shellburst, hands flapping for something to grab. His shoulders dropped toward the ground, levering his hips off the seat, and then he was on his side in the gravel. Looking up he saw a face he couldn't name, though its length and flat aspect certainly inspired recall.

"You're the prick that stole my oars," the face said. Dean Stone was the name swimming up through Marshall's uncertainty. While swollen with malice, an institutional control seemed riveted to Stone's voice, jacketing the possible outcomes. This guy thought he wanted to stomp Marshall's ass but, Marshall could see, he was going to let something hold him back.

"You and your little shit sidekick raided my camp and took my oars," Stone said. He had bent to talk to Marshall, as if meaning to conceal the spirit of the conversation. By then Marshall could see why. A pair of older gentleman stood by one of the trucks. They wore fishing vests, khaki pants, and floppy hats with brims all the way around. They peered with consternation at Marshall lying on the ground, a certain concern underlying the confusion. They might be teetering on the verge of coming to see if he was OK, but still trusting their guide and his instincts.

Marshall was surprised he hadn't started to panic yet, given what he'd heard about Stone and his buddies. But it was obvious Dean Stone wasn't absolutely sure he had the right guy—pretty sure, but not absolute—and there were those clients . . . no, nothing was going to happen here. Marshall needn't panic. Furthermore, if there was one lesson Marshall had learned from interfacing with his father, it was how to bug the shit out of agitated people. He used this opportunity to roll onto his back at Stone's feet. It was either that or stand up, and he liked the thought of relaxing in front of this furious man. One of Marshall's eyes squinted while the brow over the other one vaulted into an arch. "I *heard* about somebody losing some oars up on the Blackfoot. Couple guys guiding without licenses? Was that you?"

"You got a problem, why don't you just come at us face-to-face?" Stone said. Marshall heard it as "face-to-flat-face." Stone added, "Hey, I'm serious, asshole."

Marshall locked his hand behind his head and lay back against the gravel, staring dreamily at the sky. He said, "Why, I never," then closed his eyes.

Marshall lifted one eyelid to see Stone staring down at him, fuming, his jaw working like a cow chewing cud. "Aren't your goobs over there wondering what you're doing?" Marshall asked. Stone didn't move. Marshall could no longer see the two older fishermen without resorting to contortions. He wondered if they were still watching, realizing his musing had the ring of hope about it. He looked at Stone, summoned all the ennui he could, laced it with false kindness, and said, "Do you need some help getting your boat out?"

"There's gonna come a day, when the time is right, and then you'll be as sorry as you can remember," Stone said. He stomped off, and Marshall watched his ass wiggle. Did Stone know his ass wiggled when he stomped? How could anybody take rage seriously when it was accompanied by such a silly ass-wiggle? Marshall climbed back into his truck and managed to drift back to sleep before Stone could load his boat and pull away from the takeout. Marshall slept another hour before Alton tapped on his door frame. It was nearly dark.

"How was fishing?" Marshall asked.

"Epic. You actually would not have believed the PMD hatch this afternoon," Alton said. "Never seen a PMD hatch like that. It was . . . epic. And then the Happy Bank is just happening with caddis right now."

"Why aren't you fishing it?"

"I couldn't stand that son of a bitch for one minute more." Alton let Marshall glance over to the yellow-shirted industrialist he had guided all day, and his son. Then Alton said, "Something tells me you're not here to spill a little sunshine into my day."

Marshall told him what had happened to Molly. "Thought you might like to come along for a little night float," Marshall said. The truth was, Marshall wanted to spend a little time with Alton, trying to suss some things out. Alton jumped at the chance. He suggested the industrialist keep his tip in return for the favor of driving Alton's truck back into town and leaving it at the Fly Guys shop. The industrialist, who, following the tremendous day of fishing now thought of Alton as a man who could walk through walls and possibly talk to the animals, pushed a hundred-dollar tip on him anyway and evinced a bit too much pleasure at the notion of driving Alton's truck and boat.

"That guy's got Tonka Trucks in his background," Marshall said after the grinning maniac and his son pulled out of the fishing access, spraying gravel into the bow of Alton's boat.

Marshall drove to Superior in the dark. He kept thinking he felt headlights approaching in his rearview mirror, kept sensing a ball of light just over his shoulder, but it was only the full moon. Beyond Superior they crept along the frontage road, shining a Maglite down on the river to try to find the boat. They spotted it below the mile marker Molly's clients had told Marshall about. Alton fetched Marshall's fly rod tube—a piece of PVC with a cap duct-taped on top—and grabbed Marshall's hip pack full of fly boxes and the oars they'd taken from Alton's boat. They slid down the bank.

"This is not a fishing trip," Marshall said.

"Why not?"

"Don't you think we should go to the hospital?" Marshall asked.

"Are you a doctor now? You gonna make some great contribution there?" Alton asked. "Why waste a perfectly good night float?"

Marshall capitulated enough to let Alton drag a Woolly Bugger through the sweet spots. Marshall rowed rapidly downstream between holes, though he grew discouraged to see Alton growing consecutively more animated about working each spot. At some time after midnight Marshall found himself sitting at the oars in the hundred-yard swirl of a backwater below a point of rocks. He watched the moon climb away from them above the ragged hem of pine tops lining the riverbank while Alton cast a heavily weighted sculpin pattern into the squirrelly currents.

Marshall was primarily occupied with trying to concoct a strategy for learning just what Alton might know about what had happened in Helena. He was trying to parse out the state of everyone's awareness. He knew that Molly and Alton were occasionally shacking up, and Molly and Alton were both aware that he knew that. Marshall furthermore knew that during these occasions, no actual sex happened. Molly was aware that he knew this, but Alton wasn't. Molly and Marshall both knew that the two of them had allowed actual sex to happen in Helena. Was Alton aware of that? How to figure it out, without just asking . . .

He preferred not to bring the subject up with Molly even in the abstract, because he strongly suspected she cast him as a wild rake who would go so far as to take advantage of a good friend's inebriation. She was of course aware of his serial dalliances with Daisy Klingman, and less ongoing affairs with girls of his past. He desperately did not want her to think that he placed her anywhere near those other blips in his social life, but failed in his imagination to dream a way to clear the air. Then there was this question: did Molly want Alton to know about Helena? So Marshall felt forced to eschew his usual approach, flippancy, because in the event that Alton should soon find out what had happened that would eventually be insulting.

"So how's this dealie with Molly going to work out, do you think?" Marshall asked.

Alton bent over the bow. The moonlight was bright enough that Marshall could see the small plaid print on Alton's shirt.

"Depends on how bad her foot is. They make casts you can get wet now."

"I was thinking more of the dealie where you and Molly climb under the sheets at night," Marshall said.

"Oh," Alton said. "It's just a wounded foot."

"Hmm."

Marshall could hear the line rip from the water before he saw Alton move to strike. Alton said, "Hel-lo!" then, over the wheeze of his reel spitting line, "This is a large, large fish. Get hold of them oars— you might have to help me with this slab."

"Just bring the fish in," Marshall said, swamped in his moral conundrums.

"I'm telling you, this a *salmo twofoot*, man." Alton's rod bowed and his reel screeched as line poured from it. Marshall had seen all this before—the loosened drag, the lifting of the rod to make the reel sing. Why Alton felt the need for shenanigans at this hour of the night was beyond him. He suspected it was an evasive action in response to his questioning.

"Do you think there's like, some sort of serious relationship evolving between you two?" Marshall asked.

"I think I suckered him into eating a hook and now he wants to get as far away from me as possible and take all my line with him," Alton said.

"Again, I was thinking more along the lines of you, Molly, and the shacking up."

"Get ready to go with him," Alton pleaded.

"Please."

Alton now had both hands on the rod handle, lifting the tip then dipping it to his right and left to counter moves by the fish. Then the trout arrowed off downstream and Marshall listened to the sound of Alton's reel zinging away line. The heavy fly line made an arc before it cut into the water, and even in the dark Marshall could see that the fish was way ahead of them. Then the line went from thick to thin as backing began to run from the reel.

"Come on," Marshall said, "quit showing off."

Alton said, "If I lose this fish because you're dicking around . . ." He let that hang as if the imagination of it were punishment enough, and then the fish lifted from the water, a brassy slab of enormous trout twisting in the moonlight, and Alton's line went slack.

Marshall looked at his friend with big eyes and said, "I didn't realize how big it was!"

"I goddamn sat here and told you."

"I thought it was the usual," Marshall said, realizing the rest of the night would be a bad time to ask anything about Molly. "I'm sorry."

It took them an hour rowing to reach St. Regis, hard rowing that made Marshall's shoulder joints burn. Each breath sucked a cool column of night air into his lungs. Alton sat in the front of the boat and intermittently groaned variations on themes of loss and disbelief. At St.

Regis they found Molly's keys in the gas cap of her rig, where her shuttle driver had left them, and wasted no time loading the boat. Alton drove them back to Marshall's rig on the frontage road near Superior and they drove separately back to Molly's house. Marshall had couched the notion of possibly leaving the rig and the keys and heading off without waking Molly, who must have been sleeping at this ridiculous hour, exhausted by her busy, busy day and the light-dimming sleeping aids no doubt assigned by the medical professionals, who these days liked to believe that they managed for pain. But he forgot to get ahead of Alton during the last stage of their drive, found himself hung up on a traffic light and a good three or four minutes behind Alton's arrival.

When Marshall trod into the kitchen, he could hear faint voices coming from Molly's bedroom. It occurred to him, not without a stab of . . . of something swift and unpleasant . . . that Alton probably had spent the night in Molly's bedroom before. Marshall never had, but he now wanted to be in that room with the two of them, or rather see to it that they were not in the room together and alone. It occurred to him that eventually he was going to have to sit down and figure out just exactly what was going on with him. Later, though.

Alton sat on the bed beside Molly, whose forehead strained to lift her eyelids. She wore a T-shirt. The covers were bunched and kicked around in such a way as to release the flesh-colored bulb of an Ace bandage wrapped around her ankle. To distract himself, Marshall asked some questions about how she felt and what the prognosis was, and she told him fine and tedious.

"Hey, I saw your friend the flat-faced guy today," Marshall said next, aiming for an amusing tone, some humorous distraction. "He threatened to beat me up."

"Who?"

"Oh, what's his name, that rogue that hangs around that Ripley punk? The one we stole the oars from."

"Dean Stone. He's not the fighter," Molly said. "He's a hound. He lets Jimmy do all the fighting for him."

"Why do I think you admire those guys?"

"I don't think admire is the word. I just know them," Molly said.

And Marshall put a halt to it right there, because he sensed that he might actually be feeling jealous, and that this strange new feeling would lead him to spray wild and unsupported accusations. "Anyway," he said, taking careful aim as much at Molly as at Alton, "we don't want to keep you up."

"I can work for you tomorrow," Alton said to her.

"I'll do it," Marshall said. "I hung a sign on the door for the spring creek clients, and I brought all my gear in. Makes more sense."

"When was the last time you floated?" Alton asked. "Do you even know what's happening on the rivers?"

"It's not a big mystery, Alton. Nymph, PMD, nymph, caddis? The same things happen pretty much every year," Marshall said, taken aback by what he experienced as zealotry. He was trying not to look at Molly because he didn't want to see what she was making of this display. "What about your Shadford people?"

"I've been dying to call in sick on that bastard," Alton said.

"That's stupid," Marshall said. "I'll cover Molly."

"Why are you getting all cheesed off?" Alton asked.

Marshall rolled his eyes and accidentally took in Molly, who seemed to be either too slowed to follow the volley or coldly calculating the implications involved, depending on whether your interpretation of the vacuity on her face allowed for pharmaceuticals. "I'm not all cheesed off," Marshall said. "I don't even know what that means."

"Then back off."

"Fine. Take tomorrow, I'll take the next day's."

Molly said, "Alton, will you go out in my truck and see if there's a little billfold-like thingie in my glove box. It has my ID and money in it."

Alton rubbed her good leg and stood up. There was a visual exchange between him and Marshall, but the intent was unclear. Then he was headed outside.

"So's that broken?" Marshall asked.

"Torn ligaments."

"Oh," Marshall said. "Hurt?"

"Not now," Molly said. "A little throbbing. How about you? How are you doing?"

"I'm a throb-free individual," Marshall said.

"I'm actually more worried about stuff with me and you," Molly said, lifting her leg then lowering it.

"How so?"

"Helena."

"Oh, we're going to talk about this now?"

"I'm under duress here," Molly said. "I'd like it if you'd be nice."

"Well, Molly, there are all kinds of circumstances," Marshall said.

"That sounds like fancy dancing."

"There's the whole business with you and him," Marshall said, his head jogging toward the back door.

"And that can't be settled?"

"What do you want, Stetsons and six-guns?"

"The return of smart-ass. You're so see-through, Marshall. You're like a shower curtain."

Marshall thought he should check her shower curtain on the way out. He said, "All I'm saying is, it seems to me that the settling needs to happen in two directions."

"I don't think that's impossible," Molly said, "but I think I'd like to know if that's what *you* want to happen."

Alton's footsteps sounded on the floor, heading toward them even as the screen door slammed in his wake. Molly looked hard at Marshall, who wanted to say something. But Alton walked into the room holding a small wallet. "This it?" he asked.

"Yeah," Molly said, trying new cheer, but hampered. "That's the one."

"And on that note," Marshall said, levering himself to his feet, "I think maybe I should head on out of here. Come on, let's let her get some rest."

"I'm going to stay," Alton said.

"She needs some sleep and I need to get into your house," Marshall said.

Alton handed him a set of keys and said, "I mean for the night."

Marshall looked at Molly, who returned his gaze with an earnestness that defied diminution. Marshall tried to transmit the gist of a *What am I supposed to do here?* hamstringing, but he gave that up quickly and said his good-byes. Outside Marshall paused in the yard. Molly's boat was parked on its trailer in the driveway. Street light glimmered like greasepaint smudges on the boat's trim, casting a dusky shadow beneath the beam arc of the hull. He thought of Molly in there—on the spot and indefatigable. What was this he was feeling, an insurrection of emptiness? *You,* Marshall thought, *are shithouse crazy if you don't fall directly in love with that girl.* Just the thinking of it made him chuckle.

•   •   •

In the morning Marshall stopped in at Molly's to see if there was anything she needed before he headed back to the hinterlands. He walked
into Molly's room and found her lying in her bed, on her side, curled
like a sleeping squirrel. Her shiny blonde hair tousled over her face,
and the sheets were strangled at the bottom of the bed. When he said
something, Molly made a sound that was half word, half whimper, a
protest against consciousness and its attendant discomfort, which
drew him around the bed until he was sitting beside her head and
brushing the hair from her face with his fingers.

"Hurt?" Marshall said.

"Mmmm-hmm." He couldn't help it; the tiny tone of her voice made
him remember lying beside her in Helena, afterward, listening to how
fast she was breathing. He could smell the river on her skin and in her
hair. Molly's hand came up to his wrist and tugged.

"Lie with me," she said. This, too, was frail.

"I need to get going, Mol, and it looks like you could use some
sleep," Marshall said.

"Mmmmm," she protested, eyes still shut. "Lie with me."

Marshall looked at the bed, at her body, the T-shirt twisted up to
reveal the waistline of her pinkish underwear climbing high over her
hip. He also couldn't help but notice the dent in the sheets; that would
be where Alton would have slept.

"I need to go," Marshall said. "I just wanted to make sure you're
OK. Is there anything I can get you?"

"Yes, if you come here," Molly said. Her eyes were open now, and
her words clearer, but still weakened by complaint.

"Molly—"

That did it. The slither-quick sound of her sliding across the sheets,
wrenching her body, and sitting up was as startling as the flurry of
movement that got her there.

"Would it kill you, Marshall, to lie down here and hold me for a
minute? I mean, you didn't seem to mind it so much when we were
both naked in a hotel room."

"That's real nice," Marshall said.

"Well?"

"Come on," Marshall said, his going slowed by the twin and
equally powerful fears that everything he said next was going to sound

like commitment or a lack of commitment. "I'm sitting here looking at the exact spot where not two hours ago Alton was lying, and now you want me to climb into it because he's gone? It kills me how you see all this as me and manage to completely overlook your choices. You think I like knowing that Alton slept in this bed last night?"

What Molly liked was that he would finally come around to saying that. But she found herself, besides sedative-addled, grouchy, and riddled with guilt, also painted into a corner where, like any animal, she could be counted on to respond viciously.

"How was I supposed to tell him not to?" Molly asked.

"How about, 'My foot hurts, I need some sleep, you should go'?" Marshall said.

He had, of course, missed the real question, and she stared at him for a long moment waiting to see if he'd catch it. *How was I supposed to know to tell him not to?* While he watched, her face tucked toward a focal point between her eyes. "Go away now."

Marshall immediately leaned forward, snaked a hand along her shoulder with the intent of looping his arm around her, but she slapped and batted at his hand.

"Get out of here," she said.

Marshall redoubled his efforts to wrap some comfort around her, but she struggled with his arms and then she made a fist and rocked his jaw with it.

"All right, all right, all right," he found himself saying as he backed away, hands raised to shoulder height and flashing open palms. "I'm gone."

The drive to the ranch became an exercise in how thin he could stretch disappointment in himself over organic misery.

Marshall straddled his mountain bike—back from the repair shop after the collision with the Cadillac—alongside the pond. The cloven hoofprints of deer pressed into the soft mud around his feet. On the other side of the pond he spotted a coyote stalking the grass, eyeing the buoyant rafts of cinnamon teal and widgeon out on the water. Two royal blue kingfishers sat on branches of the small aspens along the water's edge. One of the kingfishers held a sliver of minnow in its bill, which it dropped onto the pond's surface. Both birds sat, staring at each other, Dennis the Menace coifs in profile, until one of them unleashed a ratcheting chatter. Then the second kingfisher dove headfirst into the water and returned to the tree with the minnow speared in its long bill. Two days ago Marshall had been moving rocks and slipped and kicked a log while regaining his balance. Huddled in a seam of dank wood exposed by the shift, he counted five dark salamanders with racing stripes of yellow like decals on their shiny sides. What did he know about salamanders?

Nothing. About the kingfishers Marshall knew that he was witnessing an adult teaching one of its young to hunt. He knew kingfishers mated for life and both participated in raising the offspring, so it could be a mom or pop tutorial. He knew they nested in cavities in riverbanks, digging straight back into the mud, and that they wasted no time papering their nest—rather, they made a mess of things until the place was no longer utilitarian, strewn with feces and inedible remnants of prey, then they moved Junior out into the big world and took turns teaching him how to hunt. Same process every year, which must, if a guy could only find the right application, prove enlightening. He knew kingfishers were in trouble, too, that their populations declined at a rate of almost 2 percent annually. Mainly they were casualties of flood control and trophy homes.

Marshall was learning, but there was just so much to find out. He felt quite proud that the little kingfisher family unit he watched was an unwitting beneficiary of his own brand new habitat enhancement. He liked the way that pride felt, following his heartbeat around like some sort of swelling. He didn't feel so proud of the fact that he hadn't talked to Molly in the three days since her accident. She'd left a message the day before, and he was going to have to return it. Apparently Alton kept calling in sick to Fly Guys and taking her clients out, and so Marshall hadn't had to. He found himself surprised at the level of relief he felt over not having to guide again. Did he dislike guiding that much? Well, he must. But he didn't sometimes. There had been loads of people he'd truly enjoyed taking fishing over the years. It was the sensation of being bought that rubbed him so wrong, the notion that simply because somebody was willing to plunk down five hundred dollars he had to be his fishin' buddy for the day.

He'd paused at the pond in the first place on his way back to the house after checking in on the fishermen working the creek. These were four guys from Manhattan, none of whom were older than him.

He had visited with them when they arrived at 7 A.M., already smoking greasy cigars. Their gear had shined. Even their T-shirts seemed freshly bleached. They had all donned speckless waders and boots. Perfectly nice guys. He had laughed with them for a few minutes before turning them loose on the creek. He liked them. Midmorning he'd felt compelled to go over and see them while they fished. There was nothing wrong with any of these guys. They were just rich.

Eventually he'd have to overcome that. Not all rich people were his father and his father's philandering cronies, but it was easier to make generalizations and not be disappointed. Now he was on his bike and riding down the tractor path toward the road. The sound of a two-stroke engine tickled his ear from afar. Marshall turned to the south and examined the distance. He spotted a small herd of Klingman cattle, black Angus these days, milling about and plodding in a mass toward the river. A man on an off-road four-wheeler rollicked over the landscape, flanking them. Too small to be Kyle. Looked like Bruce rather than Randy, based on the madcap way he bent and held the handlebars, elbows out, face tilted down to eat wind. As the cows filtered into the trees along the river, Bruce hinged away from the herd and throttled up. Marshall heard the engine rev a moment after he saw Bruce accelerate to chase a stray.

The 4x4 did its best to approximate the romance of cowboys on horseback, cantering and bucking through the field, and then suddenly Bruce was high in the saddle clawing at the handlebars. Next he slipped sideways through the atmosphere. His boot heel caught something on the machine and the 4x4, its throttle stuck wide open, dragged him in long flat skips through the pasture. A bump loosened Bruce's heel and the 4x4 shot on alone for a while, seesawing at speed. Then the machine bucked, sunfished, landed and launched itself again skyward, rear wheels pinwheeling over the handlebars so that it landed upside down with a *whump!* Marshall heard a split second after the dust poofed up.

He jumped on his bike and pedaled madly across the bridge, then dismounted, threw the bike over the barbed wire, and slipped between strands. Remounted, he rode across the cattle-cropped pasture, pumping his knees. His thighs burned and his breath came short so quickly it surprised him. Still his legs fired on and he slalomed sage bushes. The wheels of the bike fishtailed when he locked up the brakes and skidded to a halt looking straight down at Bruce Klingman.

The old man lay on his back with his mouth open in a round shallow suck. He had the pallor of a stunned mullet and the same bulged, unseeing eyes. Still trying to catch up with his own galloping lungs, Marshall bent and peered at the man on the ground and wondered if he was dead. Bruce's limbs, akimbo, looked sticklike. His ankle turned oddly, maybe broken. One of his arms bent into a right angle at the elbow pointing up, and the other bent pointing down. Bruce's skin was translucent along his temple, and a blue vein burped blood into his brain.

Marshall knelt, and began to touch Bruce's throat. After fifteen years of guiding he was well versed in first aid and CPR. He bent his face to Bruce's to feel for a faint breath on his cheek. Bruce's eyes snapped into focus and he bolted a deep breath. Marshall jerked upright. Bruce slapped at the hand Marshall had left resting on the pulse of his throat.

Startled, Marshall rocked back on his heels. "You OK?"

"Hell yes," Bruce croaked. He struggled to prop himself to his elbows.

"Just checking," Marshall said, involuntarily flipping into an open-palmed "hands-off" gesture.

Bruce rolled away, pressed himself to hands and knees. Marshall collected his bike. Bruce hacked twice, then gathered his feet beneath him and levered himself upright. He wobbled a step backward, then an awkward, too-long step forward. Marshall started to drop his bike, moving to catch Bruce. But Bruce reeled his balance in and Marshall resnatched the bike instead.

"You sure you're all right?" Marshall said.

"Jesus Christ, you want a note from my mother?" Bruce spat. He turned, waved an arm at Marshall, and limped off through the field toward his turtled vehicle.

Later that afternoon, Marshall phoned the Klingman house. Colleen Klingman answered. Marshall asked for Daisy.

"Wanna go for a hike?" Marshall asked her.

"A hike?" Daisy said.

"Yeah. Up Hayden Peak. It's only six o'clock. Won't be dark until ten."

"Um, sure."

Marshall drove to the Klingmans'. He hoped to stand around and wait for Daisy to be ready and while doing so snoop about Bruce's condition. The old man had worried him, looking so dead. But Daisy skipped down the porch steps as soon as Marshall's truck reached the end of the drive. She wore a T-shirt that said, GUN CONTROL: USE BOTH HANDS, and a pair of khaki shorts that would certainly fall thread from thread in three or four more washings. She'd pulled her hair up in a knot behind her head.

Marshall drove on through the Klingmans' barnyard and up the dirt two-track that connected to Forest Service logging roads. This route, like the Klingman bridge and the road over it, were technically Klingman property, but Marshall held a legal right to use them. When Bruce's Crazy Uncle Bud had completely lost his mind (Bruce's view), and sold Marshall's father his three sections of land and moved to Fountain Hills, Arizona, an easement in perpetuity to the road and bridge came with the parcel. The legal inability to stop Marshall from driving those roads ranked among Bruce Klingman's chief annoyances, but today Marshall felt no lift from his potential to goad his neighbor. He felt sad instead about the old man.

Marshall turned onto the Forest Service road, which crested a saddle that formed the upper shoulders of the ridge that fingered into the Fly X, and eased down onto the bench where the Fountainhead spring spurted from the ground. Upstream from the Fly X, the West Fork ran bracketed by steep slopes, pouring down from thousands of square miles of the Scapegoat Wilderness Area. The road headed that way.

"How's your pop?" Marshall asked.

Daisy sat sidesaddle in the bucket seat, one booted foot planted on his dashboard. She had been humming along to a Nancy Griffith tune. "Fine," Daisy said.

"He OK?"

"Why wouldn't he be?" Daisy asked. With her hair pulled back and her eyes shining, she looked girlish and eager. She could do this, though sometimes she chose not to.

"He didn't tell you," Marshall said. It wasn't a question. He told her about what had happened that afternoon. "He didn't look good when I got to him."

"Oh, Daddy," Daisy moaned. "He told us the four-wheeler died. That was all. Now I want to go back and see if he's OK."

"We can."

"Typical, though," she said, apparently locked in an argument with herself. "You could light him on fire, he'd just say, 'Bet that's gonna hurt later' and keep on doing whatever he's doing."

Daisy had already lost her fresh-faced look because an indiscriminate annoyance riddled the frown of concern pressing her forehead. She allowed that if he had been OK when she left the house he probably would be for a while, and they should continue with this hiking plan. Undoubtedly she wondered what the sudden hike was all about, and Marshall knew it. In the old days spontaneous activity invitations were rough equivalents to foreplay.

He parked his rig at a wide spot on the berm and they began climbing through the pines along a trail that didn't officially exist, though locals had used it for decades. They were hurried partly by the congealing clouds that threatened evening rain, but also by unspoken competition. Both understood the need to prove they hadn't gone soft since last they'd hiked together. They climbed fast and silent, panting breaths audible above footfalls. Being able to move quickly through the woods had always been a point of pride, one neither felt willing to betray, though Marshall's legs began to sizzle after a half hour and his knees felt sharply creaky just after.

The weather came from across the valley, great skeins of precipitation hanging from the sky like windblown curtains through an open window. They passed through a glade of pine trees, uncut for over a century so that the vertical trunks striped the green of the forest canopy at every glance. A filtered light slid from beneath the storm clouds. Raindrops filled the interstices between the pine trunks, each drop fat and glistening in the sidelong sun.

"You want to keep going?" Marshall asked.

Daisy shrugged. Wet hair dripped alongside her face. She wouldn't quit. "Long as there's no lightning."

They broke from the lodgepole stands into grassy upland parks studded by towering ponderosa pines. While they'd been climbing, it had already rained hard up here. Now it was only sprinkling but the trail was mucky and slick. Slopping along, Marshall slipped and reached to break a fall. He didn't stand erect again, instead knelt in the mud.

"Look at this," he said. Daisy stepped beside him and bent to look at the ground. Beside Marshall's hand was a deep pockmark fringed at its topmost edge by a fan of four ovals, each of those crowned with a dot. "Know what it is?"

"It's a dog," Daisy said. "I wonder whose, way up here?"

"No," Marshall said. "Put your hand over it."

Daisy stretched her fingers open and placed them lightly over the track in the mud. Her hand—fingers and palm—didn't quite span the length and width of it.

"It's a wolf," Marshall said. "And it just started raining up here a little while ago."

Daisy dropped down on a knee beside him. "Did you hear them the other night?"

"What night?"

"Must have been last Tuesday, Wednesday? They were howling like wild."

"Why didn't I hear them?"

"I don't know. They were somewhere between our house and your house. Some of them were. Some were up on the hill. They were howling back and forth. It was pretty cool."

"Why didn't you call me?"

Daisy shrugged. "You've been sort of aloof."

"Oh, come on," Marshall said. "God, I would love to hear that."

"You wouldn't like to hear what the boys at our house were saying about it," Daisy said.

The wolf that had left its track couldn't have padded through more than fifteen or so minutes before they had reached the spot. There hadn't been mud too much before that, and rain would have smeared the print's sharp edges if exposed too long. Maybe they had spooked the animal. Probably. Marshall exulted at the thought of sharing this space with a wild wolf. It was out there, ahead of them, not far. Daisy watched him be amazed, respectfully still. Then an idea occurred to Marshall and he searched around until he found suitable rocks. He formed a ring around the footprint with potato-sized rocks, then capped it with a wide, flat stone. He would come back the next day and make a plaster cast of it, a totem to the moment.

They hiked again, coming to skirts of black granite scree. Picking over loose rocks, they summited in a controlled sprint and stood for a moment on the ridge, looking into the confusion of peaks that reached miles back into the Scapegoat Wilderness Area. Marshall felt the breeze sucking his wet shirt to his body. Up this high the wind felt wild and edgy. Daisy sat on a flat slab of rock and Marshall sat beside her and pushed his hand through his hair to move it off his face. Then Daisy pushed her hand through his hair, and he turned to face her, and she leaned into him like she might kiss him.

"I, um . . . I may be seeing someone," Marshall blurted.

"I figured," Daisy said. She smiled faintly and sat easily back away from him. The whole lean-in-to-kiss move now appeared a clever gambit designed to bait Trouble and get it dancing around the floor. "The row-your-boat girl."

"Well, Molly, yeah," Marshall said. "I don't know, but—"

"So why do you feel the need to tell me?"

Daisy was a genius at asking the question that sat right beside the question he thought she was going to ask. He'd like to see more of these things coming. He said, "I don't know that either, but it's been feeling necessary."

"I guess that's what you ought to figure out," Daisy said.

Why did all the women with whom he involved himself feel so clever around him? It pissed him off and made him feel a little pedantic. "Though I'll tell you honestly," he said, "I *wasn't* seeing her when you made your little . . . display at Trixie's. You know it's exactly that kind of stuff that's always kept us from working out."

"No it isn't." Daisy could have been peeved, but instead seemed to understand completely what she was talking about. She adopted a tone of patient instruction. Her face was open again, her eyes clear, her mouth relaxed. "You're what's kept us from working out. Your terror of a real, intimate relationship. You're no different from a million other men."

"Well," Marshall huffed, "glad to know I'm so predictable and ordinary."

"You are, Marshall," she said, "Oh 'I grew up rich but nobody loved me.' Well, boo-*hoo*. I grew up poor and nobody loved me, either. You don't have to take it out on everybody who cares about you later in life."

"That . . . that is a gross oversimplification. First of all, you're not exactly poor."

"How many layers of remove do you use at any given time?" Daisy asked. He didn't know whether the words or the serenity of her delivery made more sense. "Pot, booze, fishing, work . . . But really, it's that as

long as you can keep something between you and opening up to someone, then you never have to worry about anyone treating you shabbily.
Or about their shabby treatment hurting you. I swear this fish pond of
yours is about the first thing I've ever seen you actually care about."

"It's not a fish pond." This was an unfair attack. Guiding, for instance. He'd taken guiding very seriously. And before that, the whole
process of learning rivers. Very, very serious stuff in his younger mind.

"I mean *really* care."

"It's more than just a goddamned fish pond," Marshall said.

"I know what it is, Marshall. It's an intricately developed spring
creek fishery, with the ability to entice well-heeled fuckwits to fork out
cash. Blah blah blah. I'm just curious; what are you going to do when
you realize you've succeeded at this? What are you going to hide behind then?"

"I don't think what you're saying is true at all. I think any reti-
cence I've had about a lasting relationship has to do with wanting to
make something of myself first." It was a private theory. He hadn't
never thought about why he failed to connect to women, to love inter-
ests, in meaningful ways. He'd thought about it at clever lengths, and
this was the trope he decanted to shush that discourse, though he was
not oblivious to its potential toward solipsism. It was an "I will be,
therefore I'm not yet" sort of trick. Though of course what she was saying was not deniable.

"Well, here you are," Daisy said. "And here I go. I'm going down."
She stood, pressed on her butt with both hands and arched her back
in a long stretch. Her head swiveled and she cast a measuring gaze on
him. She gave no indication whether she approved of what she saw before turning and walking down the trail, her T-shirt untucked and
swaying loose over her waist.

It seemed absurd to Marshall to be thirty-three years old and not exactly sure if he was "seeing someone," particularly when the last time
he had actually "seen" the person in question, she had clocked him on
the jaw. Some things were just funnier than others, though Marshall
floundered when he tried to figure out where to post all this on the
could-be-funny/could-be-sad scale.

While Marshall had not seen Molly since she'd punched him, they'd
spoken several times on the phone. Molly called and apologized. He

apologized back, and they had skipped the fault-finding, both feeling culpable enough. Then Molly said, "Let's act like everything's changed."

Marshall thought about that, thought it sounded like a fine idea, but he wanted to know more. "Like what?"

"Why sweat the details?" Molly asked.

"But what if some things haven't changed?" Marshall asked, thinking about Alton, but still mainly oblivious.

"Can't you just get with the program?" Molly asked.

Marshall left that conversation feeling like he should have known a lot more than he did, but she seemed dissatisfied when they hung up. He called her the next afternoon and talked about her foot and guide days and then about some kingbirds he was watching sally for insects out front and how clouds were mottling the high peaks of the Scapegoat—just blathering about what he was looking at. Molly listened, occasionally asked for a clarifying detail. When she told him she had to go, he had no idea what she might be thinking.

And then it was Saturday, the day of Palmer Tillotson's wedding, and Marshall woke at six-fifteen because that was when Katy arrived in Palmer's pickup with her maid of honor and started pounding on the door. Marshall stood around bleary-eyed in the kitchen. By 8 A.M. his most significant contribution remained brewing a pot of coffee. He'd seen women get married before, but not this close up. Eventually Marshall discovered that if he wandered off and looked busy, he could escape much of the drilling. At one point he set up a pair of folding tables and covered them with a plasticized tablecloth, which needed taping down. Then he unloaded bottles from the caterer's van and set up the bar. There was a portable dance floor to assemble, a series of parquet-looking blocks that fit together like a puzzle. He managed to turn that into an hour-long affair. Then there were tables for guests, all of which needed to be covered and taped and festooned with favors. That all this was happening before noon to accommodate a wedding scheduled for four o'clock seemed a marvel to Marshall.

Katy came sprinting by, hands waving beside her face, her long hair fanned out behind her, shrieking, "He can't see me! He can't see me!" For a silly moment Marshall wondered if she was declaring herself invisible to one of the caterers. But he looked around and noticed a group of men sitting in a dark blue rental sedan in the driveway, followed by an extraordinarily clean Chevy Blazer. Palmer was wise enough to tinker around in his father-in-law-to-be's rental car, giving Katy dodge time. Marshall walked over to them. Eventually Palmer, his father, Katy's father, Katy's surviving grandfather, Katy's twelve-year-old brother, and the best man got out of the vehicles.

"How's it going?" Palmer asked. Until now, Marshall had been feeling a little sorry for himself about the dog-and-pony show he was working his way through, but then he saw the stiff beam shellacked onto Palmer's face and realized where the real pressure was being brought to bear. As smiles go, this one was a lemon.

"Everything's fine," Marshall said. "Couldn't be any better." He was introduced to Katy's grandfather, father, and brother. The grandfather was on the distaff side. The father particularly looked meek, whereas the grandfather appeared to have some affinity for fresh air and green grass. He looked like he could kick his son-in-law's ass any day of the week, and perhaps years of just this juxtaposition contributed to Katy's father's passivity. What Marshall knew about Katy's family was that they were, through her mother, heirs to a tremendous fortune amassed during the early part of the last century by coal barons in northeastern Pennsylvania, and fattened by shrewd investment managers ever since. He also knew that Katy and Palmer had insisted on paying for the wedding themselves. No stranger to the miasma that wealthy families can sink into, Marshall was pleasantly surprised to discover the lower key Katy's family seemed willing to play.

Marshall realized he knew the best man—a stout young man Marshall had always envied for his upper arms and shoulders, and, more disconcertingly, a hanger-on of the Jimmy Ripley-Dean Stone camp. This revelation soured further when the best man—Tom was his name—stretched his huge arms and said, "Can't wait to rip some lips."

Marshall had closed down the spring creek for the day so that Palmer and the wedding party might fish it, a little relaxation before show time. What he wanted was to go with them, but much remained to do, so he instructed Palmer and the others on how to get to Klingman's bridge and the spring creek.

"Are there lots of fish in there?" Katy's younger brother asked. Marshall stared at him. Then he realized how much courage the twelve-year-old had mustered just to speak.

"Lots," Marshall said. "You'll catch a bunch. And if you don't, come get me and I'll help you get some."

Then they were off, and Marshall went back to looking for things
to do. Scotty the Wad and Billy Mills arrived at eleven o'clock followed by a truck emblazoned with the logo for Montana Party Time.
From this truck two young men withdrew the makings of a huge tent
and soon the morning clanged with the sound of stakes being
pounded into the ground. With Marshall, Mills, and the Wad as
hands, the tent guys flung their canvas structure quickly into the sky,
its towering white cone a sail against the blue-green of the mountains
beyond the river. While Marshall helped tighten lines it dawned on
him that he was about to throw a party to which were invited Billy
Mills, Scotty the Wad, Shadrat, and, in all probability, Jimmy Ripley
and Dean Stone. He tried to imagine if he could ever have imagined
that, and failed.

Alton and Molly arrived together around noon—Molly with her
ankle in a wrap and a clean white brace—and the moment they did,
Marshall handed Alton the line he was using to tie up one of the tent's
removable wall panels and walked directly into the house, as if something there urgently demanded his attention. Marshall strolled through
the kitchen, amazed at the humming and bustling activity there. His
father's famous cocktail parties had never felt so congenially *busy*. He
sneaked into the mudroom, snatched his Winston 3-weight, a box of
flies, a pair of sunglasses, and slipped out the back door, headed for
the river.

Marshall stole down the river, waded across it, and worked his
way to the spring. Strung out in the distance he saw the wedding
party fishing. He moved through the high, yellow summer grass to a
roll in the landscape and tried to identify one of the shapes as Katy's
little brother. He'd doubted Palmer Tillotson would get so wrapped up
in being a basket case that he'd leave the kid to himself, but was
happy to see that was exactly what had happened. Marshall spotted
the kid where he thought he might, by the pond.

Though he found it interesting that the boy didn't seem at all surprised by his arrival out of nowhere, Marshall greeted him with a simple, "How's it going?"

"I'm not catching any," the boy said. Marshall could see the boy
found this fact both irritating and usual.

"You seeing them?" he asked.

"Nope. Only sometimes, when they come up to the top."

"Yeah," Marshall said. He peeled his sunglasses from his head and handed them to the boy. "Here. You can see them with these. You done much of this fly fishing?"

"Some."

"Let's see you cast one out there."

The boy whipped his rod back and forth about half a dozen times and flung the fly ten feet into the water, his line collapsing in loops around it.

"OK," Marshall said, "Here . . ." He reached his arms around the boy to show him how to hold the rod, when to stop the backcast, how to use his left hand. For a half hour Marshall coached him on casting. The boy was as excited by his newfound polarized vision, which revealed the fish hanging in the pond water before him, as he was frustrated by his inability to cast without spooking them. Marshall tried to get him to pitch a ZAP PMD out onto the pond's surface and just leave it until a trout cruised by, but the kid was restless. He imagined strikes and yanked the fly like he was setting the hook. When fish genuinely approached his fly, the boy shuffled like the soles of his feet were on fire, and everything got twitchy. Cripples need absolute stillness.

At length Marshall said, "All right, that was just practice. You ready to go down and catch us some fish?"

During his years of guiding he had learned to speak to all of his clients as if they were twelve-year-olds. He walked the boy downstream through a few bends in the stream and stopped at a small pool. For reasons he could not fathom, Marshall badly wanted this kid to catch a fish on this day. He stood behind and just to the left of the boy and felt desire with every fiber of his being while he watched the kid's hopeless casting.

The boy blew his first strike because he was looking around at a soaring hawk, its red tail fanned like poker hand, when the fish came to his fly. What was missing, Marshall came to understand, was the expectation of catching fish. The boy missed a second and third strike, even while he watched the fly on the water, seemingly stunned into inaction by the halo of water being sucked from the surface with his fly. Marshall's own childhood had taught him what happens when kids are treated like short adults. He didn't say anything about the boy's failure to strike back. He pretended to be just as amazed by the appearance of the fish. "Holy smokes!" was one of his favorite things to say to kids when they were seeing wild trout coast up to suck flies from the surface. He had a number of different intonations and stresses and kept the phrase fresh.

"When I was your age, I used to come down to the river and fish at night, in the dark," Marshall said.

"Why?" the boy asked, but some of his adolescent disdain was riddled out of that retort.

"I don't know," Marshall said. "Just to get away from everybody. I liked it. Nobody bothered me."

Marshall moved the boy down to another hole after one more missed strike. From behind he reached around the kid's shoulders, held his hands on the rod and moved with him. Together they threw a beautifully simple little cast. Marshall knew he was making the boy nervous by hovering with his hands just off the rod, but he also knew the fly was about to be eaten, and when a trout rolled to the surface, Marshall clamped down on the boy's hand, flipped his wrist up and set the hook. Then he backed off.

"You got him. He's all yours," Marshall said. "Keep a bend in the rod."

The boy held the trout so tightly that he forced a long series of tail-walks across the surface by practically preventing the fish from sinking back into the water. Then he allowed enough slack to fall into the line that it buckled in a long downstream curve. But Marshall knew that fish was hooked well, and doubted the kid's inexperience could let it off. He stood back in the bright sun, feeling the grasses and sedges under his feet, and watching the individual tickles of current run along among others to describe a whole stream. Under the surface an agitated twelve-inch rainbow trout raced around, while on the bank a young boy in pair of baggy soccer shorts struggled with his first wild fish. Marshall didn't pretend to think that he had launched something in the boy, but he knew that his own day was already complete.

The wedding ceremony took place on the lawn just south of the main house. Two clusters of folding chairs were arranged in a few shallow rows on the freshly clipped and raked grass, with an aisle between them lined in cream bunting and lilac bouquets. Marshall stood off to one side, as did a number of younger guests, deferring to the older folks in terms of the chairs. Whatever pressure Palmer had been feeling when he had arrived hours earlier had lifted, and he stood tall and with a slight backward cant, smiling as he waited for his bride. A band consisting of a mandolin, fiddle, banjo, and upright bass plinked and sawed the wedding march and the bride sailed down the aisle with imposing grace in a simple, off-the-shoulder, knee-length white dress.

Amy Baine, who looked marvelous in a saffron silk blouse and a brown wraparound skirt, read a passage from Rilke, and a justice of the peace began the joining of wife and husband. Marshall stood near Alton and wondered how he could bear Amy Baine's spry, fresh-faced beauty on this day, knowing that she had come with, and would leave with, Shadrat. Molly crowded closer to the proceedings, as if being closer would somehow make a difference in time. Marshall could not hear everything that was said, but he caught something in the Rilke passage about loving the differences between them, and standing together against an immense blue sky. This pleased him, as he watched the couple standing together against an immense blue sky, and the mountain ridges beneath it. Because he was not glued to the ceremony, he noticed a slight breeze ruffling the cottonwoods and alders down by the river. The multitude of flittering leaves seemed to applaud.

The bride and groom stood and said oaths to each other. Watching, Marshall understood he knew almost nothing about love. He was a master of infatuation, but not a follower-through. Was that something a person could undertake to change? It would be nice if it was, he thought, and the key might be paying attention to what he wanted on an ongoing basis. Checking in. Marshall's attention turned to the cows grazing on the hillsides of the Klingman ranch, dark splotches that carried just enough distinction in their angular hips and shoulders to be the shapes of dumb, blocky animals. He saw a kestrel beat its wings into a blur while it hovered, then released, dipped, and climbed again to create a still flurry while its head craned forward to search for field mice in the brome. Up on the bench where the spring originated a cluster of mule deer, two does and three fawns, munched unconcerned. He could hear the suss of the river moving far behind the ceremony. What a beautiful way to begin a life together, he thought.

Marshall would have the opportunity to rearrange his opinion later, when, during the reception, the best man swerved up to the cluster of instruments under the tent to begin a toast. Palmer's immediate family consisted of his divorced parents—his mother had brought her new spouse—and some cousins. Katy's family occupied the three tables closest to the wedding party. Her maternal grandparents and paternal grandmother sat with her mother and father, her younger brother, and even younger sister. Two more tables were occupied by aunts, uncles, and cousins.

By toast time, Jimmy Ripley and Dean Stone had arrived, wearing Carhartts and T-shirts and looking for all the world as if they'd pried themselves from some very important dirtbag activity for the occasion. Marshall watched the way they eyed Alton. Against his better wishes, he found himself fearing they would do something, somehow destroy his property, retaliate for the oar stealing. They had brought with them and turned loose the biggest chocolate Lab Marshall had ever seen, and the dog roamed the reception, thrusting his snout into private crevices.

The best man, Tom, stood before the collection of musicians—who paused in their rendering of John Prine, Emmylou Harris, and Bill Monroe tunes—and lifted a plastic champagne glass outward until he figured he had everybody's attention. Then he smashed the glass against his head. A confused whooze swept through the crowd while people tried to figure out how they felt about this display. The shattered plastic had sliced Tom's forehead. A crooked line of blood dribbled between his eyes, and he grinned.

He reached for another plastic champagne glass and then said, as loud as he could, "I was with Palmer the night he met Katy. We had spent the summer driving around, trying to fish every river we could. We didn't have hardly any money, because, you know, we were just *fishin'*. Well, we got to Thermopolis, Wyoming, one night, and we had zero dollars between us. We were at this gas station, trying to figure out which one of us had enough credit on his card to buy a tank of gas. Just then a car pulls up and it's full of girls, and one of them says, 'I'll buy you some gas if you come out for a drink with us.' That girl was today's lovely bride, and she was talking to Palmer, and there were sparks flying right off the bat. Well, to make a long story short, we followed their car to a bar and pounded some cocktails." Tom raised his glass as if cocktails were the very essence of his story and, perhaps, his life.

"When the bars closed, the girls asked us where we were staying and we told them, hell, we were just going to pitch a tent somewhere. And they were all, 'No, come stay at our house.' And, like I said, Katy and Palmer had obviously hit it off, so we went back to their place and had a few more brewskies. Katy and Palmer were sitting on the couch when I passed out, and they were engaged in *deep*, uh, conversation." He paused to let people laugh and one person did—Jimmy Ripley. Tom continued: "I knew that night that it was true love between the two of them, because I was sleeping on the floor and I don't know, two, maybe three in the morning, I woke up because I had to pee so bad, and when I started wandering around looking for the bathroom . . ." he paused to allow everyone to imagine how cute he must have been, wandering around looking for the bathroom, his fingers clenching his peter, "I looked over onto the couch and I saw some *movement*, you know, some *steady* movement. I mean, there they were, Katy and Palmer, just met each other at a gas station, and they were introducing themselves to each other, if you know what I mean . . ."

A huge, solo whoop echoed alone through the tent, and Marshall couldn't help but notice that Jimmy Ripley was the one clapping his hands behind it. Marshall took in the expressions on the faces of Katy's relatives. They all kept trying not to look at each other. A small murmur of chuckles tried to force its way through the crowd, as if this were everyday tomfoolery with the new generation. Marshall's gaze could not draw away from the grandparents, their mouths involuntarily opened, their eyes hastily blinking. Marshall wondered if any guests would mind if he ducked into the house, snatched his twelve-gauge, and idly pumped a few rounds into Tom. He imagined a scene where everybody watched the bloodshed, considered the crumpled body, and then felt themselves gratefully liberated to return to their splendid afternoon. A stillness descended on the celebration even as Palmer casually stepped up to the mike and moved his friend aside and the band whipped up a frantic rendition of a Seldom Scene tune. Marshall wandered beyond the confines of the tent, hoping the lovely day outside would rid the sour taste of Tom' s toast. Molly lurched up beside him and said, "That was awful."

"Worst thing I've ever heard," Marshall said. He looked at Molly, seeing her as separate from all that was happening for the first time that day. Her blonde hair held a luster he'd not noticed earlier, glistening in the sunlight. She'd changed into a cotton print sundress, which hung by spaghetti straps from her shoulders. He looked at her feet and saw that she wore sandals with heels—well one, because the other foot was wrapped and braced—and that the sandal somehow added to his impression that she was taller and slimmer than she'd ever been. Back at her face, he saw a gentle stillness that made him wonder what else he hadn't noticed about her. She'd seemed off-limits for so many of the years he'd known her, though standing here he couldn't imagine one realistic reason why.

"You look radiant," he said.

"I've been drinking," she said.

"OK," Marshall said, understanding that looking at her like this, beginning to feel that he liked everything he saw farther down the road, meant that he would have to try to get there on foot. Just for something different to say, he said, "So what are the odds Ripley and his buddies are going to, like, destroy something of mine?"

"Never know with them," Molly said. "I'd like to think they'd be on their best behavior, but they hate your ass."

"What is it you see in them?" Marshall asked.

"I don't see anything in them."

"Why do you want to be their friend?"

"I just don't like being an enemy," Molly said.

Then Marshall felt foolish. Oddly he wanted to take her hand, just hold it, and that made him feel even more foolish, so he said, "What a beautiful day for it."

"It was such a pretty ceremony. You did a great job."

"I didn't do anything," Marshall said, feeling oddly defensive.

"Don't be a punk," Molly said. A long pause followed during which Marshall knew what she was saying, but didn't agree.

"What is it about weddings that makes women look so beautiful?" When Marshall finished the question he found himself caught by Molly's gaze. He wanted just to stare, but couldn't, though he noticed that she had no problem looking at him without answering.

"It's not just women," Molly said.

"Jesus barefooted Christ, why didn't someone just tackle him?" Alton asked as he walked up.

"Yeah, it was awful," Molly said.

"The worst," Marshall said.

Now music fiddled through the air and the ching-ching rhythm of the mandolin strummed a gay counterpoint to the evening's long waning. People danced and a small knot of fishing guides collected and told lies. Marshall danced a slow tune with Molly, holding her in place and swaying back and forth because her ravaged ankle precluded real dancing. But he felt her breasts press against him, cones of warmth reaching into his chest. He felt a little like he was in a movie, as if he and Molly were featured in a star-crossed love affair, dancing before a crowd that understood their eventual demise. He wondered if he could talk her into hanging around until everyone left, maybe spending the night. He wondered if they could do that without Alton noticing.

When they were finished they returned to Alton, who stood and watched Amy Baine dancing with Shadford. Watching Shadford try to dance was horrible enough, and seeing Amy either enjoying or pretending to enjoy it was just devastating. Scotty the Wad sidled up and asked Marshall, "You ever think about selling this place?"

Marshall had never thought about selling the place primarily because he understood that his father had—but also because, of course, he didn't own it. Nevertheless he found it interesting to gauge how he felt, hearing somebody ask him about it. Particularly now, after he'd spent so much energy transforming the stream. And he recognized that this juxtaposition had the potential to send him on a comprehensive exploration of his thoughts about the matter if the person asking the question had not been Scotty the Wad. To Scotty, probing the notion of buying somebody's home out from under him was meant as a compliment, no matter how backhanded.

"Hey, what's the name of that dog your buddy Ripley brought?" Marshall asked in return.

"Buck."

"Buck?"

"I didn't name it."

"That dog has the biggest head I've ever seen."

"Pretty good duck dog," the Wad said. "But dumber than wood."

Daylight had bled out from the sky, leaving a translucent blue-purple ring around the horizon. Everything above was rushing toward starlight. The strings of lights inside the tent and lanterns staked around the yard blanked everything in the horizontal plane beyond them. When the food was all gone, Marshall went inside and pulled elk steaks from his fridge. He'd never been to a wedding where there was enough food and he'd defrosted all the elk steaks he had for just this reason. Back outside, on his way to the grill toting an armful of meat, Marshall felt a presence beside him and knew he wouldn't like it.

"So this is the wanna-be-famous Fly X Ranch," someone said. Marshall knew right away it was Jimmy Ripley. Marshall said nothing, kept moving. He'd never felt malevolence so tangibly, like a sour breath on his skin.

"I think your number's coming up," Ripley said.

"Maybe later," Marshall said, inviolate in his approach to the grill. "Got mouths to feed. No time for testosterone and adrenaline."

"Definitely later," Ripley said.

"Frig off," Marshall said. He nearly counted the beats until Ripley caught on.

"What did you just say?"

Marshall let a grin expose some teeth. He hurried off with the elk steaks, gave them to the caterers, and showed them where the open-pit grill was. He was helping lay fillets on the grill when Shadford wandered over and said, "You know I've been thinking . . . if you put up a guesthouse here, had a place for clients to stay, you could make a fortune."

"Every time I ever saw a guesthouse it had guests in it," Marshall said. Shadford was undoubtedly right for no other reason than, like Marshall's father only on a lesser scale, Shadford had a talent for appearing in situations where money was being made. Marshall mused about what would have become of him and Shadford had they remained friends. Maybe they would have been real players in their limited world, honchos of fly fishing. Friendship. Marshall couldn't manage a relationship that involved romantic love, but give him a friendship—even a bad one—and he'd hang on to that until the damned thing was kicked to death.

By now Shadford was staring into the shadows beyond the edge of the tent where the forms of people were visible primarily as movements—except for two figures who held perfectly still: Alton and Amy Baine, talking with their faces close together. Marshall couldn't help but notice that Alton looked as if she had just told him she was dyeing her hair red and hitting the road with a Motown cover band.

"I wonder when this bullshit is going to stop," Shadford said.

"Come on," Marshall said, "they've got a lot to talk about."

"What?" Shadford asked, standing with his slim hips thrust forward. Shadford had worn shorts and Marshall wondered if it was an effort to emphasize his thighs, which, at age forty-five, were remarkable, but also his best feature. The stance led in that direction. Marshall was not without sympathy for Shadford and his personal travails. When Marshall had first met him, Shadford was a plump man married to a pretty woman who ate antidepressants the way moviegoers paw popcorn—more a function of preoccupation than desire. She didn't, according to Shadford, enjoy sex, fishing, or any activity that required either gear or enthusiasm. She was happy when she could fly someplace and acquire something, a lifestyle that Shadford—newly minted successful small businessman with big American dreams—shambled right into for a while, until something went terribly wrong.

In the final six months of their marriage Shadford's wife slept with ten or a dozen different men. As more lurid details crept to light, people began to wonder how much Shadford's wife didn't like sex, versus how much she didn't like Shadford. Perhaps Shadford's infatuation with Amy Baine had to do more with long-lost innocence than last-chance prurience. Not that it wasn't nonetheless pathetic, but Marshall felt comforted by the organic teleology of the former assumption. Nobody likes to discover a pervert in his address book.

"Don't you feel the least bit guilty about it?" Marshall asked.

"About what?"

Marshall would have cared more about Shadford's blitheness had he not seen Molly, standing on the other side of the dance floor, also staring at Alton and Amy Baine in the darkness. Just then a cry rose from a few feet away, near the grill, then general laughter, followed by a voice that could have been vamping had it not been accompanied by a genuine animal yelp. Marshall focused in time to see Jimmy Ripley hauling his dog, the chocolate Lab, by the scruff of the neck toward the grill. The dog had an elk steak clamped firmly in its teeth. Although it seemed to have otherwise submitted to whatever disaster was at hand, the dog refused to unclamp the meat.

"Oh, hey, it's fine," Marshall called, rushing forward to redirect any rupture in the good cheer. "It's no big deal."

"Animal's gotta learn its place," Ripley said. Marshall was too far away to anticipate what happened next in time to stop it. Ripley lifted the dog in his arms against his chest. He grasped one of the dog's forepaws in his hand and pressed it against the black bars of the grill. Marshall could hear the dog's pad sizzle before he heard the squeal. Ripley managed to hold the writhing animal for ungodly seconds. The dog screamed as if it were being skinned alive. Marshall froze, seeing the hand pressing the dog's paw to the grill, smelling the burned flesh, then watching the dog twist free. The animal fell in a heap at Ripley's feet. Ripley's face held a triumphant grin, as if he'd taught everybody nearby a lesson he'd been holding secret for a long time. The dog cringed and limped in a tight circle at his feet, alternating between crying, licking its paw and looking up at Ripley for . . . for what? Deliverance? Forgiveness? What could make an animal look that way at a human that had treated it so horribly?

Marshall was moving forward then, among a converging crowd. His hands wanted Jimmy Ripley's throat, but he found himself jostled aside. People were shoving, as if an attempt to rearrange everybody's position might change the situation. Marshall scooped the dog's head in his arms, the animal's cries incessant. The burned foot extended away from Marshall's grasp, and the dog tried to lunge forward to lick it.

"Leave my dog alone," Ripley said.

"You don't have a dog anymore," Marshall said. He felt, despite the crowd that had gathered, Ripley tearing at his arms. The dog's struggles and Ripley's thrashing forced Marshall's utmost concentration just to hang on. He felt a looping punch ring against the top of his skull and another crash into his cheekbone. The dog's cries climbed even higher.

"Let go my fucking dog!"

Marshall wasn't letting go. He sensed more than saw Alton flying by him, and the fists stopped raining on his skull. He found himself in a calm space, although around him he sensed furor. He heard nothing beyond the howling of the dog.

Then he heard Alton yelling, "You're done! You're outta here!"

Marshall looked up to see a wall of men between him and the flailing Ripley. The mass tottered and staggered about a small area. Dean Stone, Tom the best man, and Scotty the Wad arrayed themselves beside Ripley in various positions of support against virtually every other able-bodied man in the place. Billy Mills looked nervous and tense, ready to smoke anybody he could sneak a sideways lick on. Katy's grandfather braced amid the bunch, a handful of Jimmy Ripley's shirt clenched in his fist. Marshall had no doubt the grandfather would take on anybody in the place, whereas Ripley was considering whether decking the old man would help his mission. Marshall saw

Alton striving for Ripley, his legs driving. Without any of them directly interceding, the various vectors of Dean Stone and Scotty the Wad, and even Palmer Tillotson, interfered with Alton's progress.

"Give me back my goddamned dog," Ripley said, spraying the words through gnashing teeth. The grandfather still held his shirt, but Ripley moved as if he were a free man. Marshall recognized a situation poised at the brink of disaster and understood his role in it.

Marshall stood with his knee bent so that he might keep his hand clasped to the dog's collar. The animal's keening seemed to reach an even higher pitch.

"Let me have him," Ripley said. Marshall understood he wasn't talking about the dog anymore.

"Let him go," Marshall said. He looked at the grandfather and was pleased to catch a sliver of approval before the man let go of Ripley's shirt. But none of that mattered. The minute Ripley swung free, Alton and, Marshall was surprised to see, Shadford, burst into his path.

"Get out of here!" Shadford yelled at Ripley. "Get out of here right now, before you get into trouble you can't get out of!"

Scotty the Wad and Dean Stone tugged at Ripley. Marshall could hear them saying things like, "Not here, man," and, "Another day, Jimmy. Another day, another place."

"I'm coming after my dog," Ripley roared.

Marshall stayed with the dog.

"Your ass is so fucking dead," Ripley shouted.

"Get out of here now and don't you ever come back," was the best Marshall could come up with. Later he would dream of all the good comebacks he could have voiced. In fact, for much of the rest of the evening, he would talk to people, yet find running through his mind a mantra of better things he could have said to Ripley. *I'll wipe you out. I'll beat you like an egg.* But, "Get out of here now and don't you ever come back?" *Shee-it.*

While Marshall took the dog in the house, cleaned the burn, and wrapped gauze around the foot, his other preoccupying thought was that, regardless of others' heroics, it was Shadford who had preempted the brawl. His advocacy had been enough to freeze Wad and Mills, and even Dean Stone. Ripley himself seemed cowed about taking shots that might land on Shadford's face. A silly reason to place respect, Marshall thought: a fly shop.

What he felt like next was a lot of drinking. But that, he understood as soon as the impulse struck him, would go badly in all regards.
In fact, even without booze the evening had already seemed to lose
focus, the events swirling in his short-term memory. There seemed like
something he had wanted to get back to, something he had wanted to
find out more about. But his attention was all swept away with caring
for the dog, and by the time he had the Labrador settled down and
comfortable, by the time he ventured back out into the night, guests
had dwindled. There remained few people he wanted to talk to. And
Molly was nowhere to be found.

Marshall sat on the porch, listening to disturbing news on the Montana
Public Radio evening edition: somebody had killed a wolf in the valley.
It had been the female, the wolf that had made such an epic journey to
this place, to find a mystery mate, to give birth to a litter of pups. Her
radio collar had been found in the West Fork River, cut cleanly. There
was no sign of the carcass, but Fish and Wildlife agents monitoring her
radio collar noted that the signals kept coming from the same place for
a day or two running. They moved in and found the collar, sliced neatly
by a sharp knife. On the radio, biologists were speculating about the
ability of the male wolf to raise the pups on his own.

Marshall's heart swelled and he actually thought he might cry.
Had he been so close, up on Hayden Peak, to the wolf that died? Was
it her footprint he had a plaster impression of curing in the barn? Nobody was speculating about who shot the wolf. Marshall wanted to
think: *Klingman.* On more than one occasion Marshall had been working outside late at night and heard rifle shots booming through the
darkness from the direction of Klingmans'. He assumed the Klingmans poached a deer or two in the winter—folk wisdom held that in
these parts more deer are killed by a .22 in the winter than a .30–06
in hunting season—and maybe an elk now and again. Marshall worried when he saw moose tracks.

It wasn't Bruce. Bruce didn't care much for hunting, thought it a
bit of extravagance. "I'll shoot an elk as soon as they start making
them with zippers," he'd heard Bruce once say. But Randy Klingman
imagined himself in a high-stakes game with wildlife law enforcement
officials, a sort of Robin Hoodish affair wherein Randy didn't redis-
tribute the wealth so much as simply display derring-do and uncanny

woodlore. That more than half the time law enforcement wasn't playing didn't seem to affect Randy's outlook or enthusiasm.

But the truth was the Klingmans weren't the only people in the valley who viewed fish and game laws as quaint suggestions. Nor were they the only wolf haters. In fact, Marshall might be the only pro-wolf faction around, and nearly anybody else in the valley could be suspect in the killing. The dog, Buck, came limp-trotting into the yard and something was wrong with his mouth. Marshall hadn't noticed the big chocolate Lab wandering off. In the few days since he'd taken the dog, Buck had generally refused to move anywhere but exactly where Marshall was about to step next. But clearly he had gone somewhere and now was back, skulking in from the direction of the river. His body posture announced he'd done something that would provoke consequences.

The dog's head seemed more red than chocolate and fringed with a strange white-gray mist. When he drew nearer Marshall saw rows of porcupine quills wagging with the dog's trot. Buck stopped at Marshall's feet, opened his mouth, and tried to gag out a ball of quills, but they were all firmly anchored in the muscle of his tongue. *Oh good Christ,* Marshall thought. His first reaction was to be furious, but one glance at the dog told him any act of punishment was already upstaged.

He looked at the dog and said, "You're one of those dumb bastards, aren't you?"

Buck turned his head sideways and peered up at him. Marshall fetched his Leatherman and used the wire cutters to clip the tip of each quill before using the pliers to grip them and yank. Clipping the quills allowed them to deflate, making them easier to remove, but still Marshall cringed as the dog's flesh stretched with the apex of each tug. Buck was a remarkably submissive patient, allowing Marshall to peel back his lips and dig at the spines wedged deep in the gums between his teeth. Each quill brought a welling of blood with it.

After an hour Marshall had to pause to stop his hands from shaking when he went to work on the tongue. He poured some water from the spigot into a bucket for Buck to lap at, though the quills in his tongue made it awkward. Then he got Buck down on the ground and knelt with a knee on either side of his head. Buck held his mouth open and breathed in a high whine while Marshall gripped the barbed tubes driven beneath the dog's tongue and ripped them out with quick, violent plucks. This was not Buck's first clambake, so to speak. Marshall wasn't able to get all of the quills—some broke off deep in Buck's gums and tongue—but at a certain point the dog's patience ran out and he wiggled free. He plunged his head in the water bucket and drank at length. Marshall rocked back on his heels and looked down the front of his blood-speckled self.

By the river the low sun lit the tops of cottonwoods and slid in among the heavy branches as they snaked through bustiers of leaves, while beneath the trees deep shadows began to run out into the meadows. Behind the nearest ridgetop the light shone pale and watery blue through a picket fence of silhouetted pine trees. The moment he spotted splotches of color moving against the yellowing grass across the river an adrenaline jag spiked his chest. Nobody was scheduled to fish that day. It was about eight o'clock, just in time for the evening hatch.

Marshall backed his truck from the garage shed, then led the dog in, and shut the door. He drove to the spring creek parking area, got out, and strode through the field. Long before he reached the pond, Marshall walked up on the first interloper, another in the endless streams of Mr. Johnsons. Except this one was a Japanese man. He seemed to be done fishing where he'd been and was starting to head in the same general direction as Marshall. "Uh, excuse me," Marshall said, "can you tell me who booked you onto this stream?"

"Oh," the man said, "Mr. Billy did."

"Mr. Billy," Marshall said.

"Right," the man said. His speech was truly Japanese rather than Japanese-American. "Mr. Billy Mills. He's only up the stream. From the Fly Guys fly-fishing store in Missoula? It's OK. You only have to call the main house and tell the man you are going fishing."

"Really?" Marshall said. They were walking along now, side by side.

"Yes. But the number of fishermen is limited. And it costs money. One hundred dollars."

"A hundred bucks?" Marshall asked. *A hundred bucks?* "Bah. Highway robbery."

"You only paying for the most best fishing," the man said. They passed a second man, also Japanese, who stepped away from the creek and fell in a little behind them, which made Marshall paranoid.

He wandered into Billy Mills, crouched on his knees, waving his rod and tossing a fly out into a long run. A third Japanese Mr. Johnson stood back, watching. Marshall observed: here was Billy Mills, with people who were clearly clients. Had Shadrat given Mills a guide's license, too? Was there no end to this travesty? Mills's previous fishing experience, as far as anybody knew, consisted wholly of purse-seining for shrimp out of Galveston, Texas. Mills had admitted he was "all brand new to this trout-fishing business" when he had applied for the Fly Guys clerk job the summer before.

"Howdy, Bill," Marshall said. When Mills's head turned, Marshall beamed a false grin and perked his eyebrows. "Came to meet your clients."

"Oh, yeah, hey, this is the guy I was telling you about," Mills called up to the three other men, who had collected in a loose knot behind Marshall. Mills was rising and moving up the bank toward them and saying, "He built this whole stream."

Marshall blanched at the sound of that. He turned, though, to shake hands with the men, who introduced themselves. Marshall heard: Bill Johnson. Nice to meet you, Bill Johnson. The first guy he'd talked to had no idea what to say and didn't even offer a name.

Mills said, "I thought you were going to be at that whirling disease meeting in Great Falls or I would have phoned ahead."

"Yeah, I decided not to go," Marshall said. "So you're guiding now?"

Mills's face colored. "These guys are friends of mine. I had the afternoon off, thought I'd bring them out here and show them your place." He made it sound like he'd done Marshall a favor.

Marshall twisted toward the collected Johnsons. "Really? You guys go to school together or what? How long have you known Bill?"

"We met him in the Fly Guys fishing store," one of the men said.

"They just dropped into town," Mills hastened, "and we met up at the shop and I told them about your slammin' creek. They were pumped to come fish it." Marshall noticed that Mills had taken to smiling viciously, as if to say, *you wouldn't dare.* He wondered if Mills had noticed his jangled condition and felt emboldened. Marshall felt emboldened himself, more by meanness and the fact that his chest, arms, and legs were covered in blood spatters. But he understood how tricky this could get.

"Actually, we were thinking about naming it that—Slammin' Creek," Marshall said. "So this isn't an actual guided trip? What a charming turn of events for you all." He rocked back on his heels and surveyed the three men. They all looked primarily bamboozled. "I'm glad you could get some fishing in together with Bill. Hope you find the place to your liking. You want to just settle up now?" The last he directed suddenly at Mills.

"Uh . . ." Mills was hit. His glance flitted all over. "Uh, we thought we'd settle up on the way out," he mumbled.

"Bill, I wish I could accommodate that." Marshall was positively beaming now, and nodding back and forth between the Johnsons and Mills. "I really do. But today, of all days, I'm probably not going to be around later. Any other day, hey, no problem. But tonight, see . . . so it's sixty dollars each." He let a smile press into his lips, but squelched it before teeth were bared. Marshall waited a long beat before he heard what he was waiting for. One of the men, muttered, "Sixty?"

Mills moved between him and the other men, casting an eye-slap at Marshall. "Uh, they were all going to write a check to me and then I was going to cash out and pay you."

That was when Marshall fully understood just who was being scammed. Not only had Mills boosted the fee to a hundred dollars, he hadn't planned on running them through either Marshall's or the Fly Guys' books. Mills stood to pocket the whole shebang. Marshall chuckled to himself. Rage was radiating from Mills. Marshall assumed there would be some interpersonal consequences farther down the pike, but standing in the sunny summer evening, he knew Shadrat and Mills would wind up clawing each other over the short end of this stick.

"I wish that would work out," Marshall said. "I really do."

Then Mills said, "Dude, killer thing is, I think you've got a bigger problem up the creek."

Marshall tilted back in his newfound ease. "Really? What's that?"

"There's some guys up at your pond fishing with worms," Mills seemed back on top of his game, smiling spite. "They're whackin' and stackin' 'em. I put the quiz to them, but one of them said he was your neighbor and it was no big. Hey, what'd I know?"

"That's a question you could spend some time delving into, Billy," Marshall said. Addressing the Johnsons while he collected the cash from one of them, he added, "Gentlemen, this is so kind of you, coming out here today. I sure hope you get a chance to tell Mr. Shadford down at Fly Guys what a fine time you've had. It helps me tremendously if you can stop on in there before you leave town and tell him personally what a great time you had with Billy, here. If you can't stop in be sure to give Mr. Shadford a call, or drop him a letter. He loves to hear it from the source. Now I've got to attend to this other thing."

He watched Mills's grin go sheepish and would have liked very much to revel in that, but it made not a splash in the hollow pit dropping through the bottom of his stomach. Instead, moving away, upstream, he exercised extreme concentration in an effort not to dash to the pond. As soon as he could flick a glance over his shoulder and see he was beyond the realm of Mills's dupes, Marshall broke into a gallop. He stopped running a hundred yards or so before he broke over the embankment and into view of the pond. It would probably look foolish to come sprinting up. You come blasting out of the weeds onto somebody and instantly there's the question of *What next?* Too, it would be nice to be able to breathe.

Before him spread a cozy tableau: three men slouched in the waning daylight, a jeans-and-T-shirt crowd, work boots splashed with mud. Angling. Two of them sat near a red Igloo cooler that stood in an inch or so of water at the pond's edge. All of the men had arranged themselves so as to dangle their feet in the pond's water. They kicked back in the slanting sunshine, casually regarding red-and-white bobbers out on the pond. Randy Klingman had brought a lawn chair for his recline. Behind them a scattering of crushed aluminum cans winked on the grass. As Marshall drew closer, he spotted near Randy's chair a pile of about a dozen fish heads, dark across the noses but bright white and florid pink where the flesh had been severed.

When Marshall's approach was brought to his attention, Randy twisted in his chair and stared for a moment as if thinking to himself: *what a pleasant surprise!* Marshall strode up to Randy, looked at the fish heads and nearly cried. They had been beautiful fish and some of the pond's largest. Marshall made a quick take of the two men Randy had with him. They were much like Randy: ruddy and ragged and in need of showers, also swaggering and bulletproof. They'd come to watch a fistfight.

"Tate, I had no idea the fishing over here was so goddamned good!" Randy said. "Kyle told me, but shit, I didn't expect this." He gestured to the fish heads.

"I think you better leave my property," Marshall said. His vision threatened to dissolve in a mucky cloud of rage. Marshall thought: *cool as jelly*.

"Hey now, Marshall, we're just using that stream access law you were telling me about the last time. Waded along the river and then made a left turn right up the creek, stayed between the banks all the way," Randy said. Marshall could tell he'd been wanting to say that for some while. "I'm telling you, I don't know why you wave them fly poles around all the time. These fishies are starving for nightcrawlers."

Marshall snatched the fishing rod from Randy's grip and in a looping continuation of the movement grasped the rod with both hands and brought it down over his knee. But the rod whipped and didn't snap and then that was just embarrassing. Marshall opted not to try again. He heard a chuckle bounce back and forth between the two bystanders. Meanwhile Randy had come to his feet.

"What are you doing with my rod?" Randy asked.

Marshall tossed the rod into the deep part of the pond. Randy came at him. Marshall saw a panel of black flash on and off across the entirety of his vision. He felt an impact on the side of his face and, in a process similar to what happens when you stove your finger, instantly realized that there would be pain involved, though it hadn't come yet. There may have been other impacts. When everything settled down, Marshall found himself on his back in the grass. He propped himself on one elbow and hurled a pointing finger in a general direction. "Get out!"

"I've got a right to fish here," Randy said. "You told me about it yourself. Stream Access Law."

Marshall pulled his feet under his buttocks and stood on them. He could see that the two companions were grinning like mad despots. They were pretty certain they'd pulled off a marvelous sneak-job. They were thinking they were some real rascals.

"Don't make me come at you again," Randy said.

"Did you actually read the Stream Access Law, Randy?" Marshall asked, his lips feeling too big. He experienced a strange sympathy for the man, the way a teacher wants badly for an idiot child to learn something. "It doesn't apply to springs. It very specifically cites waterways with historical usage and navigation. The question you'll want to be asking yourself is, how could there be a history of usage and navigation on this creek if it wasn't even here two years ago?"

"See, you're just making shit up now because you know I'm right this time," Randy said, leveling an index finger at Marshall and squinting to sight down it. "You're mad because I have every legal right to chop up your precious little fishies."

"Either of you other dipshits want to chime in here?" Marshall asked the other two. He felt fairly bold now. He knew either the punching was over or he would get his ass thoroughly thrashed. But the first part didn't hurt much—yet—and he was a lot less scared now that it had happened. "Well then, here's the deal: you just assaulted me on top of which you're trespassing, which makes me feel real confident about how a visit from the sheriff might turn out. You can wait for the deputy here or go on home and change into something comfortable for your sleepover down in Missoula."

"You rotten little piece of shit—" Randy started.

"Wait now one minute, Klingman," one of Randy's companions said. "You said this was a no-brainer."

From the mouths of babes, Marshall thought. He lifted his chin at Randy and said, "Your daddy is going to be so proud of you."

Marshall strode over the field toward his rig, not paying attention to what Randy and his gang were doing, but he knew they'd be on the skedaddle. He could hear Randy screaming, "We're gonna shut your ass down!" but it sounded shrill. Marshall's heart wasn't really in it anymore, either. He had no intention of pressing charges. He was right about the access law. He could have Randy hauled to the hoosegow for the assault, but that would just ratchet everything up one notch higher. In terms of the blows to the head, some things you had to take. A fairly good case could be made that he had it coming, and anyway, one didn't run and cry help against Randy Klingman. One let it be known that one could take it and whatever else.

Marshall looked up at the bench to the west, gold in the early August evening. He saw the pine-clad ridges above it. Beyond them, though he couldn't see from this perspective, he knew that mountains jutted from the forest like the skeleton of some dead beast piled in a mossy grove. Everything around him rose so far above his head. Blood whapped in the swelling skin beside his eye socket.

He could call the sheriff, have him come up just to generate a little dinner table conversation at the Klingman household. But—the tangled web. Marshall was mainly concerned that Randy didn't try that stunt again. He didn't know how many insurgencies the pond could take. There had been at least ten heads in the pile. He knew that in the morning, before any clients arrived, he would have to go and clean the mess up. He should do it now, but he feared he would break into tears. Two had been big browns. A couple looked like pure cutthroats. In the energy suck created by the dissolution of the violence, Marshall felt like he might cry over those fish. Or maybe it was what happened with Molly and that aftermath, because as right as everything seemed to be going with the spring creek, his plans and their fruition, there was always something else going just as wrong. Thirty-three years old and he might just sit in the field where the russet-tipped brome reached over his head and pull his hands through his hair and cry. Yes. All those beautiful fish.

There was no way Marshall could scoop up half a million dollars, but he was resigned to the actuality that he'd have to shell out for legal advice to figure out how to avoid it. He did not want to be afforded an opportunity to sit down with his neighbors under the auspices of an authoritative figure and settle their water rights dispute. Rather, he hoped there was some legal trickeration he could deploy to get a retroactive water right filed and end-run the opposition. There was just the matter of tapping into the right legal mind. While the early season had exceeded his expectations in terms of paying visitors to his spring creek, now in the doldrums of summer people were returning to their familiar waters. Attendance, while still regular, was not on pace to provide windfall.

Marshall was a little pissed off that he'd let himself buy into the early giddy success. He supposed there was a "business" name for what he was learning: cash flow or income cycles, some such. Didn't matter. At the moment, a thorough scan of his receipts and due bills left him facing a choice. He could (a) skip the insurance premium payment, (b) leap into the water rights mess without legal advice, or (c) not eat for a while.

He concocted a compromise in which he would put off an insurance premium until the last possible moment, hoping for a windfall, and, in combination, would not eat for a while. Why, he wondered, were Klingmans taking so long to file a claim? Stuffing all their jacks in their boxes, no doubt. This was the state of his thinking when he checked the mail and thought longingly about breakfast, and the very act of longing made him remember Molly at the wedding. He had never seen her look so lovely. The sad part was, the very best he had ever seen her look was when she stood at the edge of the light from the tent and watched Alton discuss something passionately with Amy Baine. It was the disappointment, Marshall thought, that made her so beautiful.

Affairs of the heart added to money trouble, he thought: *the root causes of 95 percent of the criminal acts in the republic.* Within the hour, the dog erupted in frenzied barking, startling Marshall, who was used to long stretches of silences interrupted by nothing. But now he had a dog living with him, a dog with a bandaged and crippled front left foot, and a scab-splattered muzzle. The dog suddenly leaped onto the couch and, facing the window that overlooked the driveway, tilted his head back and bowweled out a long series of strained barking sounds. A few minutes later Shadford arrived with a group of fifteen clients in two vans. Part of Marshall thought: *Wow! Here's $900, minus whatever 15 percent is! Standing in the yard in front of my house like they were rubbed from a lamp!* Whereas another part of him flared. *Whatever happened to the six-rods-a-day limit?* And so there was a neat little clash between ethics and economics.

On three legs the dog danced around the people who poured from the vans, his tail wagging hard enough that he staggered to not fall over. The vet had told Marshall that the dog might never be able to place its weight on that foot again, that the burns had been deep enough to do serious nerve damage. It was all wait and see. Marshall sized up the crowd, a tourist group from Toledo, and counted not an angler among them. He doubted they could do much damage to his creek, but that was not the point. The point was two other gentlemen from Duluth had booked for the morning and they deserved the aesthetic experience that only limited access could provide. It was what they paid for. They did not deserve fifteen screaming meemies, thrashing the water and terrorizing its denizens. And yet—nine hundred lamp-rubbed dollars! Maybe he could offer the Duluth boys another day—one all to themselves.

But then here was Shadford, showing up unannounced with an overbooking, putting Marshall on the spot in front of fifteen Toledans who probably sold insurance. Scotty the Wad had come along, driving the second van. As Marshall pondered and Shadford stood before him with a devious glint in his thin-man's eye, this very group of Rotarian souls clustered on the yard, craning to peer at the massive log structure of the ranch house, pointing at flickers and mountain bluebirds on the fence posts, asking if they could see the river from here, and were there any grizzly bears? Though raised on *Gentle Ben* and *Grizzly Adams*, everybody feared the griz.

"Talk to you over here a sec?" Marshall said. Shadford followed him a few steps away. Marshall said, "What's this your idea of?"

"Your buddy Alton's been calling in sick on me," Shadford said. "But there are persistent rumors of him guiding someone else's clients on the river."

"What that has to do with this situation plumb escapes me," Marshall said. "Even if Alton had come to work this morning, he could take two of these folks for a boat ride, which would make two less people in your van, or thirteen—and yet the limit here has been six all summer long."

"There's no point in being rigid just because you know how," Shadford said. "Got to learn the pivot. All the good big men learn the pivot."

"That's a sports metaphor?" Staring at Shadford, straining not to just shoot the moon and tell Shadford to go hump a goat, an inspiration came to Marshall: live to fight another day. "Tell you what we're gonna do," Marshall said. "You're going to take exactly eight of those folks down to the river. There's over two miles of river on the place and then all that up above if you stay in the banks. The seven others can fish the creek."

"I think they'd all like to—"

"And tortured souls want out of hell. Bottom line is, I have other folks," Marshall said, "It's a decent compromise and the best you're gonna get given the carnival you've trotted out here."

"Come on, Marsh. To be honest with you, it's getting so since we've started doing business together we're not even treating each other like friends anymore."

"I'm not sure we ever were friends." Both Shadford and Marshall took a beat to let that sink in, each in his own way as shocked that it found air. Then Marshall glanced up to see Daisy Klingman behind the wheel of a pickup bouncing down the drive.

"Well—" Shadford said.

"Right-o," Marshall said, and headed back across the grass toward the knot of would-be anglers and asked them if they could please lay out on the grass all the gear they intended to use. Daisy drove up onto the lawn but slid out of the pickup in an entrance much less dramatic than her usual fare. She twirled the keys to the rig absently around her index finger, leaned against the truck to assess the situation. Marshall found himself picking up a cheap thrill out of the danger she always brought with her.

"What's with the gear inspection?" Shadford was asking. He was holding in the atmosphere, like a raven. Marshall watched him visually cruise Daisy. Marshall walked over to her. She looked slightly abashed and, with that revelation of human decency, infinitely more alluring even than usual.

"Good morning, beautiful," Marshall said.

"What's with the sugar?"

"More flies."

"Keep it up," she said.

The dog trotted over and planted his nose in Daisy's crotch. She nonchalantly pushed it away, but gave Marshall a "what's this?" look.

"Got me a new dog," Marshall said. "Gonna teach it some old tricks."

"It's already learned your best one."

Marshall wrapped his hand in the dog's scruff and with Daisy walked him over the lawn toward the house. He led the dog into the house, reached to a shelf just inside the door, and collected an armful of squirt bottles, which he took back across the lawn to Shadford. "Spray everything," Marshall said. Shadford started to argue, but Marshall explained that he'd been to four whirling disease meetings around the state this summer. He wasn't taking any chances and was brooking no bullshit about it. "It's just a mild solution of denatured alcohol diluted with distilled water," Marshall said.

"Bad PR is what it is," Shadford said.

Marshall walked back to the house where Daisy stood just outside the door. He hooked his head for her to come inside. He held the door open and let her walk in front of him. Marshall stuck his head outside the door and yelled, "Shadford! Eight and seven! I'm counting!"

Gliding onto Marshall's couch, Daisy's posture was more tired than most days. There was her usual brashness, but it seemed hanging by its last pins. It left her with a ragged beauty, and, not fearing this, Marshall sat beside her on the couch.

"Little party this morning?" she said.

"More like a disagreement in principle," Marshall said.

"You seem to have those with everybody." Which was a concept that might not have always registered, but was also something he didn't need to grapple with in public. "What's today's?"

"Oh, my allegedly good buddy Shadford brought out about twice as many people as I allow."

"Tell him to pound sand," Daisy said.

"Problem is I'm too friendly."

"Well, you know us Klingmans," Daisy said. "Where there's a will, we'll make dead people."

"Is that what you're here about? That Klingman battlin' spirit?"

"They don't know I came," Daisy said, to get that out of the way. "Look, Randy did something stupid and that's what he does best. But everybody's a little scared now. Well, Dad's ape-shit. Randy's figuring this whole jail thing could turn into a bummer deal."

Marshall had never had any real intention of pressing charges. The Klingmans couldn't have known that, but still, how much of Randy was ulterior motive, stacked up against just plain excuse? "You remember how it was?" he asked. "Jail?"

"It wasn't so bad. But that was just the one and only time for me. Randy's got some misdemeanor assaults. Another one could turn the wrong judge into misunderstanding his unique sense of joie de vivre," Daisy said. She said *joy de veever*, though he knew she understood how it was pronounced.

"So you hustled on down here to try to take my mind off the whole shebang," Marshall said.

Daisy pressed both her fists into the couch cushions beside her and glared at him. "You've been a lot of things to me, but you've never been cruel."

He knew what she meant. They'd gone back and forth. She'd never been a real option except inasmuch as she always was. He thought an apology would be cheap.

"Do you really think I'd put Randy in jail?" he asked.

"I didn't used to." She stood with a tired grace he would have never guessed she could put together, and walked across the room. It made him wonder just what he had done to her, or her family. She stood staring out the window toward the river, back to him, fingers wrapped around her triceps. Her hair tumbled down her back like a wild animal.

"I didn't call the cops when it happened. Why would I do it now?" Marshall said. He took that moment to peek out the window and saw that Shadford had all of his people loaded into their vans. It seemed sudden. Marshall glanced around for the spray bottles. He saw them standing on the gravel of the drive on the edge of the lawn. Even from the distance he could see they were all completely full. Daisy turned around when the screen door slammed.

"Hey hey hey hey!" Marshall ran across the yard screaming and waving his arms at the vans. Shadford sat in the passenger seat of one and Scotty the Wad navigated for the other. Marshall aimed for Scotty's van, which was in the lead. He let the heel of his hand thump against its front and held his other hand up to the windshield. Scotty halted and Marshall moved back to Shadford's van.

"I thought I said spray everything," Marshall said.

"Oh, phhhfft," Shadford said. "It's almost all rental gear from the shop."

"I don't care," Marshall said. He felt the bitterness he had wanted to direct toward Daisy now find its stride. "Spray everything."

"That's crazy. We don't have a problem here," Shadford said.

"A problem with what?" the driver asked. Scotty the Wad had left his van and leaned in to hear from behind.

"We're about to have a problem here," Marshall said. "Scotty, get all your people's gear out and spray it with those bottles. It's either that or no fishie."

"What are we spraying for?" the Rotarian behind the wheel asked.

"You're making something out of nothing," Shadford said.

"You're making yourself unwelcome," Marshall said.

"Hey, hey," Shadford said, starting to haul on the door latch in an attempt to get out. "What's wrong with you? There's no need to make a scene about this."

"Except here we are, in the middle of a scene. And I happen to know how this one turns out: you spray that gear or you don't fish here," Marshall said. He aimed at the van and said, "Folks, I have to ask you to spray your gear purely as a precaution in the unlikely event that any of this stuff has been exposed to whirling disease."

"What the hell did you have to say that for," Shadford spit. He was hot now, and he forgot to get his tone low enough.

"This is the thing I was telling you about," somebody deep inside the van said, and there followed a stir. "I read about it," one of the men said. "It's a worm that's killing all the fish. It eats their head and makes them swirl around until they get too dizzy to eat." He seemed in danger of pronouncing everything he thought he knew about whirling disease.

Marshall put a stop to it. "Yes, well, no matter what you've heard, most of what is knowable remains unknown in this case. Lots of the rest is conjecture and imagination. But I'd like to take no chances. I've got an extremely pristine piece of water, as you all will see. And, in an effort to keep it that way, I'd like you all to squirt your gear. That includes any footwear you may intend to use while fishing. It's all purely precautionary. I apologize for the inconvenience, too."

The van's side door rolled open. Scotty the Wad's head tilted back and he trudged off to his van to announce the change in protocol. Shadford stomped a few yards out into the field grass and seemed to be waiting for Marshall to join him. Marshall only stared and shook his head. He stuck around until the gear spraying had begun, then sidled up to Scotty the Wad. "No more than seven on the spring at a time, OK? I'm trusting you because . . . well, because you're the guy I trust here. OK? I'm coming over to count."

"Sure. Hey, nice job pissing off Jimmy at the wedding. First you steal his oars, then you steal his dog," Scotty said. He sort of laughed.

"What oars?" Marshall said.

"They're looking to hang you out to dry, man. And he doesn't fight fair. I'm just warning you."

"For now can we just deal with this fiasco? You can count to seven, right?"

"Watch your ass with those guys," Scotty said. "I'm being serious."

Marshall chose to ignore the fuming Shadrat standing on his lawn and stalked back to the house. He walked in to find Daisy returned to the couch, her head turned away from the door. When he walked through she looked at him and she was crying, or had just stopped. He thought: *Oh Jesus.*

This was honest crying, not the tortured performance she sometimes staged to win a capitulation. This kind of crying rinsed the bravura from her and let Marshall see in her downturned mouth and her furrowed eyes all the doubt and hopeless fear of the little girl he had known so many years ago. Of course he'd seen none of that then. He recognized an anger that gnawed at her better wishes, eventually pulling the rug out from under her most warmhearted gestures. Marshall knew he was deep-down mad about some things, but that most of his anger came from not having the guts to face up. He couldn't even touch the undercurrents rending Daisy.

"Your new dog puked on the floor," Daisy said. She scooped at her eyes with her fingertips.

"You're kidding."

Daisy pointed with her chin to a pile of half-digested dog food on the carpet beside the couch. White shards of bone stuck up from the babyshit yellow pile. Buck stood across the room, his head lowered almost to his feet.

"He looks so sad," Daisy said.

Marshall looked at the dog, which seemed to shrivel under his gaze. "Aw, buddy," he said. Marshall crossed the room and petted the dog, which lowered himself to his elbows and twisted his head under Marshall's lowering hand.

Marshall said, "It's OK. You're fine. You feeling OK? You're fine," and petted the dog until the dog stopped licking at his hands. To Daisy he said, "He just doesn't know it's OK to be sick."

Marshall hurried into the kitchen and returned with a roll of paper towels and the plastic garbage bag from the kitchen trash can. He mopped at the puke, feeling its warmth seeping through the paper towels into his palm. Daisy watched him without commenting and when he sneaked a glance he saw that she was staring at him just for someplace to rest her eyes. He stuffed the mess into the garbage bag. On his way back into the kitchen he looked at Daisy and said, "You want a drink?"

"*Do I want a drink?*"

"If I were smart I'd just shut up."

"That's why you never do."

He guessed she wanted him to go to her, and he guessed he didn't really want that, but he knew he would. He had known the moment she turned her head and looked at him with the tear tracks over her cheeks that she'd end up in his arms. Actually he assumed they'd end up in bed. But Daisy wanted to say things.

"Why does this never end?" She stressed never, as if she'd all along expected some end to be inevitable.

"I don't know what to say."

"I try not to do this, but you're so . . . damned . . . *available*."

Marshall was crestfallen. For years he had thought that was exactly how he felt about her. He'd coddled that simple tenet as his excuse for so long. And now she'd said it out loud first. He held still a moment. Then he said, "Maybe I'll have one of those much ballyhooed drinks."

"It's nine o'clock in the morning," Daisy said.

"The o'clock didn't seem to be an issue last time we had a drink at your house," Marshall said. He walked into the kitchen, opened the refrigerator and cracked a beer.

"It had been a while," Daisy said when he came back. Her crying had transformed her face into a terrible pout. "Plus you were pissing me off."

"Huh." Marshall looked outside at the cottonwoods like a series of green fountains along the river. In the sky clouds in ranges dwarfed the mountains below. "Why'd you quit fishing?"

"I didn't quit," Daisy said. "Nobody takes me."

"You could go by yourself."

"That was never what I liked about it."

Marshall stepped beside her and put his hand on her hair. He gathered the curls in his hand and squeezed them in his fist, reminded of how her hair seemed to spring back against his hand. He used to do that all the time. He remembered driving up the Forest Service road with the world closed down by pine trees to the strip of dusty tan road in front of them and the near lodgepole trunks, so many so close together as to form a green-black stockade at eye level. If Daisy wasn't feeling bratty, she might slide over and sit beside him on the pickup's bench seat, and he would squeeze hanks of her hair, feel it spring back against his palm. Back in Rhode Island, at boarding school, before it ever happened, he dreamed of driving around in a pickup truck with Daisy scooted over beside him. Then it came true. Then what? Then so many things. Then this. He sat down beside her on the couch, calmly now, and spoke to her as if she were someone he spoke to every day.

"Do you remember your Crazy Uncle Bud?" Marshall asked. He set the open but untasted beer down on a table beside the couch.

"What about him?"

"Well, that. What do you remember about him?"

"He's my dad's uncle, not mine," Daisy said. She seemed calmed, but inches away from another outburst, like a wild-eyed colt temporarily at bay. "I don't remember him well. He was ugly, I remember that. He was a tough old cod. We figured nobody was ever going to get anything he put together. That's why they tried to have him . . . well, that's why nobody could believe he wanted to sell the place to your dad."

"I never saw his place before we built this house," Marshall said.

"Oh, Bud lived in the house that was here forever, not much better than a homestead. Electricity was the end of his world, everyone said." Daisy's affect was as flat as if she were detailing the events of a dull day. "I do remember one time he showed up at the house, he must have been in his sixties or seventies, and he couldn't walk. Dad asked him what was wrong and he said his toe was all stove up, so they had a look. Dad said, 'Christ, man, you're going to lose your foot.' It was just an ingrown toenail, but it had been abcessing for weeks. They decided to have some surgery in the kitchen. Real cowboys, you know. Dad lit up the old gas burner on the stove and roasted the blade of a steak knife till it glowed. This was after they opened a bottle of whiskey. They wanted Dad's brother Hank to help hold Bud down, but Hank said, 'I can take a gallon of pus out of a horse's ass, but just show me one minute of that and I'm throwing up.' So Hank had to drink as much whiskey as Bud. I had to go outside and get a nice thick stick and clean the bark off, and Bud lay on the floor and put the stick in his mouth. Hank held his arms down and Dad sat on his legs and sliced open the toe and dug the toenail out. It wasn't that easy. There was screaming and twisting. I had to keep taking the knife over to the stove top, to keep it sterile, Dad said. I was just a little girl. Talk about your bad smell. Shit, it was awful." She breathed more easily the more she talked. Her nostrils lost their flare.

"So he owned just the three sections we bought?" Marshall asked, wanting to keep her going.

"He owned these three sections plus the section that those Ballou people bought. I think four sections altogether, plus the odds and ends. He was the one that dynamited that old bridge upstream because he thought somebody could run his cows across and back into those Forestry Service roads and disappear them. He had a son that was a skydiver. The son—Jerry, his name was—he was in the Marines and then when he got out he'd do that trick stuff at air shows. He was over at the Livingston rodeo, was going to parachute into the arena to start off the show with a bang, he and five other guys. His chute never opened. But he did fall right into the arena. They said he hit so hard he bounced three times. Right after that is when Bud put the ranch up for sale, and then along came you handsome Tates. The rest, as they say, is conjecture and imagination."

"Nobody says that," Marshall said. It saddened him that she could be so flip about it if only because he never could. She had a connection to this place that he realized all the digging around and moving of water still had not granted him, the kind of connection you can play fast and loose with because, as cheaply as you treat it, it never plays out. If he had something like that, he realized, it would be his most prized possession.

"You just said it outside," she said. " I heard you."

"I thought you were busy in here, seething and hating me and whatnot," Marshall said. He smiled and she smiled back at him a little, then moved onto him so that her cheek pressed against his shoulder, and that fragrant bouquet of hair bloomed beneath his nose.

"There are so many ways I feel about you," Daisy said. Her voice seemed far away, as if he were hearing her through his chest. "But none of them are really hate. And you know it."

"I know," Marshall said.

In this way they came to the part where they were bound to end up in bed. Inevitably, but with a pace that allowed them to think it wasn't really happening until it already had started, they made love. When they finished she lay beside him on the bed. A column of sunlight angled through the window, glistening in her hair. Marshall touched her shoulder, ran his finger down the bumps of her spine. He saw on her shoulder two faint scars and remembered how she had been standing beside the corral when a horse bit her. She'd been nine or ten years old, and she'd turned to sneer at him about something. The horse reached over the rail and nipped at her shirt. It was a charming mannerism of this particular horse, but this time it bit too deeply and crunched into her skin. Now the scar was barely visible, a pale oval, like residue from a pair of lips.

How, Marshall wondered, could this be here, this wanting and the finding . . . how could this be here now that there was his new sense of Molly? He doubted love would be so duplicitous, or so obtuse. He should know something by now. Just look at him.

BAETIS

Marshall, Alton, and Molly had been drinking at the Rhino bar for a long time before the subject of fishing came up. Actually, none of them were drinking much. Marshall mused and carefully measured the rate at which he sipped his beer, the first he'd allowed himself in public since he'd decided to cool the drinking jags. Alton jabbered and Molly seemed on pins and needles, which was what Marshall found himself musing about. Fishing had come up right away, of course, long enough for them all to concur that through separate experience their mutual conclusions were the same. Alton veered into complaining about Fly Guys and Molly bitched about rowing with her foot still tender, and Marshall started, for the umpteenth time, talking about building himself a drift boat during the off-season, none of which they considered talking about fishing. That was business. Until Alton mentioned trying to get down to the Big Hole.

"Last fall I moved a fish in that river that scared me it was so big," Alton said. "I had on this Pepperoni Yuk Bug, and I missed a strike on a smaller fish so I was just sort of sweeping the rod to make another cast and the fly was kind of skittering along the surface, and this monster brown rolled up. Scared the shit out of me."

"How big?" Molly asked.

"I don't know. I botched it. Saw the fish coming and got all excited and yanked the fly away before he could get his mouth on it. But this fish was huge."

"Pepperoni Yuk Bug?" Marshall asked. "Where do you come up with these things?"

"It was fall. The browns were moving. Shit works, man," Alton said.

"Is this a plastic fly like your Skwala bugs?"

"Those are foam."

"It's plastic," Marshall said. "You might as well pitch crank baits."

Molly watched with little real interest. Alton had stepped into his cocky rooster stance—chest out, arms pulled back, fists gripped; a cartoon banty man. Marshall was willing to go with this, as indicated by the catty tone with which he had spat out "crank baits." Molly knew the routine. They'd start playfully insulting each other, challenging relative skills. Alton might even slap Marshall in the head eventually. It was a strange turn of events, this return to normalcy, and for a moment of suspended time, Molly didn't care that she was involved with both of these men in a way that could only turn out badly. For the moment they were all getting along as swimmingly as she thought they could.

"Need I say the North Fork of the Blackfoot? Last July?" Alton said, "Twenty-nine-inch bull trout, and you caught—?"

"You caught one fish," Marshall said.

"One monster fish," Alton said. "And when was the last time you caught a twenty-nine-incher in a stream?"

"I'm just going to say Happy Bank, August, caddis. That's all I'm going to say," Marshall said. "Oh, and also this: zero."

Molly laughed, recognizing the reference immediately. On a rare day that all three of them had off the previous summer, they'd floated the lower Clark Fork between Huson and Petty Creek. Nearing the end of the evening a blizzard of caddis erupted from the willows along the river's left bank. The Happy Bank on a summer evening was bread and butter, if you could talk clients into staying on the river that late. Caddis swarmed over the water, weaving wild dances into a moiling blanket inches above the river's darkening surface. At times you breathed with your mouth closed or sucked bugs. Trout heads tipped up behind every rock. But every time Alton cast, a fish rose just before his fly hit the water. It was all fluke. At one point he cast a fly and bounced it off the head of a fish rolling up to eat a natural.

"Name the river, the stretch, and the day, and we'll go head to head any time," Alton said to Marshall.

"Do I get to name the fly, or are you going to throw plastic shit?" Marshall asked.

"I'll fish you on dries," Alton said, chest puffing and a big grin splitting his lips. His blue eyes popped from his head. "I'll fish you on seven-X tippet with midge emergers."

Marshall leaned back on his stool, his chin tilted up so he could look down his nose at Alton. "I wouldn't waste a day on seven-X water over you," Marshall said.

Alton hopped off his bar stool and stood almost as tall as Marshall did sitting. "Or maybe you want to take a walk out in the alley and settle it there?"

"You're going to decide who's the better fisherman in the alley?" Molly asked. She was laughing.

"Maybe I'll just kick him around for a little while until he comes to his senses," Marshall said. Whereas Molly drifted along in the belief that this could be just like old times, Marshall felt edges on the exchange. He was sort of thinking about Alton with Molly, and how Molly seemed disinclined to clarify any of that. He was feeling profoundly bewildered and tired of it, and fearing, besides, that he was allowing the motivations of other people to provoke his thinking about what he wanted. Things were getting complicated. He suspected Alton knew something was up, sensed it even if he wasn't fully informed. So just at the moment he was thinking along the lines of kicking the situation around a little, seeing if anything came free.

"Back it up, big boy," Alton said.

Marshall planted his feet on the floor and stood. He was easily five inches taller than Alton and outweighed him by twenty pounds, although some of that, Marshall understood all too well, was fat. He'd seen Alton with his shirt off and knew Alton was basically ripped. Marshall made his way across the wooden floor toward the Rhino's back entrance, wondering if it was fair that he felt so angry at Alton, and that Alton didn't know it. That didn't seem at all fair. Whatever happened in the alley, Alton undoubtedly expected high jinks. He would be thinking in terms of theater, and would be caught with his pants down should art start imitating life. Outside the alley lay dark, sandwiched between the brick walls of buildings and paved with asphalt. A glitter of gravel pebbled the alley's surface, glowing in the neon wash of beer signs from the bar's windows.

"We gonna punch or just wrestle?" Marshall asked.

Alton started bouncing around on his toe tips, "You're the one that's going to kick my ass around for a while. You make the call."

On another day this was nothing more than brothers agreeing to roughen up the horseplay. Alton clouted Marshall on the ear with an open palm. It took a moment for the blow to sink in, but then Marshall felt an upwelling of frustration that poured out as motion and contact. Marshall snatched one of Alton's wrists, then parlayed his grip into an overhook of Alton's shoulder. He felt he could do what he wanted, that Alton's defenses were mere inconvenience. Marshall pivoted beside Alton and tried to drive him to the asphalt. Alton whirled to stay in his face, ripping at his clothing for a hold and catching him across the bridge of the nose with a glancing forearm. Marshall shoved Alton away, and when Alton came back in, Marshall arm-dragged him to the ground, although somewhere along the way Marshall's grip slipped and his head bounced on the pavement and he could feel the gritty grate of pebbles in the flesh of his cheek. He recovered quickly enough to spin around behind Alton—who struggled to reach his hands and knees—and keep his chest on Alton's back, pressing him into the alley.

"I can knock you into late last week if you want me to," Marshall said. He looked down at the other man, at his head buckled under his shoulder. Marshall raised his fist, ready to pound on the back of that head, but felt his vision expand in a strange upward spiral, until he seemed to be looking down at both him and Alton. He could see his raised fist, and Alton helpless. The fist fell, but opened into a half-hearted slap when it whapped against Alton's head.

"Get off!" Alton said.

Rising, Marshall forced Alton sprawling onto the asphalt. Marshall dusted the gravel from his knees, feeling pretty bad about things, while Alton rolled over and sat up.

"I think you broke my freakin' arm," Alton said.

"I believe I'm concussed," Marshall said, vaguely remembering conking his head on the asphalt.

"We'd better have more beer," Alton said.

Marshall reached out a hand, hauled Alton to his feet, and they walked back into the humid bar. Marshall felt a singed warmth on his cheek, and for the first time, felt liquid. He reached his fingers to it and found blood dripping down his face.

"So who's the better fisherman?" Molly asked, while Alton poured their glasses full of Fat Tire.

"I think he broke my arm," Alton said.

"I'm going to exsanguinate," Marshall said.

"You don't look so good," Molly said to Marshall.

"Yeah, well feel this," Alton said, digging through his hair with his fingertips. "There's a goose egg the size of a goose egg up there."

Molly touched Alton's head.

"And my elbow's starting to swell," Alton said.

"And you're bleeding all over the bar," Molly said, nodding at Marshall. "What tough fellas." Marshall reached across the bar for a cocktail napkin, which he plastered to the split in the abrasion over his cheekbone.

"So who won?" Molly asked.

"Oh, he kicked my ass," Alton said, disgusted. "I can still outfish him."

"Maybe," Molly said, lightly stroking Alton's hair above the lump on his head, "what we should do is get you both home and patch you up so you can work tomorrow."

Alton looked at her like she'd just killed Lassie. "I've got beer to drink."

"I'm not going home," Marshall said. "If I go to sleep I might die."

Molly glanced at him askance.

"That's what happens when you get concussed. You fall asleep and you drop into a coma and you never wake up."

Molly glanced askance again.

"Seriously," he said, leaning closer to her. "Look at my eyes."

She did.

"Do they look dilated?"

"Kinda hard to tell."

"Well, are they beady?"

Molly guffawed. She reached out to touch his face, to hold his head still, but brushed against the cocktail napkin stuck on his cheek and he pulled back. "Who would know?"

"You hanging out with tough guys now, Molly?"

Molly's head swung slowly, but before her eyes lighted on him, she knew who it was and what it meant. She only wondered how many he'd brought with him. There were three: Jimmy Ripley, Dean Stone, and Scotty the Wad. Ripley's hand crept up her back to her shoulder, rubbing her as if she'd asked him to.

"Aren't they fierce?" Ripley said, ostensibly to Molly, but he was staring at Marshall.

"Oh, we're just screwing around a little, we're just having a little fun." Molly felt like including herself with Marshall and Alton's fun might somehow change the dynamics of what otherwise was looking a lot like the opening credits to a free-for-all. She liked that Marshall and Alton were letting her do the talking so far, but didn't know how long she had before they assumed breakout roles.

"Must just be fun, because nobody got hurt enough to be a fight," Ripley said.

"You know what, Jimmy? Now would be a really good time to just leave well enough alone." Molly stood as she spoke, turning into Jimmy Ripley. She consciously thrust her chest forward, pressed against him, which caused Ripley for a moment to glance away from Marshall and down the scoop neck of Molly's white blouse. But her trick only lasted a second. Ripley lifted an arm and scooted her under it, twisting as he moved her past him, then turning back to lean his forearms on the table. "What you guys fighting about?"

"Just screwing around," Marshall said. He was trying to get a feel for Alton's mood, but could see nothing behind the glassy eyes of his friend. Alton was either truly puzzled by this approach, or he was sarcastically acting overinterested in Ripley. Marshall thought they could still get out of it OK.

"They're the kings of screwing around," Scotty the Wad said. Marshall didn't like the way Scotty seemed to be apologizing for knowing them.

"Not fighting over my dog, are you?" Ripley asked.

"We had a disagreement over who was the more accomplished angler," Alton said. The timbre of Alton's voice—way too loud—provoked Marshall's vision of a peaceful ending to spend. Add the slight singsong Alton fell into and the absurd cock of his head, and even Ripley couldn't miss the picture. "We've decided to settle all those kinds of disagreements in the alley."

"What makes you think either of you are any good?" Ripley asked.

Alton looked at Marshall like: what an astonishing question! Molly reinserted her arm across Ripley's chest and shifted her hips trying to get leverage to pull him away from the table. Marshall kept looking at Ripley, the blond crew cut over his too-wide forehead, the nice cheekbones, square jaw, short slash of nose—all pleasing and pleasant features. But it was the hooded eyes that gave away the thug in him, and the dull blank behind them.

"Jimmy," Molly was saying, less subtle in her efforts to wrangle him away from the table. "Now would be the time to kind of fuck off." Behind Ripley, Dean Stone opened his mouth in what would have been a laugh if sound came out. Maybe, Marshall thought—

"We're the best damned fishermen on the river!" Marshall said, pounding the table with his fist, letting a lunatic grin spill over his face.

"You guys think you're good fishermen?" Scotty the Wad slapped his hand on the table, exuberant if nothing else. He'd caught the drift.

"That's right!" Marshall said, pounding the table again. "I can out-fish anybody in this town!"

"Really!" *Slap!* on the table from the Wad.

"You betcha," Alton joined in, pounding away at the table. "You name the river, you name the day!" But then he lifted off his stool to shout across the table at Ripley, "Hey, why you wrestling with that girl?"

Molly had dug in, lowered her hips and was hauling on Ripley, try-ing to get him away from the table. Ripley's arm flailed as he tried to keep it from Molly's grasp. He was drunk enough that she was able to move him.

"Any day! Any river!" Scotty the Wad said, *Slap! Slap!*

Dean Stone had taken a couple steps back. Alton came off his stool and stood. Marshall thought he'd better, too.

"Hey, Wad, how come your Califuckya buddy here is wrestling with a girl?" Alton said.

The California reference, it turned out, was probably all it took. Alton probably didn't even need to reach around and grab a handful of Ripley's worn T-shirt in his fist and pull, stripping the fabric away. Rip-ley watched his shirt rip, shrugged Molly off for just long enough to step forward, say, "Oh really?" which made no sense to Marshall, any more than Ripley's hand made sense, shaped as it was like a fist, but holding the neck of a beer bottle that poured beer down upon himself and Molly and the table as Ripley raised it and then brought it crashing down on the crown of Alton's skull. Marshall felt the beer splattering him even as he watched the bottle strike Alton's head and Alton's head strike the table. And then Alton was sliding to the floor and blood bloomed all over the place.

It made no sense, either, the way everybody surrounding the table appeared to be ducking away at the moment Ripley struck. Wasn't anybody going to try to help Alton? Did he, Marshall, appear to be ducking down and away, too? Because he wasn't. He was lowering himself in preparation to launch at Ripley, which he did just as Dean Stone and Scotty the Wad and Molly all moved forward, creating a jam of collisions, none of which affected Ripley, who ducked. But the ensuing pile did land on him, forcing him to the floor, and somebody managed to pry the bottleneck from Ripley's fist, terminating the maiming.

"Help! Somebody help us!" Molly screamed from somewhere in the pileup.

Marshall struggled beneath he didn't know how many bodies. Ripley was beneath him, though, and Marshall was doing his best to come up with something he could do that might hurt. He found a thumb and began wrenching it back toward the wrist it came on. He didn't have all the leverage he wanted, but he pulled hard enough that he heard the thumb pop, then felt the joint go loose. But he heard nothing of protestation or pain from Ripley, so he tried jamming the thumb in another direction. Nothing. Then he was being lifted and kept being lifted—beyond the point where he should have been able to swing his feet under himself and get upright—continuing to rise until he felt himself sweeping over a short distance and then dropping, face-first, back onto the floor.

Molly, the moment she felt the bartenders and bouncers pulling her free, made a lunge for Alton, who lay tangled and motionless under the table. She didn't hear herself, but Molly was mumbling, "Somebody help us!" over and over as her fingers splayed and hovered over the shape of Alton's head, unsure of where to touch him. Blood glistened on the floor and in his hair. Molly backed out from under the table and screamed, "Call the ambulance!" Then she ducked right back under again.

At the hospital, Marshall felt like he wanted to be holding her—wrapping her hand, at least, in his—the entire time. As much as benevolence,

he longed for Molly's reciprocal touch. They sat on low white-pine furniture with tweed seat cushions in a fleshy mauve color. The carpet
was just deeper mauve. Somebody had thought it would be nice to
paint long stripes on the walls coming at them from all the way down
both hallways. The halls were mainly silent once they left the emer-
gency room waiting area and moved up to this one outside of surgery.
Marshall thought: *there's not a readable magazine in the pile.* The beer
from earlier in the evening lay in his brain pan and congealed. An ER
nurse had insisted that she pick the pieces of bar napkin from the
fresh wound on his face, and had slapped a gauze bandage over the
scrape. "How'd you get this? A little hanky-panky?" she had said.

Which he didn't think was at all funny. The white edge of the bandage lingered unfocused in the near periphery of his sight. Waiting was
grinding away at the thin hours of early morning. Intermittent checks
of the clock told him this was taking longer than he ever thought it
could. Molly had never been so keyed up in her life. She had been
scared when they arrived after begging a cop to give them a lift in the
back of a squad car, scared in the visceral, sensual sense. Six hours
later she still felt adrenaline pooled in her stomach, only now she had
time to frighten herself intellectually as well. She felt every moment
like she might vomit. Something told her that Marshall didn't really
believe what was happening the way she did. They'd both seen the
same things, both seen the white flash of skull beneath the spongy pink
blood, both seen the absence of Alton when the EMT peeled back his
eyelids, both noted the drool spilling unchecked from the corner of his
mouth. But she didn't think Marshall believed—knew in his soul—that
Alton could die tonight.

Why then, wouldn't the stupid son of a bitch just tell her everything would be all right? She couldn't see how that was too much to
ask. But Marshall only professed to not know a thing. "He's in the best
possible hands," Marshall told her. "They're doing everything they can."

He's in the best possible hands? How could she think she was in
love with someone who could utter such crap? But, credit where credit
was due; Marshall was being steady all night. Molly had felt herself
swing from elaborate forms of panic to desolation and abandoned
hope, from self-buttressed positive thinking to a collapse of energy.
Marshall, though a bit inward, had held the line. "I don't know," he'd
said when she'd asked him what the surgeons were doing. "I don't

know anything about it," he'd kept saying, "but they do. They'll do whatever it takes to pull him through." Marshall kept his chin up—physically—and steadily replied to every splinter-driven question she asked him. It was just that she sort of wished he'd lie to her.

They had arrived at the hospital at 11:45 P.M. By about three in the morning, Marshall could almost feel the stretch of his veins from the coursing adrenaline, now gone. He imagined those veins looked like the elastic in the waistband of an old pair of briefs. His tongue tasted fudgy. He had an occasion to see Molly while she stared down the hallway, and to watch her for a long moment. She sat, unguarded, her chin resting on the heel of her palm, fingers curled so that her knuckles touched her lips. He realized instantly what made her so beautiful, how the urgency of her feelings infused the tired face before him. Even glassy-eyed her gaze charted the depth of her concern. Marshall had never seen her sad before, and he loved her the moment he did. He'd always loved her, of course, though he never knew quite how—apparently not in the way she'd wanted him to, at any rate. This knowledge matched his sadness like a puff of wind revealing its shape on still water.

"I want to say some things about the . . . situation between you and me," Marshall said. For a long moment he did not know if she'd heard him or not. So he said, "The way we've been talking to each other, I don't like it . . ."

Molly's words came glazed in distance from lips that barely moved. "The situation has changed some."

"I know, but it makes me want to talk about the other."

Again a pause awaited him, then a thin, flat voice. "I am talking about the other. And that situation changed."

"In the bar—," Marshall said, seeking clarification.

"I'm talking about Alton. I . . . we sort of . . . you know," Molly said.

Marshall felt something inside break loose. In a dubious whisper he said, "When?"

Molly was looking at him now. "I don't owe you answers," she said.

"No," he said. "Prolly not." Whatever had broken loose seemed to have also punched a hole in him, and he felt some vital draining. In an instant, he no longer wanted to be there, no longer felt that waiting would help anybody. He wanted to be back at the ranch. He stood, prepared to stalk off.

"Marshall," Molly said. He felt like she was calling, but the word was a simple softness, the drop of snow from a branch to snow drifted just beneath it. He looked at her again and saw her face open and clear.

"I'm sorry," she said. "It just happened. Nobody planned it."

"How long?"

Molly hesitated, as if deciding whether to let him have this. "The night of Palmer's wedding.

Marshall let his head fall back and stared at the ceiling. "At the wedding I wanted you to spend the night with me. I wanted to see if . . . and I was trying to figure out how to ask you to."

"You wanted to see if what?"

"If Helena was real."

"Was I supposed to know that?"

"I thought I was showing you. I was trying to. Then there was the thing with the dog, and then everything kind of got away."

"Everything always seems to. Look, what happened in Helena was . . . it was really nice," Molly said, then seemed to change her mind. "Except no, it wasn't really nice, really. I mean sex is never that good the first time, not like it is later, when there's something to share. On top of that, we were drunk. So how nice could it have been?"

That seemed to Marshall far harsher than it needed to be, though perhaps he could reexamine whose needs were in focus. Apparently his expression failed to veil the scalding his ego cringed from, because, by way of further explanation, Molly said, "Marshall, I can see how as a gesture you might have thought it was nice, but then there was no follow-through. Think about it. I mean, who knows with you?"

"Who knows what?"

"Anything." Molly returned her stare down the long hallway with its striped wall. "Who knows if you're ever going to call? Who knows if you're ever going to let anybody know how you feel? Who knows when you're going to fall back on Daisy Klingman."

"That is—," Marshall said, but he felt too exhausted to go on. His original intent was to finish with *not fair*, but that sputtered and died. In its place, he felt himself wanting to concentrate on identifying something he could be right about. "This is exactly why I thought the whole thing would be a disaster from the minute I heard you were hooking up with him. Exactly this confusion of loyalties and all these . . . cross-purposes. I could see it coming six ways from Sunday."

"Marshall, you're not available—not to me, or anybody else, re-ally—not on any sustainable or meaningful level." Molly held her eyes steady on him while she spoke. He expected her to sound more stri-dent than she did. Rather she spoke in discrete elements, as if she were laying out a complicated story problem. "Everybody playing this stupid little game knows that. I suspect even you. And I don't know why you won't let yourself be available. Maybe you will one day. I don't even know if that's exactly what I want, not really. But I do know what I don't want: I don't want to waste my time and energy hoping for something with such little promise."

"Don't," he said, coming back now, falling away from his mean surge of jealousy. "Just stop talking for a minute, please." He let one foot take a step. He let his other foot take a step, but he knew already he wasn't going anywhere. He glanced at Molly again and saw that now her eyes held the vacancy of a mirror the moment after sunlight fin-ishes glinting on it. He sat back down, and they remained in the room together for more hours, each inhabiting vastly different spaces. Molly felt . . . not *good*, but stable, within herself. She'd been afraid to say what she'd said, and then she'd said it, and her feelings were *out there*, occupying the room and rubbing up against both herself and him.

Marshall, meanwhile, plunged into a funk, wondering why it was that people seemed compelled to tell him things about himself that he wasn't dying to find out. First of all, how did they know these things? And then, did feeling like his nose was being rubbed in the carpet constitute a healthy, adult response to what Molly was saying? That "probably not" popped right into his mind did not supplant a certain craving to whimper. You could learn something, he thought, but it might take a while to actually know it. When the doctor strode down the hall, he didn't know which of the two of them to address. The band-age on Marshall's face may have tilted him toward Molly.

"Are either of you family?" the doctor asked.

"Yes," Molly answered.

The doctor took a long look. He guessed the truth, but said, "It's up in the air still. We've got the bleeding under control, but there's been a lot of swelling on his brain. We're not going to know for a while how much damage has been done. It's going to take a while."

"He's going to live?" Molly said.

"He's stable for now," the doctor said, but his tone indicated that she had asked the wrong question. "Look, you two aren't family, and there's policy here—"

"We're the closest thing he's got here," Marshall said.

The doctor took another moment, then sat down on the arm of a chair. "OK, he's resting, but with the swelling around the brain, we just don't know. Anything could happen. We just can't know and we won't know for a while. And you won't be able to see him for a while. It's best for you two to go home and sleep. Come back in the morning."

Marshall watched the doctor's mouth making words about Alton, releasing the words "anything could happen," into the waiting room, and felt with the force of a slow but steady dissolve many of the things he had wanted to be so upset about not mattering anymore, not one bit.

The next morning Marshall climbed the canting metal stairs to the back door of Fly Guys. The weather conspired to continually douse his mood as a hemisphere of grainy sky filled the Missoula valley, the clouds fitting like a gray cap over his sense of space. Consequently, though mired in mid-August, the morning was cool. He had slept only in short spots throughout the night, but had awakened at the sound of nurses' sneakers squeaking on linoleum as they moved through the halls, or the *click-clack* of doctors' well-heeled feet. Shortly before dawn it had occurred to Molly that Alton would have clients this morning, and she said something to Marshall, whose first reaction was: who cares? But then Molly wondered aloud if Alton had health insurance.

"He should be covered through the shop," Marshall said. All the anxiety that had boiled between them in early conversations had washed away with the night. Both spoke as if they had nothing but the other's concerns at heart.

"Isn't he an independent contractor?" Molly asked. "Isn't that what all that contract hoopla was about this spring?"

"Yeah, but he's also employed at the shop as a full-time clerk. I'm pretty sure he told me a while ago Shadrat gave him some sort of policy through the shop," Marshall said.

"Wasn't that when he was talking profit-sharing and a bunch of other stuff that never came true? You know Shadford. What are the odds he's going to pay if he can figure out a way not to?"

The Fly X spring creek could stand Marshall's absence for a few days. He realized this was the only thing that made any sense, and just that quickly he was back in the guiding business. So he picked up Alton's rig and boat, drove to Fly Guys, and marched up the back steps. He noted Shadrat's Suburban, parked in the space behind the shop. He planned, essentially, to walk in and order Shadford to give him Alton's clients for the day. He had access to Alton's boat, all of Alton's gear. He knew that nothing would go that easy. Shadrat would make him sweat, because that was what Shadrat did. The first person he saw, when he swung the door inward, was Amy Baine. The morning's swipe of lip gloss shined on her mouth, and her hair fell damp along her shoulders, leaving swaths of wet marks on her white silk blouse, but her eyes looked pinched. She seemed to be stretching to keep them open.

"I just heard," she said. "Nobody told me."

Marshall didn't know what to say to that.

"Is he OK?" Amy asked.

"We . . . ," Marshall started to say, then considered the potential colorings of the pronoun. "Nobody knows yet."

"I just . . . I don't know what to do."

Marshall looked at her, touched by her earnest tone and the confused plea in her eyes. "I don't know what to tell you, Ames." He felt an urge to launch into a long exposition about what he thought she should feel, but then thought that perhaps he had no standing to tell anybody what to feel. And then Shadford stepped from his office and said, "We just heard. What's going on?"

Marshall said, "Don't know. It's bad. He's out of surgery but still critical."

"What happened?" Amy Baine asked. Marshall saw that Shadford had tried to move beside her, but that she'd come a step forward, closer, and away from him.

"Somebody rapped him on the head with a beer bottle," Marshall said.

"Why?" Amy asked.

Shadford: "It was a bar fight, right?"

"In the Rhino. That Ripley punk was mouthing off and then the next thing you know he hit Alton with a bottle. They were jawing at each other, but Alton never did anything to provoke a beer bottle to the head. Alton reached out and grabbed the guy and ripped his shirt. That's it."

The back door to the shop swung open and Billy Mills's head popped into the opening. He smiled, then followed his face into the room. Scotty the Wad followed Mills. His eyes couldn't meet Marshall's, instead fell sidelong.

"Heard your buddy got whacked," Mills said.

Like a herd of deer watching a wolf trot through a meadow, all faces pivoted to Mills. Amy Baine's glance dripped away first and her lip began to melt into a curl. Scotty the Wad had sidled around Mills, moving himself as far as possible from Marshall while remaining in the reaches of conversation. Marshall's glare flipped from Mills to the Wad. Throughout the night, his mind had changed channels from imagining what was going on in the surgical suite to nostalgic recall of things he and Alton had done together to conjuring vivid fantasies of revenge. He had imagined the various ways he might beat Jimmy Ripley senseless. Some of the versions had Marshall moving on to batter Dean Stone when he tried to interfere, and then even Scotty the Wad, who, though he had nothing to do with the attack, suffered sorely by association. To Shadford, Marshall said, "Got a minute?"

"Dude," Mills said. "How about disclosing some more tale?"

"What do you need to know? Man lies near death in hospital after being whacked over the head by asshole with beer bottle. Read the paper."

"They arrest the other guy?" Shadford asked.

"He went for a ride in the police car," Marshall remembered, "and he wasn't sitting up front."

They stepped into the office and Shadford closed the door behind him. Marshall slid over and shifted his butt against the desktop edge. Shadford stood in the middle of the room with his arms folded across his chest. "What kind of help are you going to give him?" Marshall asked.

"To be perfectly honest with you, that's tricky," Shadford said. "He can't get workman's comp because he wasn't injured on the job."

"Is he covered on your insurance policy?" Marshall said.

"He's an independent contractor," Shadford said.

"But he's also a shop employee. I remember him telling me you were going to give him some insurance."

"True," Shadford said, sighing as if he wished things could be different, "but frankly, I'm engineering my coverage in a sort of unique way."

"But if you offered him benefits—"

"No, what I'm saying is . . . do you know how expensive insurance coverage is? Do you know how many small businesses go out of business after they offer employees insurance coverage?"

"I don't care," Marshall said.

"Well, I arranged a coverage structure—"

Marshall thought: *what do people see in me that makes them feel so clever?* "I don't care what you arranged, Mike. What I want to hear is, 'Don't worry, it'll all be taken care of.' "

"The situation is a little fluid. I . . . am thinking about changing carriers to provide more complete coverage and—"

Marshall sighed. "You didn't pay the premium."

"I—"

"You let it lapse," Marshall said, the note of discovery in his voice genuine.

Shadford shuffled forth a little laugh, a snort or two intended to let Marshall know he couldn't possibly understand all the implications. "Things are just never as simple as you seem to think they are."

"I bet it'd get a lot simpler if I told Amy what you're pulling," Marshall said.

"This has nothing to do with Amy," Shadford said, as suddenly vicious as Marshall had ever seen him. "It's not your concern, either. The only reason I'm willing to discuss it with you at all is that we used to be friends. Now, I know you're wound up. You're emotional. But you and I have a relationship. Alton and I have a relationship. Amy and I have a relationship. They're all different relationships, and in the real world they don't mingle."

Marshall let the air hang for a long moment. He decided to wait for Shadford to make another fidget, any kind of move. When finally Shadford shifted his weight to one foot, letting his bony hip cock, Marshall said, "So, how do you think that went over?"

"Look, the important thing is that Alton gets better," Shadford said. "Then we can figure out all the details."

"No, the important thing is this insurance business gets taken care of, pronto. I'm going to give you two days to figure out that Alton's covered on your shop insurance policy and the premium is worth paying before I tell Amy that you think it's not," Marshall said. "In the meantime, who's guiding Alton's clients?"

"That's another problem. I may have to for a day or two until I can get something figured out."

"I'll do it," Marshall said.

"You will?" Emphasis fell on *you* rather than *will*. "That's, that's uh, awfully nice of you. To offer. But you're not an employee of mine and you're not on my outfitter's license."

"I have my own outfitter's license. I'm covered. I'll sign whatever you need me to sign whenever you want. I'll save Alton's guide fees to give to him, and you can have the rest." Marshall nodded, lurched away from the desk to stand up straight.

Shadford pivoted to make space for Marshall to swing by him and said, "I really don't appreciate you putting the squeeze on me on this other thing."

Marshall didn't respond. In the shop Amy Baine grasped his upper arm and said, "I need to talk."

She pulled him into the stockroom, amid cardboard boxes stacked nearly to the ceiling. The room held the rubbery odor of unused waders, the plastic smell of new pile fleece, and also stale feathers and rabbit skins from the fly-tying supplies. Amy put her cheeks in both palms so that Marshall was looking at the perfectly straight pink seam of scalp parting her glossy brown hair. He reached around to Amy's back and, without pulling her closer, gave her his arm to lean against. He let his hand, splayed open against her shoulder blades, rotate in gentle circles.

"I don't know what to do," Amy said, her voice wrenched by the crying. "I want to be there for him. I want to be there when he wakes up. I feel like I've screwed up everything and now it might be too late."

"This is not your fault," he said.

"But given everything that's happened—," Amy said. She'd lifted her head from her hands, and Marshall felt her beseeching him to forgive her, to say anything that would mean all the previous mistakes might have been casual, and that the critical bent of this situation would make it now different. Her mouth fell from the words. "Is he going to be all right?"

He said something about making it this far, having a better chance the longer things go. Jabberwocky. Then Amy began a series of phrases that weren't completely comprehensible: "God, I . . . I couldn't stand . . .

we just were . . . I thought, and then I . . . I can't believe this could really happen." Marshall felt her heaving against his arm. He wondered what Alton would think if he woke and found Amy at his bedside—heaven-sent or just a mess? He knew Alton well enough to suppose the reaction would have a lot to do with whether Amy sat there unencumbered, or whether Alton felt she was still under Shadford's thrall, just off crusading. And also how Alton was thinking about Molly.

"We all get ourselves into ugly situations," Marshall said. "It's how we get out of them that matters."

Amy's head lifted and he watched her eyes flicking back and forth to each of his. A clarity settled over her face. "I'm going over there right now," she said.

Marshall remembered that Molly was still at the hospital and took a small moment to imagine how interesting that little waiting room was going to get in a short while. When he walked out of the stockroom, the back door was closing on Amy. Shadford stood just inside, staring at the door's glass window. Marshall began to sift the fly bins looking to stock up for the day's float trip. He noted how low the fly stocks were. Alton's ZAP patterns were gone, except for a few individual flies littering their bins like crumbs from a feeding frenzy. The caddis bins were chewed thin. Mills stood at the bins talking to two women. They looked ready to fish and Marshall guessed these would be his Johnsons for the day. Mills was saying, "I belong to the twenty-twenty-twenty club. Do you know what that is?"

"No," one of the women, the taller and stockier of the two, said. She had salted gray hair that had been sculpted by a hairdresser who cared. "What's that?"

"When you catch twenty fish over twenty inches on a fly under size twenty in the same day," Mills said. He took a step back, leaving them room to be impressed. Intellectually, Marshall gagged.

"Really?" the other woman asked, smaller but more lithe, more attractive in every but a regal sense.

"Yep. Did it on the Bitterroot one day this summer," Mills said.

Marshall stepped up to the women and by way of introduction said, "Hi. My name is Marshall and I'll be your guide for today. I won't be telling you stories like that one."

Mills stood with thumbs jacked into his jeans pockets. "You guiding Alton's people?" Mills asked.

"Yeah. What, were you thinking you might?"

Mills stumped himself into silence.

Marshall turned to the women. "This is a little problem we've had since that *River Runs Through It* movie. There's been a surge toward hyperbole, as if it wouldn't be enough just to float a Montana river and catch some wild trout. I gotta tell you, I've been guiding here for fifteen years and I've never heard of anybody catching twenty twenty-inch fish in one day, never mind the size of the fly. On the other hand, what I *can* promise you today is a lovely float on a gorgeous stretch of water and a chance to catch a whole bunch of really beautiful trout. We may catch more than twenty, and we may catch some twenty-inchers. I won't make you fish with No. 20 flies unless you want to. We'll fish big attractor patterns, throw fuzzy things by the rocks, and we'll have ourselves a time."

"I think," said the older woman, "I like your style, Marshall. My name's Dianne and this is Kristen." Her companion kept casting side-long glances at Mills, as if his approach might be a scootch sexier.

"Where you going?" Mills asked, his narrow face thrust forward, eyes tight, as if the answer might prove Marshall's undoing.

"Blackfoot."

"Which section?" More of the interrogation mode, including a sharp hand gesture that was almost finger-pointing.

"Box Canyon."

"Got a gun?"

"Why would I need a gun to float the Box Canyon?"

Mills's hands flew up, a protestation of who was he to say, but— "I'm just saying I floated it two days last week and I saw mountain lions both times. It's Kitty City up there, man."

"Get attacked?" Marshall asked.

"Suit yourself," Mills said, "but FWP gave us a warning."

To his clients, Marshall said, "I'm extremely not concerned about mountain lions. I doubt there's ever been a case of a mountain lion swimming across a river to attack a boat."

Two hours later Marshall perched on the rowing seat of Alton's green boat as it wended its way down the Blackfoot River. Outside of the Missoula Valley, the sky cleared and bright light ran lambent up from the river over the trunks of trees, showering into the upper branches where the flittering action of certain leaf formations set off temporary starburst effects. Overhead the sky was as clear, achy blue. Beneath him the current chimed and jingled over its bed of yellow, green, and brown cobbles. It was hard to believe Alton could be lying in a hospital bed on a day like this.

Marshall spent a bit of time trying to ascertain whether his clients were lovers or mutual enthusiasts. He didn't care in any personal sense, but as a guide that kind of thing could matter. The uncertainty confounded him when he tried to think of one of them as Mr. Johnson and, for the first time he could remember, their actual names—Dianne and Kristen—stuck with him. The two women—Kristen in her late thirties and Dianne a decade older—took turns fishing from the front seat. It seemed they had no interest in fishing simultaneously, but much preferred to observe one another. They offered each other casting tips, and hints about reading the water. The fish were eating mayfly duns off the surface right from the start. Over and over they watched slow, lazy plucking turn into a violent, twisting *sploosh* and the zinging of line when the fish realized what they had eaten. The women took great pleasure in each other's hookups, and each closely examined the fish landed, invariably commenting on the beauty of the individual trout. The net effect of their mutual admiration left Marshall feeling useless save as an instrument of locomotion. He tried conversing, noting that they seemed like proficient casters and asking where they had learned.

"Well, Kris," Dianne said for her partner, "is from outside Detroit, Bloomfield Hills, and she learned in upper Michigan on the Pigeon and the Toussaint and the Au Sable. I'm from Grosse Pointe, and my father belonged to a club in Ohio called Castalia Springs."

"Sure. Outside Sandusky. It's a big spring creek. I have a spring creek," Marshall said. "On the ranch where I live. It flows into the West Fork. You might like to fish that sometime."

"Aw, I'm not much interested in spring creeks anymore," Dianne said. She hadn't turned her face to talk to him, kept watching the river. "That Castalia place, you know, it was all manicured. The lawns were all clipped right up to the stream banks. They had branch cutters on poles for if you hooked your backcast up in a tree. Benches to sit beside the stream and tie flies. It was just . . . landscaped. Like fishing on a golf course. I mean, I'm glad it's there or I may have never picked up fly fishing, but it's just a bit unreal."

"Well, that's what I mean. My spring creek is natural," Marshall said, realizing at once that he was lying and then sort of prevaricating. "All the fish in it are wild. They live in it when they want or drop back down to the West Fork, no barriers. That's why I thought you might find it interesting by comparison."

Now Dianne let her cast drop and the fly drift. Placing one hand on the gunnel as a support, she twisted her upper body around and tilted her face to peer out from behind her sunglasses at him. "I'm sure your spring creek is very nice," she said. Dianne went back to fishing, and kibitzing with Kristen.

At a long left-hand sweep of river, Marshall rowed into a deep hole that he liked to fish. He had Dianne set up to cast along a run of water that girdled a rock face. Something about the landscape looked more familiar to him than usual, though he realized he hadn't floated the Blackfoot all year. He realized he hadn't floated any rivers all year, save the one trip down the West Fork with Kyle Klingman and his girlfriend, and the first early spring drift down the Bitterroot with Alton and Molly—the last time he had fished with Alton. Perhaps the last time he would. That seemed unthinkable, so Marshall tried to remember a season during which he hadn't floated the Blackfoot, then began a dreamy sort of argument with himself about whether staying up on the ranch and off the rivers was going to be healthy over the long term. His internal monologue was shattered by the tremendous *ka-sploosh!* sound of something blowing a hole in the water just beside the boat. Dianne's head whipped to spot the source of the noise. Another *sploosh* split the quiet water, and then another, in a steady spaced cadence. Marshall glanced to the bank and saw a man, probably in his late fifties, standing atop the high bank, hurling river rocks down at them. The man was perhaps twenty feet above the river and he lobbed the projectiles like shot puts.

"What's going on with him?" Dianne asked.

"I have no idea," Marshall said, and in that instant he recognized where they were. One night earlier in the summer he and Alton had had swum across the river here and stolen the oars from the boats on the other side. The man on the bank must have been one of the owners of the property—Jimmy Ripley's or Dean Stone's father.

Marshall called up the bank, "Knock it off!"

The man, dressed in a white polo shirt and brick-colored knee-length shorts, said nothing. He lobbed another two-pound rock into the pool Dianne was fishing.

"How rude," Dianne said.

"This is crazy," Marshall said, but he knew it wasn't, or at least not in the sense where crazy meant anything unusual.

"What's going on?" Kristen asked.

"That guy owns the land along the river. Apparently he doesn't want us fishing here."

"Is that legal?"

"We're completely within our rights." What he didn't say was that generally this was the sort of thing that gets dealt with outside the legal system and sometimes gets people's heads contused. The man stood now, hands on hips, staring down at them.

"Are you going to let him get away with that?" Dianne asked.

Up to that point, Marshall hadn't thought about any other option. He saw the dismay in Dianne's gaze and wondered what she had to prove. Then he remembered he was a guide again and said, "I don't guess so."

Marshall put the boat in against the bank and tried to muster some anger that he could consider earned, but he mainly felt tired. The man on the bank could be the father of the guy who smacked Alton on the head with a beer bottle, which should have been enough to boil some blood—but what did the father have to do with it? Well, he kept saving the kid from his legal scrapes. Still, Marshall felt as if he were wading against the current even as he cleared the river and began to hike. For a few moments as he lumbered up the bank he wondered what an eye in the sky would see: a tall, lanky guy trying to be pissed off, pretending to hustle after an old man who was pitching rocks in the river. Did he look angry? Were his movements aggressive enough? It was a funny image, but he didn't think it was supposed to be. Then Marshall wondered if he'd just discovered the great joke about life.

The man in the polo shirt strode toward him with a vigor that made the loose flesh of his thighs vibrate like a tuning fork. The man wore an immense shock of white hair over a nose redder than a squashed tomato. His lips appeared joined by a solder. He waved his arms like a football referee calling off the clock. At a loss for any applicable outrage to spout, Marshall said, "What?"

"You're on my property!" the man shouted.

Marshall paused to consider a retort, but decided it better to continue his approach. The two closed the distance between each other and the atmosphere seemed to wheeze like an accordion squeezing shut. The white-haired man stopped, plunked his hands on his hips and stared, his silence seamless. Marshall felt the shock wave of the other's halt bring him up short. He stood with his arms at his side, at a loss for a gesture.

"You're trespassing!" the man said.

"Look, we're fishing the river," Marshall said. "That's all we're doing." He despaired at his inability in this crucial moment to draw from his reserve of outrage. It left him feeling floaty, removed from the scene.

"How sick do you think I get of you money-grubbing guides dragging your clients through my property?" the man asked. He seemed sincere about wanting an answer.

"I don't care," Marshall said. *I don't care?* He couldn't even muster up a good *screw you.* "The rule is, we stay inside the banks, we can fish wherever we want."

"That's what you think," the man said, pointing to indicate who the "you" in question was.

"I don't—" Marshall started. "Look, I don't even want to be here right now. I'd be happy just rowing by. But you can't heave rocks at people and expect them to float by."

"I played quarterback at Stanford," the man said. "If I threw rocks *at* you, you'd by God know it."

"I don't know your name," Marshall said, and felt compelled to thrust his right hand forward, as if an introduction were in the offing. "My name's Marshall . . ."

He stood still until it became apparent that his hand meant nothing. Then he said, "I don't mean to cause any trouble with you. I'm just trying to show these people a nice day on the river. We weren't planning to stop."

The man looked at Marshall with his eyebrows unsettled. "That's my hole. I paid two million dollars to own that hole."

The price tag sparked the anger Marshall had been looking for. "You own the box of wood you sleep in," Marshall said. "You want to own a river, move to Snoborado, where whole flocks of assholes like you think they can own a river. Here you're just about ready to get in-volved in an assault charge."

"I'm an attorney, you dumb shit," the man said. "You think I don't know the law? There's no law against throwing rocks in the river."

His grin bespoke a man constantly in a position to turn the screw another notch. It pissed Marshall off more than anything that had transpired to this point, and he was suddenly able to equate the arro-gance of this man with Alton lying in a bed with tubes in his nose. He closed the distance between them and was surprised to see the man flinch, throw an arm up before his face. Marshall felt himself freed by intent from the inanity of the exchange. "See, now you've confused the actor in the assault charge I was talking about."

He moved toward the man, and, in a flash of reflection, understood that he meant to hurt him. His hands found the man's shirt collar. The man swung his arms in an inside circle to bust Marshall's hands free. Marshall felt the shock but held tight. He held on long enough to prove his point, then jammed his fist against the man's collarbone. The man tripped a few steps backward and his eyes swam back in his head. Marshall saw his face in a moment of pure weakness and understood that this was Dean Stone's father, not Jimmy Ripley's. He wondered if there was a difference. A wave of disgust twisted him on his heel and he staggered back down the bank. The women said nothing as he pushed the boat into the river and straddled himself aboard. Shaking his head, Marshall moved the boat back into current, let it drift on through the pool and downriver.

"Can you believe that?" Dianne asked. She seemed suitably mor-tified, though aimed her perturbation at Kristen. "Who would have thought . . . in Montana?"

"Things are going to hell," Marshall said, "here more so than most places."

A mile or so downriver they stopped for a late lunch, during which the women seemed not to notice anything he said. He envied their self-prepossessing ease. Though some buried instinct whispered to him that he should, as a guide, be thrilled to have clients who felt completely con-fident in their ability to catch fish without him, this was an awful day to feel useless. After lunch Kristen took the front seat and Dianne ob-served from the rear. An hour or so downstream Kristen had caught six or eight smallish trout, mostly cutthroats or hybrids that pinwheeled along the surface as she dragged them to the boat. Marshall began to imagine a crusade, the purpose of which would be to capture a fish for Kristen that was longer and heavier than the two sixteen-inch rainbows Dianne had landed earlier in the day. Though he noted that Kristen evinced not a hint of desire to one-up her partner, Marshall became imbued with the notion that it would be just and right, as truly as the act of laying hands on the white-haired man had revealed itself not to be.

Below them the river veered sharply to the right, leaving a high, shallow shelf of water peeling off to the left over a submerged gravel bar before rejoining the main current. Marshall knew that along the right bank ran a deep seam. It was a tiny niche, didn't appear large enough to hold good-sized fish, which left it overlooked by anybody who didn't make a careful study of the river. Marshall leaped overboard and stood knee-deep in the cold stream. He grabbed the gunwales and hand-over-handed until he was holding onto the stern, hauling the boat to a standstill in the rushing water.

Full of purpose, he called up to Kristen, "I'm going to walk you up this bank. There's a pocket there, see the foam? Cast to the foam line. A little inside the foam line, if you can mend and get a drag-free drift."

Dianne, a woman whose round Irish face Marshall found mischievously gorgeous, peered down at him from her seat high in the stern, perusing with a glance designed to ferret out whether what he was doing might be macho. Finally she sat up straight to monitor the accuracy of Kristen's casting. Kristen did exactly what he said and across the silvered layers of rushing waters a very large brown trout raised its head, opened its mouth, and chomped down on the fly. Marshall heard line ripping from the water as Kristen set the hook, and the fight was on. The fish blasted into current. Kristen's line threw a spray of droplets into the sunlight as it sliced the surface at an angle behind the fish.

"Oh my, Kris," Dianne was saying. "Just look at it!" she cried when the trout turned and ran all the way across the river, cutting upstream. For her part, Kristen alternated between smiling and pressing her lips together grimly. Once, she whooped. Marshall couldn't help but wonder if this was the same fish Alton had pulled out of the same pocket the year before. Fat chance, he knew, but it *could* have been.

Marshall loosed the anchor cleat, dropping the lead pyramid. Kristen fought the fish masterfully, although her cause was enabled considerably by the big brown's refusal to turn and shoot downstream, where it could turn its broad flank to the current and initiate a critical standoff. In ten minutes Marshall could see the trout washing back onto the gravel bar. His polarized glasses allowed him to watch the sweeps of the fish's tail. The trout would link together four or five explosive blasts from its tail—so fast and fluid as to be indistinguishable as individual movements—and jet upstream ten or fifteen feet. Drifting back down it fanned the water almost casually, body arcing to scoop current into its effort, head turning to point its eyes in a search for this baffling danger and the next potential escape route.

Marshall opted to take no chances and netted the brown for Kristen. He slid the aluminum lip of the net onto the boat's rail so that the mesh held the fish against the side of the boat. He unclipped hemostats from Alton's gear bag and used them to back the fly from the fish's mouth.

"Want a picture?" he asked.

"Oh, absolutely yes," Kristen said.

Kristen plunked overboard without hesitation, stumbled when the current pushed her feet into places she hadn't expected them to land. She staggered and kicked water into splashes, grasped Marshall's arm, and caught her balance. Marshall wanted Dianne to have the shot all lined up so that he could hand the trout to Kristen, get the picture, and drop the fish back into the net before it realized that a wriggle or two might set it free. But then he saw that the camera was a manual-focus 35mm, and that the shot was going to take some arranging.

"Focus on Kristen," Marshall said, "and figure everything out before I get the fish out."

"Give her the fish so I can see how it's going to fit in the frame," Dianne said.

He knew what was going to happen, and yet he followed the instructions. He wetted his hands, then used both to heft the fish. The trout's markings were a leopard swirl of black on butter brown, the bright red dots burning like cigarette tips in the dark. Its lower jaw was pronated, hooking up to touch its snout with a ball point. Marshall realized how old the fish must have been, how long it must have lived in this river. He imagined that it very possibly could be the same fish Alton had caught, though it showed no obvious hook or handling scars.

Kristen was holding her hands, both palms cupped upward. She was going to drop the fish moments after he handed it to her. He looked at the trout as if he would never see it again, trying to examine all of its markings, memorize its whorls and the mossy webbing of its translucent tail fin and the gradations of yellow-brown on its flanks.

"Be ready to snap it," Marshall said to Dianne. To Kristen he said, "Get your hands wet." She dipped them in the water and lifted them again—ready, but still wrong.

"Just hand it to her," Dianne said, "and move out of the picture."

Marshall handed the fish to Kristen. She cradled her fingers beneath, lifted it to her chest. The fish's body snaked in an S curve and then it was free-falling back into the stream. One wriggle. It splashed heavily into the water.

"Did you get it?" Kristen asked.

"No," Dianne said, "Oh Kris. It was such a beautiful big fish."

"Oh no," Kris said. "Oh damn."

"I'm sorry."

"No, no."

"It was such a gorgeous fish," Dianne said. "Oh, it would have made the best picture of the trip."

Marshall listened to them go on for a moment, but his eyes dropped, from habit, to the water. There, due to the miracle of polarized lenses, he saw the big fish, exhausted from its recent ordeal, holding in the current in less than three feet of water. In the bright sunlight the current, broken into thousands of threads by the cobble of the gravel bar, cast continually unfurling shadows of turbulence against mottled stone bottom. The trout's body undulated as if it were a piece of the current itself, a solid representation of the liquid's movement.

He would have to do this perfectly the first time. With Dianne and Kristen still bemoaning the loss of spectacle, Marshall shuffled a few steps forward against the rush of water, bent at the waist, and stabbed his hands into the river. In the instant he felt his fingers bump a firmness he understood sensually was too soft to be rock, his hands clutched like talons. He lifted the big fish, water pouring from its belly, back into the sunlight. Marshall thought: *he's got to be thinking life just turned Kafkaesque.*

He proffered the fish to Kristen, who still stood beside the boat. "Here you go," he said.

The camera came to Dianne's face like a rake handle when a cartoon character steps on the upturned tines. Marshall showed Kristen how to hold the fish by wrapping a hand around its tail, then wrapping her fingers under the fins.

"Move closer to her," Dianne said to Marshall. The picture happened in a flash. Marshall plunged the trout back into the water. He held it in the current a few moments, letting oxygen gush over its gills, until he felt the twisting muscles flex against his hand. Then he slowly opened his fingers. The fish did not hold long this time, but shot across the current and was gone. Marshall turned to see the two women beaming at him and, for a brief moment, remembered what it felt like to be a fishing god again.

On the drive back to town, Marshall's cell phone rang. Only Molly and Alton—and his father—knew this number. His heart kicked when he heard the chirping and a small panic zoomed through him while he hesitated to answer the call. He actually thought to himself: *am I ready for the worst?* Then he excused himself to his clients and answered.

"I've got some things to discuss with you," Skipjack said.

"Oh," Marshall said, "good." In any other instance an unscheduled call from his father would be decidedly not good.

"Good what?" Skipjack asked.

"Oh, Alton's in the hospital. It's real serious. I thought you might be someone calling about that."

"What happened to Alton?"

Marshall told him there had been a head injury, but felt uncomfortable elaborating with clients in the truck. "I'll tell you all about it later. I'm guiding for him right now."

"All right, listen," Skipjack said. "Have you got that water rights situation straightened out?"

"Not yet," Marshall said. Marshall's father, as deedholder, had been sent the same notices by mail that Marshall had received.

"Well, goddamnit, I'm going to come out there and straighten it out. You're going to wind up giving the whole place away."

"Dad, I am not." Marshall tried to keep his eyes on the road, and avoided appearing to glance at his clients. He didn't need to know they were watching. "It's all under control. You don't need to involve yourself."

"I'm going to hire a goddamn water rights lawyer and come out there and end this. I'm tired of it. Ought to just sell the whole place and be done with it. Who's that guy we had last time we had water rights problems? Buttermilk? Something like that. You call him and find out when he can meet with me and I'll fly out."

Marshall felt a heaviness he put on like a coat. "No. Just . . . I'll handle it."

"You're not exactly handling it so far. Not so well."

"Can I talk to you later about this?" Marshall asked, trying to recoup his tone a little.

"How's everything else?" Skipjack asked. "How's the spring creek?"

"Busy. Bookings are solid for the next few weeks. It's doing great."

"Well, don't neglect that to run around taking care of your buddies' clients."

"It's kind of a serious situation. I'm just helping out—"

"That's Shadford's problem, not yours. I'll call you on Sunday."

"Right."

Marshall dropped the two women at Fly Guys. Dianne curled a fifty-dollar bill into his palm when he said good-bye. Marshall stuffed it in his pocket, to save for Alton. He checked the book to see that Alton was scheduled to guide again in the morning. Marshall examined the booking form, trying to glean any helpful information about the morning's clients, but it was a bare-bones entry. He told Mills he had completed his entire float trip without having to shoot any mountain lions.

Mills folded his arms and leaned back to peer at Marshall and said, "You know, I don't think I like your attitude."

"Fine by me," Marshall said.

He left the shop and drove to the hospital.

"How is he?" Marshall asked Molly in the waiting room.

"Steady but not out of the woods," Molly said. Her broad shoulders sagged, wrapping in toward her chest. "They let me go in and see him for a minute—"

Marshall's look said, "And?"

Molly's eyes fell away and she shook her head. She visibly shivered.

"Did Amy come over?"

Molly jogged her head toward a corner of the waiting room where Amy Baine lay curled in a chair, asleep.

"We need to get you home," Marshall said to Molly.

"I can't."

"It's not a contest, Mol. You need to rest and eat."

He drove her to the Bridge takeout where they got slices of pizza to go, then swung through a convenience store and picked up a six-pack of Pacifico. Molly drank a beer while Marshall drove. The windows were down and he could feel the evening cooling into night on his hands and face. Molly sat slumped, blown back in the seat. He took her to her house. They sat at her table and ate the pizza and drank the beer while he explained his guiding day. "It was weird, to be out there again."

"Did you like it?"

"I don't know," he said.

He told her about the man throwing rocks at them, and where it had happened. She asked him what the guy had looked like.

"He had a gin drinker's nose, a halo of white hair, and a sunburned scalp," Marshall said.

"That's Jimmy's dad. He's probably here to deal with Jimmy."

"I was at the shop; Mills told me the dad already got him out on bail," Marshall said.

"Jimmy's dad is one of those big-time lawyers. This is a small town," Molly said.

"Guy's a sociopath," Marshall said. "How's a guy get like him? I mean, it seems like he could have turned out normal."

Molly took a long swallow of beer. She said, "That scene with the dog at Palmer's wedding? That's the perfect metaphor for how Jimmy is in his family—handsome and useful as an idea but sort of an outlet for fury when things don't go exactly right. I'm not saying his dad burned his hands or anything, but, emotionally? He was raised by really cruel people."

"You've been involved with him, haven't you? Way back when, or whenever," Marshall said. He was pretty sure he knew the answer. "It doesn't matter."

"No," Molly said. "Not Ripley."

Marshall was surprised by her answer, then heard what she'd said. "The other one?"

Molly tilted the beer bottle back to drain it, but kept her eyes on him. That was her answer.

"You have so much more going for you than that," Marshall said.

Molly thought: *isn't that the pot calling the kettle a pot?* "It was a stupid little thing during a very didn't-have-a-clue-what-I-was-doing phase of my life," Molly said. "It wasn't even, you know, full-on. Don't you dare tell Alton."

"Why is it OK for me to know and not Alton?" Marshall asked, feeling the triangle the three of them had formed suddenly swing up onto a pivot point.

"Because you don't hate people. They annoy you, or disappoint you. I don't think you care enough about people to hate them. Alton despises people he decides not to like. If he knew I did that, no matter how innocent it was, he'd hate me forever."

Marshall admired how cleanly she'd described the differences, and wondered why he couldn't care enough to hate someone. It appeared to him suddenly as a tragic flaw. "Why is that, do you suppose?"

"It's all the things he hates about himself," Molly said.

"You don't think I ever hate anything about myself?"

Molly reached a hand to slide along his thigh. "Yes, Marshall, I do." Somehow this seemed like perhaps the sweetest thing she'd ever said. "But the people Alton despises all represent some part of himself he hates. Or they point out a weakness he thinks he has. It's not something you would understand. He sees his flaws in other people. You, for some beautiful, beautiful reason, keep all your flaws on your own terms." Molly's eyes would not leave his alone now. "None of us are as uniquely messed up as we'd like to believe. And you know that. Alton and I don't."

"But you just said it."

"I know it here," Molly said, pointing to her head, "which is very different than knowing it here." She ended with a gesture to her heart.

They lay on the sofa, and somehow Marshall found himself lying back with Molly's head cradled in the pocket of his shoulder, a juxtaposition that allowed them to say things without facing each other.

"I'm tired of hating myself," Molly said.

"Why do you need to?" She heard his voice softer than she ever had, as if every bit of surety were gone, all the words yielding to caution.

"When I was with Alton I felt so guilty for wanting to be with you. And when I was with you, I felt guilty because I knew how much it would hurt him. I hate the going between."

All Marshall could say was, "Molly."

"What if he dies?" she said.

"He won't," Marshall said. His words sounded to her like smoke from a campfire blaze.

"He could," she said. "He might." Marshall felt her fingers tighten on his T-shirt.

"I can't think that," he said.

"When my brother died . . ." Molly started. Marshall had known about her brother's death—the long battle with leukemia, machines eventually trickling off to recordings of a boy's passing. It had happened before Marshall knew her, but she'd talked about it in bits and pieces. When he first met Molly he had sensed a wall of sadness that nobody could penetrate. She had seemed so lost for so long, until really the last two years.

"It won't be like that," Marshall said. He didn't know if he believed it, but wanted to say it to her as if he did.

Molly sat up in a rustle, her head turned to his face. "How do you know?"

"I just have such a strong feeling that he's not going to leave us."

Molly said, "When my brother died I remember seeing his body there, on the bed, hooked to the machines. He was so bloated. It didn't look anything like him anymore. But I'd go in and talk to him. I'd lay my head on his chest and talk to him. The nurses said that when we talked to him, you could see the numbers jump on the machine. His heartbeat jumped and his respiration got stronger. I wanted so badly to believe that it would be enough, that if I just went in there and talked to him enough I could get him going again. He died anyway . . . and when it happened, when he was finally gone, I remember thinking that the one good thing that could possibly come from this is that I would never hurt that much again. In the few days after it happened, I thought there was nothing that could ever hurt this much again. Nothing. And a month later, I thought the same thing. It was worse, but I thought it couldn't possibly get any worse than that. Only it did. It just got worse and worse and worse. I used to cry until I threw up."

Marshall tightened his grip on her shoulder, pulled her closer to him. He ran fingers through her hair. He could feel her tears on his chest. He wanted her to pull away from people who had left her, to think about people who still had a chance.

"I think it must hurt to die," Marshall said. "Even on the machines. I think it must hurt like hell to make that final release, or otherwise why would people fight so hard to stay alive? I think it's a physical pain, but a pain in your soul, too, knowing how much it hurts to leave people. I think Alton's thinking about that right now. At some level, he's thinking about how much it would hurt to leave us all. And he's a tough, tough guy. I think he's going to win, Molly. I do."

He could not tell if she heard him, because he felt her body jerking with sobs. He wondered who the outbreak was for—a lost brother, a dying friend, herself—and then hated wondering if he deserved to know.

Marshall remembered that he had a dog. He jerked awake with this awareness at four-thirty in the morning. Flat on his back he stared at what he could see of the room, trying to figure out where he was. Molly's couch. Perhaps there was enough time to get to the ranch and then back in town in time to meet Alton's clients. He crept into Molly's room and jostled her shoulder. She made a sleepy *mmmmm* sound.

"I gotta go home and try to get back here. I'll see you at the hospital later, OK?"

Another *mmmmm* sound. Marshall slipped from the room. He noticed he was still dressed in river gear. Maybe he could grab clean shorts at home. Marshall flew his one-ton over the highway. False dawn had risen over the West Fork Valley, revealing it to him in a wash without color. The gallery forest of cottonwoods marking the river course stood like a hedgerow in the distance. Marshall sped along the gravel road to his house, watching for the shapes of deer that might be standing too close to the road. Contemplating how many piles of dog shit he was going to have to scrub off the carpet, he turned into his drive and renewed speed, hurling a thick dust cloud into the sky behind his rig. He could not be mad at the dog, he told himself as he drew nearer the house. No matter how bad the mess was, it wasn't the dog's fault. In the distance Marshall could see a light on in his kitchen. He seriously doubted he'd left it that way.

Marshall skidded to a halt in front of the house. The front door opened and Buck charged from it, his weakened paw lending a slap-dash teeter to his progess, as if every gallop might end in a crash. To complicate matters the dog wagged his tail in such rapid, enthusiastic swaths that he threatened to knock his own ass over. He clenched a

filthy, mealy tennis ball in his jaws. As Marshall stepped down from
his truck, the dog planted both forepaws on his chest, shoving him
back against the side of the vehicle.

"Hey hey hey," Marshall was saying, confusing the dog with a tone
that was both appreciative and admonitory. Buck leaped and whined
so hard he nearly squealed. Daisy Klingman came out the door and
stepped off the porch.

"What are you doing here?" Marshall asked. He ripped the tennis
ball from the dog's mouth and threw it. Buck wheeled and devoted his
manic energy into a dashing pursuit.

"I read about your friend in the paper. I tried to call you, to see if
I could help with anything. You weren't home and weren't home, and
then I remembered the dog." She shrugged the rest away.

"How'd you get in?"

She blinked and shook her head. "I've known where the key is for,
like, fifteen years."

"Was it a mess?"

"Not bad at all. Poor guy, he did his best. Just one pile, but it was
right by the door, in the mudroom. How's your friend?"

"Touch and go," Marshall said. Buck cantered up to him and with
a flip of his head tossed the tennis ball against Marshall's leg. Marshall threw the ball as far as he could and the dog tore off across the
yard after it. The sun crested the rim of the valley and poured rich,
sweet light onto upper slopes of the ridges to the west. The yard twinkled with dew. The morning smelled fresh and moist, and the air held
perfectly still. He looked at Daisy, seeing her again as if he hadn't believed what he'd seen the first time.

"Do what you need to do," she said. "I'll take care of the dog. If you
want, I can come over in the morning, take the money from your clients
or whatever—"

"Aw, Daisy, you don't have to . . . I can just do outfitter bookings
and collect later."

"I'm not doing anything much," she said. "We're just haying. It's
mostly done."

"Daisy, you're . . . ," Marshall didn't know what he wanted to say,
only that he felt a suddenly ineluctable surge to say something that
would tear from inside of him, something that would capture the
wooze of feelings washing through him. "I, um, you're so—"

"Just stop," Daisy said. "Just can it."

They stood looking at each other, separated by a few feet of ground. Daisy shifted her weight to one hip and Marshall thought her eye narrowed ever so slightly, just for an instant. But she wasn't going to smile. So he did. A tennis ball bounced against his leg.

Three hours later, when Marshall again appeared at the Fly Guys shop, Shadford was hiding in his office. Marshall opened the door without knocking, thinking it might give him a little edge. He needed one because the truth was, he felt nervous enough to be sick over what he might find out.

Shadford was on the phone. Marshall stepped into the room, closed the door behind him. What followed was a genteel sort of standoff in which Shadford made his best effort to pretend Marshall was not present, all the while prolonging his phone conversation, straying into the subjects of duck hunting, people he and the caller could duck hunt with, Labrador retrievers, Lab breeders, people Shadford and his invisible talking partner knew, and what they were doing now—all the while Marshall stood in the room. He argued with himself about strategy. Should he sit? Make himself comfortable? That might get across the impression that he wasn't leaving until he'd got to business. But standing seemed more authoritarian. It seemed to suggest an upper hand. Although Shadford might appear the more comfortable, seated, looking out the window, jabbering away about the last time he saw ol' so-and-so. *I'm going to have to figure these things out,* Marshall thought, *if I'm going to keep trying to assert myself.*

He did know a thing or two about patience, though, and eventually Shadford's phone pal ran out of things to listen to. Shadford put the phone down, watching himself do it like a man turning over hole cards.

"What's the story on insurance coverage for Alton?" Marshall said.

Shadford blew a short piece of breath from between his lips. "You know, Marshall, I'm going to be honest with you," Shadford said. "You're pretty goddamned naive about how the world works."

Marshall paused for a moment to reflect that, indeed, that seemed to be the case. "What's that mean, you don't have it?"

"My policy lapsed," Shadford said. "We're between policies here. That's all there is to it. It's just rotten timing."

Marshall thought: *Jesus.* "It's not one of those deals where the policy lapses, but then it's reinstated if you just pay the bill, is it?"

"I've been in the process . . . ," Shadford started, but something about Marshall's expression seemed to truncate the folderol, and he said, "It's been lapsed for a couple months. I've been trying . . . hell, you just wouldn't understand what I've been trying. You wouldn't know the first thing about trying to make ends meet." By the end, his words were awash in spite. "You've never been able to move two inches without stepping in Daddy's money."

It was instructive, Marshall noted, that while he heard plenty to be angry about in that little sortie, instead what he mainly felt was a great swooping of sadness. It seemed like he was going to be able to understand, in both his head and his heart, that this was not about him, that Shadford had to bring the action, and that he was standing right here, in the way. A part of him wanted to keep it going, to make Shadford pay with, at a minimum, some measure of guilt—because he knew Shadford well enough to know that he'd find a way to rationalize out from under it. But that wasn't going to be Marshall's job this time. There would probably be a long lawsuit in Shadford's future, involving Alton's health care creditors. Maybe that would keep it all fresh in Shadford's mind, if he didn't figure out a way to cast himself as the little-guy victim fighting the big, bad insurance industry. Anyway, who knew what visited Shadford in the small hours of the night? Not Marshall. Not anymore. He had to be done with it.

Out in the shop, Amy Baine cornered him near a rack of Patagonia fleece jackets and asked him what he'd heard. He could tell her nothing. "I went to the hospital," she said.

"I saw you there. You were sleeping."

"I don't know . . . ," Amy said.

"What did you expect?" Marshall asked. He had always thought Amy was attractive in the way pretty twenty-three-year-old girls can be, but he saw in her sadness an opening to the deeper cavities of beauty within her, the sort of soulfulness and caring that could arise with lovely resonance throughout her lifetime.

"I feel so removed," she said.

"Is that a choice you made?"

"Maybe it was a mistake," she said. "But what if it was a mistake I couldn't ever make up for?"

"How could you have known?" Marshall said. "Don't punish your-self like that. If this hadn't happened, where would you be?"

"Honestly? Unhappy."

Marshall reached out to squeeze Amy's shoulder. "Well, that's probably another story. And it may honestly be too late for some things. But it's not too late to care," he said. "It never is."

Alton's—now Marshall's—clients for the day waited, a large barrel-chested man with broad shoulders, who, within moments of introduction, let it be known that he had once played linebacker at Nebraska. Marshall could see in his beady eyes a certain passion for destruction, an expression so diluted by intervening celebrations of past glories that he doubted the man could sort out the difference between making remark-able tackles and telling the tales about them. The man wore thin gym shorts that hung like curtains around his scraggly legs, providing the impression that the lower half of his body had nothing to do with the broad-chested beast above. He had with him his son, a gangly, straw-blond kid who was, Marshall recognized, terrified by his father—the kind of kid who just wanted to play guitar, or maybe his Sony PlayStation.

"I want this boy to catch some Bitterroot River rainbow trout and I hear you're the man to get that done," the linebacker said.

Marshall had a number of different things he wanted to say to that, but he settled on "Bitterroot is a hard river to do well on."

"I just read an article in *Fly Fisherman* magazine that said the Bitterroot was one of the best big-fish rivers in the West."

Marshall was able to wheedle from the man that he had "just" read the article the previous January. "In March and April it's great, but this time of year it's a hard stretch of water. Real fickle," Marshall said, "Now the Blackfoot—"

"I came out here to fish the Bitterroot and that's where we're going to fish."

"I'm fishing the 'Root today," Billy Mills said. He was standing be-side Marshall with a hand reaching out to tap Marshall's shoulder. He said, "Dude, can I talk to you a sec?"

Marshall immediately grew wary as he excused himself and let Mills twist him away. Mills said, "I got this thing going . . ." He left a long pause to indicate what sort of thing it was.

Marshall let Mills look at him for a while. Marshall definitely knew. This was the second occasion he knew of Mills kiting clients from Shadford's shop. He found it sort of charming that Mills thought he understood Marshall's enmity toward Shadford enough to believe it didn't extend to his own self.

"Well, I want to go Woodside to Bell. I heard it's fishing hot, dude, *en fuego*," Mills said. "My boys were up there yesterday rippin' lips. Just utterly."

"Who's this?"

"My sources, dude, my peeps. They said it was a meat market. You should seriously take this goob up there, in which case, you know, I need a shuttle and you need a shuttle so I was wondering if we could maybe use one together?"

"I'm just going to call Palmer," Marshall said.

"Yeah, well, maybe you could just inform him to do my rig, too," Mills said. "Maybe on the q.t.?"

This was not his job, either, dealing with Mills's duplicity or his obliviousness to the notion that things might catch up to him. But it fell right in Marshall's lap. There was making good, and there was getting even; Marshall wasn't sure exactly which he was aimed at, and at the moment it didn't seem to matter. What he saw was an appropriate outlet for some pent-up frustration. "I'll take care of it," he said. "You got the money?"

"Oh, dude, that's so killer cool," Mills said, digging into his jeans pocket. "And we'll stay away from your boat, no shit. Hey, can I pay you after?"

"Sure," Marshall said. "You putting your keys in the gas cap?"

"Right on. It's the white Ford with the rack on the back. Tell Palmer. He'll know it."

Marshall returned briefly to his clients, advised them on some flies to purchase, then stepped away to call Palmer Tillotson. When Palmer answered, Marshall updated him on Alton's condition, then said he had a rig to shuttle, Alton's Toyota pickup, and yes, that would be the only Fly Guys outfit to shuttle on the Bitterroot today. "I think Mills is fishing up there today, but he's running his own shuttle," Marshall said.

When he had guided for a living, Marshall had wanted to learn something from every client he worked with. This day rang with midsummer brilliance and as he walked through the back door of the shop Marshall could see the Clark Fork River running dark in contrast to the thin blue of sky. Green saturated its banks. Already Marshall noted wisps of cloud floating above the Bitterroots, and he took this as a harbinger of midafternoon showers—exactly what he wanted to happen. The ex-football player and his son followed Marshall down the wrought-iron staircase and when the voice croaked, "Buddy, your tip today is going to be a dollar for every fish my boy gets to the boat," Marshall realized that this day would be a lesson in why he quit guiding in the first place.

Among its many other foibles, the Bitterroot was a light-sensitive stretch of water. Marshall stood hip-deep on the inside turn of a riffle and watched in amazement as the entire expanse of water above the riffle—a flat, featureless section with nothing to recommend it—exploded with fish, which the football player's boy could not catch. The football player either sat in the raft and smoked cigars or waved his own rod back and forth until his fly snapped off in the bushes behind him. A regular sequence unfurled: Cumulus clouds sailing like spinnakers across the sky drifted away from the sun, leaving a hard, warm light; *Baetis* popped up on the flat surface, adjusting their own translucent sails; then another cloud drifted across the sun, dimming the glare, and the fish turned on, blasting the surface like a bank-to-bank minefield.

It was Marshall's superstition that when western Montana trout keyed in on *Baetis*, they would look at almost nothing else. He understood this belief was the kind fishermen always hold dear; he had no idea if it was true, but he believed it helped him catch fish. The hatch lasted almost exactly two hours and then the whole river shut off. During the window of opportunity, every now and then, in an act of suicidal sacrifice, a fish would leap to the surface and impale its mouth on the boy's hook. Marshall felt distracted and unable to help the kid. He realized another reason he did not want to come to this river: it made him remember the last day he had floated with Alton the previous spring—the skunk, Molly's hidden spot, the confrontation with Dean Stone. That had been so typical of spring Bitterroot fishing, where one thing may happen or another, seven days may be terrible and the eighth unbelievable. The wind blew, then it didn't. But in the spring on the Bitterroot, when everything came together and you happened to be there, the days became relics, banners commemorating a decision to be in a place and hope it's the right time.

Meanwhile, on this day, the boy in his boat caught little. His father had not been kidding, either. At the end of a long day, he handed Marshall a wad of bills that totaled ten dollars—five for the number of fish the boy had caught and five extra because one fish had been over fifteen inches. Marshall must have failed to disguise his chagrin.

"Jesus, guides are the same everywhere," he heard the man telling his son as they walked away back at the shop. "You pay them to go fishing and then they resent you for it."

Marshall remembered fondly just the previous day, the two women who had appreciated this one little thing he knew how to do well. So long ago. The sky held a pale shade just short of dark, making ghosts of the mountains surrounding town when he drove to the hospital.

Molly, who looked her own sort of ghoulish, sat bedside and had nothing to report beyond what Marshall already knew—that Alton was stable, that he was recovering, that every day was good news, that they would just have to wait and see what kind of front temporal lobe damage had been done.

Alton looked barely alive, his head wrapped in gauze, his body covered in sheets. His face had been shaved and the skin looked tender and wounded. A clear mask was taped over his nose and mouth, from which a mint-green corrugated tube jutted and snaked around to the machine hissing at the bedside. An IV stand held two bags of clear liquid, dripping into the tubes that disappeared in a needle under another patch of tape on the back of Alton's left hand. Marshall could see so little of Alton's body, and in the places he could—swaths of face, forearms—Alton's flesh looked like the carcass of a newly dead baby bird. Around the bottom edge of his head bandage, Alton's skin shone. The rest of his body seemed deflated. Marshall couldn't imagine Alton's frail arms capable of once rowing boats.

"I've gotta go to work tomorrow but I can't," Molly said. "I can't find anybody to cover me."

"I gave Kyle Klingman a guide's license," Marshall said. "He's fine up on that stretch of the West Fork at our place."

"Daisy's brother?"

"Little brother. I've floated it with him, he knows where the fish are. He's a viable option."

"That sounds so ridiculous, but I might have to."

Marshall felt disappointed at how easily she gave up her objection to hiring Daisy's brother. He glanced around the room, surprised not to see Amy Baine, until Molly told him she had gone to pick up Alton's mother at the airport. He wondered what it was like, the two of them sitting in the same room for so many hours, worried about the same thing. He suddenly didn't want to be there when Amy Baine returned with Alton's mother. Though he'd known Alton for over ten years, Marshall had met his mother only once. He felt much the same about his own mother for years. Marshall could still see his mother, an accidental beauty who bore a striking resemblance to the young Natalie Wood, sitting in the kitchen of the house she bought in Canandaigua after the divorce, eating jelly beans from a bag. Her brown eyes yawned huge and vacant, and she seemed to have moved out of herself. He had thought he had lost his mother then, that she would never come back to him, though he had been too young to understand what he feared. At the time he had only felt a grainy, malicious malaise.

His mother came back in her own way, years later. Skipjack married a thirty-year-old socialite, which pissed off Sarah Tate enough to goad her into living well, and papering her luxury with his money. It was she who eventually taught Marshall that open rebellion was a waste of time, given that Skipjack paid so little attention to either of them. "It's one thing to prepare for loss and another to demand it," was the thing his mother said that grew talons and clutched the inner curve of Marshall's cranium. Rather, Sarah taught him how to live on his father's ranch and endeavor to make it a better place than his father possessed the imagination to picture. From those exhortations sprang the spring creek. And by then the evolution in Marshall's thinking had him believing that he might do more than just improve his father's land; he might even teach his father how it had happened.

Marshall wondered what Alton's mother meant to him. What lessons had Alton's mother taught him? Why would you not know that about so dear a friend? His hand rested on Molly's shoulder. He tried to assemble what he knew about her mother: divorced, teacher, lived in Havre. Never really approved of her daughter's life choices, but there was the whole brother-who-died thing. Dying people always seemed to wreak some kind of havoc.

"Let's get you out of here for a while," Marshall said to Molly.

She reached up and squeezed the hand and twisted her head to look up at him. "Not yet," she said. "They'll be back soon."

Marshall thought, *who?* but then knew: Alton's mother . . . and Amy. "Molly," he chided.

He felt her grip tighten on his hands, grinding his knuckles together. "I'll go home later," she said.

Marshall drove to Alton's house and stood looking at Alton's bed, which featured grimy blue sheets on top of which, like the cast-off husk of an emerged insect, lay a wrinkled sleeping bag. *Thirty-two years old and he's still sleeping in a sleeping bag.* It occurred to Marshall that probably this was exactly where Molly and Alton had recently consummated whatever it was they were consummating, and, furthermore, the sheets had likely not been changed since. The couch grew more charming. Marshall stretched out, feeling his face press into its woolly tweed. He prided himself in being able to conk out anywhere, but this time sleep's sweet suspension took forever to slide under his consciousness.

In the morning he wasted little time waking, rising, and making coffee. While it brewed, he called the Klingman ranch. Without any introduction he asked for Kyle, and when the boy came on he said, "You want to play guide for a few days?"

"Aw, boy, now's not a good time. I mean, I gotta help Dad finish the haying."

"Hay? You've been wanting to guide all summer and I've got three or four days of legitimate float-boat guiding with real clients who pay cash money tips and you're going to *hay?*"

"We gotta hay, Marshall."

"You're going to make two hundred and fifty dollars a day plus tips. You can hire someone to take your place stacking the damned bales."

"Yeah," Kyle said. A long silence followed. Marshall listened to Kyle breathe, imagined him working this one through. He smiled into the phone mouthpiece, thinking about Kyle on the other end, sweating, until Kyle said, "Well, all right then."

For some reason Marshall felt flush with victory—he actually double-clutched his fist in the classic *yes!* gesture when Kyle said he'd do it. He drove straight to Fly Guys. Inside Palmer Tillotson, wearing a T-shirt so old it had rents like wounds across the shoulders, was standing near the front of the shop talking to Shadford. Shadford shot

Marshall a look of warning, which Marshall assumed had something to do with Amy Baine jumping ship, but Shadford remained up near the till when Palmer broke off the conversation and moved back through the shop toward Marshall. Already a few clients stood near the fly bins picking out the day's offerings.

When he drew close, in a tone guarded from the other customers, Palmer asked, "Hey, what the hell went on with Mills yesterday?"

"Huh?" Marshall said, though some vestige of his sense of humor was dawning on him.

"Mills called me last night at about two-thirty, three in the morning from some all-night gas station, all livid because I didn't shuttle his rig. He said you were supposed to set it up," Palmer said. "You told me he was handling it."

"This is going to be one of those things I don't know anything about," Marshall said.

"OK," Palmer said, his grin cutting to the chase. "Bad night for Mills. He apparently took the wrong channel on the Woodside-to-Bell float. You know if you stay river-right through all those channels you wind up in a channel that's an irrigation canal, but this time of year it doesn't have enough water in it? It takes you out into a ranch and then just kind of stops? Apparently he made that mistake. He had to drag his boat all the way back up the channel—meanwhile it goes pitch-dark on him—he gets back to the main stem by about midnight, and at two in the morning he arrives at the takeout to find he doesn't have a rig because nobody called in a shuttle for him. I guess he had some people with him. And then he hitchhiked to a gas station and called me. He was six different kinds of pissed off."

Marshall wanted to laugh about that, but his attention was drawn to a sudden raising of voices near the cash register. Two men stood there, yelling at Shadford. Marshall recognized them as the same two guys he saw Mills leaving the shop with the previous morning. He tilted his head toward them and said to Palmer, "These are the pipers, coming to get paid. Stick around. Things are about to get real interesting."

"Huh-uh, man, I'm outta here."

Palmer left and Marshall overheard one of the men chewing at Shadford. "—paid good goddamned money to be guided by an *experienced* guide and you set me up with that bozo . . ."

Shadford shuffled through the guide book, mumbling, "Who was your guide?"

"Bill Mills."

"He's not one of our—"

"We met him right here in this shop yesterday, didn't we? Are you telling me you don't know who your own guides are?"

Marshall sidled on up toward the front. Shadford caught his eye, but Marshall gave him a visual shrug of the shoulders. He eased over to a fly bin and casually picked through some grasshopper patterns, but really he was there to watch Shadrat twist.

HOPPERS

"He's awake," Molly said. She moved toward him in the hallway outside Alton's room. Marshall was finished with his fourth day of guiding Alton's clients. Nobody was getting his best efforts, and he'd shut today's people down around four o'clock in the afternoon. Now it was past six.

"Why are you out here?" Marshall asked, pulling up before Molly reached him.

"They're changing his sheets."

"How is he?"

"Frail. Kind of out of it. But awake."

"Where's his mom?"

"She's been here all day. He woke up around noon. Amy took her back to Alton's to get some rest."

Marshall swept forward and wrapped his arms around her. He squeezed hard, wondering why he'd waited so long to do it. "This is great," he said. "This is great, Molly."

A nurse pushed open the door to Alton's room. "Can we go in?" Marshall asked.

"He's really tired," the nurse said. "Just for a minute."

Marshall hurried into the room. A second nurse hovered bedside, fussing with Alton's IV bags. Beneath puffy lids, Alton's eyes rolled to

track Marshall's entrance. The blood vessels of his corneas had exploded, turning the whites of his eyes red. The intubation mask was
gone from his face and his skin looked pale and papery, the complex-
ion of an octogenarian. Marshall slid into the chair beside Alton's head
and laid a hand on his shoulder. Molly stood at the foot of the bed.
"Hey, buddy. How you feeling?"

"Don't do that," Alton said. His speech was slurred and Marshall
had to lean close to hear some of the words.

"Do what?"

"Don't touch me. I don't like being touched right now." His voice
was rough and raspy, cutting in and out.

"OK," Marshall said. He lifted his hand and put it in his lap.
"Sorry. How you doing?"

"Tell him what you did with your breathing tube," the nurse said.

"It bothered me," Alton creaked.

"He pulled it out."

"Ouch," Marshall said.

"I woke up and found that thing down my throat. I was scared.
Now it hurts to talk."

"Can I get you some water or something?" Marshall asked.

"They only let me suck on these things." He lifted from a cup on
the bed tray what looked like a rock-candy swizzle stick, except where
the candy would be was a knot of greenish sponge, sparkling with glu-
cose wetness. Alton plunked it in his mouth and sucked on it. Then he
pulled it back out.

"Oh, man, you don't know how good it is to hear your voice," Marshall said. "Do you hurt?"

"I'm drugged," Alton said. He lifted a handheld clicker. "Morphine."

"They gave him Versed, too," Molly said. "It makes you forget how
much things hurt."

"Do you remember what happened?" Marshall asked.

"I don't care," Alton said.

"Do you remember any of it?"

Alton made a faint nod toward Molly. "She told me. I don't even
remember being in the bar."

Molly leaned in and tweaked Alton's blanketed foot, eliciting an
instant, if feeble, reaction—just a face that let Molly know everything
she needed to know about touching him again.

"Sorry. Hey, I'm going to get a Diet Coke. Marsh, anything?"

Marshall said no and Molly ducked out of the room. Marshall looked at Alton, and their eyes met. Marshall searched to find what was in Alton's, but the pupils were pinpoints and the focus blurred.

"I gotta get out of here," Alton said.

Marshall raised a hand to clasp his shoulder again, but caught himself and dropped it instead to grip the mattress. He said, "Hey, buddy, don't you worry about anything but getting better. I'm guiding all your clients and socking all the money away. Everything's fine on the outside."

"No, I gotta get out of here. They have me tied down. I can't move," Alton said. "Get me out."

"We'll get you out just as soon as we can."

"I want out now."

Marshall felt Alton's birdlike grip on his forearm and looked into Alton's eyes. He found a wildness there he could not quantify, and then it passed as Alton's lids slipped shut and his head dropped back on his pillows. The nurse returned and placed a paper cup full of more swizzle sticks on Alton's bed tray. "You'll have to leave soon," she said to Marshall, then she left the room again.

"You think it'd be OK if I took Molly home for a while?" Marshall asked Alton.

Alton's eyes opened and he pulled into a frown, which seemed to cause him some pain. "You're going home with her?"

"I'll crash on the couch maybe. She's been here all day, every day. She needs a break, but I think she might need you to say it's OK."

"Why?" Alton asked. His concentration was swimmy, his eyes tightening, then letting go.

"She's real emotional right now," Marshall said, "and she maybe doesn't see that you don't need her here every waking moment."

"I don't need her here at all."

"Maybe don't tell her that."

"I've got all these nurses and doctors," Alton said, "My mom. Amy's here all the time. I have too many people around, if you want to know the truth."

"OK," Marshall said, "I'm just saying everybody's a little fragile right now."

Alton's expression seemed to accuse Marshall of taking sides.

"We're all here to help you get better and get out of here," Marshall protested. "I'm just saying, you know, Molly's a tough kid, but she has some soft spots, too."

Alton's eyes flashed. He said, "Don't treat me . . ." His voice clipped out and Marshall had to twist his head to indicate he hadn't heard. Alton surged forward weakly and said, ". . . like I'm weak."

"I'm not," Marshall said. "I don't mean to. She's relying on you more than you may know, is what I mean. Maybe so much she doesn't realize she's waiting for permission to take a breather."

Alton dropped his head back on his pillow. He seemed unable to puzzle out the intricacies of what Marshall was saying, and the effort had overwhelmed him. He struggled to compose a casual expression, as if he had forgotten how to make his face look relaxed. He said, "So what have you been doing?"

"Nothing, man. Guiding. Just guiding for Fly Guys. I'm sure Shadford would send his regards, if he had any."

Marshall convinced Molly to walk a few blocks downtown to eat burritos in a shop on Higgins. Marshall could see now how worn she was, how the tension of waiting out Alton's coma had broken with his emergence into consciousness, but how the initial elation of seeing Alton awake could not lift the incredible grinding of worry and psychic deal-making she'd endured for days.

There was a loveliness to her exhaustion, aroused perhaps by empathy, perhaps sheer admiration. She was, for the few moments while they walked through the town's summer evening, letting him take care of her. And, while he was not very good at knowing how to do it, her very gesture of making the option available let him feel a deepening in himself. *This*, he thought, *must be the kind of thing that makes love possible.*

For two weeks Alton lay in the hospital bed. Alton's mother, a small woman with hair hard and shiny like a tin roof, endured the worst of it. Late one night, after a day of guiding Alton's clients, Marshall sneaked into Alton's room and found Alton's mother at the bedside, reading. She looked at him above narrow, gold-framed reading glasses. Marshall said hello, asked how Alton was. Maureen Summers told him that Alton had been resting hard for a while and probably should for a while longer. He'd had a big day, talking and looking around. Marshall asked if he could just sit for a while, bedside.

Maureen seemed to think about that, shifted to sit more upright, then said, "Sure. Do you want me to leave?" She liked to move her jaw a lot to get words all wrapped up.

"No," Marshall said, "no, not at all. I just want to, you know . . . be here."

Maureen nodded, seemed to approve of the sentiment. She made a show of returning to her reading. Marshall felt her distance and wondered if it was an effort not to impose, or just the sort of device she needed to trudge through this vigil. He felt a bit guilty about changing the space.

"How are you doing?" he asked, emphasizing the "you."

Maureen looked up over her glasses again. Her tongue sat forward in her mouth, filling up the space just behind her teeth. She said, "Fine."

Marshall had a third idea then, that perhaps he was being tarred with the brush of blame, part of what made her be here. He didn't want that either.

"Are you getting out to eat and everything?" Marshall asked. He knew it was a stupid question before she gave him the look. "Are you getting outside at all? Getting any fresh air?"

Maureen appeared to decide to abandon the book for a moment, tilting her wrist to let it fall away, and let Marshall know he had her full attention. "I'm fine," she said. "I eat at the cafeteria."

"How's that?"

"It's not bad. They have salads."

Marshall nodded, realizing how the thread he'd started now blundered its way into a dead end. Maybe she'd known that was going to happen. The politeness fell away from him then, and he said, "I miss him."

Alton's mother continued looking at him.

"I miss his smart mouth and just being around him. I never thought I'd . . . I never thought I'd have to miss him. It's weird."

"Are your parents still alive, Marshall?"

"Yeah. Divorced. I've lost all my grandparents."

"It's different, isn't it?" Maureen said.

"I don't see my mother very much. And my father doesn't really see me."

"Alton lost his father when he was very young."

"I talk to my mother, on the phone. She doesn't like it out here. Reminds her too much of my dad."

"Do you ever go see her?"

"At Christmas," Marshall said. "There's really not a lot for me to do there."

Maureen nodded. "Do you ever go places with her?"

Marshall pushed his lips together. "Like where?"

"Anywhere," Maureen said. "When Alton was in college, he and I went to Costa Rica together." Marshall vaguely remembered Alton making the trip. They were just getting to know each other at the time, and Marshall, a callow college sophomore, had made a great sport of Alton traveling abroad with his mother. "We saved up and Alton found some cheap airfare. It was terrible; we sat on the runway for four hours in a sweltering heat. I don't like to fly to start with. And then they sent the plane back and we all got off and waited another four hours. I thought I'd go crazy. And when we got there, Alton had arranged everything and the place we were supposed to stay was supposed to send someone to pick us up, but they weren't there because we were so late, and so we hired a car, but the last part was a muddy road and the driver wouldn't take us the rest of the way. And it was the middle of the night by then. So we had to walk the last mile in the dark down this road through the jungle with the bugs and all those creepy sounds, and we didn't even know if we were going the right way. It was the best trip of my life."

Marshall smiled. "Sounds like it."

"It really was. I found out things about myself. I found out things about Alton, too."

Marshall thought about his own mother, how she'd handle a situation like that. She was a tough cookie, his mother. Marshall had always thought of her as broken by the end of her marriage, but when he was seeing it with some remove, he understood that she'd bounced and found a way to live that she liked. He thought: *I bet on a muddy road in a foreign country on a dark night, I bet she would have trusted me.*

Engrossed in the act of remembering, Maureen continued skating off on her own. "God, when Alton was little his father and I used to tell him and his brother and sister that we really only ever wanted two kids and if they didn't behave we were taking one of them back," she said. She tried a lazy grin to let him know it had been a joke at the time. Then her smile cavitated. "I could kill myself for saying that."

Marshall tried to assure her that he doubted she had scarred her son. "He's never once mentioned it."

"Nowadays most people—and by 'most people,' of course, I mean people whose opinion I don't respect—think children are little pieces of precious pottery or something," Maureen said. "It was different when we raised our kids. Trying to run a household and raise three kids. There was about a ten-year period where I never slept. Now of course everybody goes to therapy to find out where their parents screwed up. But I think my kids came out great. I think they're good kids."

"You raised good kids," Marshall concurred.

"Except for things like this," Maureen said.

"This wasn't Alton's fault. This was just . . . things got out of hand. And the guy he got tangled up with is a seriously bad actor."

"When Alton was a boy he spent all of his time outside," Maureen was saying, again seeking shelter from the present. "He'd crawl around in the dirt and mud looking at bugs or lie in the grass and watch birds. I could never understand why it mattered so much to him which ducks were back on the river when, or which finches were at the feeder. But it sure did. And then he kept all those insects in his room . . ." Maureen made a sucker face that meant *Yuk!*

"I was kind of like that," Marshall said. "Not the same extreme maybe."

"What do you think of Amy?" Maureen asked with a sly suddenness. Marshall understood from the cool crinkly wrapping in which the question was presented that there was a certain way she expected him to think of Amy.

"I've always liked Amy," he said. "She's young. She makes young-person mistakes."

"She and a few other characters around here."

"But I think her heart's in the right place," Marshall said, deciding to ignore what could have been a swipe at him instead of deducing whether it was.

"I wouldn't know," Mrs. Summers said.

"Have you not met her before?"

"This is the first time," Maureen said. "Alton went to her house for Christmas last year instead of bringing her home." An occurrence for which Amy Baine was clearly not yet forgiven.

"I know," Marshall tried, "that Alton cared a great deal for her for quite a long time."

Maureen chuffed. "She's too pretty," she said.

"She's also been at the hospital every day this week," Marshall said.

"That prettiness, it's a flaw. Alton doesn't need a pretty face. He needs somebody more sturdy. He needs somebody more like that Molly."

Marshall must have frowned out loud, because Maureen waved her hand in front of her mouth and said, "Not that Molly's not pretty. She's just not . . . *too* pretty. Molly's not going to let prettiness distract her."

Still not able to rally an appropriate reply, Marshall let his eyebrows arc, hoping that let her know he was taking all this quite seriously.

"You know men fall in love with perfection," Maureen said, "but they stay in love with potential."

"I did not know that," Marshall said, still nodding.

An awkward silence descended, and Marshall felt cheated. When the conversation had been about mothers and sons, a brief flash of illumination had revealed an amorphous opening in the inner caverns of possibility. But then the light flicked away toward more obvious passages, as if Maureen had never even seen the recess that caught his attention. Shortly thereafter more awkwardness ensued as Alton's eyes came wide open. Alton was either terrified to be awake, or to remain unconscious.

"It's huge!" Alton gasped.

"What is?" Marshall asked, caught up in the elevated panic levels. He looked to Maureen for cues.

"It's huge! Right out there!" Alton croaked.

"He's been dreaming," his mother said.

"It was gonna take me down. Suck me down. They were fishing and it came up from under me . . ."

Marshall watched the ideas drop through Alton's consciousness like the metallic balls of a Chinese pinball game working their way through the silver pins, each contact warping the expression on Alton's face a new way. He felt helpless in the face of Alton's fear, even as he realized Alton was not completely awake. Marshall wanted to reach his friend, hold out a metaphorical steadying hand. Then Alton's hand clasped his forearm, forming a band of cool but relentless pressure. Marshall felt himself being pulled into the man on the bed, yanked into him, and, startled, he pulled away. He beseeched Alton's mother, who had been watching her son with one long-lasting shrug. It wasn't until she glimpsed Marshall's fright that she stepped in, stood beside the bed, folded Alton's grasping fingers in her hands, held them to his chest. "You're all right," Maureen said. "You're OK, now. You're fine. Come with us now. Come talk to us . . ."

And gradually, through a litany of murmurings, Alton subsided into another sleep—this one festering with tics and twitches—without ever breaking into lucidity.

"The drugs," Maureen said. "They make him dream the craziest things."

Later, as his emergence gained momentum, Alton told wild stories of the things he saw in his drugged haze. He swore the doctors were screening blue movies on the monitors in his room. He claimed the nurses were fishing in the hallway. Giant water creatures, usually fishlike with additional insect characteristics—wings, six legs—lurked beneath his bed. One night he'd seen a roomful of people standing silently around his bed, poised as if about to laugh mockingly at him. He knew these images were fantasy, but seemed to find them fascinating, as if the dreams had assumed more significance than his waking life.

His muscular coordination was slow to return. His fingers seemed reluctant to close over objects, and when they did they held scant pressure. Sometimes his hands had trouble finding his mouth. When finally he was able to eat food, he repeatedly spilled the liquefied menu items and fruit juices down the front of him, which resulted in a dress code that on any given day lent the appearance of a mad artist in his smock. Most disturbing was an odd little smirk that etched itself onto Alton's face. He seemed to be remembering a joke so dirty he couldn't tell it in present company, though Alton seemed to have no control over, nor awareness of, the inappropriate expression.

Alton's doctors quickly inferred that Molly and Amy Baine would be doing the caretaking during Alton's home recovery. While she remained in town, the doctors addressed every bit of news first to Alton's mother. But once his recovery seemed imminent, Maureen Summers flew back to Seattle to work and wait and see what the next step would entail. After that what passed in doctor-speak for the long drawn-out conversations were directed at Molly and Amy. They told Molly that it would take a long time for Alton to regain simple states like equilibrium, and longer to move comfortably around even familiar places like his home. He was going to be brittle and frangible. His moods would soar and plummet, but mostly plummet. His personality might not be the same, they said, though they failed to divulge how that could be so. Alton would likely be subject to fierce headaches, and unreferred pain in seemingly unlikely spots on his body. They were in for a long, strange trip.

After nearly three full weeks in the hospital, Alton was released in late August. On his third day home, in the evening, Molly and Marshall stood in Alton's kitchen by the sink. She rapidly deployed clean dishes into a rack. Marshall wiped them with a dish towel. He had started attempting to place dishes in the shelves and had reached a frying pan into a cupboard beside the range when a querulous plaint floated from the bedroom.

"That doesn't go there."

Marshall swung around and looked at the bedroom door, half opened. He could see, stuffed against the wall, the duffel bag Molly was living out of, but he had no clear view of Alton in the bed.

"How could he know that?" Marshall said to Molly. He trusted the splash of water from the faucet and Molly's clanging of flatware and cookware to cover his voice.

"I don't think he really does," Molly said, her tone low, too. "But the odder thing is he didn't used to care at all. Organization was not something you expected to find at Alton's house. Yesterday he made me alphabetize his spices. He's only got about five different spices."

"Weird," Marshall said. He imagined Molly spending her days reshuffling items in the cupboards, or chasing dust bunnies beneath the bed. He knew she was reading to Alton. She'd started *Moby-Dick* while he was in the hospital, reading to him while he was unconscious just to keep the sound of a voice flowing into his head. Then he'd come out of it and demanded that she start over at the beginning.

How all of this affected Marshall's own life had ceased to matter at a certain point. Whereas he had felt a festering unease about the jumbled dissilience the three of them had managed to create prior to

Alton's injury, those concerns now burbled in a low-grade background noise.

"I talked to the other guides at Fly Guys, Karl Hager and Charlie Duggan and those guys," Marshall said. "They're going to work it out so they cover Alton's clients, and they're going to put the money in a fund for him. I may have to do another day or two here and there, but they're going to cover it from here. I'm pretty much done."

"Good of them," Molly said.

"When are you going to get back on the river?" Marshall asked.

"I don't know," Molly said. "I made some phone calls, lined up some other guides to take my people. Kyle Klingman got a bunch of them. He's done a good job. I cleared the next three weeks."

"Three weeks?" Marshall said. This was really too much. He lowered his voice. "Molly, I'm worried about you. I'm afraid you're losing yourself here. I think you ought to get back to work."

"I don't know if I'm going back to work," Molly said.

"You're just going to hang around here and play nurse all day? He won't need that after a while."

Molly laid a broiling gaze on him. "I think, yes, this could take some time," Molly said. "And then after that I don't know what I'm going to do. I don't know if I'm going back to guiding full-time."

The detached voice sliced in from the bedroom: "I can't hear what you're saying, but I don't like the way you two are talking to each other."

Both of them turned as if they could see the voice's flight path. Then they checked each other. Marshall dropped the pan he was drying back onto the rack. "Why would you do that? Quit guiding?"

"I don't care about it anymore," Molly said. She had noticed this, rather than arriving at it. She had noticed that being here—in Alton's apartment, or her own house, or sitting outside under a tree as college students walked by, or running to the grocery store, or bumping into people she knew—she didn't miss being on the river. She talked to guides every night, checking with Kyle Klingman and the other guys she'd rounded up to cover her clients. She asked about the hatches, asked about the water, knew what people caught. She had noticed that none of these conversations made her want to step into a fly shop, trade banter, or sit in the Rhino and brag about fish. None of them made her want to row people downstream, telling them where to place their next cast. "Christ, Marshall, you quit guiding, why can't I?"

This did beg the question, Marshall thought. He kept hearing Molly's words as repudiation of his own life choices, was why. But there was a budding realization that seeking validation by proxy was, perhaps, not the game of champions. It probably wasn't very fair, either. In a last sputter of petty self-righteousness, he said, "I quit to do something else."

"Well then, that's what I'll do," Molly said.

Despite his auspicious beginning with it, Marshall remained both concerned and fascinated by the whirling disease epidemic infesting the state's rivers, and when a stakeholder's meeting had been organized by the state Department of Fish, Wildlife and Parks, Marshall had called in and signed up. Life was staggering onward. There seemed no ducking it.

Marshall rose early for the drive and reached Butte before sunrise. A heavy rain had fallen just before he crossed the Divide so that when he rolled down the eastern slope onto the alluvial plain near Whitehall, heavy clouds hung seemingly just above his reach. The slopes of the Tobacco Root Mountains shone black with wet trees. Sunlight sliding in low from the east fired the cooled air so that tendrils of steam rose from the valley floor wherever the earth was green. Flimsy patches of fog hung suspended between the bottoms of the clouds and the steaming ground. The sun sautéed the grass and shrubs so that a green aroma seemed to rise from them.

Marshall had embarked on this trip full of the sense that something would come of it, that he would empower himself vis-à-vis whirling disease. He felt potential, all of which had drained away by the time he reached Belgrade. It had been—a year?—a while since he'd driven to Bozeman in daylight, and the cream and brown and plywood-colored panels he saw rising across the farmlands between the Bridger Range and the Gallatin Mountains shocked him. As far as he could see into the distance, shiny new houses stood. Around Belgrade they clustered in vast tracts, big and boxy, roomy homes built for brawny families, the type of which energized the suburbs of all the nation's cities, large and small. He felt certain their owners thought these structures beautiful. Farther into the distance housing starts had become the primary cash crop in the former ranch land of the Gallatin Valley.

Marshall found himself shocked by the runaway development, which led him to cascade through his own memory in an effort to determine when he had last driven through here. When he first moved to Missoula permanently he had been in college, and had very early on met Alton. The two of them knew other people, boys and girls interested in rock climbing, backcountry skiing, trekking, but Marshall and Alton recognized in each other an impatience for the exertion of energy in topographical zones that did not contain rivers and streams. Nor were either of them particularly interested in sitting in a plastic kazoo, wrapped in neoprene, paddling through washing machines or suckholes. They were fishermen and neither had to explain to the other just what they found romantic about spending nine hours in a pickup truck, eating beef jerky and sunflower seeds and drinking Schmidt's beer, listening to bad country music—all as a prelude to the moment you step out of the vehicle and breathe new river-flavored air and hear the sounds of a new stream and see for the first time the features that everywhere define rivers—rocks and current and bank and sedge and leaf and log and light and swirl and sweep—unfurling before you in a brand new arrangement you have never before imagined, yet one that appears inevitable and organic.

Even before they had mastered the water near Missoula, Marshall and Alton had run all over the streams of south-central Montana, shooting over for weekends on the Madison and the Yellowstone, the Gallatin, the Beaverhead, and Jefferson. They'd sneaked onto the Ruby back when ranchers were offering to shoot fishermen in that valley. Once or twice a winter the two of them drove seven or eight hours to the Bighorn, floated for an evening—usually by full moon to avoid the hordes of floaters on that magnificent water—then turned around and drove home. They'd started with the big, well-known streams and over the years eventually trickled into the Boulder, Stillwater, and Elk Rivers; Slough, Hellroaring, and Frenchman's Creeks; nameless springs and sloughs that dribbled through remote ranches; and the high-country ponds and lakes that stipple those mountainous valleys. At one point Alton had read that the most remote place in the lower forty-eight in terms of distances from roads was the Thorofare region of Yellowstone, which inspired them to round up a canoe, paddle across Yellowstone Lake, and hike ten miles into the Upper Yellowstone to fish fat, wild cutthroats under the hazy gaze of grizzly bears. It was too early to tell, but Marshall realized the possibility that the Alton who emerged from his collision with the beer bottle may never want to drive over the Divide to go fishing again.

Marshall had entertained notions of moving to Bozeman at one time. This was during younger days, when he generally felt more openly rebellious than he had energy for now. During and after college he had seriously resented his own lack of initiative and the idea of living on Daddy's ranch. Probably, he recognized now, the very tension of that angst churned out many of the drunken grinds that characterized a good portion of Marshall's college career. He had some bad feelings about ol' Skipjack during those years.

Marshall pulled into the Doubletree in Bozeman at 8:55 A.M. and stretched his long legs for a brief moment before rushing in to piss out the truck-stop coffee he'd been swilling all morning. In the hotel hallway a felt letterboard sign told him the Montana Department of Fish, Wildlife and Parks whirling disease stakeholders' meeting would be held in the Oak Room. The room held an array of banquet chairs set up to face a podium. Men wearing jeans sat in most of the chairs. Men wearing khakis sat in the other ones.

The same young man in the same olive pants who had spoken in Helena rose and addressed the gathering, setting forth the agenda, which would include another presentation by state biologist Kipp Wessel, and then a group workshop designed to elicit concerns of the people who had gathered and propose solutions to them. Wessel rose, his body seemingly too scrawny to hold his head, which itself seemed overloaded with cranium. Again Marshall found himself surprised and then charmed by the rich, booming voice that flowed from Wessel's mouth.

Wessel reeled off a list of streams now known to contain whirling disease, and any remnant hope hidden in Marshall's soul hissed away as the list unwound. If it seemed to him that the disease was marching westward, he soon enough realized that the lab and scientists were all based in Bozeman, and were merely working naturally from the Madison to the Jefferson, Beaverhead, Big Hole, Little Prickly Pear Creek. And so forth. They'd reached the Clark Fork near Butte, and the Little Blackfoot, both of which tested positive, which was all Marshall needed to know. A disease present in the Clark Fork would suffuse his creek eventually. Same watershed.

Marshall heard Wessel say a lot of things then, discussing bird vectors and the ground-up fish heads placed on slides under microscopes.

The initial infestation was thought to be pinpointed in an illegal fish dump of infected trout in the Madison. A hatchery truck driver was delivering fingerlings to a private pond. The pond owner wasn't ready for them. The driver stopped and pumped the fish into the Madison. Widespread death and pestilence ensued.

"Why was the infection so virulent in the Madison?" Wessel said. "One of the factors we think we've isolated is water temperatures. The disease spores apparently are far more virulent in warmer-water temperatures. In fact, we think we have discovered that when trout spawn in water temperatures below sixty degrees, they're fairly impervious to infection. Analysis of spring creeks in the area has shown us that in the springs, where water temperature is constant and usually around fifty-five to sixty degrees, we have very little infection."

That was what Marshall would take home. It didn't mean he was out of the woods, but it was a hope to plant a flag on. That was worth driving over for. He would try to forget what followed when, during the open comment period, the opinion was voiced that perhaps the rivers should be closed to angling pressures while they recovered from the parasite. At that a man in jeans and a shirt with broad stripes in too many colors stood up and strode to the mike. He had on a clean, new pair of Wrangler jeans and a cell phone clipped to his belt. His chest and shoulders stuffed the shirt, and his jeans seemed too tight in disturbing places. Marshall tried to tell if any of the shirt stripes were the same color as any of the others. A staged expression of deep pathos called the man's sincerity into doubt before he even opened his mouth. "I'm Bryan Ebzery and I'm president of the Montana Fishing and Hunting Guides Association." There followed a long explication of the beauty of rivers and the beauty of men with clients fishing them, before Mr. Ebzery said, "And I'm here to ask, by golly, who is going to speak for these rivers? Who's going to take the responsibility to say what these rivers want to say to us?"

"Do we need to guess?" a man in the crowd said.

Ebzery stepped back, clutched his chest as if shot by the accusation. "*I* can't speak for the rivers," Ebzery said. His face opened up as if this admission should be surprising. "That's my point. *I* can't any better than *you* can. We don't know what the rivers want."

"What do you want us to do," the man in the audience asked, "all go stand on the riverbank and listen to what it says?"

The men and smattering of women in the room all laughed, but the guide went on in a state of excited concern. Marshall tuned out. Later, though, as the conversation spun wildly away, he would think that it wasn't a bad idea. Maybe they could all stand to walk out by the river and listen for a while. Some of them might even benefit from holding their heads under the water for a long time to see what they could hear.

"Have you noticed that everything in this room is designed to handle meat?" Molly said. She was struggling. The room was the kitchen in Alton's house, and there was a predominance of fry pans, cleavers, and fillet knives visible on the shelves. She rolled open a drawer and pulled from it a meat thermometer, held it aloft for Amy Baine to see. "And there are no paper products outside of the bathroom."

"That paper products ban was a conscious choice," Amy said "The other, it used to have more . . . other stuff." Amy Baine said.

Of course it did, Molly thought, *when you lived here.* She pitched the meat thermometer back in the drawer and turned and leaned against the counter.

Alton lay in his bed, asleep, and the door stood wide open. From where she stood Molly could see Alton's legs under a navy blue blanket—Amy must have brought that—and one shoulder and the beginnings of his head, his chin, and cheek swaddled in white gauze. Amy Baine sat at the kitchen table staring at a crossword puzzle in the newspaper spread open before her. A cup of coffee steamed beside her. Molly had walked in a few moments before and had yet to settle into a place. Amy seemed not the least disturbed from where she had been. She wore a printed cotton tank top—pink flowers the predominant motif, with a darker pomegranate band around the waist, which ended short to leave a slice of tanned midriff exposed.

Amy's hair, straight and brown, sheened in the morning light, glossy as a wet seal. Just the tips of her ears divided seams in the long flow. Her face, like her body, was long and narrow, with a vaguely distant cast—the countenance of a civilized mystic. Amy looked up and caught her staring. Molly fought off the urge to flick her glance away. She wondered what Amy was finding in her face, if Amy saw a jealous glare or the sort of puzzled admiration Molly was feeling. Amy was, after all, a beautiful woman. Even if she was only twenty-three, she should be used to being seen through comparative moods.

Neither of them spoke and Molly felt the moment stretching. She didn't seek a pissing match, but she wanted to be on the level. This was going to take a while, she knew, and they were going to have to get used to each other. She sensed how important a peace was going to be to Alton's recovery. That was a thing she wanted to get across without sounding self-righteous. She thought she saw Amy knowing it.

"You wonder what I'm doing here," Amy said.

"No," Molly said. "I know what you're doing here."

"You wonder why," Amy said.

No, Molly wanted to say. No, what she wanted to know was what had happened before, how Amy could possibly have ever left Alton for Shadford. And before that even—how Amy found herself attracted to Alton. At the heart of it, what Molly wanted to know was if Amy was just a bored suburban girl getting her hands sort of dirty in a fairly safe way. Wasn't she going to look back at this period of her life one day and think it was wild and cool and completely not who she really was? Wouldn't she talk about it to her bridge club, leading her reminiscences out with phrases like, *back when I hung out with the fishing guides?* One day, Molly had always suspected, Amy would look around her and suddenly long for Upper Arlington or Oak Park or whatever ritzy midwestern suburb had spawned her and she would be gone, leaving Alton slack-mouthed. In the end it had worked out worse—she'd taken up with Shadford.

"You think it's guilt," Amy said.

"I'd like to think it's concern," Molly said.

"It is. Both." Amy watched to see how honesty was registering.

"Why don't we just concentrate on the concern," Molly said.

"Do you know what it feels like to feel like you're wasting yourself?" Amy asked.

"Are we going to do this all at once?" Molly asked.

"OK," Amy said. "Forget it."

Molly pushed herself away from the counter, nodding at the bedroom. She walked past Amy and into Alton's room. Alton lay on his back, pillows propped up behind him to elevate his head and shoulders. She saw a book on the end table, assumed it was something Amy was reading to him—Turgenev's *A Sportsman's Notebook*. Crafty. Molly stood beside the bed, then sat in the chair Amy had pulled to the bedside. Alton's face remained discolored in deep, dark scythes under his eyes. The puckered lips of stitched gashes dashed his left cheek and temple. His hands seemed small, unable to wrap around an oar grip and pull. Molly was glad his eyes were closed at the moment. She sat and watched him breathe.

Amy's slim figure filled the doorway. "I do need to talk about some of this."

"What do you need to say?" Molly gestured that they should return to the living room.

"First, I want you to know," Amy said, when they'd reached the other room, "I mean, I've heard some guys say this . . . not a lot, but some people, some guy guides and some wannabes, well, I've just heard some people say that you're just a gimmick, a girl fishing guide. I'm sure this is no secret to you. But I want you to know that I've never thought that. I always thought you were real."

Molly thanked her, sensing it was heartfelt.

"I always knew, too, that he wanted you," Amy continued, nodding at Alton.

"What are you talking about?" Molly said. "He was crazy about you."

"Maybe," she said and smiled shyly, "maybe for a little while. But long term, you had everything he ever wanted." Molly sat too befuddled to reply. Amy said, "I never worried a whole lot about it from a competition standpoint because you were so obviously after Marshall."

"I was?" Molly asked, her inflection bringing the question *where did you get such an idea?*

"Yeah," Amy said. "I always worried that you would just wind up hurting him. Alton. I figured you'd hook up with Alton on one of those overnight float trips or something, and then he'd realize he was all in love with you. But I figured you'd eventually wind up with Marshall—and break Alton's heart."

Molly had no idea what to say, which had to be apparent to the other woman. Amy stood for a while, looking back at the room where Alton lay. A hint of smile gently curled her lips, as if she had gone on to thinking about something entirely different, some warmly remembered morning, or a gesture she once loved. Then she looked back to Molly who, despite not wanting this at all, felt tears beginning to well in her eyelids.

"I know you two are together. Have been together. Whatever," Amy said. "And I know you never thought I was any good for him. I know you thought I was not his kind of girl. He knew it, too. I don't . . . ," her breath caught. "That wasn't fair. It should have been for us to decide. I guess what I'm trying to get at is, I always get cast as the evil bitch, but you had a lot more to do with what happened than you let on."

Molly couldn't believe she was going to sit in front of this girl and let tears stream down her cheeks. She saw Amy lift her own chin, point her face away, and quickly wipe at her eyes, too. Molly wondered at how remarkable this was, the two of them holding their places in the same room, Alton asleep just a few steps away. Then from the bedroom came the sounds of Alton stirring. Both women brought hands to their faces, rubbing those tears into their fingers.

Marshall had a cheap face mask strapped to his face with a snorkel extending beyond his ear. He wore only shorts and sandals and waded along the spring creek, every now and then bending and placing his face into the water, examining the bottom structure. A pair of little brown birds, ouzels, skipped from rock to rock in the creek, then dove beneath the water to walk along the bottom, grazing insects from the streambed before hopping back into the air, shaking themselves briskly, and moving on. After more than three solid weeks of guiding and a run to Bozeman, he simply needed a day back in his creek. He needed to literally immerse himself in it. In the deeper holes he swam down to peer under logs and cutbanks. The world beneath the creek's surface was different than any dry-land observer could imagine. Already some of the cutbanks extended five feet under the bank. Marshall could barely discern movements of what he knew must be huge brown trout living back in those dark recesses. One submerged log had thirteen fish finning near or under it.

Marshall snatched grasshoppers from stalks of grass on the bank and threw them upstream from a big hole, then dipped down and watched trout blast off the bottom after them. He watched the way the fish held in the current, anchored in eddies or the slipstreams behind jutting rocks. In many places, at the bottom of the stream, in the few inches just above the bed, there was almost no current at all. Marshall lay down behind a big boulder, submerged in the creek. He pointed his nose into the current and stuck his head out from behind the rock, feeling the cold water sweeping against his face, the stream of bubbles, the constant reeling film of small debris and insects rushing by.

Then he ducked behind the rock again and just listened, trying to hear what fish hear: the gush of current, the squeak of mixing air, loose stones clattering over each other on the bottom.

He moved upstream on his knees or in a crawl, staring at the bottom. In shallow water a round brown rock caught his attention, until he realized it was not a rock at all but a type of aquatic vegetation—mounded and fuzzy and pocked by tiny air bubbles. He was fascinated at the variety of plants that grew underwater—duckweed and elodea and watercress he'd known of, but there were countless others he had no names for, and they'd all colonized the creek on their own. This one seemed like a large cap of soft algae. Then he stared harder and realized he was looking at a flop of cow shit. Marshall popped out of the water, forgetting to clear his mask as he looked wildly around the banks of the creek. He pulled the mask from his head. No cows in sight, but the transplanted willows along the bank were trampled and three small aspens now titled at crazy angles from the earth. Hours of backbreaking work, undone with the casual swagger of hundreds of pounds of hamburger on the hoof. Black mucky suckholes marked where the cows had wallowed in the soft banks. Black and brown shit splats mushroomed all around the grass.

Marshall jumped out of the creek. Sometimes, when the sun was bright, he could glance across the meadow to where the plain began a gentle tilt toward the Fountainhead bench and see animals moving and know right away that they were deer or elk. The elk shone golden and the deer this time of year took on a reddish cast. But at other times, when the sun was shaded by cloud as it was today, he saw big shapes moving and had to stare for a moment to know what they were. In this case, a few seconds of watching the way the animals moved told him what he feared: he was seeing cows, lots of big, black cows, aswim up to their bellies in the high grass of his pasture.

Marshall headed overland where he had left his bike. He climbed on and, mask still looped around his neck with the snorkel clipped to it, pedaled in the direction of the Klingman house. Two white-blond kids were sitting in the dirt in the yard. The little girl pounded the ground with a garden hand rake. The boy pointed a pellet gun at Marshall as he approached. Marshall had no idea who the children belonged to. Bruce, his wife, Colleen, Randy, and Kyle were the only real constants on the Klingman ranch. Daisy came and went. A brood of God knew how many kids—there were older sons and daughters Marshall had met as a kid who seemed to have, over the years, fallen out of favor and simply evaporated—as well as nieces, grandkids, and stepchildren showed up, stayed various lengths of time, and disappeared again, kids belonging to this daughter or that loathsome cousin Marshall had never met.

"*Pa-choo. Pa-choo,*" the boy said. "I'm shooting you."

"You couldn't be so kind," Marshall said.

"You're dead."

A quick scan of vehicles strewn in the yard beside the house revealed a goodly percentage of the adults were probably gone. Marshall mounted the porch and rapped on the door. It didn't open for a long time and he pounded again, then stepped back and turned to overlook the yard. The two kids were watching him unabashedly, wide blue eyes in fascinated stares. Then the girl said, "You've got a tube sticking out of your neck."

Now that it was pointed out to him, the boy seemed to think this was a perfect reason to shoot Marshall again. The door yawned open to reveal Randy Klingman in jeans and an untucked white T-shirt, hair in a ratty swirl. The T-shirt held freshly pressed wrinkles. Randy took a look at Marshall with the mask and snorkel around his neck and immediately grew wary. This was beyond his realm of everyday experience and clearly required his most crafty approach.

"Randy," Marshall said, aiming for Western Cordial: a willingness to do business pasted on to a don't-mess-with-me undercarriage. "Got a bunch of your cows over in my place. I was hoping you'd come get them gone."

Randy reached a hand to scratch the back of his head, then let the motion carry into a long stretch. It accentuated the ball of muscles at his bicep. He yawned and said, "Shoot, Marshall, I'm kind of right in the middle of something."

"A nap?"

"A rancher's work is never done. Gonna be a while before I can get to them. They ain't gonna starve to death over there, are they?"

"No, but it'd be a shame if they all ended up in a meatpacking truck headed for Des Moines."

Randy chuckled into a long, lazy laugh. Marshall couldn't do anything like that, and everybody on the porch knew it. Except in a few municipalities, Montana was open range country, which meant land-owners were responsible for fencing cattle out; ranchers were not responsible for fencing them in.

"They're not out of there by end of the day, I'll tell you what I will do," Marshall said, because this was about his only recourse aside from charging Klingmans a few measly dollars for a day's worth of pasturage and whatever he could prove the ruined seedlings and tender transplants had cost him—which was nothing, "I'll let my new dog go over there and chase them till they puke. He's not real smart, but he's a real go-getter. A retriever. Hell, I might even go over and shoot guns in the air just to pump up his enthusiasm. Hot day like this, we could just melt the weight right off those little dogies."

Randy's eye shone with a dullard's mean glint while he calculated how much trouble he thought Marshall was willing to cause him, compounded against what having a bunch of exhausted, skinny cows would do for his stead with the old man—as opposed to just firing up a four-wheeler and driving the cows back across the fence line.

"Kyle'll be home soon. I'll see if he wants to help me get 'em back."

"That'd be ideal. I'll go fix the fence," Marshall said. He'd have to find the hole in the fence and patch it before the process of booting cows off the place became circular. "Mind if I borrow your wire stretcher?"

Randy considered the request a moment, then hooted.

One evening Marshall strolled through Alton's front door full of false cheer, but faking it like a champ. He came into the room calling, "Anybody in here with a head wound I can talk to?"

"Couple of us," Molly said. She sat in the chair beside the bed, a paperback copy of Jack London's *Tales of the Pacific* opened in her lap. "One more overt than the other." She wore hiking shorts and a yoke-necked T-shirt, and Marshall noticed that while she wasn't exactly what one would call gussied up, she looked fresh and clean. She had just finished squeezing Alton's hand when she said that.

"How are you doing?" Marshall asked. He suddenly noticed something tickling the inside of his nose, but didn't want to explore it in front of Molly.

Alton wore his inappropriate smirk. He said, "I'm doing good as I can." His words were slightly chockablock, as if his tongue had been stuck in his mouth at an uncomfortable angle.

"Well, you're looking good."

"Never going to look like I used to," Alton said.

"Nonsense," Molly said.

"I've accepted it," Alton said, as if he were talking about faith.

"I think you're looking great," Marshall said. The nose thing didn't feel dried or snotty. It felt like a tiny probe. "Feeling any better?"

"Feeling as good as I can," Alton said.

Marshall hooked a thumb at Molly and said, "I was thinking maybe later I'd steal this one away and get her some dinner. You mind?"

Neither Molly nor Amy were exactly living at Alton's house, but it worked out that one—and often both—was almost always present. One of the two always spent the night on the couch. Marshall dropped by as often as he could. He felt constantly dumbfounded in terms of what he could do to help with Alton's care, but what kept rising to the top was the notion that he could provide for Molly some breaks, a little away time. The attached truth was he missed her friendship.

"That's fine," Alton said.

"Actually, if we're going to," Molly said, "I'd like to run by my house and pick up some new clothes."

"Why don't you do that," Marshall said. "I'll sit here and chat with the gentleman of the house while you get your stuff gathered."

Molly rose from the chair and began stuffing items in the duffel bag on the floor near the doorway. The dull rips of zippers followed. Molly swung from the room, her duffel slung over her shoulder. "You want to pick me up in a half hour or so?" she asked.

"Sure," Marshall said. Molly headed out the door. Marshall went to the refrigerator and pulled out a can of Diet Coke, took a swig and headed into Alton's room.

"Could you get a coaster for that?" Alton said.

Marshall looked at the pop in his hand. "What if I don't sit it down on anything?"

"Please get a coaster," Alton said. It was no request. Marshall shrugged, went back into the kitchen, and opened a drawer. Not finding a coaster, he opened a second drawer. He heard Alton say, "Other side." He moved to the drawers on the other side of the sink, opened the top one, and found a coaster.

"Close that other one," Alton said.

Marshall looked at the first drawer he had been in. It gapped open about two inches. He pressed his lips together and glanced toward Alton's room. *How does he know these things?*

He sat in the chair Molly had occupied, held the coaster in his lap and balanced his Diet Coke on it. He reached his fingers to his nostril and pinched lightly at the opening. Whatever it was, once it started moving it seemed to come from a long way inside his head. He pulled his head back and examined what he had withdrawn from his nose. It was a reddish brown hair. Dog. Buck. He was tickled by how much he liked the way that felt.

"Are you making moves on her?" Alton asked.

Marshall had to review for a moment. Molly, he must have meant. "Alton, my goodness. The things you think about," he said.

"I've got a lot of time to think," Alton said. The smirk seemed to suggest most of his thoughts were evil, or at least ornery, though Marshall doubted that. It was simply a new and discomforting facial tic. "I've been thinking a lot about being happy."

"What about it?"

"Well, you spend your whole life and you're not happy and you can't figure out why, and then one day you just decide, I should be happy. I should love my life and be happy for the people in it who love me, and just be happy to be alive every day. And then you are happy."

"Huh," Marshall said. He'd all along suspected it would take a blow to the head for some process like that to happen. "So you're happy now? Or happier—"

"That's right," Alton said. "Thankful. I've got good friends. You and Molly. I love you two and I'm thankful to have you in my life. Amy, too."

"That's great," Marshall said.

"I think you should tell people when you're happy about your life," Alton said.

"Sure," Marshall said. *Tell people when you're happy* . . . well, that was one he'd have to come back to. "We're going to have to get you back out on the river."

"Marshall, if I don't ever get on the river again, I'll be OK with that."

"We'll get you back out there in no time."

"I'm telling you it won't matter."

"I think it will."

"You don't know," Alton said. His voice was resolute. "I'm telling you, I'm going to be happy either way. I'm going to be happy if you and Molly end up together, too."

"Don't talk like that right now," Marshall said. "There's something much bigger going on now."

"I know, and I'm thankful for it, and all of you deserve happiness," Alton said. "That's what I think."

"OK," Marshall said. "All right. Well, did I tell you I finally made an appointment with a water rights attorney?"

Marshall met Tripp Laudermilk in an office carpeted in rich, golden-olive swaths of pile. The office was three floors up in a plain—ugly, actually—brick building in downtown Missoula. Laudermilk came out to fetch him in the lobby, a hand stretching out for grasping, the palm turning open, even while the man was yet ten strides away. His suit was a lighter olive than the carpet, the jacket cut boxy and loose, hanging open, split down the front by a swank mustard-colored tie that Marshall knew right away was silk. Marshall meant to cut short pleasantries. This guy was costing him two hundred dollars an hour, and they had some background to cover. Treading behind Laudermilk to the conference room, Marshall couldn't get over how beautiful the carpet was.

Before a broad oak conference table, Laudermilk extended his hand, waving Marshall to his choice of any of the high-backed, upholstered swivel chairs. The table was waxed to a gloss Marshall could see himself in. "So you've got yourself a water rights dispute?" Laudermilk said. He smiled as if his teeth demanded sunlight, and his demeanor seemed to indicate that a water rights dispute was the best possible thing Marshall could have.

Laudermilk plopped a redbone file on the table and sat down opposite the chair Marshall had chosen. He seemed far away across the table. The lawyer appeared to be reading through the file while Marshall explained his problem, every now and then prompting Marshall with a "Yes" or "I see." Marshall didn't like the way certain sheets of paper launched surprised scowls on the man's face, because it made him suspect that Laudermilk hadn't even reviewed the case before this very moment—although the "Yes" and "I see" prompts were all impressively placed in appropriate spots.

As a test, after a long description of the Fountainhead, Marshall said, "In several of the springs I sank a six-inch pipe into the ground and directed them to a central stream. In one I took an eight-inch pipe," and stopped speaking, inflecting the phrase as if it were the end of a sentence.

Laudermilk looked at him from beneath a tilt of black eyebrows, the hairs groomed slick, and smiled. "Yes. And what did you do with the pipe?"

Convinced, Marshall told him the rest of the story. When he finished, Laudermilk said, "Well, Mr. Tate, you're in violation here, that much is clear. And, should the Department of Natural Resources and Conservation inspect your property in response to a claim violation filed by your neighbors, and they see the unpermitted development you've done, you could be on the hook for tens of thousands of dollars in fines. My question, then, is who are Kyle and Daisy Klingman?"

"Why does that matter?" Marshall asked.

"Because, Mr. Tate, your only strategy, should the DNRC investigate, is to throw yourself at the mercy of the Water Court and plead for leniency. But here's a thought: you keep talking about Bruce Klingman, who is the deedholder to some of the land described by the Bar K-L ranch property. But the records I have indicate that ownership of that ranch is divided several ways, via a trust instrument, which has been amended several times, once quite recently. At the moment, Colleen Klingman owns a large majority percentage of the property. Randall Klingman holds significant portions, as well. There are a couple other names attached to various minor slivers. The acreage of primary interest to you, the piece that Alice Creek runs through . . ." Laudermilk slipped a piece of paper onto the table and pressed his fingertips on it, then used them to spin the paper for Marshall to see it right side up before sliding it across the table to him. Marshall was looking at a plat map. He could see immediately the shape of Alice Creek and the way it wound over and across schematic property lines. A large square had been outlined in blue pen. Laudermilk slid another piece of paper toward him, this one a legal deed. "Well, two pieces. The title to those pieces are held by Kyle Klingman and Daisy Isabelle Klingman."

"What do you mean—they're the designated inheritors or something?" Marshall continued looking at the drawing purporting to represent the grassy field through which Alice Creek wove a strand of willows and water.

"No. They actually hold title now," Laudermilk said. "It's a fairly common practice for large landowners to disseminate the burdens of liability. I assume these are relatives?"

"Offspring," Marshall said. His eyes flicked up to see Tripp Laudermilk favoring him with a varsity smile.

"It's probably just a fiduciary strategy, quite common actually, but if these people—Randall, Kyle, and Daisy Isabella—are involved enough to hold title, can you talk to them? Would they be amenable to some sort of resolution?" Laudermilk asked. "That might obviate a visit from DNRC until we can put together some sort of request for waiver from fines for unadjudicated development. It's not unprecedented for them to waive excessive fines. They're a reasonable regulatory agency, particularly if you can solicit some supporting letters perhaps from some neighbors, and perhaps—well, I'll be frank, the heavier the hitters the better your chances."

A lightness began spreading across the inside of Marshall's head with the creeping ease of a benevolent stain. He said, "What do I owe you?"

"Excuse me?"

"How much?"

"Well, we're just getting started," Laudermilk said. "Didn't my secretary go over the billing procedures on the phone?"

"She did. I've been here what, an hour?" Marshall stood, dug his wallet from his pocket and pinched a sheaf of bills from it. "That's two hundred. That all right?"

Laudermilk stared at the cash, pursing his lips. "That's uh . . . unusual. But fine, I guess," he said

Marshall lifted the two sheets of paper from the shiny table. "You make me a copy of these?"

By early September, after Alton had been walking for a couple of weeks, a strange hitch plaguing his gait, Molly and Amy took him for a drive. Alton remained weak, and his coordination had been jarred

askew. Always a small man, he was now gaunt and pale. He had lost
nearly twenty pounds. Alton wore a baseball batting helmet with the
Frontier League Missoula Osprey's logo on the front. He wore it any
time he left the house and would have to for months.

The proximate spark for the drive was a phone call Alton had received from the Missoula Police Department, informing him that due
to a jurisprudence schedule packed tighter than a canned ham, a trial
for Jimmy Ripley, who remained free on bail, would not occur until
late fall. Even though Alton's face showed little range of emotion since
his injury, Molly detected an eerie chill even in his unfocused gaze
while he listened. Troubled, Alton's attention seemed to float, ghost-
like, beyond reach of the words he was listening to. Profoundly
spooked, Molly panicked and, in a not atypical response, organized an
activity. She wanted to take him farther away from where all this had
happened, away from the town where his attacker strolled the side-
walks. Even understanding that they would have to return soon, Molly
hoped the simple change in surroundings could jar the creepy effect
the phone call seemed to hold over Alton.

She drove Alton and Amy up the Bitterroot Valley, dodging the
mad drivers and kamikaze deer, then climbed Chief Joseph Pass, and
spilled over into the wide, sage-clotted panorama of the Big Hole Valley. They took Alton's rig and he leaned back in the passenger seat as
he watched the veiny, willow-lined creeks that coalesced to form the
headwaters of the Big Hole River. The three of them zoomed along the
open road, flying over small hillocks, and dropping into curving hollows as the Big Hole ran beside them. Alton sat silently, and Molly
wanted to pay attention to that silence, learn what lived in it. But Amy
must have feared the stillness, because she filled the trip with words.
At first it had bugged Molly, but she wanted to maintain a pleasant atmosphere, and since Alton wasn't responding to much of what Amy
said, she felt she had to. Eventually she realized that Amy would keep
chattering whether anybody seemed to be listening or not, and in a
way Molly found this comforting, like listening to a baseball game on
the radio. She only had to tune in to the highlights. The remainder of
the drive she spent watching landscapes twirl by, and watching Alton.

Molly pulled in at a fishing access alongside the Big Hole River. A
few wooden picnic tables stood beside the river. Three were occupied.
Two rafts were tied up at the bank. Amy took Alton's elbow while they

walked to an empty picnic table. Molly brought from the truck a bag
full of Italian prosciutto and fresh mozzarella and a loaf of rosemary
focaccia. While she arranged lunch on the table, Alton made a few
stiffly architectural strides toward the river. Molly moved to accom-
pany him. Alton let her draw even before he said, "Go back to what you
were doing. I just want to look at the water."

"That's fine. I'll go with you." She could actually hear how blue-sky
she sounded. *"That's fine—"*

Alton tilted his head toward her and shoved her, hard, the heel of
his hand jarring her shoulder.

"You and her," Alton hissed while his hands described an imaginary shape the size of a basketball, "you just *hover*. Why can't you just
leave me alone for ten minutes?"

"Don't hit me," Molly said, instantly aware that she had snapped
it. She felt a bubble of fear rising through her, and enabled by that moment of vulnerability, thought she saw in Alton a parallel fear, though
not one borne of what he'd done. Then it was gone, her own fear and
her ability to see his. "We're trying to help, Alton."

"I just want to go look at the river," Alton said. "Is that asking too
much?"

"No," Molly said, "I'll—we'll make lunch." She watched Alton turn
and hobble away, aware of a throbbing on her shoulder and, more
acutely, a scraped sensation inside her chest. It felt just like a little
desolation. Then she felt Amy's hand on her arm.

"He doesn't mean it," Amy was saying. "He's just frustrated."

Before she knew how to stop herself, Molly was wrapped in Amy's
arms. Molly felt her shoulders shaking and saw the distant blue
mountains shimmer through a screen of incipient tears as she set her
chin on Amy's shoulder and tried not to cry. Amy patted her back and
kept saying things until Molly finally roped in her ragged breaths and
straightened. With the side of her hand she squeegeed the wetness
from her cheeks. Amy knew enough to back right away.

"OK?" she asked.

Molly looked at her for the first time since the outburst began. Amy
stood with her neck angled forward, her head held toward Molly with
her eyes looking out from beneath genuinely hopeful brows. No wonder
Alton had fallen for her.

Molly bit her lip and nodded. She sniffled and said, "Yeah."

"I used to think," Amy said, "like, if I could get people to fall in love with me, well then that's what it was all about. But this all makes me realize that it's so much more important to just give it to them. I can get so much more out of it if I just keep that in my head." When she saw Molly looking dubious, Amy hastened to add, "I don't know if that helps any—"

"I don't either," Molly said. She walked over to the picnic table and started doing things. That's how you got things back. Make the lunch. Slice the bread and cheese, peel off the prosciutto. Everything would be fine. Just a momentary lapse. A speed bump.

After lunch they took the cutoff road up and over the mountains to Anaconda and Georgetown Lake, then followed Flint Creek back to the interstate. Molly found herself trying to characterize the change she felt in Alton. Something was gone from him, the playful glimmer had flickered out sometime after the beer bottle had thudded onto his skull. She wouldn't say he'd found religion. More like he'd found dogma. He didn't claim to know anything more than he had before, but what he knew he knew like granite. There was no questioning and his certainty was so unshakeable as to seem aggressive, though he pushed nothing on anybody.

Alton began agitating to go fishing after he began to move around on his own. His insistence grew with his mobility, until he had walked down and looked at the Big Hole River, stood at the water's edge, and just watched. After that he'd become adamant. Marshall thought it was a wonderful trend—it had been his idea for Molly to drive Alton to the Big Hole. Molly had a different tilt at it, because she had witnessed Alton's return to fly tying. One afternoon Alton rose from his bed and sat at his tying bench.

"I have to start doing this now," Alton said.

"You don't have to now," Molly argued. "You might be pushing things."

"I have to start now. I have to get it back."

Molly meant to blunt any potential failures and started mentioning the patterns that would probably be a lot harder than others to get back to. She kept it light, teammate talk. "Boy, it might be tough to wrap a parachute post," that sort of thing. She watched him pick up his whip finisher and twirl it slowly beneath his stare. He picked up a bobbin, held it upside down, then put it back on the table. His fingers felt the vise, and for a moment Molly thought he might be trying to force the vise open from the tip.

Molly sifted through some hooks and set one in the vise for him, then held up the bobbin. Alton took it and started wrapping thread on the shank. But his wrist would not make the supple turns and the thread slipped from the shank.

"Easy," Molly said. Their faces were close together. "You'll get it. It just might take some time."

Alton peered at her with a disgusted sneer. He pinched a piece of prespun dubbing and started dressing the hook by hand, but the wrap was too loose and the tag end dribbled off the shank.

"It's just going to take a little time," Molly said. "Don't get discouraged."

"You don't have to be with me," Alton said.

"This is going to come, Alton, but it's going to take time. The docs told you that."

"I mean," Alton said, letting the dubbing go, dropping the bobbin to the table, and sitting back in the chair so their faces were farther apart, "you don't have to be with me, just because of what happened before. It's different now. I'll understand."

Molly scrambled to elude this little bit of blindsiding. She said, "Right now I think the thing to concentrate on is getting stronger, don't you?"

"I'm just telling you. I'll understand."

Molly thought, though, that perhaps it wouldn't do to coddle him. Perhaps she should treat him like an emotionally fluent adult. He was probably astute enough to notice things about her. Molly could see the Clark Fork through Alton's bedroom window, and she took a moment to watch the water wobbling down its watercourse, mixed by obstructions beneath the surface. She liked looking at it. She liked knowing that she could conjure the smell of willows along its banks. She liked knowing what it felt like at the end of a day when she'd been standing in the river, when her skin held a sensation almost like the thinnest of glazes from the river water drying on it. She knew the slushy, rushing sound the current made against the hull of her boat when she held water. She *knew* it. She didn't need it again every day. She'd noticed this, and had started listening to herself about it. She'd been sitting right beside

Alton while most of this transformation occurred. He could perceive the change—why not? After a moment of tensile quiet, Molly said, "If this . . . hadn't happened to you, do you think we would be together?"

Alton did not hesitate with his answer. "Maybe. Before it happened we seemed to be getting closer."

"Do you think we would have kept getting closer?" Molly asked. "Do you think we were going to get closer and closer as time went on, or were we just getting as close as we ever could be?"

Alton took a moment to visibly calculate, then said, "I don't understand the question."

"I know," Molly sighed. She had asked feeling a degree of security in suspecting she could forecast the answer. Part of her wanted to explain it to him, word by word, but he'd never indulge her that.

Alton responded with inflexibility. "You can be with Marshall. I'll be fine with that. I'll be happy."

"We'll just get you better," Molly said. "We've got that part, easy."

"I know you're not going to stay with me," Alton said.

Molly didn't argue. She floated a broad, don't-be-silly smile. There were things she knew now and one of them was that she didn't need to react to everything he, or anybody else, said. She didn't need to give people all the things they wanted. What she would do next could stay with her.

Alton returned to his vise. He picked up the bobbin and, with his free hand, used a finger to press the thread's tag end to the shank while he tried wrapping. But he couldn't point the bobbin at the hook and describe an ellipse. Molly watched and felt tears well heavy on her lower eyelids. Alton's wrist had once been a supple blur. This time the thread plinked the hook and broke. Molly loosed a gussied-up guffaw and said, "I hate it when that happens."

Alton threw the bobbin at the wall, then punched the vise with the heel of his other hand. He stood and lifted a foot and kicked at the vise. Molly watched, caught from behind by shock, before she shook it and rose and wrapped her arms around him. Her arms seemed too roomy for his body, as if she could gather him using only her forearms. He felt like a burlap bag full of sticks. He flailed a few moments, but the spastic movements were soon overhauled by long jerking sobs. She held her chest still against him, letting herself absorb the waves as they broke from him, feeling a redolent recognition of the kind of fear that rises from the inability to move in any direction, the stemming of flow.

So Molly was less excited than Marshall about taking Alton fishing. She'd told him about the incident in the briefest terms, preferring not to flap Alton's private breakdowns in this particular breeze. Marshall kept pushing, which fed Alton's own fixation. Molly felt at first trapped, as she had so many times by these two, until eventually she gave way to herself and granted herself absolution for any possible outcomes. Molly decided her best recourse was to see that he was safe. Let the rest come as it may. A little more than a week after the Big Hole trip, Molly and Alton and Amy Baine climbed into Alton's Toyota pickup and headed up the highway to the Fly X. Though far from town, Molly thought of Marshall's place as close to safety. Marshall knew they were coming, but he was working in the field and would find them eventually. Molly parked and Amy helped Alton out of the rig.

They walked slowly across the field to the spring creek, Molly and Amy strolling and trying to pretend this was the pace they'd have preferred. Each step kicked sprays of grasshoppers into the long grass before them. The water of the creek was beautiful, flat and gin-clear. In the slow runs, long trout held against the outside turn of the bank, their forms blue shadows in the water. And they were actively feeding. All around, Molly heard the silence of the big open punctuated by the splash of trout slurping hoppers and other bugs off the surface. The water was so clear Molly could see the fish tip up from the bottom, drift back, tilt their noses under hoppers struggling in the surface slick.

"You go," Alton said. So Molly joined up her rod and strung line through the guides and tied on a foam hopper. She moved upstream and found a run of faster current where the creek bent and poured water over a shallow gravel bar. Alton stood along the bank and watched. Amy stood at his side. Molly could see fish on the gravel bar with their backs out of the water. She started catching fish on almost every cast, strong, sixteen-, seventeen-inch fish, thick through the shoulders. They were deep fighters, not flashy, but serious about it.

"Now I go," Alton said, after a while. Molly felt dread rise through her, and a quick stab of anger at Marshall for not having arrived yet. She stood knee-deep in the clear, crisp water and stared up at Alton on the bank above her. He wore a queer, thin smile, as if he were no more certain than she about what would happen next. For a moment she thought she glimpsed what she had seen in him in the moments before he attacked his fly-tying vise and just after he'd shoved her at the Big Hole—it was a fear that seemed formless.

She slogged ashore and Alton waited for her with his strange, supplicant's smile and both hands extended, palms up, as if she were about to present him with a sword. A quick glance at Amy revealed an expression that Molly was sure mirrored the one she wore: a mask of sad doubt.

"Sure you want to do this?" Molly said. "No reason you have to. We could go on home, come on back later in the week . . ."

Whatever happened in Alton's mind was lost to her then. Molly handed Alton the rod and moved to his left shoulder, stood behind him a half step, ready to reach and help him move the rod. Without thinking she had moved into the exact stance she used to instruct beginners. Molly waited, poised, and when nothing happened, she sneaked a peek at Alton. He was glaring at her. She understood and backed away. Alton raised the rod tip and pulled some line from the reel. He began jerking the rod back and forth, trying to load it with line. He moved too fast and forgot to pause and Molly cringed.

"Wait," she said, "let me get some line out for you."

Before he could argue, Molly reached for the rod tip and pulled line out through the guides. "Now go."

It was the worst thing she'd ever had to watch. Alton moved the rod tip back but with no snap, no speed, and the line draped around his shoulders. He tried to whip it forward and off him, but succeeded only in tying a noose around his neck.

"Help him," Amy said.

Molly stepped in, but met a thump on her shoulder as Alton pushed her away. His other hand, still holding the rod, madly twirled line in an attempt to clear the loop from his head and shoulders.

"Wait!" Molly said. "You're going to hurt yourself." Alton glared at her and she let him see how emotional she was for a moment, then softened. "It's gonna take a while, sweetie. You're going to have to go slow. Let's start over."

Whether it was his brain failing to communicate or his muscles failing to execute its commands, Alton's hands and arms moved with disastrous dysfunction. On his second attempt the rod tip drifted back then twitched forward and the line caught in the grass behind him. Molly unsnagged the fly from a stem, and carried it out into the stream. Alton seemed to be calculating what this failure meant. His skin was so pale that his face almost dissolved against the white of the summer sky. Molly was ramping up her patience, prepared to stand there all day, until he got tired. Again Alton tried to cast. Before the line could flow back behind him, Alton pitched forward and a huge loop tied itself over and under his arm. This time Alton broke into a flurry of dislocated movement and before anybody could stop him he had hurled the rod into the creek.

Molly splashed after the rod. Alton flung the line from his body and turned and staggered back the way he had come. Amy Baine followed. As she chased the rod into the creek, Molly could hear Amy trying to tell Alton it would be all right, how much better it was all going to get later. Molly fetched the rod from the water and gathered loops of line and stepped back onto the bank and then she saw Marshall, standing twenty yards off in the tall golden grass. She stood at the bank with her hands dropped and knew from Marshall's face that he had seen enough of it.

Molly wanted him to come to her. She wanted someone to start talking about how horrible this all was, so she could say *yes, yes* and let loose herself. If Marshall would only say one word, any word, she could start.

Marshall's hand reached to pinch the bridge of his nose, and when he let go he wiped his fingers across his cheek. His other hand opened and the palm turned up. Molly thought she saw him shake his head, and then he turned quickly and stalked off in a direction opposite Alton's exit.

Two days later, Marshall and Daisy climbed through the forest, each of their deep breaths spiced with the smell of pine. The day was far along, and its heat cooked up a potpourri of aromas—dirt, hot rock, bitter grass, the pine. The dog trotted ahead of them, the faintest of limps still plaguing his gait, his rear legs a tick faster than the front so that the rear pair kept swinging out to the side like they meant to pass. They moved along a game trail worn into the shoulder of the hill, angling up until they broke from the forest and into a meadow at the crest.

Daisy said, "That dog of yours is out of alignment. You ought to take him in, get his paws rotated."

In the open, grass shadows painted the trail in a blue groove arcing across the contour of the slope. Wind blew in gentle gusts, tossing the tall stems. The ridge they had climbed overlooked the bench from which the majority volume of Marshall's spring system sprung and as he squatted then lowered his butt to sit on the grassy hillside, he could see below him the ribbon of the spring creek, winding across the pasture toward the deep seam of river.

Although when they had walked along the banks of the spring the summer's vegetation covered most of his sculpting efforts, from this height and angle Marshall could see how the gouges he had carved flared from the more natural contours of the landscape. His creek looked new, the banks still raw and bare compared to the wetland stringers that marked tributary creeks up and down the valley. From up high, the grass along the spring creek seemed thin, like hair coming back after chemotherapy. In a few years tules would fill in around the deeper pools and the pond and rushes and sedges would coat the banks of the stream. In ten more years aspens and willows would fill in. In fifty years cottonwoods would grow sturdy, tall and thick, and nobody would ever know that this stream was an invention, that it hadn't flowed precisely in this form, snaking from the hills to the river, since the beginning of time.

Beyond the river, the handsome house his father had built looked tiny and no different in scope or grandeur than the Klingman farmhouse and outbuildings hiding under their own collection of tin roofs far to the south. To the north and east benches rolled toward the high country. The sun canted down so the sky to the east filled with a rich azure, and distant patches of granite on the peaks shone brown and slate blue. The mountains themselves looked vital and seething, as if to suggest they had plans involving sweeping movements of rock and light.

On those distant slopes the trees lost their individuality and turned into broad green smears, with darker shadow illustrating the topography beneath the canopy. Far away, on a mountainside back in the Scapegoat, the plume of a wildfire threaded into the sky but dissipated shortly after it filtered from the green backdrop into the blue. Daisy sat down beside him, and Marshall pointed at the tableau before them, his father's ranch and the watercourse he had built. Far below he saw a client at his spring creek, a form wearing a bright blue shirt standing by the creek.

"I didn't know if you'd ever seen all this before," he said.

"I have," Daisy said. She leaned back on her elbows and straightened her legs down the slope of the hill. She wore jeans and hiking boots and a gray T-shirt that had "King Ropes" on it, and she chewed a two-foot-long stalk of timothy. "I came up here and checked it out as soon as I heard what you were up to. Springtime sometime. It was right after I got back home."

"Oh—trespassing."

"Oh—bite me," Daisy said. Her T-shirt was too short to stay tucked in. Marshall could see the beltline of her jeans floating loosely around her waist. It would not be hard, he thought, to look at her all the time.

The dog quit zipping around the meadow sniffing things and sat on the grass uphill a few feet from them, then lowered himself onto his elbows. "You never leave here anymore," Daisy said. "You used to go to such neat places."

"There's too much to do," Marshall said.

"Don't you get tired of just being here?"

"It's important—for me—to be here now," he said, chagrined that she wasn't getting it, that she could probably understand in her bones why people like her father felt it was important to be here, but not why he did. "It matters."

He pointed out the willow-lined course Alice Creek scribbled as it poured from a crotch in the hills. Since mid-July he had been afraid to look closely at that water, afraid he would find it reduced to a trickle. But one day, a week or so back, he'd sneaked a peek and, to his everlasting relief, saw that Alice Creek was no lower than any other year.

"Know who owns that part?" he asked.

"We do," Daisy said.

"No," he said, "*you* do."

He told her that she and Kyle owned the land they were looking at, and the water rights attached to it. She looked at him level and said, "My name's on some of the deeds. It doesn't mean anything." She shifted her elbows, tilting her upper body at a less oblique angle, but otherwise seemed content to stare down at the land below her.

"Don't you care at all what happens down there?"

"That's Dad's business," she said.

"Your dad's trying to shut me down, Daze. I don't know why, maybe he thinks I'm stupid. Maybe he wants the place and thinks he can pick it up cheap if he runs me under. I don't know. But he's perfectly positioned to inflict real damage on what I'm trying to do." Marshall tried to convey to her that now was the time for a serious exchange. She pursed her lips and nodded in a gesture that resembled acquiescence.

"It's mostly my brother," Daisy said. "Randy. I get the feeling Dad's been kind of test-driving him." She shrugged. "Maybe you, too."

"I don't ask anything from those guys. I just want to live on our place and do my thing." He examined her, searching for telltales that she thought this was fair. Daisy's eyes seemed hard, as if she were glaring at conclusive evidence. "What I need in this mess, Daisy, is you on my side."

"For a minute there I thought you were going to say 'by' my side," Daisy said.

"I'm talking about life stuff, Daisy. You know you'd never stick around long enough to be *by* my side." He spoke flippantly, imagining this as her out. The truth was that *he* knew she wouldn't stick around long enough. He knew that, despite all their shared history, she didn't know him well enough to want to.

"I don't know what sticking around has to do with it. We could go anywhere," she said. "Successful fish farmer like yourself? The world's your oyster, pal."

Marshall let himself laugh. He waited for things to settle a moment. Then he said, "We're what's next around here, Daisy." He pointed first at the Klingman property, "You," then at the Fly X, "and me. Don't you want to have some say? I mean, your dad's setting up a situation that pretty much guarantees twenty-acre ranchettes when he kicks over. That place has had everything to say about you; don't you want something to say about it?"

She seemed poised to quip, but pulled up short, changing the shape of the corner of her mouth. A puzzling series of intuitions angled her brows together. Then they released. "What about Kyle?" Daisy said at last. "You gonna bring him up here and talk his pants off, too?"

Marshall's first instinct was to feel undone, but he remembered to whom he was talking and let that slide over him. She gave him a look that said, *Who you kiddin'?*

"I'm not worried about Kyle," Marshall said. "I've got a plan I think he's going to like, something both of you could like if you'll get interested. You and Kyle and I would need to do a little conniving, but I think Kyle'll come right around. He respects you, for starters, and . . . Kyle's got a lot of his mother in him."

"How does that help? She's more redneck than any of us," Daisy said.

"She's the only one of you tough enough to stand up to the old man."

Daisy blew a little snort as if to say wasn't it ironic, knowing that. She let her gaze scroll up and down Marshall's long body, before fixing on his eyes, and Marshall could see that everything had changed. Daisy moved so fast he couldn't have stopped her even if he saw it coming. She pushed his back flat onto the grass and scooted a knee over to straddle him. Her knees pinned his biceps to the ground and her hands gripped his wrists up beside his ears. She laughed at how easy it had been, then laughed that she could laugh so easily and he found himself caught up in it. Marshall giggled like a boy. He felt like he *could* laugh . . . he couldn't imagine when they would have to stop laughing. He had a visceral flashback from the things Daisy would do to him when they were kids, holding him down and beating a tom-tom on his chest until he thought he would go insane, or dangling some part of a dead animal over his face. He smelled the warm dirt of the hillside beneath him, the dry grass. He remembered it smelling just this way when he was young. Above him, Daisy drew her eyes nearly to a squint. Her jaw set. She said, "It has really been something, knowing you, Mr. Tate."

The dog lay ten feet upslope, watching what happened next with eyes half-closed, panting slightly.

Marshall had offered to take Alton for a float in a one-day-soon frame of mind. He had been surprised when five days after the spring creek debacle, Alton phoned him and said, "Will you still take me fishing if I want?"

Marshall said he sure would, any old time, because he felt like what he needed to be more than any other thing was supportive. He could drop anything to do it.

"I want to go tomorrow," Alton said. "I want to do the Box Canyon float on the Blackfoot. I want to get started about eight in the morning."

"I think it's supposed to rain like hell tomorrow," Marshall said.

"I want to go tomorrow," Alton said. "Do you want to take me or not?"

"I'll take you," Marshall said. "It's just supposed to rain. I don't know if that's healthy for you."

"I have rain gear. I've fished in the rain before. I want to go tomorrow."

"OK," Marshall said. "Tomorrow at eight."

After watching Alton fail so desperately while trying to cast on the spring creek, Marshall thought it imperative to rekindle Alton's feel for the river before the memory of that frustration suffused everything. They would fish or not fish, but Alton would have to spend all day on the river. If he tried to cast and failed, he would have hours of floating to overcome it. Or he would try all day and eventually get it right. Or not, and then he would know something.

When Marshall arrived the next morning, the sky swelled with latent precipitation. Once it started, it was going to be an all-day soaker. Alton was in his garage, lining up gear. "He's been out here for two hours, getting things ready," Amy Baine said. "Laying it out, rearranging it, picking flies."

Alton handed Marshall the fanny pack he had always used to carry his fly boxes and tippet. Marshall thought he saw how weak Alton was when he tried to lift the pack to Marshall's grasp, but then the fanny pack dropped into his hands and Marshall realized it was far heavier than it should have been. He unzipped it and saw a chrome handgun in a leather holster tucked in the space normally allotted to fly boxes.

"What's this?"

"Desert Eagle .44 Magnum," Alton said.

"OK," Marshall said, "but why?"

"Mountain lions," Alton said. "You told me they've been seeing mountain lions on the Blackfoot."

"I told you Mills said that. Consider the source. And that was over a month ago."

"I can't get away from a mountain lion, not in this condition," Alton said. The wonder of his adamancy was not in any heightened tone, but rather in his lack of excitement.

"You're not listening. There's no—"

"I don't want to get killed by a mountain lion," Alton said. "I'm not as strong as you. I'm taking my gun."

"Fine," Marshall said. "But can we put it, like, in the dry bag, or somewhere safe and out of the way?"

Alton agreed to stuff the gun in a dry bag, but left Marshall feeling shaken. This was not the way they had argued in the past. There was about Alton something impenetrable.

On the water Alton sat up front in his rain gear like a blue figurehead, and stared at his surroundings as if trying to rebuild the river from memory. Where a plug of gravel had built itself into the center of the stream, a ridge now colonized by willows, cottonwoods, and various tough riparian plants split the water into two separate flows as it leaned into the turn. The channel on the right had, over time, gouged a narrow flume and bashed directly into the cliff wall before being bent right.

"I heard they've been seeing mountain lions along in here," Alton said.

"Alton, Mills said that. Nobody else is seeing mountain lions. Hell, nobody's even seeing Mills anymore. Remember I told you he kited some clients and wound up taking them down the wrong channel, all that? Since then he's just disappeared. He never came back into Fly Guys."

"Do you know you told me that twice?"

"Well, we talked about it twice."

"You told me that twice," Alton said. "The part about Mills saying that. You told me that twice."

"Well—"

"I just wanted you to know. I wanted you to know that I knew it."

"OK," Marshall said. He was quiet for a long time. He talked to the dog, which sat in the stern with his paws looped over the rail, eyes examining the rain-pocked surface of the water at the end of his nose for hours on end. The dog looked up when Marshall spoke, but quickly returned to his intense perusal of the river. Marshall found it nearly impossible to imagine things to say. Alton seemed to exist in another state of consciousness, one inaccessible to him. They made the whole float with Marshall rowing. Alton never picked up a rod. At the foot of a sweeping leftward turn, where car-sized boulders chopped up a broad pool, Alton turned so Marshall could see his profile and announced that he had caught a twenty-nine-inch bull trout from this spot the season before.

"That was farther up," Marshall said, remembering the fish.

"It was right here," Alton said. "On a Pepperoni Yuk Bug."

"It was above River Junction on a green Sculpin on a bright sunny day," Marshall said. "I remember it well."

Alton turned back to the river. "It was right here."

"Alton, I was there. It was—"

"Here. Right here. Right behind that rock." He pointed to one of the boulders.

If Marshall had hopes of connecting in any visceral way to Alton today, they washed away with the swish of the water coursing through that pool. He felt patient, felt he understood the role time would play in this. Today would be only a first step. He held both oar handles with one hand long enough to reach back and scratch the dog's ears. Buck groaned and pressed his head into Marshall's hand, but did not break his fascination with the water's surface.

The Sperry Grade takeout was a ramp scraped in the dirt on the right bank of the river. A steep, rocky rise cupped that bank as the river made a gradual turn leftward. Sperry Grade was not an officially recognized takeout, although guides and locals had been using it for years. At the water's edge the ramp jutted with smoothed rock, and most boaters dragged their craft up the hill a few yards before attempting to load onto a trailer. Rigs were parked in a clearing out of sight from the river. Alton's truck, which Marshall had paid to have shuttled, waited there.

Marshall hauled Alton's boat from the water through a bed of reeds and left it on the downstream side of the ramp, landed, but just at the water's edge. A white boat occupied the ramp. Marshall glanced to see Alton, his batting helmet shining in the streaming downpour, going through a dry bag. The dog trotted up the muddy bank and stopped, looking back and forth between Marshall and something out of Marshall's view over the rise. Typically this was the way Buck acted just before taking off to roll in a rotting deer carcass, so Marshall leaped from the boat and trotted up the incline. The dog waited until Marshall was clearly coming, then raced away from him.

Sitting on a rock, twenty yards away, Marshall saw Jimmy Ripley hunched over, knees spread, rain dripping off his head. Buck wriggled at Ripley's feet, tail tucked, huffing breath through his nose. Ripley put his hand on the back of the dog's neck. Then Buck saw Marshall and twisted free. Ripley let loose a savage, "Hey!" and tried to snatch his collar, then clench the loose skin of the dog's nape as the dog slipped it, but Buck escaped and pranced back toward Marshall. Marshall grabbed the dog, squatted, and wrapped an arm around his neck and shoulders. He looked up at Ripley, wondering what he was doing here. Waiting on a shuttle, no doubt. Marshall thought: *what an awful coincidence.* Ripley wore a storm jacket, but in the ellipse of the hood, through rivulets of rain, Marshall could see his face bulging like a trout, his forehead bulbous and lower jaw stocky. He was chewing gum with an open mouth and regarding Marshall with brand new amusement.

"How's my dog?" Ripley said. "Looks like you feed him good."

Ripley's eyes drifted away, and Marshall followed to see Alton standing still amid a swath of hip-high yellow grass, his feet frozen, but his body leaning forward as if he'd spotted something worth stalking. Alton looked swamped in his rain gear, like a boy with a too-big jacket on. Marshall wanted to reach him, tell him quietly to let it go, to pick his battles. Wait, Marshall was going to say, until you're ready.

Ripley assessed first Alton and then Marshall again. He didn't bother to stop hunching. Marshall saw the entire landscape saturated by rain, the distant pine trees tiered by water falling, the yellow grass almost yearning to turn back to green. A screen of rain made the mountains more distant than ever. Marshall thought about how close he was to home, how if he could just get through these next few minutes he could go home and sleep.

Scratching under his batting helmet, Alton walked past Ripley, around to the passenger side of his truck. He leaned in. Marshall rose and started leading the dog to the back of the truck. Ripley stood. "You can quit worrying about taking my dog home," he said. "He'll be coming with me today."

Alton backed out of the truck cab and came around the front of the vehicle. He drew closer to Ripley than seemed wise. Ripley, too, seemed surprised at Alton's approach, but tickled by it, as if he were about to get a chance to prove a point he'd been trying to make his whole life. Marshall felt an intuition that things were going to turn badly, but he had no idea how to stop it. He heard Alton say, "Hey, this your knife?" at the same time Alton tossed something silver at Ripley. Ripley flinched to catch the object.

Marshall found the slack of Alton's face chilling, and something else about the mechanics of the gesture was bothering him. Furthermore, as Marshall saw what Alton had thrown, he could not understand the wisdom of providing a weapon—a folding stainless steel skinning knife, in this case—to a violent young man. Ripley looked at the knife in his hand, a nifty circular item that opened one-handed with the flip of his thumb. Ripley nodded appreciatively at the blade as he tested its sharpness with a scrape against his thumbnail. He looked up at Alton, a long, hungry stare, then smiled, and said, "Naw."

As Alton's right hand tilted up from underneath his rain jacket, Marshall realized what had bothered him: Alton had tossed the knife with his left hand—he was a rightie. Alton's right hand, it turned out, was filled with the big chrome pistol. Marshall had no time to say anything. Ripley's smirk died on his face, and that may have been moment enough for him to understand what had happened to his life. Alton fired the gun and a burst of orange licked the rain-filled air around his hand. Ripley dropped as if his spine had been vacuumed from his torso. A slash of red blood leaked from around his chest, but he offered no dramatics; he was dead.

"What did you do?" Marshall asked. "What did you do? What'd you do? What'd you *do?*" He felt an antic grinding in his head and the desire to press his skullcap down with the flat of one hand, and he did that.

Alton looked at Marshall. "You saw the knife. He was coming at me with it." Alton's voice was singsong, the rhythm of a little girl explaining how one of her dolls had been bad and needed the punishment it received. "He's already attacked me once and he was going to do it again."

"Jesus Christ, Alton!"

"That's the way it happened. You saw it."

Marshall saw Alton watching him, waiting to hear from him, and just that suddenly understood everything he had known about his friend was gone.

"Yes," Marshall said, because what else could he do? "I saw it."

Marshall swam through the next hours in a milky daze. He spent hours at the takeout waiting for an ambulance to haul the dead person— Marshall tried to think of him as a man, but it kept coming to him as "kid"—away. He had called the authorities on his cell phone, then sat in the cab of Alton's truck and waited while rain swam down the windshield in marbled gray sheets. The space was dense with the smell of wet dog, but underlying it Marshall still had blood and gunfire packed deep in his nostrils. Buck had gone over and sniffed Ripley and licked his dead face until Marshall loaded the dog in the truck. Alton stood outside in the rain for much of the time, then eventually wandered over and sat beneath a big larch tree near Jimmy Ripley's body. He sat with his elbows on his knees and stared patiently at the corpse as if waiting for Ripley to tell him something.

Marshall tried to talk Alton into getting out of the rain but was met with silence. After that they didn't exchange a word. The sheriff's deputy arrived first and invited Alton into the backseat of the squad car. Marshall went back to make sure he was OK, but the deputy stopped him, told him to go sit in his truck. Marshall drove behind the sheriff's car all the way to Missoula, not seeing any of the rainy river corridor, not hearing the radio or his tires *slishing* on the road, just driving.

At the facility in Missoula, Marshall and Alton were kept in separate interrogation rooms. The sheriff opened the door to Marshall's room and sat across from him at the small table. He brought a Styrofoam cup full of hot coffee. Marshall told them the story Alton wanted him to: They had come off the river. Ripley was there waiting. He and Marshall had words about the dog. Alton came up and tried to go to his truck. Ripley had a knife in his hands. It looked scary. Alton shot him.

"The guy nearly killed him once before," Marshall said.

"We've a more than passing familiarity with the deceased," the sheriff, whose name was Pyle, said. The sheriff seemed to want to believe his story, too, but felt compelled to ask the same questions from various angles. Finally he spoon-fed Marshall a self-defense statement. Sheriff Pyle asked, "Is it your opinion that Mr. Summers feared Mr. Ripley, that he feared for his life?"

"Yes, it is," Marshall said.

"Did you fear for your own life and safety?"

"I'd been threatened previously. Told to watch my back. I had reason to believe there might be some sort of attack."

"Did you fear for your own life and safety this afternoon at the fishing access?"

Marshall knew what he had to say. "I was afraid something bad would happen every time that guy was around. I was afraid today that he might harm either me or Alton."

"Did you fear that harm could be life threatening?"

"I've seen what the guy could do," Marshall finally said. "He almost killed Alton before. So, yes."

Sheriff Pyle stared hard at Marshall, a moment during which Marshall knew he was being seen through. He could not remember ever telling a deliberate lie so gillnetted in other kinds of truth. He wanted to let himself feel good about the complications, but instead despised their necessity. Nevertheless Pyle released Alton and asked Marshall to see that he got home. By then it was almost midnight. Molly and Amy both waited for them at Alton's house. Amy dropped her forehead into her palm, but then visibly decided to react differently and crossed to Alton and hugged him. He did not return the gesture.

Molly's mouth opened and closed, and she dropped down into a chair and started asking questions. She wanted to know everything. Marshall gave her the official line, though he tried to convey with pauses and glances that there was more to the story. Every answer Marshall gave her seemed to heighten Molly's mortification—although she directed her horror at Marshall, as if he had failed exactly as she suspected he might in his responsibility to not let something like this happen—until Marshall finally stopped and said, "What, Molly?"

"Well, Jesus Christ!" Molly hissed. "He shot someone!"

By then Amy had followed Alton into his room. Marshall could see them both seated on the bed, Alton frowning at the wall while Amy stroked his hair and murmured to him.

"*He* shot someone," Marshall said in an angry whisper. "*I* didn't."

"You were with him." Molly's jaw clenched.

"I didn't have anything to do with it. I didn't even see the gun. He threw Ripley that knife and as soon as Ripley touched it, as soon as he opened the blade, Alton shot him," Marshall said, aware that a creeping concern he had felt all day was developing into a discrete concept: *calculation*. He remembered how adamant Alton had been about floating that particular stretch of river on the particular day. It was hard to tell. Alton was adamant about everything now, but Marshall couldn't help but recall that they'd never taken a gun fishing before.

Molly sat in the chair looking at Marshall standing by the counter. They stared at each other for a long time with sad, sad eyes, wanting someone to understand how devastated they felt, each trying to catch up to the rapidity with which their lives were changing, and hoping the other would have the decency to document it. Marshall felt himself wanting to know where to put this, how to place it. Even the dog seemed to understand something terrible had happened. He curled in a ball on the kitchen floor and covered his nose with his tail, peering up at Marshall from time to time.

That night Marshall spent at Molly's. Molly slept at Alton's—on the couch—while Amy Baine slept on the floor. In the morning Marshall had driven back to the ranch without stopping by Alton's or talking to anybody there. Never in the time he had known Alton had Marshall wanted to place space between them the way he did now. Two days passed with only one phone call from Molly, a few bits of information exchanged in dull monotone. He had just enough sentience to know that Molly was as stunned as he was. What happened on the ranch, Marshall didn't really perceive. Some people came fishing. What he did with two days, he would never, later, be able to say. Some walking around. He remembered driving the tractor a little. He drank some coffee. Took the dog swimming in the river. Frowning—the muscles in his forehead told him he was doing a lot of frowning. It kept raining.

The Klingmans brought him out of his long, strange swim. Marshall was sitting on his front porch, watching a merlin and two kestrels perched on posts of the split-rail fence that separated the yard from pasture. The merlin looked like a small prairie falcon, though bare yellow-orange legs from the knee down provided an easy visual distinction, as did the lemon-yellow spot at the base of the bill. The kestrels sat angled with regal bearing, skullcaps and sideburns adding a costumed formality. Dozens of flickers and magpies were scouring the yard for grasshoppers. A certain sequence unfolded in a recurring loop, presented each time from a slightly different angle: the merlin scanned the gathering, and when a flicker moved close enough to its post, bombed down and latched its talons into the flicker's back; the flicker screamed with heartfelt opprobrium and fluttered and cranked its head to peck at its attacker; the merlin let go; both birds flew off a little ways—the merlin uttering a frustrated chirrupy cackle as it returned to a fence post, the flicker pausing momentarily to consider this startling injustice, then dipping its bill to pick more grasshoppers.

The process repeated itself for some time. What captured Marshall's otherwise thoroughly dislocated attention was the fact that the kestrels, heretofore perfectly content plucking grasshoppers from the lawn, began mimicking their larger cousin, dropping down on the flickers and the much larger magpies. The merlin had all along failed to accomplish much beyond outraging the other yard birds, and so Marshall figured he was watching an exercise in maladaptive learning, which seemed poignantly applicable to the recent past. Then Daisy brought her brother Kyle over, and even the strangeness of what had happened to his world could not stint the jolt of Kyle's enthusiasm for a plan Marshall had almost forgotten he'd conjured. They had a long talk, during which Marshall could not escape the motion of life beginning again, pulling him out of an eddy of stillness and forward into the swirl of events, activities, plans, and lives. Daisy started things slowly, but Kyle's eyebrows arched like two bucking colts, and he bounced around the room looking for paper to draw maps and charts on.

A scheme came out of it, such that two days later, at around six on a clear, bright evening, Marshall walked across the lawn of his father's house to his truck. He opened the door to get in and felt a rusty rush as the wet-smelling dog hurtled under his arm and up onto the seat. The dog moved across to the passenger seat with such calm deliberation that Marshall never thought to kick him out. Instead he climbed in, turned the key, and dropped the transmission into reverse.

Daisy had called a few hours before and invited him to dinner. Had he been less overwhelmed he might have paid attention to the fact that he'd never been invited to the Klingman house for dinner. Instead he realized he'd been sitting around the house for hours without any food in his stomach—he'd forgotten to eat breakfast and also dinner the night before, and he'd neglected to sally out for groceries. Plus, the whole thing was planned, and though it had slipped his mind, he had largely planned it. It was proposed as a night of great theater. *Either way things worked out,* Marshall thought, *might as well find out.* So much was suddenly different and the next part of his life was going to call for adaptive change. Might as well figure out up front what sort of scale he would have to rearrange.

He had considered a bolo tie, but decided not to overdress, and likewise eschewed his fancy cowboy boots. But he did wear a shirt with a collar and his newest pair of jeans. Marshall drove along fallow pasture, vaguely noting herds of skinny-legged deer, their heads buried in forage. Recent rains had left a rich, saturated gloss on the grasses, and the fields seemed to glow around the chocolate-colored deer in the early September light. The dog held his head out the window, tasting the wind. His ears flapped wildly as if his head might fly away. Marshall watched him, trying to imagine the sensation. He knew a dog's sense of smell was highly developed, but it had evolved before the advent of motorized travel. Marshall wondered how it must taste or smell to have all those scents rushing in and by. He imagined it as a delicious drug, a swimming paisley drenching of flavor.

It was a lovely evening, warm and dry with a kiss of autumn cool beginning to slide into the light breeze. He drove slowly enough to not raise dust. Across the bridge, Marshall slowed his truck, then stopped it, but never moved the gearshift from drive. He sat with his foot on the brake, staring back at the fields the spring creek ran through. *Time to find out what all that was for,* he thought.

Marshall drove on until he turned into the long Klingman lane, trying to note any changes since he'd come to confront Randy about the cows. He could see none. Antiquated machinery still grew weed piles around it. The closer the junk had been to operation, the closer it stood to the house. Nobody was on the porch, which Marshall took as a bad sign, until he saw the door swing open and Daisy step through it. Marshall pulled his truck over and parked it. The dog turned his head, seeking information. "Stay," Marshall told him. He left the windows down for the dog and slid from the truck.

Daisy's face and hair held a soothing shine in the lowering light. They paused on the porch for a moment, though Marshall couldn't be certain if she knew how nervous he'd suddenly become. They both looked back at the dog seated in the truck, his head hanging out the window, watching them with ears perked, hoping that any second one of the people on the porch might provide cause for him to bound right over.

"You know that feeling you get when you walk into a room to do something and you know there's a reason you came into that room, but you can't for the life of you remember what it was?" Marshall said.

"Sure," Daisy said.

Marshall nodded toward the dog. "I think his whole life is like that."

Daisy swatted him on the back lightly and left her hand there for a moment. "You ready for this?" she asked. She sported a blithe grin, leaving Marshall reminded that, historically, in times of trouble, the Klingmans herded up, turned their butts inward and showed the world the curve of their horns. He wondered if times had fundamentally changed that much under this roof.

Daisy said, "You'll do fine. Just be the person your dog thinks you are."

She led him through the family room, past the two children he remembered from his previous visit. The kids stared at him as he passed into the kitchen where Randy sat on a ladder-back chair in front of the set table. The place settings shone with white plates and the dull glimmer of flatware. A small forest of drinking glasses ringed the table, leaving open a bare expanse of wood in the center. Marshall's nose was pleasantly assaulted by the aroma of cooking. He smelled broiling meat and onion and pastry and heard something sizzling in butter. Randy sat at the table holding his hands close to his chest and picking at the fingernails of one of them with a pocket knife. He glanced up at Marshall, favored him with a handsome—if somewhat crazed—grin, then looked at Daisy.

"What's he doing here?" He turned to Marshall. "You run out of food where you live?"

"He's having dinner with us," Daisy said. "You have a problem with that?"

Befuddlement clouded Randy's face. He let the ensuing silence and his narrowing eyes tell Marshall and Daisy all about the problem he had with it, but then let his face perk up with his rogue's grin and said, "Hell, one time my oldest sister brought an Indian home for dinner. Full-blooded Blackfoot, right here at our kitchen table. If I could eat through that, I'm sure I can eat through you."

Bruce Klingman appeared from a doorway that led to a back staircase. His eyes shifted to Marshall and paused before his glance rolled on by. Bruce moved into the room and pulled back a chair at the head of the table. It took him a slow moment to ease himself into it. Bruce rested his forearms on the table and stared at the settings, apparently content to say nothing and wait. Marshall heard the muffled sound of a toilet flushing and water cranking through pipes deep in the house. He felt a push of air behind him and smelled perfume, then turned to see Bruce's wife attempting to slide past him.

"Oh, excuse me," Colleen Klingman said.

Kyle entered through the back door at the same moment. He flashed an anxious huddle of teeth at Marshall, but seemed genuinely pleased about his presence.

"Have a seat," Daisy said, pointing to a place setting flanked on one side by an empty chair and the other by a seat Randy occupied. "It's all ready." She must have seen Marshall glancing askance because she tugged him by the arm, flicked her fingers against the back of Randy's head and said, "He won't bite."

Randy looked at him for a moment as if to suggest that you just never knew.

Marshall sat but did not scoot his chair completely up to the table. A guarded chaos followed as Daisy and Colleen Klingman began filling the table with steaming food dishes. A juicy roast crowned the assembling spread, flanked by mashed potatoes featuring pools of melted butter, a glistening heap of peas and carrots in a large serving bowl, and another bowl globbed with applesauce that Marshall knew just by looking was homemade. Warm rolls hid beneath a cloth in a wicker basket. A third bowl held fruit cocktail from the can—about four cans' worth. Nobody spoke as the family began mechanically picking up dishes, ladling servings onto their plates, and passing things along. Marshall was included in the dish-passing rotation, but not addressed directly. Daisy dropped into the empty seat beside him. Marshall was flopping dollops of mashed potatoes onto his plate when he felt her reach under the table and dig her fingers into his thigh down near the knee. He nearly came out of his chair. Then she was back up to fetch a pitcher of iced tea.

Colleen Klingman took plates into another room, where the two small children were apparently eating, then returned to sit with the adults. At the table the meal progressed into a deliberate ritual of consumption, the sounds of chewing, gulping, and swallowing accompanied by the ringing clink of flatware on china and the occasional slurp of liquid. Marshall ate slowly and tried not to be noticed spying on his hosts. When he caught Colleen Klingman's glance, she made a sound he interpreted in the affirmative, a full-mouthed *Umm-hmmm* that sounded vaguely evangelical, though he had no idea what she meant by it. Randy seemed determined to consume the entire joint of beef in the roast pot before anybody else could. Marshall had seen Kyle eat before, but never when there was so much food in front of him.

"So Dad . . . ," Daisy said.

Though her rhythm did little to indicate she intended follow-up comments, Daisy's voice stuck a hitch in the eating. Randy let his forkful of meat drop back to the plate and looked up, still masticating and waiting to be amused. Bruce held his spoon full of applesauce half raised and glanced at her over it. He deliberately stuck the spoon in his mouth, lifted his chin, pointed the handle up high, and withdrew it, empty.

"Marshall here," Daisy said, "our dinner guest?"

"I know who's eating our dinner," Bruce said.

"Marshall here has been telling me some pretty interesting stuff lately," Daisy said.

Bruce inverted his spoon and jabbed it toward Daisy. "Who you associate with in your own private life is your own foolish business, but don't think I aim to listen to your tales about it during my supper," he said.

"Oh, I think you'll like this one," Daisy said. "He was telling me about this water rights argument you all are having."

"I knew that's what this was gonna be about," Randy said. Even his voice had a pounding effect. Seated directly beside him, Marshall found himself flinching, waiting for a more physical connection. "You're trying to come at us through her. I knew you'd stoop to that."

"Well, wait, Randy," Daisy said. "I think you're going to like this, too. You know that piece of land with the water rights you're all arguing about? You know whose names are on the deed to that?" Daisy stopped, eyes opened wide. She opened them even wider, indicating Randy should try to guess. Marshall took a peek at Kyle and thought he caught a stray sparkle in his eye.

"Of course I know. It's ours," Randy said. "This is just bullshit and nonsense."

"You watch your language at the table!" Colleen Klingman exclaimed.

"Well, for Christ's sake," Randy said.

"I mean but *now*!"

"Who owns it technically is me," Daisy said. "Me and Kyle. Isn't that right, Daddy?"

This brought Randy's strangling protest to a sudden halt, and everybody's attention to Bruce. Bruce cocked his head and sneered first at Daisy, then Marshall, then back to Daisy. There was calculation brewing. Marshall could see a squall of blame coming his way. Daisy wore the fierce grin of a raptor. He felt an upwelling of admiration for her based solely on how much she seemed to relish her control of the situation. This was a girl skipping through a field of flowers, casually lobbing hand grenades at the adjacent tract houses.

She said, "Were you ever going to tell us, Dad?"

"When I was dead and gone, the way any decent human being would," Bruce said.

Marshall took in Randy now, who flicked his eyes back and forth, from speaker to speaker. His lips formed a tight circle of outrage, but the fresh sting of rebuke held his tongue deep behind his teeth. That, Marshall thought, was exactly Randy's problem. He never understood relative magnitude.

"Look," Bruce said, "how I structured the ownership of our property is nobody's business but my own. Certainly not yours, Missy. And not your smarty-pants boyfriend, either. There's things you just do to keep the tax man off your ass, that's all. It don't mean anything."

"I think what we're doing is wrong." This was a new voice in the conversation, and Marshall was surprised and a little thrilled to see that Kyle had propped elbows on the table, pushing his biceps into massive wads, and was staring at his father with open rebellion. Marshall thought: *Oh my my. Oh hell yes.*

"What do you think this has to do with you?" Bruce glared at his most recent progeny in a posture that seemed to suggest he was about to rise and clout the boy on the cheek. The posture also looked worn and rehearsed.

"I'll be eighteen in a couple months," Kyle said. "That seems like something for starters."

"And do you think you and your sister are going to just suddenly lay claim to that pasture? Maybe move out there and grow sunflowers or something? Build a nice two-bedroom house with a redwood deck and a satellite dish? My suggestion to you is you think about your options before you start feeling a bunch of starch in your pants. I can change those titles quicker than shit through a goose."

"Not quick enough, though," Daisy said. Her voice had gone sweet, as if she were talking to a much weaker father than hers, someone she pitied, perhaps, or at least felt empathy for. "The way we see it, our other options are to sit here and watch you give this whole place to Randy so we can keep on fighting with all the neighbors and have things be just business as usual."

"What's so wrong with business as usual?" Randy asked. He was leaning away from Marshall as acutely as Marshall leaned away from him, and Marshall felt the intensity of Randy's blue eyes burning a hole in the side of his head.

"I don't like it," Daisy said, then swept her head to include Kyle and said, "We don't like it. So we've arranged to make a little deal with our neighbor . . . excuse me a moment." Daisy rose. She smiled and winked at her father, and left the room. At the table, silence roared.

Then Daisy was back, with a sheaf of legal papers. With a flip of her wrist, she extended them to Marshall. He took the papers and placed them beside his plate. "This here's a buy-sell agreement," Daisy said. "Kyle and I are going to sell the Tates our piece of the ranch."

"*What!?*" Randy cawed.

"For a dollar," Daisy said. "You got that buck?"

Marshall shifted on his hip, slipped his wallet from his pocket. He withdrew a crinkled bill. He watched Bruce, who was biting a smile. Marshall was glad to see Bruce held some appreciation for farce and understood who was being gigged.

Daisy scowled at the dollar Marshall handed her, then said, "You got a newer bill? This one won't even work in a Coke machine." Across the table Kyle smirked.

"You drive a hard bargain," Marshall said. He took the bill back and leafed through his wallet for another one. Daisy dug a ballpoint pen from her jeans pocket and handed it to Marshall. "Sign here."

"This is a sham," Randy said. "This is bullshit. I swear the amount of bullshit we have to put up with in the name of you—"

Colleen Klingman slapped the table with her palm. In a ring all the way around the table, the silverware jumped. "Randy Klingman!" she shot.

"Well, these goddamned kids think they know everything," Randy said. He flung his spoon onto his plate and shoved himself violently away from the table.

"Randall," Bruce warned.

"I will not hear that language at my table!" his wife shouted.

"That one's a scheming bitch," Randy said, jabbing a finger in Daisy's direction, "and she's been a scheming bitch since the day she was born!"

That reached the end of Colleen Klingman's tether. She leaped from her chair and wrapped her fingers into Randy's shirt and hair, hauling him from the table. "Nobody talks like that in my kitchen!" she screeched. She bull-rushed Randy into the living room. "Get out and stay out until you learn how to speak like a decent human being."

"Bitch!" Randy shouted as he was shoved from the room, "Bitch! Bitch!" but that faded when the slapping sounds started, and small surprised yelps replaced the epithets. Daisy's face held a wry pleasure. Kyle frowned, apparently surprised that things had spun so out of control. A few seconds later the slamming of a vehicle door was followed by the cranking of an engine, and then gravel popping. Marshall looked around the table and, though nothing physically was untoward or out of place save Bruce's clattered spoon, what he saw was wreckage. He could not imagine an appropriate response.

"Is this what you came to see?" Bruce asked. Marshall realized Bruce was talking to him, and understood the audience was waiting for his turn to take the stage. He sensed, though, that waiting would be best now, and sat silently. Daisy settled in beside him and put a hand on his arm.

"We know we don't have the power to sell any piece of this ranch," Daisy said. "We know it's not set up like that. This isn't even a buy-sell agreement." She lifted the papers and handed them to her father. "It's a different kind of agreement. I . . . we just feel like if you're going to leave part of this to us, we should have some input."

"Look," Marshall said, recognizing his cue to be involved, "it's stupid for us to be at each other all the time. Not too long ago I saw you skipping across the prairie behind a runaway four-wheeler. What if something happens to you? Then what happens here?"

"What the hell do you mean, what if something happens to me?" Bruce asked. Colleen Klingman now stood in the threshold to the kitchen, her arms crossed over her bosom. Marshall saw the concern with which she seemed to be studying her husband, and knew instantly that embarrassing the old man was the wrong move. He said, "If something happens to you, and the kids can't get along, they split the place up into little pieces and sell it off for the quick cash. You're the one who told me there's no future in ranching, that the best thing you can do is build the value of this place. Look around at who's buying big pieces of land and what they're doing with them. Cattle outfits? Huh-uh. It's people who want recreation, second homes, retreats, what have you.

"Your land has as much springwater on it as ours does. If you let Kyle and me develop it, rehab it, like I did mine, the value of this place skyrockets. I talked to a realtor last year who told me a productive spring creek can increase the value of the land a million dollars a mile. And we can make money while we're putting it all together. Next year I'm raising my rod fees to a hundred dollars a day, and I'll get it. People are already booking for next summer. If we can get your springs in shape, fold the two fishing operations together, we could have enough stream miles for fifteen fishermen a day. Fifteen times a hundred? That's around forty-five thousand dollars a month if we can really build it up. Yeah, we may spend some time not fully booked, and yeah, we split the profits, but when was the last time you made fifteen or twenty thousand dollars a month for doing nothing? You open the stream June through November. Close for the winter while you calve."

"Plus," Daisy said, "Kyle has a job. Tell that part."

"Kyle and I will be the riverkeepers. We'll do all the administration, handle all the clients. We'll keep it completely out of your hair. Between the two of us we'll see to it that someone is on site every day, making sure the clients don't interfere with your cattle operation. Maybe even we plant some alfalfa over on our place and work a trade so we can keep the cows out of the sensitive areas when the feed's real low."

"I'm not going to start a *fish farm!*" Bruce said. He carried a high tone, as if he were preaching a gospel they all should be familiar with, something about easy sins.

"It's a good idea," Kyle said, "just hear him out."

"We'll have some start-up costs," Marshall said. "Won't lie to you about that. There's insurance, some development outlays. But FWP just got a huge slug of money to deal with whirling disease, and one of the things they're doing is offering grants for rehab of spawning streams. We can get twenty, thirty thousand out of them and get started for almost nothing in construction costs. Kyle and I can do the work. We already know how."

"I've got a whole bunch of ideas. I made some maps," Kyle added. He had been practically sitting on his hands, waiting for the moment to jump in. Bruce's eyes narrowed as they cut to his son. Marshall could almost see Bruce thinking, *maps?* Kyle unfolded a piece of yellow legal paper from his shirt pocket.

"That's a lot of goddamned people wandering around my property," Bruce said.

"That's what Kyle does. He manages that part," Marshall said. "And you're in control to dictate where they can and cannot go."

"We talked about this for a long time," Daisy said. "We decided things didn't need to be the way they are. Just, there are other ways to do things and we think it would be nice to try them. Right, Kyle?"

"He worked hard to get that spring creek going," Kyle said, cutting a glance to Marshall. "So did I. That's what I'm saying. And this is a good opportunity, Dad. I've been thinking a lot about it."

Bruce Klingman took a long look at these two children of his and found neither lacking in the steely will he prized in his bloodline. They'd ambushed him, and he'd have to prove he wasn't toothless, but there were different avenues to grace in that sort of escape. He pressed his lower lip under his upper and leveled a measuring stare at Marshall, who met it and found something he'd not before seen in the old man's eyes—he was within the margin of error, he knew, but he felt nearly sure he was looking at respect. Bruce seemed to decide something then. He nodded almost imperceptibly, still looking at Marshall, and almost let the corners of a secret grin tickle his lips. But he pressed that back and turned to Daisy. "Say good-bye to your company," he said, "then we'll hash this over." They all watched the awkward feat of Bruce Klingman pushing away from the table and levering himself to stand. He stopped to let a last scathing glare settle on Kyle.

"I'm not above throwing the baby out with the bathwater," Bruce warned.

"I know it," Kyle said.

"I'm not."

"We know, Daddy," Daisy said. Bruce shuffled without further comment out of the room. His wife followed. A silence bloomed for a few seconds during which the three people remaining in the kitchen stared at the table and each other and gathered deep breaths.

"Dinner at the Klingmans'," Marshall said. "Who knew?"

Marshall went out the back door, hoping to avoid any chance encounter with a sulking Randy, possibly returning from revving up his violent streak. Daisy walked out with him, stepping down into the cooling evening. Overhead the sky had gone pale yellow, with a touch of fire painting the lowest edges of wispy clouds to the west. He could hear the breeze in the trees around the house. On the edge of the green lawn a black-and-white cat crouched in mid-stalk, its head turned toward them. The cat did not appreciate the interruption.

"Be interesting to see how things settle out," Daisy said.

"I owe you," Marshall said. "Big."

"No," Daisy said, "We're all settled up." He could not remember her appearing so content and in control. She reached behind his head with both hands and brought his face close to hers. Daisy gazed at him as if she knew things she suspected he would guess soon. He felt her kiss swish through him with the same mysterious thrill that he'd known kissing her almost twenty summers before. He felt no barrier between where his lips ended and hers began and her tongue came to him like an endless surge of warm sugar melting in his mouth. The kiss broke in a long linger.

"You'll be hearing from us directly," Daisy said.

But even on this evening that seemed so triumphant for them both, even as he stood on the lawn and watched her walk back to the door, he felt the sad longing he had always felt, since they were kids, when he knew she was keeping some of herself from him. He watched her retreating, a figure of brightness fading against the gray-white wall of house and the darkened lawn, and struggled to balance that image with what had been right in front of him only moments before, touchable and in touch.

Marshall drove home as the sky was darkening, swimming in a viscous mélange of goodwill, sweet nostalgia, and an indefinite yearning, yet keen enough to marvel that just a matter of hours before he'd been awash in the days-long vestigial ugliness of the scene at Sperry Grade. Alton's act had kept him deeply disturbed, but for the moment the more immediate display of Klingman character held that at bay. How many times had he looked at someone and thought different things?

The dog tilted at Marshall with his nose, though Marshall couldn't understand what the animal was trying to tell him. He wanted something, that much was clear. Food probably. Marshall thought it must be trying to be a dog. You depend on a person for everything. You have to wait to eat and drink water if the bowls are empty. When it's time for the bowels to move, you have to find someone to let you out. Driving down the lane to the ranch house he saw a rig flashing in his headlights, a white Toyota 4Runner parked in his drive. He saw Molly sitting on the steps to the porch, wearing a T-shirt and shorts. She sat there while he pulled in and doused his headlights, then climbed out of the truck. The dog hit the ground with all four legs braced and started woofing. Then his head dropped and he raced to Molly. His tail burst into rapid slashes as he nosed under Molly's chin. She held his head and endeavored to stand.

"Where have you been, all dressed up?" she asked.

"Dinner at the Klingman ranch," he said in a way that let her know he found it as odd as she would. They walked around to the side door, which he held open for her. They walked through the mudroom and kitchen and into the living room.

"What was that like?" Molly said behind him.

"Oh, it was just the craziest thing."

Molly sat on the couch while Marshall returned to the mudroom to feed the dog. Buck pushed his big head into the bowl before Marshall could get it all the way to the floor.

Marshall walked back into the living room, thinking there was something else he had to do. He said, "What's going on with you?"

That Molly would be as disturbed as he by what Alton had done at Sperry Grade was as clear as the notion that she'd be equally unequipped to deal with it. Marshall felt the actuality as a sour, rotten pain that made him want to pull pieces of his body off and throw them away. He wanted respite from it and knew there was none, that he would have this discomfort for . . . well, until he didn't anymore. Molly was the only person who could feel it hurt worse.

"I'm taking Alton home," Molly said.

"To Seattle?" Marshall asked. He was rocking on his feet, trying to remember other things he had to do.

Molly nodded. "Soon as he's well enough to travel." She perched on the edge of the couch, not daring to let herself settle.

"Alton in on this?" Marshall asked.

"He needs to be someplace where people can take care of him. He's going to need a lot of physical therapy. Probably the other kind, too."

"Think he's going to get better?"

"Better than what?"

Marshall found himself infused with both sadness and relief. He was glad Molly had decided not to take this on herself, yet he heard in her voice a confirmation of his fear that Alton was, in the ways that would matter to his own life, gone. They both let their eyes fall around the room. They could hear the dog pushing the bowl across the floor as he chomped his food.

"Is it OK legally?" Marshall asked.

"Jimmy's dad is agitating, but we cleared it with the DA's office. They're not going to bring charges. They're going with your . . . with the self-defense. There may be a civil suit later, but Alton's free to move about."

"What's Amy doing?"

"She's going to stick it out here," Molly said. "Be on her own for a while. Figure out what she thinks."

"How about you?" Marshall asked. "Change your mind about going back on the river?"

Molly gave her head a quick shake. "I'm going to do one more guide trip. I'm booked with the lieutenant governor again. I'm going to bring him here. It might help you with your water rights problem later on down the line. Can't hurt anyway."

Marshall started to argue, "You don't have to . . . ," then halted when he watched her expression stiffen to stalwart. "Thanks for that," he said. "I appreciate it. What about after?"

Molly rose and walked to the window where she crossed her arms and stared out at the lawn, barely visible in the gathering dark. "The river," Molly said, "I did that. What was good and fun about it isn't fun anymore. Isn't even *there* anymore. I want to move on to something . . . that lasts longer."

Marshall wanted to say, *the river lasts forever,* and argue about notions of endurance. But he knew she wasn't talking about the river, but rather their time on it, the run of seasons when, to them, each river was only the river. So instead, he said what had first come to his mind: "I'm glad."

"On my own," Molly said, her tone corrective. She turned her chin to her shoulder and didn't exactly look at him.

"We'll still be—"

"We will, of course," Molly said quickly. What she didn't say was that the kind of friends they'd still be would have a lot to do with him, the initiatives he felt willing to take. Or that she had real hope that, given some time, they could build a tremendous friendship, a mutual understanding far deeper than the one they had before recent events, the one so misinformed by—and she had to smile when she thought this—confusion of loyalties and cross-purposes. "But I'll need some time first. It's going to be different than before."

How? Marshall wanted to ask. Rather he took the moment to examine the notion, rising through his consciousness, that his soul bore none of the injuries inflicted by an unsentimental world, not really. All of the dramas of his life had been self-generated. Losing what Molly had offered was only the most recent example. He'd have to get himself ready to absorb that kind of thing. He was going to want the possibility. He understood it now, and felt Molly had everything to do with this opening. He stepped up beside her. "My life isn't going to change very much for a while, I don't think," he said, and even he was confused about whether it was part apology. He nodded at the window and everything outside in the darkness. "I'm learning so much here. It feels like important stuff."

She shifted her weight, moving closer until her shoulder almost touched his. That was it, she thought. It had never been about her, or Daisy for that matter. Marshall had voted with his feet: he'd stood on his ground. It was either everything he wanted, or all he could see.

"I'd like to find a place like that," Molly said. She felt his hand on her back, felt it as a distant sensation, like watching somebody else being touched and imagining how it feels. But Molly wanted him to know what he'd had to do with her looking toward what came next. She turned and slipped her arms around him and locked on. Marshall pressed right back, reaching for the part of her that was leaving. At this last moment, he felt certain he had it in his grasp.

They held on to each other for a long while, until Molly was first to break the embrace. Marshall kept his eyelids pressed down while he felt her pull away, and when he opened them, she was gone. Out a window he glimpsed her striding across the drive in the dark. A flash of white T-shirt was all that remained of her, then taillights fading down the lane.

A week later, the last week of September, Marshall sat in the shade of his porch at the peak of the afternoon heat, drinking a glass half filled with sun tea and half with lemonade, and fondly remembering the gin and tonics of his past. Later he had work to do, but for the moment he had allowed himself to slip into a floaty space where neither fantasy nor reminiscence seemed particularly foolish, and he could truly enjoy his wist. There was much to be wistful about—which didn't mean he wasn't aware, too, of the moment. He could hear bluebottle flies sizzling against the windowpanes, trying to get into the house. The lawn and meadows beyond, refreshed by late summer rains, held every conjugation of green and yellow. Letting his eye drift along the lane, he saw raptors on a pair of power poles, red-tailed hawks.

Cedar waxwings, their dandy, Peter Pan caps and black masks apparent in profile, perched in a pine near the house, making quick and deadly sallies for midair interceptions of insects, then returning to the tree. With binoculars he could see the waxy red "droplets" along their wing feathers that gave them their names. A pair of crickets bleated madly at each other. Whitetail does stood just beyond the yard fence, their coats already losing the summer red, preparing to fade to autumn's gray.

This was what Marshall loved about doing nothing. Then pretty soon he was doing something—namely, rising to greet Daisy Klingman, who strode around the corner of the house in shorts and a blouse with a pronounced tropical motif. He hadn't seen her coming. Daisy mounted the stairs and climbed onto the porch.

"Half and half?" Marshall asked.

Daisy made a face to indicate she didn't know what he was talking about, then shrugged. "Sure."

Marshall ducked inside to mix Daisy some lemonade and iced tea. He wondered if she'd come in as well, but this time Daisy seemed comfortable conducting her business in the light of day. Marshall sat on the porch's loveseat, giving her the chance to sit beside him. She took it. She made a pointed glance at his binoculars on the end table and nodded when he said, "Birds." She took a drink, then an appreciative longer one. She set the glass down on the porch boards and stared off into the distance, as if she were looking for birds of her own.

"I'll be taking off here soon," she said.

"That so?"

"Yep."

They both sat and stared out at the sky, where the birds might be, and some were. Marshall waited, trusting her to tell him what he needed to know and not a whole lot more. He remembered the inchoate sadness he had felt driving away from his dinner with the Klingmans, his sense that Daisy knew something she was waiting for him to figure out. Daisy's legs were crossed and her heel swung like a metronome keeping jerky time to their silence. *Appropriate accompaniment,* Marshall thought. Then Daisy started talking, keeping it aimed at the blue sky.

"When you said we're what's next around here, you weren't talking about you and me. Not like that. You were talking about you. Maybe Kyle. I'm not what's next around here. Anyway, a friend called a while back, a friend I met from Reno." Daisy paused, and retrospectively Marshall would understand she was struggling with pronouns. "They've got a sailboat and they're going to take it down to Mexico, sail up around Baja for a while. Zihuatanejo, we're starting in." She said it again, her tongue exaggerating the allure she found in its exotic rhythm. "*Zihuatanejo.* Doesn't that sound cool?"

"It does." Marshall nodded at the tropical blouse. "Leaving right now?"

"I'm just trying things on," she laughed. "Have you been there— Zihuatanejo?"

"No," Marshall said.

"Well, I'm going to go do that with . . . them for a while. Just kind of see how it goes. I've never been on a sailboat."

Marshall heard the "him" in "them." He doubted she was here to see if he'd put up a fight. The presentation was far too even-keeled for all that. "Well," he said. *Well* . . . "Sounds like a blast."

At last she turned her face to him and beamed and he could see that the grin was no longer one designed to engage him. This was all wide mouth and shiny teeth. "You know how I like the margaritas," she said, as if it were a wholly tenable weakness, described in all the literature.

"I know," Marshall said, "how you like the margaritas."

"I guess I'm going to help be the crew."

"That seems right. You'll be great crew."

"Time I get back, you and Kyle will have this whole fish farm scheme of ours up and running," Daisy said, twinkling her fingers, flicking just enough dubiousness into what she was saying to excuse herself from taking it—or, he realized, him—too seriously.

"Sure," Marshall said, thinking he'd been saying good-bye to her pretty much the whole time he'd known her, and he was tired of it. "Lot of work to do, but—"

Daisy slapped her hands on her thighs and stood up. She looked down at him as if expecting him to stand too. Marshall felt stupid not standing, petulant, which, he could see, was a corner she'd constructed around him. He had to rise. For a moment he saw her eyes soften, and her own nostalgia complicated her laissez-faire. She let him see her, then, like she had the night a few months back, when she'd arrived at his house at 3 A.M. Or the morning she'd appeared amid a misunderstanding with Shadford and told him the story of her Uncle Bud. This was a clean exchange, and that in itself felt like a gift.

"This way," Daisy said, and it was clear to him she wanted to be forthright for a moment, "we'll still always have that something to wonder about, when our regular-life stuff goes to hell."

"Right," Marshall said. "That." He felt a tight, evaporative sting, zapped into him by the sense that he was just standing there watching, but just as quickly evanescing with the understanding that, were he of a mind, he would have made choices about Daisy a long time ago.

"Don't cry on me," Daisy said.

Marshall instantly smiled. The thing was, part of him really did want to wrap his fingers around his eye sockets and weep. But this was his past, peeling away and taking the adhesions with it. "You're going to have a great time," he said. Then, feeling absolutely no need to guard against it, he nodded and, with pure candor, said, "I guess the hard part for me is thinking about all this . . ."—he made a gesture shuttling his hand between the two of them and swirling it to mix them up—"everything, as . . ."—frown, then wide-open eyes in a gaze straight into hers— "as a waste of time."

"Aw, but Marshall," Daisy said, "we wasted it *well*."

He had to give her that. Marshall walked down off the porch with her and around the yard to the red pickup truck. At the driver's-side door, Daisy stopped, held her arms wide, and said, "I'll want a hug."

He wrapped her in a heartfelt one that, in the second he eased up, felt too short. But by then, what more could he do with a hug?

"Bye-bye, sweetie," Daisy said. "I'll see you soon."

Marshall said good-bye.

Alton sat in the passenger seat of his own rig, hurtling down I-90 through the wheat stubble and channeled scablands of eastern Washington. Molly drove. A CD they had been listening to and were now tired of was stuck in the dashboard CD player. Just the edge of it rimmed the slot. Alton tried to pinch it with his fingers, and the disc would suck back into the dashboard, though it wouldn't seat itself properly to play. Then a tiny engine whined and it would reappear in the slot, a glimmer edge. Alton kept pinching.

"Stop that," Molly said. "You need tweezers."

"I've got tweezers in here," Alton said, and unbuckling his seat belt, twisted to start tearing through the boxes stacked in the backseat.

"You'll never find them," Molly said, thinking: *He's like working with a trained ape.* It had already been a long drive.

"Yes I will." Alton ripped the tape from one box top and started rooting through its contents. He tore into another one.

"Are they even in here?" Molly asked. "Maybe they're in a box in the back."

"Pull over," Alton said.

"What's the biggest fish you've ever caught?"

"An eighty-pound tarpon off Marathon Key. I know those sons of bitches are in here."

"Biggest trout?"

"Twenty-three-pound steelhead, Hoh River, 1992," Alton said. "Pull over for a minute."

"We're not going to pull over to look for tweezers," Molly said. "Alton, you've got to let go of the little things. Now put your seat belt back on."

Molly had reason to regret saying that as Alton returned to his seat and strapped himself in. His eyes aimed out the windshield in an unfocused stare, and Molly felt the presence of low-grade fear again, fizzing as silently as background radiation.

The interruption of a life's flow was how she chose to think of it now. Hers had been diverted—not something to overlook—whereas his had been stanched. Though of course nobody's could be truly stanched, not really, unless you were dead. His life was already pouring in a new direction. It would be up to him to figure out a way to define the speed and course of that flow. Alton would have to shape it.

Molly distantly wished she could have a hand in that shaping, but understood inherently she could not. The processes were over her head now, and she had her own carving out to do. Maybe, she had been thinking in the last few days, she would take up one of her long-term guiding clients who kept offering some stake money to partner in opening a new fly shop. Become a businesswoman, get involved in the community, promote more responsible uses of the rivers and the fish. God knew Fly Guys survived primarily in the old-fashioned way—by sheer dearth of competition. She could steal the show.

Something would come. She could sell Sage. She could go back to school and become a podiatrist. First there would be leaving Alton in Seattle. They had already dropped his boat off at Marshall's for storage in a shed at the ranch. Marshall had promised to get it wet now and then. That parting had been awkward and short. Nobody knew what to say, and there seemed to be a mutual agreement not to try to say it. Marshall had hugged Alton—no touching be damned—and said, "I'll come see you soon, buddy."

Who knew if Alton believed him, because who knew what Alton believed at all anymore, so diverted was his neural circuitry. Who knew what he would believe in a month, or next year?

But Marshall *would* see him soon. Marshall believed he could still matter in his friend's life, and he would visit Alton regularly—more so even than Molly and far more than Amy Baine, who would never see Alton in Seattle. For the first few years Marshall would make the trip at least once a season, sometimes with Molly, other times undertaking the nine-hour drive alone, running over even for a two-night visit when he found the time. Eventually, as it became obvious that Alton either could never, or had simply no desire to, return to any distinguishable semblance of his former life, Marshall's trips trickled out, though for the next decade, until his friend's health took a serious turn for the worse, he would make the drive to Washington at least once a year.

Molly kept pointing the vehicle down the highway, listening to the rough roll of the tires on the asphalt. The wind out here pushed against the side of the rig in unexpected shoves. It moved across the wheat fields like vast herds of small, invisible animals. Alton squinted at the horizon. Molly wondered what he saw. The sun would set out there if he looked long enough.

Kingfisher, she thought, *that would be a cool name for a fly shop.*

In the light before sunrise Marshall stood on the lawn behind an aluminum tripod, staring into a spotting scope. It was the end of September now, cool mornings and warm afternoons, and the slender stems of grasses had yellowed and browned. He watched through the scope, as across the river and half a mile away, a wolf trotted the pasture. Marshall had spotted the animal from his window just as the gray light of dawn lifted on a field of silvery dew. He'd noticed its motion, been jolted with the recognition that the animal's pace was completely unfamiliar as anything he'd seen in fifteen years on this place, and had immediately run to the lawn and set up the spotting scope. He stood on the grass wearing only a pair of threadbare boxer shorts and some shearling moccasins.

The wolf was black, with long legs and a thick ruff around its shoulders. From the aimless, leggy gait, Marshall had the sense it was a young animal, one of the pups now, at the beginning of autumn, nearly full-sized. He watched as it moved along on soft feet, pausing to bite at the ends of long stems of grass as they bent with the weight of morning dew. *Grasshoppers,* Marshall thought. *She must be eating the grasshoppers that are still too wet from the dew to fly.* He guessed the wolf to be female because it never stopped to lift a leg—something he'd read wild male canids did on a systematic, if not obsessive, basis.

Marshall watched over the course of a half hour as the wolf meandered through the open ground, then began to climb the bench. The wolf stopped two or three times to survey the meadow she had just crossed, leaving Marshall to wonder if another pack member was somewhere behind her, but he could spot nothing. When she crested the ridge, the wolf broke into a trot and disappeared within seconds,

heading for the Forest Service boundary and the high ridges beyond—
though who knew where she might actually go.

Marshall scanned the meadow again through the eyepiece, then
stepped back and looked at the scene without the help of the scope. In
the distance he saw the ridges, their cover of larch dense and smooth.
He thought he noticed a slight lightening in the green of the larch,
their needles already starting their fade to yellow in advance of falling
off for the winter.

Marshall leaned an elbow on the tripod and continued to stare
around. *A wolf,* he thought. *Wouldn't Alton get a kick out of that?* He
remembered how hard Alton had worked when he'd helped to develop
the springs, tie them together to make a creek. Molly, too, had seemed
to share his dream of a spring creek, trout-laden and coursing through
a broad meadow. Those two had once treated the Fly X as if they were
a coterie of its inhabitants, if only on an itinerant basis.

*A wolf. Have to keep the dog from straying, keep him in eyeshot
from now on. Wolves hate dogs, kill them every chance they get. Something to be aware of.* His thoughts gave way to the warbling of the
telephone. Marshall hesitated, remembering it was Sunday. He knew
who the call was from and didn't, for a moment, feel like taking it. But
then he made two long skips and broke into a jog, running inside to
answer.

"Son."

"Father." Marshall annoyed himself by falling immediately into
the half-sarcastic tone he used to protect himself from conversations
with his father. Time to cut that out.

"What's going on out there?" his father said.

"It's pretty quiet," Marshall said.

While he talked to Skipjack, Marshall fed the dog, then wandered
over to his bookings calendar to see how many fishermen he could expect that day. He wondered what time they would start arriving. This
led him to wonder if he shouldn't offer some sort of breakfast—coffee
and pastries, at any rate—for the early comers. Could be a revenue
source . . . *do you need a license from the Board of Health for that?*

He walked outside, still chitchatting with his father on the cordless, still wearing only old boxers and ratty moccasins. The dog followed. Marshall told his father about the wolf.

"Jesus, we don't want those around," Skipjack said.

"They're fine, Dad. We don't have livestock. They won't hurt anything."

"Wolves, for God's sake."

"Are you kidding? If clients can see a wolf while they're fishing? They'll love it."

"Until somebody gets eaten."

"You sound like a Klingman," Marshall said. "Wolves don't eat people. Those are the fairy-tale wolves. Little Red Riding Hood and the Russian steppes. Real life isn't that way."

Marshall told him how the Klingman situation had been averted, that all was well with the water rights—at least until he could get some applications and pleas for leniency cobbled together. As he explained, it dawned on him that there might soon come a time when he could visit the Klingmans and ask Bruce exactly how far ahead of Marshall he'd been, and just when he'd got there. *Why else had he changed the deeds when he had?* There was, Marshall saw, still much to be learned from studying his neighbor.

Meanwhile, news of a squabble avoided cheered Skipjack. "We could throw one of our famous old bang-up cocktail parties out there next month," he said. "A big autumn fly-fishing weekend party on the spring creek. Surprise those big brownies spawning. I'll get Nick Price to bring up a bunch of boys from Sun Valley, and Eric Ruberg can fly his plane up from Jackson with a group. We'll have a game feed and fishing outing. Be good for business to introduce some of these guys to the place, let them word-of-mouth it in the right circles—"

It took Marshall almost no time to say, "You know what, Dad? I don't think so."

"You don't think so?"

"I think it's a bad idea," Marshall said. "I have way too much to get started on here."

Perhaps there was a new timbre in the flow of Marshall's voice. Or perhaps his father was newly attuned to hearing an undercurrent that had started flowing with more force. In any case, Skipjack said, "Hmmm. Well. Maybe next spring, then. We could probably plan a real whizbanger for, say, April. If I have enough time to put together a crew . . . that could be something."

"Listen . . . ," Marshall said, paying close attention to his own voice, trying to hear how this sounded, "Look, Dad, do you think maybe you could just come out this fall instead? Just you? I'd like to show you all this. What I've done here."

When he hung up, Marshall opened the door for Buck—who had been bouncing off the door panel earlier, confined inside while Marshall was out watching the wolf. Marshall kicked off his moccasins and followed the dog back outside into the brightening morning. Buck raced around the yard, nearly knocking himself over in the struggle between sniffing night smells and tearing around, burning exuberance. A splash of movement snatched Marshall's gaze away, toward the bridge and the road on the other side of it. Marshall saw a dust plume arrowed down to a red pickup, making speed along the dirt road in his direction. He gazed idly toward the main road and saw a vehicle coming from that direction too. Possibly, he thought, clients for the day. He glanced back at the flowing funnel of dust coming from the direction of Klingmans', wondering who was driving, if it was Bruce or Randy, or Kyle. He was curious about the resolution of the drama that had begun at his Klingman dinner.

He wondered if the driver was Daisy, living life at high velocity and blasting out of his orbit for . . . ? How long until he might see her next, and what would that be like? What Marshall couldn't yet know was that their previous conversation would be their last. After a quarter century of knowing her, Marshall would never see Daisy again.

What he *could* know was the feel of the shadowed grass, cool and slick under his bare feet. He could see the sunlight coming across the valley, a bright front sweeping down from the high country. He let his focus settle on the galleries of cottonwoods lining the river. He remembered being a boy and stealing through the fields at night, to the river. Behind him the jangling lights and noise from the house would whirl into themselves until he escaped their vortex and felt the stronger spaces of the night swallow him. He had learned, during those stealthy outings, to trust his movements in the darkness. In those days dawn had been a mixed blessing, lighting the waking land around him, but also tapering to a close stolen moments of peace—so precious, then. When the pale morning light gave way to the day, there was always the necessary return to the aftermath of his other life.

Now the sun kept coming on strong. Overhead a thin, cloudless blue stretched in all directions, immense and broad and everywhere he looked, so Marshall had the sense that his little valley and the mountains that surrounded it formed the bottom of a small hole in the sky. Behind him vehicles were drawing closer from both directions. One would turn in his drive. The other would continue on down the road. He would have to return to the house soon, put on some pants and meet whoever was coming his way. But he had a few more moments to spare before the sun lit the lawn and started burning off the night's dew. He had a few moments to gaze beyond the treetops to the slope of meadow leaning down toward the river, where the spring creek twisted its clear, clean way across the ground. He used all the time he had to see what he had done.

Ninemile Valley, Montana
September 9, 2004

ABOUT THE AUTHOR

Jeff Hull's writing has appeared in *Ploughshares*, *Southern Review*, *Atlantic Monthly*, *Audubon*, *National Geographic Traveler*, *Outside*, *Travel & Leisure*, *National Geographic Adventure*, *Town and Country*, *Outdoor Life*, *Fortune*, *Men's Journal*, *Fly Rod & Reel*, *Fly Fisherman*, *American Angler*, *Yachting*, and *Sailing*. He won a Fiction Fellowship at the University of Montana, where he received his MFA. He was nominated for a 1994 National Magazine Award by *Atlantic Monthly*. He has guided in Montana and remote bonefish flats in the Tuamotus archipelago in the South Pacific, and teaches magazine writing at University of Montana School of Journalism.

Ronni Flannery